# Whatever After

## BOOKS 1-3

Read all the **Whatever After** books!

# Whatever After

## BOOKS 1-3

#1: FAIREST of ALL
#2: IF the SHOE FITS
#3: SINK or SWIM

# SARAH MLYNOWSKI

Scholastic Inc.

Text pages 1–175 copyright © 2012 by Sarah Mlynowski
Text pages 176–514 copyright © 2013 by Sarah Mlynowski

All rights reserved. Published by Scholastic Inc., *Publishers since 1920*. SCHOLASTIC and associated logos are trademarks and/or registered trademarks of Scholastic Inc.

The publisher does not have any control over and does not assume any responsibility for author or third-party websites or their content.

This book is a work of fiction. Names, characters, places, and incidents are either the product of the author's imagination or are used fictitiously, and any resemblance to actual persons, living or dead, business establishments, events, or locales is entirely coincidental.

ISBN 978-1-338-10175-1

10 9 8 7 6 5 4 3 2 1     16 17 18 19 20

Printed in the U.S.A.   40
First printing 2016

Book design by Elizabeth B. Parisi

# * contents *

SARAH MLYNOWSKI

Whatever After

FAIREST of ALL

SCHOLASTIC

for jessica braun,
p.s. read (forever!)

## This Is Not a Joke

Once upon a time my life was normal.

Then the mirror in our basement ate us.

Do you think I'm joking? Do you think I'm making this up? You do, don't you?

You're thinking, Um, Abby, mirrors don't usually go ahead and slurp people up. Mirrors just hang on the wall and reflect stuff.

Well, you're wrong. So very WRONG.

Everything I'm going to tell you is the whole truth and nothing but the truth. I'm not making anything up. And I'm not a liar, or a crazy person who thinks she's telling the truth but secretly isn't. I am, in fact, a very logical person. Fair, too. I have to be, since I'm going to be a judge when I grow up. Well, first I'm going to be a lawyer, and then I'm going to be a judge, because you have to be a lawyer first. That's the rule.

But yeah. I am an extremely logical, extremely practical, and extremely *un*-crazy ten-year-old girl whose life went completely berserk after her parents forced her to move to Smithville.

Still don't believe me? You will when you hear all the facts. You will when you hear the whole story.

Let me start at the beginning.

# ✳ chapter one ✳

## The Beginning

the moment the recess bell rings, the kids in my new fifth-grade class decide they want to play tag. We *eenie meenie miney*, and somehow I'm it. Me, the new kid. Great.

Not.

I cover my eyes to give the other kids a ten-second head start (okay, five), then run toward the fence. Straightaway, I spot Penny, who is very tall. Well, taller than me. Although most people are taller than me. She's also wearing a bright orange sweatshirt that's hard to miss. I don't know all the kids' names, but Penny's is easy to remember because she always wears super-high ponytails and I just think, Penny's pony, Penny's pony, Penny's pony.

I dash over and tap her on the elbow. "You're it, Penny's pony! I mean, Penny."

She looks at me strangely. "Um, no. I'm frozen."

Huh? It's not that cold. Plus, her orange sweater looks really warm.

"What?" I ask.

Penny wrinkles her forehead. "You tagged me. I'm frozen."

"Noooooo," I say slowly. "I was it. I tagged *you*, so now *you're* it. Now you have to tag someone else to make them be it. That's why the game is called it." I blink. "I mean, tag."

"The it person has to tag *everyone*," Penny says. Her tone suggests she knows way more about tag than I do, and my cheeks heat up. Because she doesn't. "When you're tagged, you freeze, and the very last person tagged is the next it. It's called *freeze* tag. Got it?"

The LAST person to get tagged gets to be it? If you're the last person tagged, that means you're the best player. If you're the best player, you should get to do a happy dance while everyone throws confetti on you. You should not have to be the new it, because being it is not a reward.

My heart sinks. If I have to be it until every last fifth grader is tagged or frozen, this is going to be a very, very, VERY long game.

Here's the thing. I am trying to have a fresh start and be flexible about my new school. But how can I when the people here do EVERYTHING wrong?

Please allow me to present my case.

1. Everyone in Smithville calls Coke, Pepsi, and Orange Crush *soda*. Ridiculous, right? *Pop* is a much better name. *Pop! Pop! Pop!* Coke *pops* on your tongue. It doesn't *soda* on your tongue.

2. The people here do not know how to make a peanut butter and banana sandwich. The right way is to slice the banana up and then press the slices one by one into the peanut butter, preferably in neat and orderly rows. But the kids in my new school mash the bananas, mix a spoonful of peanut butter into the mashed

bananas, and then spread the whole gloppy mess on their bread. Why oh why would they do that?

3. And now, instead of tag, they want to play "Ooo, Let's All Be Frozen Statues While Abby Runs Around and Around and Around."

Ladies and gentlemen of the jury:

I do not want to call pop *soda*.

I do not want to eat gloppy banana mush.

I do not want to be it.

"I'm pretty sure the way I play is the right way," I say, my throat tightening. I'm right. I am.

"No," she states. "I'm frozen. And you'd better get going, or it'll just get harder."

Tears burn the backs of my eyes. I don't want things to get harder. I want things to be the way they used to be. Normal!

"No thanks," I say in a careful voice that's meant not to let my tears out but might sound a little squished. Or prissy. Or spoiled-brat-y, possibly.

"You're quitting?" Penny asks. Her eyebrows fly up. "Just because you didn't get your way?"

"No! I'm just . . . tired." I'm not even lying. I *am* tired. I'm tired of everything being different. Why can't things be like they used to be?

I go to Mrs. Goldman, the teacher on playground duty. I ask her if I can go to the library.

"You mean the media room, hon?" she asks.

I shrink even smaller. They don't even call a library a library here?

But the second I step into the *media room*, the world gets a little better. I take a deep breath. *Ahhhh.*

Maybe in Smithville a room filled with books is called a media room, but it smells just like the library in my old, normal school. Musty. Dusty. Papery.

The books on the shelves of the school library — media room, *argh* — are books I recognize. They're books I've gobbled up many times before. Many, *many* times before.

My shoulders sag with relief, because guess what? No matter how many times you read them, stories always stay the same.

I get my love of books from my nana. She used to read to me all the time. She's a literature professor at a university in Chicago, the normal place where we used to live.

I feel a pain in my gut when I think about my old house. My faraway friends. My nana. Peanut butter and banana sandwiches made the *right* way.

And then I shake off those heavy feelings and run my finger along the row of books. My finger stops. It rests on a collection called *Fairy Tales*, where good is good, and bad is bad, and logical, practical fifth-grade girls never get stuck being it forever.

My chest loosens. Perfect.

# ✳ chapter two ✳

## My Annoying Wake-up

*t*hat night I'm dreaming about my old friends. We're playing tag the *right* way when someone calls my name.

"Abby! Abby! Abby!"

I half open one eye. It's Jonah, my seven-year-old brother, so I pull my bedspread over my head. Sure, I love the kid, but I'm a growing girl. I need my sleep.

Jonah yanks down the covers, presses his mouth to my ear, and says, "Abby, Abby, Abby, Abby, Abby, ABBY!"

I groan. "Jonah! I'm asleep!"

"Wake up, wake up, wake up!"

Does he have to repeat everything a million times? There's a fine line between being persistent and being annoying.

"Go back to bed," I order. I have been told that I can be bossy, but come on. It's the middle of the night. Plus, it's my job as an older sister to boss Jonah around. I'm only performing my sisterly duty.

It's also my job to make sure he eats his vegetables.

At dinner, I caught him hiding his broccoli in his sock. So I told on him. Then I felt guilty and gave him half my chocolate cookie.

"But the mirror is hissing," he says now.

I squint at him. *What?* I don't even know what to do with that sentence. "Jonah, mirrors don't hiss. They don't make any sounds at all. Unless you break them." Uh-oh. I sit up like a jack-in-the-box. "Did you break a mirror? That's bad luck!"

"I don't think so." He does this weird twisty thing he sometimes does with his lips. "Well, maybe."

"Jonah! Which mirror?" I swing my legs over the side of my bed. It better not be my pink hand mirror, the one I once caught him using to examine his toes.

"The big one downstairs."

"Are you kidding me? The creepy one in the basement?"

I realize I'm shrieking, and I lower my voice so I won't wake my parents. "Why were you in the basement so late at night?" There's something odd about the mirror in our basement. It seems like it's watching me wherever I go. Like the eyes in that painting the *Mona Lisa*. But of course that makes no sense. Mirrors can't watch you. They're not alive.

He shrugs. "I was exploring."

I glance at my alarm clock. "It's eleven fifty-two!" My wrist feels heavy and I realize I forgot to take my watch off before I went to sleep. I press the light. It says 11:52, too.

Jonah shrugs again.

Jonah is always exploring. It's amazing we're even related, really; we're so different. I like reading. He likes adventures. I like cuddling in my bed with a book. He'd rather be rock climbing. Seriously. Mom takes him to rock-climbing classes at the Y on Sundays.

Patiently, I take a breath. I ask, "Did you see green?" because when Jonah was three, Dad got him a clock that changes colors. All night it stays red, and then at seven A.M. it turns green. Jonah is supposed to stay in bed until the clock turns green.

But Jonah isn't great at following instructions. Or colors.

"I know how to tell the time," Jonah says, all huffy.

"Then why did you wake me up?"

"Because I saw purple, too, and I wanted to show you," he says, then waves at me to follow him. "Come on, come on!"

Huh? He saw purple?

I sigh. Crumbs. I get out of bed, step into my striped slippers, and follow him.

"Wait!" I say, spotting his bare feet. I steer him to his room, which is next to mine. "You need shoes, mister. I don't want you cutting your foot on a piece of broken mirror glass."

"But there's no glass."

He broke a mirror and there's no glass? I point to his closet. "Shoes!" It's my job to protect all of him, even his smelly feet.

Jonah's room is bright, because of the glow-in-the-dark stars stuck to his ceiling and his *red* clock. Not purple. Red. Jonah grabs his sneakers from the floor of his closet and shoves them on. "Are you happy now? Let's go, let's go!"

"Shush!" I order. Mom and Dad's door is closed, but their room is just down the hall. Mom will not be happy if we wake her up. (She already got annoyed at me once today when I told her she was six minutes and forty-five seconds late picking me up

14

at school. I didn't mean to make her feel bad. But I have a super-cool timer on my watch, and if I'm not going to use it to tell her how late she is, then what am I going to use it for?)

We slink down the first flight of stairs. They creak. A lot. Finally, I reach to open the door to the basement.

I freeze. I freeze as if, well, I've been tagged. Because the truth is I am possibly not the bravest girl in the world. And it's late. And we're going to the basement.

I prefer reading about adventures, not having them.

"What's wrong?" Jonah asks, sliding in front of me and down the stairs. "Come on, come on, come on!"

I take a big, deep breath, turn on the basement light, and close the door behind me.

# ✳ chapter three ✳

## Mirror, Mirror, Bolted to the Wall

One step. *Creak.*

Two steps. *Creak!*

Three. *Creeeeeak!*

I stop on the very bottom stair and look across the basement at the huge and creepy mirror. It's still huge and creepy, but other than that, it looks perfectly fine. "There is not a single crack in the mirror," I say. "We're going back to bed. Now."

"I never said it was *cracked*," Jonah says. "I said it was hissing." He approaches the mirror, getting so close his breath turns the glass foggy. "It must have stopped when I left."

I stay where I am, taking in every last detail of the antique mirror the previous owners left behind. It's twice the size of me. The glass part is clear and smooth. The frame is made of stone and decorated with carvings of small fairies with wings and wands. I don't know why the old owners didn't take it with them, except . . . well, it's creepy. And attached to the wall. With big, heavy Frankenstein bolts.

In the reflection I see my shoulder-length curly brown hair. My lime-green pajamas. My striped slippers. Only, there's something off about my reflection, so I turn away. I don't know *what* exactly, but it's weird.

"It's not hissing," I say, checking out the rest of the basement. Black leather couch. Desk. Swivel chair. Lots and lots of bookshelves, all filled with my parents' old law books, which they never look at but don't want to throw away. Mom and Dad are both lawyers. Unlike me, neither of them wants to be a judge.

For the record: I'm going to be a really great judge because I'm all about peace and order. I'll make sure justice is always served, because it's not fair when bad people don't get in trouble, or when bad things happen to good people.

Like my parents making me move to Smithville.

"You have to knock," Jonah says.

His words pull me back. "What's that?"

"On the mirror," he says, his eyebrows scrunching together. "You have to knock."

I laugh. "I'm not knocking on the mirror! Why would anyone knock on a mirror?"

"They would if it was an accident! See, I was playing flying crocodile when —"

"What's flying crocodile?" I ask.

"An awesome new game I invented. I'm a pirate and I'm being chased by crocodiles, except my crocodiles can fly and —"

"Never mind," I say, regretting I asked. "How did this lead you to the mirror?"

"Well, when I was being chased by one of the flying crocodiles —"

"One of the *imaginary* flying crocodiles."

"— when I was being chased by one of the *imaginary* flying crocodiles, I tripped and smacked into the not-imaginary mirror. It sounded like a knock. I'll do it again. Ready?"

Ready for what? I'm ready to get back into my toasty bed. But to him I say, "Go ahead."

He lifts his fist and knocks.

We wait. Nothing happens.

"Nothing's happening," I tell him.

But then I hear a low hissing sound.

*Sssssssssssssssssssssss.*

My whole body tenses. I do *not* like hissing. Especially hissing mirrors. "Um, Jonah?"

"See? Now check this out. Look what happens when I knock twice!"

He knocks again, and a warm light radiates from the mirror, too. A warm *purple* light.

"See?" Jonah says. "Purple! Told you!"

My mouth goes dry. What is going on? Why is the mirror in our basement turning colors? Mirrors should not change colors. I do not like mirrors that change colors!

"This is when I went to get you. But I want to see what happens if I knock again. Three's a charm, right?"

"Jonah, no!"

Too late. He's already knocking.

Our reflection in the mirror starts to shake.

I don't like shaking mirrors any more than I like purple hissing mirrors.

"What's it doing?" I whisper. My image is rippling like the surface of a lake. My insides are rippling, too. Have I mentioned that I want to be a judge because I like peace? And order? And not rippling, hissing, purple-turning mirrors?!

"It's alive!" Jonah squeals.

The ripples in the mirror spin in a circle, like a whirlpool.

"We should go," I say as tingles creep down my spine. "Like, *now*." I try to pull Jonah away, but I can't. Our images are churning around and around and around in the mirror like clothes in the dryer, and we're being dragged toward the mirror. Jonah's right foot slides forward. His sneaker squeaks against the concrete floor.

"It wants my foot," Jonah cries.

"Well, it can't have it!" I grab him tight. "You can't have it, you . . . you mirror-thing!" I crane my neck toward the basement stairs. "Mom! Dad!" I yell. But they are two floors up and I closed the basement door. Why did I close the basement door?

I snuck into a basement in the middle of the night and closed the door? What is wrong with me? I need backup! "Help!"

With my free hand I reach out and grasp the leg of the desk. My fingers burn, but I will absolutely not let go of my brother *or* the desk leg.

*Whoosh!* Suddenly, the whole world turns sideways. Jonah and I are horizontal. We wave in the air like human flags, which makes no sense. I don't *like* things that make no sense.

"Cool!" Jonah hollers. Is he smiling? He is! He's smiling. How could he be having fun at a time like this?

My brother's shoe disappears. Disappears right off his foot and goes into the mirror.

No! Impossible!

There's a really loud buzzing, and my brother's other shoe gets swallowed by the mirror, too.

*Slurp.*

My heart is racing, and I'm hot and cold at the same time, because that could not have just happened. None of this can be happening. And why weren't Jonah's shoes tied? Do I have to do everything myself?

My slippers are suddenly sucked off my feet.

*So* not my fault. You can't tie slippers.

A book flies off the bookshelf and into the mirror. And another. All my parents' law books go — *swoop* — right off the bookshelf and into the mirror, their pages flapping like the wings of overexcited birds.

The swivel chair scoots across the floor. *Slurp!*

My brother's hands are slipping. "Abby?" he says, and for the first time tonight, my brother — who isn't afraid of anything — sounds scared.

"Hold on!" I try to tighten my grip on his hand, but our palms are clammy. Pain shoots right from my fingers to my shoulders. I ignore it. I need to hold on. I *have* to hold on.

"Abby!"

"No!" I say, holding on even tighter. He flutters in the air. His eyes are wide and glowing purple.

"Jonah!" I scream. NO, NO, NO. I will NOT let the crazy mirror slurp up my brother. I'm in charge here! I will keep my brother safe!

I let go of the leg of the desk and grab him with both hands. With a satisfied grumble, the mirror sucks us both inside.

# ✳ chapter four ✳

## Too Many Trees

*t*hump.

    I land facedown on dirt. Dirt and leaves and grass. There's a twig in my mouth. Blah. I pick it out and wipe my hand on my pajama bottoms.

"I think I just broke my head," Jonah mumbles.

"Seriously?" I ask.

"No," Jonah says, rubbing the back of his neck. "I'm okay."

Good. I'm glad he's okay. Now I don't have to feel bad when I yell at him. "WHAT WERE YOU THINKING?"

"What do you mean?" he asks innocently.

I leap to my feet and tick off the answers on my fingers. "Exhibit A: You drag us to the basement. Exhibit B: You knock on the creepy mirror. And exhibits C, D, and E: You then proceed to knock *two more times* on the creepy mirror, and when it tries to suck us in? You. Said. 'COOL!'"

"'Cause it was!" he exclaims. "Come on, Abby! That was so awesome! That was the most awesomest thing to ever happen to us."

I shake my head. I'm not sure what even happened. Where are we?

I sniff. It smells like nature. I push myself up onto my elbows and look around. I see:

1. Large trees.
2. More large trees.
3. Even MORE large trees.

Um, why are there thousands of large trees in my basement?

Wait. My basement does not have trees.

I turn to Jonah. "We're not in the basement!"

24

"I know," Jonah says, nodding. "Sweet."

"So where are we?"

"Somewhere awesome."

"The backyard," I say. "We have to be in the backyard. Right?" Except we have a tiny backyard. And our backyard has only two trees. Two scrawny trees. Not thousands of large trees.

"No way, we're not in the backyard," Jonah says, shaking his head.

"Maybe it looks different at night?"

"Nope. I think we're in a forest."

"Jonah, we can't be in a forest! That's impossible!"

"Well, maybe impossible things are possible?"

*He* is impossible. I rub my eyes. "This makes no sense. Wait. What if we're dreaming?"

"Both of us?" he asks, raising one eyebrow.

"Fine, me. What if I'm dreaming?"

He pinches me.

"Ow!"

"Not dreaming," he proclaims. He bounces on his toes. "You are one hundred percent awake, and so am I, and we are in a forest. Hey, I'm hungry. Do you have any Cheetos?"

*"Cheetos?"* I screech. "We've somehow been transported from our basement to a forest in the middle of the night, and you're thinking about *Cheetos*?"

He scratches his belly. "The mirror was hungry, so it ate us. Now I'm hungry, and I would really like some Flamin' Hot Cheetos. And maybe some ketchup."

"That is disgusting," I say. Jonah dips everything in ketchup. Even French toast.

"And it's not the middle of the night," he continues. "Look."

I tilt my head. Blue sky peeks through the tops of the trees.

Before, it was night. Now it's day.

I don't understand what's going on! I stomp my foot like a two-year-old. *Ouch.* A twig scratches my heel, because — *ohhhh,* that's right — before the mirror ate me, the mirror ate my slippers. But here I am, so where are my fuzzy striped slippers?

First I will find my slippers. Then I will figure out how to get back to our basement.

That is my plan. Plans make me happy.

Step One: Find footwear.

I crane my neck and check out the scene. In addition to me and my brother, our basement chair is lying on its side a few feet from us. Some of the books from the bookshelf are also in the grass. And there are my slippers!

"Yay!" I cheer. I run toward them and slip them on. Ah. Fuzzy striped slippers can make a person feel much better.

I turn to Jonah. "Did you find your sneakers?"

"Yup," he says, pointing at them.

"Well, put them on, and tie them this time." I wait. "Are they tied?" I know he knows how to tie them, because I taught him. And I taught him the right way, not the baby way with two bows.

He groans and laces them extra tight.

Good. We've completed Step One. Now for Step Two: Get back to our basement. *Hmm.* That one's tougher, but nothing I can't handle.

I suppose it would help if I could figure out where we are.

We can't be very far from home, since the whole trip only took, like, a minute. There must have been a tornado, or maybe even an earthquake. Yes, an earthquake! An earthquake that tossed us a few blocks from our house! Yes! We must have hit our heads and fallen asleep and *that's* why it's already daytime!

Now I just have to find our way home. Time to focus.

*Growl.*

What was that? Nothing. I must have imagined it.

*Crack.*

"Did you hear that?" Jonah whispers.

"Um. No?"

*Growwwl.*

My heart thumps. "Any chance it's your stomach grumbling because you're hungry?"

He scoots closer. "Maybe it's an animal's stomach. Because the animal is hungry."

*Growwwl, crack.*

"Hungry for humans," Jonah says, sounding a bit too excited for my liking.

*Crack, growwwl.*

*Argh!* How am I supposed to focus on Step Two of my plan with scary animal-stomach noises all around me?

"I think we should go," I tell him.

"Go where?"

*Growl, crack, growl, crack, growl, crack, crack!*

"Somewhere that isn't here!"

I grab his hand and we run.

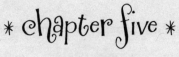

## Hide and Seek

I never knew I could move so fast.

If I was back at school playing tag — the right *or* the wrong tag — no one would ever catch me.

That's the good news about my mad dash with Jonah. The bad news is that I have no idea which way is home, or where in Smithville we are.

I also don't know what's chasing us. But guess what? Our fast-running feet may have outrun it, because I no longer hear anything behind us. Then again, that may be because my loud huffing and puffing is drowning out all other sounds.

A sharp pain stabs my side, and I stop.

"Need . . . water!" Jonah pants. "Need . . . food! Forget Cheetos. I'll eat anything! But no broccoli, please!"

I lean over and try to catch my breath. "I don't know about you, but I have yet to spot a restaurant around here. Just trees, trees, and more trees."

"Look," Jonah says, dropping his voice. He points at something up ahead.

I look, and my heart leaps when I see that it's a person! A female adult person!

"Oh, yay!" I call, charging toward her. "Hi, there!"

She keeps going, slipping between the trees. Did she not hear?

"Excuse me!" I cry. "Wait! Hold up!"

Finally, she turns around. She's old — like grandparent old, but without the hot pink lipstick my nana wears — and she's wearing a black coat and holding a basket.

I wave and smile.

She glares. And continues walking.

How rude. Grown-ups aren't supposed to be rude. My nana would never be rude.

Now what am I supposed to do?

"Excuse us!" Jonah yells. "Excuse us, excuse us, excuse us, excuse us, excuse us, EXCUSE US!"

The lady stops in her tracks and turns around again. "What?" she barks.

Yay, Jonah! I guess being persistent can pay off.

"Do you know where we are?" Jonah asks.

"We're kind of lost," I add. "We were in our basement, but then we knocked on our mirror, or rather, my silly brother knocked on the mirror, and —" Maybe it's best not to go into the details. "Well, anyway. Can you help us, please?" I give her my most charming smile. I elbow Jonah to indicate that he should do the same.

She scowls and goes back to walking.

My nana would *never* ignore two lost kids in a forest, even if they weren't us. She would walk them home, tell them to wear a hat, and bring them chicken soup.

"What should we do?" I ask Jonah.

"Follow her!"

"I don't think we should," I say. "She's mean. I don't think she really wants us to, either."

"Do you have a better idea?" he asks.

31

I chew on my bottom lip.

Jonah takes that to mean *Okay, then! Follow the mean lady it is!* and off he goes. I hesitate, then hurry to catch up.

"Quietly," I whisper, grabbing his arm to slow him down and stop him from stomping on every branch and twig.

Mean Lady goes around a tree. We go around the same tree, then hide. She goes straight; we go straight. She goes right; we go right. We are sneaky and follow her wherever she goes. Then, even more sneakily, we hide. And follow and hide and follow and hide.

"I hope she's not lost, too," Jonah whispers as he ducks behind a tree.

Ten minutes later, she reaches a path. Yay! Only, I still don't know where we are. Why does Smithville have forests with paths in the middle of nowhere? This place is so weird. First soda instead of pop, and now weird forests.

We follow the old lady for another five minutes, until we arrive at a house. It's a small house. It's painted white, with flowers planted in the front garden, and it's cute and tidy and welcoming. My chest feels lighter, because Mean Lady does know where she's going. She's going *here*. And it's better to follow a mean lady who knows where she's going than no one at all, right?

I pull Jonah down behind a tree as Mean Lady walks up the charming stone footpath.

She knocks on the door. Once. Twice.

No one answers.

She knocks again.

And finally, the curtain behind one of the windows twitches.

# ✳ chapter six ✳

## An Apple a Day

S omeone's home!" Jonah whispers. "Why aren't they answering?"

"If a meanie like that was knocking on your door, would you?" I ask him. He'd better not.

"I know you're there, you silly thing," the lady says in a teasing way. She's acting a lot friendlier to the silly thing in the house than she acted toward us.

The curtain moves and the window opens. "It's just . . . well, you see . . . I'm not allowed to answer the door," the person inside replies.

Someone *is* home! It's definitely a girl. She doesn't sound like a kid, but she doesn't sound like a grown-up, either. A teenager, maybe?

The old lady pulls a shiny red apple out of her basket. It glistens in the sun.

"Hungry," Jonah whispers. He pretends to be a zombie and makes his eyes glaze over. *"Hhhhuungry!"*

I pinch him. "Shhh!"

"I have apples to sell," the lady singsongs.

"No, thank you," the girl says from behind the window curtain. "I'm not supposed to buy anything."

"I'll give you one as a gift," the lady offers, then clears her throat. "I'll sell the rest later."

"No, really, that's okay," the girl says. "But thank you."

If I lean forward, I can see a corner of her face. Her hair is super dark, and her skin is super pale, except *not* in a zombie way. More like in a china-doll way. And her lips are really red. Really, really red. Like, bloodred, but again, not in a *bad* bloodred way. She's beautiful, actually. Also, she looks familiar, like I've seen her before. Has she babysat for us, maybe?

"But it's so yummy!" the lady coaxes, extending the

apple. "So juicy. So fresh. What's wrong? Are you concerned it might be —"

Jonah scrambles out into the open too quickly for me to catch him. "I'll take it! I'll take the yummy, juicy apple!"

Oh, brother.

"Jonah!" I whisper-yell. *"Get! Back! Here!"*

He skids to a stop at the front door. "Hi," he says, smiling at the old lady. He holds out his open hand. "Can I have one, please?"

The old lady snaps, "It's not for you. Bye-bye, now."

"But I said 'please,'" he whines. "And I'm starving."

I groan, then emerge from our hiding spot. "You heard the lady. It's bye-bye time." I grip his shoulder and lower my voice. "Plus, you shouldn't eat food from a stranger, and you know it."

"Then why can the girl inside eat it?" my brother asks.

Hmm. A red apple. A girl inside with dark hair and white skin. Something odd is happening in my head. It's a kind of brain squiggling, as if I should be figuring something out.

"She can't, either," I said, distracted. "And anyway, she's not going to. Didn't you hear her?"

To the girl, I call, "Good job on staying safe!" I give her a thumbs-up, which the old lady swats away.

"Scoot," the now extremely grumpy old lady says to me and Jonah. "Time for you to go now." She tries to smile at us, but it looks fake and a little scary. Then she turns back to the girl. "Time for *you* to eat the apple, dear one."

"Why is she being so unfair?" Jonah asks me. He reaches out, tilts the basket toward him, and peeks inside. "If she's got a whole basket of apples, then why can't she —" He breaks off. "Hey. Wait a sec. The basket's *empty*, you big liar!"

The old lady wrenches the basket from him and yells, "Go away!"

"But you said 'apples,'" Jonah insists. "You said you were selling *applesssss*, so how come you only have the one you're holding?"

"I already sold the rest," the lady says. "All right? Are you satisfied?"

My spine is seriously tingling. Something weird is going on. I turn to the girl in the window. "Do people often come to your door selling food? That never happens at our house, except for the Schwan's grocery delivery guy. And he drives a big truck, and it says 'Schwan's' right there on the side. *And* he wears a uniform."

"Girl Scouts, too," Jonah says, contributing. "They come around and sell cookies."

"True. And they wear uniforms, too, don't they?" I turn to the old lady. "So what's the deal? If you're selling apples, why do you only have one piece of fruit?" I look at her black cloak. "And is that supposed to be an apple-seller uniform? Because I've got to be honest — it's not, like, sending the right vibe."

"Take the apple," the old lady orders the girl. It seems like she's decided the best way to deal with me and Jonah is to pretend we don't exist. "Enjoy it. It's free."

"I don't think so," the girl replies, her voice wobbly.

"Take it!" Beads of sweat glisten on the old lady's forehead. Makeup starts to smear down her face. Lots of makeup.

"Is your skin melting?" Jonah asks.

The girl gasps. "It's you!" she cries, pointing to the old lady. "You tried to trick me by wearing a disguise!" Her voice catches, as if she's frightened or about to cry or both. "B-b-but it didn't work, so please, just go away!"

She slams the window and draws the curtains closed.

The lady stomps her feet. With her melting makeup, she no longer looks old. Just strange. The features of her face are all blurry, like if you spilled water on a painting. She mutters and says a bunch of words my nana would *never* use. She waves the apple at my brother. "You want my apple so badly? You can have it! Go ahead! Eat it!"

Jonah grows pale. "Never mind. I'm not really hungry anymore."

The melting old lady takes off her black cloak, exposing a tight black gown, and whips the cloak at Jonah.

"Hey!" I protest.

She draws herself tall, and something glints near her collarbone. It looks like a necklace with something hanging from it. I think it's a key, but I can't get a good enough look to be sure. Then she lifts her fists to the sky — one hand clenching the apple, the other clenching air — and roars, lion-style. She has really lost it.

She glowers at my brother. She slits her eyes, takes two steps toward him, and mutters, "You will pay for this. You ruined my whole plan."

How dare she! I wrap my arms around Jonah and yell, "Don't you threaten my brother! We're not scared of you!"

What *plan* is she talking about, anyway? Just because I have a plan, she has to have a plan, too?

Except I don't have a plan. Not exactly.

The old lady laughs a terrifying high-pitched laugh. The kind that makes mirrors not just shake, but shatter.

The kind that would scare anyone.

She throws her basket on the ground and stomps back into the forest.

I feel my brother shivering.

"I think I want to go home now," he whispers.

"Me too. And we will," I say with fake confidence. If Jonah, who *loves* adventure, is scared, then the world has officially turned upside down. And if the world has turned upside down, then that leaves me to be the brave one, doesn't it? Which is a *very* frightening thought.

Think, Abby. The plan. What's the next step in the plan? Wait, I know! Use the girl's phone! Yes! Call home! Get Mom and Dad to come get us. If they can't get here by car, they can always try the mirror. I knock on the door. Once. Twice. Three times. I'm not giving up.

"Please go away," the girl says wearily. "I told you I'm not allowed to let anyone in."

"Yes, but we aren't melty or scary," I beg. "My brother and I, we just need to use your phone."

"My what?"

"Your phone!"

"I don't know what you're talking about!"

Jonah pokes me. "Ask if she has a snack."

"I promise we're not bad guys," I say. "We're just normal kids, and my brother is really hungry. Haven't *you* ever been lost before?"

There is silence.

I hold my breath.

Then, miraculously, the door creaks open, and we see the girl for real. She looks about the same age as my cousin, who's sixteen. She's more beautiful than I first thought, despite the frown creasing her pale skin.

"I'm going to get in trouble for this," she says. She presses her red lips together and swings the door wider. "But all right. You can come in."

# ✳ chapter seven ✳

## Hello, Snow

I'm Abby, and this is my brother, Jonah," I say as we follow her into the house. Except it isn't really a house. It's more of a, well, *cottage*, but that sounds like a word my nana would use.

Everything is small. Really small. Small table. Small chairs. Small lamp. And everything is tidy. Couch cushions are plumped and upright. Table is perfectly set. Fork, plate, knife; fork, plate, knife — times eight. She must have a big family. Well, a *small* big family. But where is everybody?

"It's, uh, lovely to meet you." The girl falters. She clutches the skirt of her dress, and I get the sense she's not used to having visitors. "I'm Snow."

Snow? What kind of name is Snow?

"What an interesting name," I say, or think I say. Maybe I don't. My eyelids suddenly weigh a ton. I can barely hold them open. I yawn.

My brother pinches my arm.

Ouch! "I'm not falling asleep!" I say, although I kind of am. It's late. And we walked for miles. And it's warm in here.

He waggles his eyebrows.

*"What?"* I say.

"Her name is *Snow*," he says, and waggles his eyebrows again.

"Yes, Jonah," I say, giving him a look. "I heard."

*"Snow,"* he repeats, giving me a look right back.

Whoa, my head feels cloudy — but that's no excuse for forgetting my manners. "Right. Sorry. Nice to meet you, too, Snow. Do you think we could use your phone?"

"You keep saying that, but I don't know what you mean," Snow says.

I sigh. Who doesn't know what a phone is? But I don't say that. That would be megarude. Maybe she's homeschooled. Or one of those kids who's never allowed to watch TV or use a cell phone.

Jonah pinches me again. "Abby," he whispers. "Snow is —"

"Stop it," I mutter, and yawn again. Why is he being so embarrassing? I can't take him anywhere.

"But —"

"Shush. No talking. Zip it." When Mom or Dad tells him to zip it, he has to be quiet and silently count to a hundred.

"Would you like to sit down?" Snow asks, motioning to the couch.

*Yes!* "Thank you," I say. My whole body aches. My feet are on fire. Walking in slippers was not my best move. If I'd known I'd be hiking through the forest when Jonah woke me up, I would have worn sneakers. And kept them tied.

I collapse onto the couch. So tired. Except it's hard to get comfy. These cushions are so small. Who fits on a couch like this?

Jonah squeezes in beside me. And bounces.

"Do you have to use the bathroom?" I ask him, struggling to keep my eyes open.

44

He shakes his head back and forth. Then he giggles. He *giggles*!

What is wrong with him? Does he ever get tired?

"Can I get you anything?" Snow asks.

"Do you have any Cheetos?" Jonah asks.

Snow looks at us blankly. "I don't know what those are, either."

Her parents must be health nuts, too.

"Do you two live around here?" she asks.

At last we're getting somewhere.

"Yes!" I say. "I mean, no! I mean, can you just tell us how to get to Sheraton Street from here?" Realizing how lame I must sound, I add, "Um, that's where we live. We just moved."

"I've never heard of Sheraton Street," she says. "So you're *really* two lost kids? You're *really* not wearing disguises?"

I laugh uneasily. "Do people usually come over wearing disguises?"

"Only my stepmother."

Jonah bounces again.

"Jonah, stop," I say, and turn back to Snow. "Why would your stepmom put on a disguise?"

"So I won't recognize her."

I rub my forehead, because what she says makes no sense and makes total sense at the same time. It's like I'm being given puzzle pieces, one and then another and then another, and if I wasn't so tired, I could probably put all the pieces together and make some sort of picture.

"I'm glad you showed up," Snow continues. "Otherwise I probably wouldn't have realized it was my stepmother at the door, and I would have taken the apple. Who knows what would have happened then?"

"I do!" Jonah blurts out. "You would have eaten the apple and it would have been poisoned. That's what!"

He zipped it up for about a minute. Not bad for Jonah. Wait. What did he just say? "The apple would have been poisoned?"

"Yeah," Jonah says. "Snow's stepmom was trying to kill her with the poisoned apple and that's why she was wearing a disguise. So Snow would open the door. How could you not remember the story? Nana used to read it to you — to us — all the time!"

Stepmom.

Apple.

Disguise.

Poison.

I am suddenly wide-awake. "Oh. My. Goodness!"

"Finally!" Jonah says, and throws his hands in the air.

No. Yes. Impossible. "You're Snow White?" I say. "You can't be!"

She blinks her round blue eyes. "How do you know my last name?"

# ✳ chapter eight ✳

## We're *So* Not in Smithville Anymore

I look around the cottage at all the small furniture.

I think about the apple and the woman in disguise.

The stepmom in disguise.

"You're Snow White?" I ask again.

She nods.

"The *real* Snow White?"

"I think so. Unless there's another Snow White?"

"I think you're it," Jonah says.

"But . . ." I slump back in my tiny chair, the gears of my brain turning.

Snow White exists only in a fairy tale. That means that if the Snow White here *is* the real Snow White, then we, Jonah and I, are also in a . . . in a . . . It makes no sense. You don't just fall through a mirror and land in a fairy tale.

"We're in the story," Jonah says. "It's magic!"

"But there's no such thing as magic," I say. "Not in the real world."

"Maybe there is."

"But . . . but . . ." I strain to come up with an argument that will convince him. I mean, me. I mean, him!

"You know how you want to be a judge when you grow up?" Jonah asks, his tone annoyingly calm.

"Why yes, I do know that. What does that have to do with anything?"

He shrugs. "Judges look at the evidence, right?"

I'm silent.

"So look at the evidence," he says.

I don't want to. But I do. I study the girl in front of me:

• Black hair.

• Pale skin.

• Red lips.

*Just like in the story.*

I look around the cottage. Tiny couch. Tiny table. Tiny chairs. For tiny people. *Also just like in the story.*

I turn to Jonah. "It's really her." I turn back to Snow. "It's really you!"

I'm staring at Snow White. The real Snow White. I'm in her living room.

No wonder she looked so familiar. I used to have a T-shirt with her face on it! And didn't I once dress up as her for Halloween? And wait — she's on my jewelry box! The one on my dresser. She's with some other fairy tale characters, but she's definitely there. And I think she's even wearing the same dress with the puffy skirt and fitted top that she has on now.

"Who else would I be?" she asks.

"You're famous!" Jonah cheers. "We've never met anyone famous before."

Snow blushes. "You mean because I'm a princess?"

"Not because of that," I say. "We've heard your story, like, a million times."

"Really?" she asks, looking worried. "From who? Xavier, the huntsman? He said he wouldn't tell anyone!"

"From books," Jonah says. "You're even in the movies."

Her forehead wrinkles. "I don't understand. What's a movie?"

"It's a story," I say. "With pictures. That move."

"But I'm right here," she says. "So how can I be in books and movies?"

A very good question. "I don't know," I say honestly.

We're all silent. I'm finding this all confusing, but at the same time, I can't help feeling giddy. Because OH MY GOSH, how cool is this? I'm standing next to Snow White! I'm *in* a fairy tale!

Snow sighs. "So you know that my stepmother is trying to kill me?"

"Yeah," Jonah says. "Bummer."

"She sent Xavier, her huntsman, to kill me, but he felt bad for me," she says. "He let me run away, but then I got lost in the forest. I walked and ran and walked some more, and finally, I came across this cottage. And I was so tired. So I fell asleep on an empty bed, and the next thing I knew, there were seven little people staring down at me."

We hear a rustling outside and then the door flies open.

One little man. Two little men. Three.

"Speaking of whom . . ." Snow says.

It's really them! "The dwarfs!" I yell, and then clamp my hand over my mouth. Am I supposed to use the word *dwarf*?

"Hello," says the guy in the front. He's the tallest of the seven and possibly the oldest. He has a really loud voice. "Is something wrong?"

I remove my hand. "I didn't mean to call you a dwarf. What am I supposed to call you?"

"I'm Alan," he booms. "The guy with all the hair is Bob. The super-handsome guy is Jon. That's Stan with the big teeth, Tara has the braid, Enid has pink hair, and Frances has the cane."

Tara, Enid, and Frances? Three of the dwarfs are women? That is not how I remember it. Maybe the story never said if they were women or men and I just guessed they were men. Oops.

And they're definitely not like the dwarfs in the Disney version. No Sleepy, Happy, or Sneezy here.

"Hi!" says Jonah. "Nice to meet you!"

"Now you know who we are," Alan says. "Do you want to tell us who you are?"

"And why you're in our house?" Stan asks.

"Talk!" says Frances, slitting her eyes and lifting her cane to point it at us.

My heart skips a beat. The dwarfs are kind of scary. I push Jonah behind me to protect him.

He pushes my arm out of the way. "I'm Jonah!" he exclaims. "And this is awesome!"

Bob pulls on his beard. "Snow, we told you not to let anyone in the house when we're not home!" He really does have a lot of hair. Beard hair, mustache hair, head hair. And chest hair peeking out of his shirt. "Didn't you learn anything from the last two times you answered the door?"

"I know, I know," Snow says. "But they're just lost kids."

"Yes," I say. "We're just lost kids. Don't hurt us!"

Alan shakes his head. "But why do you keep talking to strangers?"

"A stranger is a friend you haven't met yet," Snow says, and then gets a sad look in her eyes. "That's what my father used to say."

"We're harmless," I promise as I raise my arms to prove I'm weaponless. "We'd never hurt anyone."

Snow nods. "They saved me from my stepmother. She came back. She tried to give me a poisoned apple, but they stopped her."

"Wow," says Enid. She runs her hand through her pink hair.

Frances puts down her cane.

Tara tugs on her braid.

Bob tugs on his beard.

Jon continues to look handsome.

Alan nods. "I guess we owe you a thank-you."

"Thank you," all the dwarfs say together.

I flush with pleasure. "No problem."

Jonah puffs out his chest. "Anytime."

"How about all the time?" Frances grunts. "Whenever we leave her alone, her stepmom does something awful. Do you know how hard it is to find someone to clean and cook? Hey, do you guys need a place to stay, too?"

"Cool!" Jonah cheers.

"She's not just a housekeeper," Alan says, glaring at Frances. "She's a little sister."

Little? She's twice the size they are.

"It's kind of sad that a princess has to cook and clean," I say, thinking about the unfairness of it all. "I guess you have nowhere else to go."

"I don't mind," Snow says. "It gives me something to focus on. Otherwise I'd spend all day thinking about . . ." Her voice trails off. I know she's had a hard time lately, what with her step-mom trying to kill her and all, so I don't ask for more info.

Poor Snow. I turn to my brother. "Jonah, we can't stay. We have to go home. When Mom and Dad wake up, they're going to be worried." Not that it wouldn't be cool to hang out in a fairy tale for a while. How many people get to hang out with the real Snow White?

"But we don't know how to get home," Jonah says.

"We should probably head back to the forest," I say. "Maybe if we go back to where we started, we'll figure it out."

Problem is, do I remember the way back? I should have left bread crumbs along the path, like Gretel. Hey, I wonder if all the fairy-tale people know each other. "Do you know Gretel?" I ask. "Sister of Hansel?"

"Who?" they ask.

"Never mind." I guess a poor, unwanted girl wouldn't know a princess.

"Can you at least stay for dinner?" Snow asks.

"Yes!" Jonah says. "I'm starving."

"I make the decisions around here," I say. "I'm the older one." My stomach growls.

I *am* kind of hungry. We *did* do a lot of walking today.

I'm the older, responsible sibling. It's my job to make sure we refuel before setting off on another journey.

Plus, outside there are growling animals.

And stepmoms who want revenge.

"All right," I say. "We can stay."

# ✳ chapter nine ✳

## That's the Way the Story Goes

I don't understand," Stan says, ripping into a piece of stew with his ginormous teeth. "How did you know that the peasant woman was the evil queen in disguise?"

"Because we know your whole story," I say. "We've read it. It's called *Snow White*."

"No," Jonah says. "It's called *Snow White and the Seven Dwarfs*."

Enid straightens her pink dress. "That's us!" she squeals. "The seven dwarfs! We're famous!"

"I think the real one, the one written by the Grimm brothers, is just called *Snow White*." I turn to the dwarfs. "But you guys are definitely in it."

"Do you have any ketchup?" Jonah asks.

"Is that a type of food?" Snow asks.

"Yes," Jonah says. "A delicious kind of food."

They shake their heads.

"Never heard of it," Snow says.

"So you're a fortune-teller?" Bob asks. At least, I think the words came from Bob. I can't see his lips moving under all that hair.

"Nope," I say. "We're just kids, not fortune-tellers."

"We kind of are," my brother says around his mouthful of stew. "Since we know what's going to happen." I'm surprised he's liking the stew and not hiding pieces in his sock. It's kind of gross. Snow is not the world's best cook.

Frances narrows her eyes at us. "Are you a witch? Because we don't want any more funny business, you hear?"

I shake my head. "Nope. No witches, no funny business anywhere." Well, some funny business, considering that we got here via mirror.

"Where do you live?" Alan booms.

"Smithville," I say. "Unfortunately."

Alan shakes his head. "I do not know of this Smithville."

"I'm not surprised. I'm guessing it's kind of far from here," I say. Like, a world away. "Where are we, anyway?"

"You're at our cottage," Bob says.

"Yeah, but where's your cottage?" I ask.

"In the kingdom of Zamel," Alan says.

"Zamel!" Jonah cheers. "Great name!"

Huh? "Zamel? Where's Zamel?"

Frances rolls her eyes. "Here."

So how do I get us from here to Smithville?

"Can you tell us about it?" Snow asks.

"Smithville? It's in the United States of America," I say.

"No, I mean my story," Snow says. "Can you tell us how it goes?"

"Yes," the dwarfs echo. "Tell us, tell us! We love stories!"

I look at my brother and shrug. I guess I can tell them, since it's, um, about them. But I doubt I remember the story exactly. It's the fifth story in the *Fairy Tales* book from the library. I only got through the first two today, and I haven't heard it since before we moved. "Once upon a time —" I stop. "A few years ago, there was a queen." Then what? Hmm. Oh! "And she cut her finger. And a few drops of blood landed on the . . ." I forget what they landed on. What was it? Oh, right! ". . . snow. And the queen thought the combo of the blood and the snow looked really pretty. Wait. It was the combo of the red and the white and something black, too. Jonah, do you remember where the black came from?"

He shakes his head. "I don't even remember this part."

Jonah wasn't exactly as into Nana's stories as I was. His eyes glazed over a lot. He liked to play more than he liked to listen.

"Anyway, the queen wished that she could have a baby who had skin as pale as snow, hair as black as, um, night, lips as red as blood."

"As pale as snow," Bob says, nodding. "So that's how she got her name."

"Oh," Snow says softly, her eyes teary. "I never knew that my mother wished for me. I never knew that's why I look the way I look."

"She must have loved you very much," Tara says.

"I'm sure she did," I say, and my eyes get a little teary, too.

Because what happens next is so sad. I clear my throat. "And then the queen died."

A tear rolls down Snow's cheek.

Aw. Poor Snow. I reach across the table and touch her hand. "Do you want me to stop?"

She sniffs. "No, go on. It's just hard to hear."

I nod. "The king remarried. And the new queen was really full of herself. Every night she would look in her magic mirror and ask who the fairest person in town was. And every night the mirror would say that the queen was."

Snow rolls her eyes. "She's obsessed with that mirror. You have no idea. She talks to it constantly."

"And then one night, when the queen asked who the fairest was, the mirror answered back, 'Snow White.'"

Snow yelps. "That's why she tried to kill me? Because of that stupid mirror?"

"You *are* really pretty," Enid says. "Maybe the mirror isn't so stupid."

"I had no idea that's why she wanted me dead," Snow says. "I thought she just wanted to tear down my room and redecorate. She *loves* to redecorate."

"Anyway, the queen got really upset," I continue. "She decided if she had Snow killed, then she would go back to being the most beautiful. So she asked one of her huntsmen to kill Snow."

Everyone at the table gasps.

Bob turns to Snow. "But you're still here!"

Snow looks down at the table. "I begged Xavier not to kill me. I told him I would hide and never come back to the palace."

"Why didn't you tell us?" Frances asks.

"It was just so awful," Snow says. "I wanted to forget about it."

"The huntsman felt bad for you," I say, nodding. "But he told the queen that he had done it. And I think he gave her the lungs and liver of some animal, pretending it was you."

Bob slams his fists on the table. "That's awful!"

"I remember that part!" Jonah exclaims gleefully. "Didn't she eat them?"

I grimace. Eight sets of eyes widen in horror.

Sure, *that* he remembers.

"She is pure evil," Tara whispers, squeezing her braid.

I nod. "And then she went back to the mirror and asked who the fairest person in town was, and the mirror still said it was Snow."

Stan grunts right through his big teeth. "She must have been really miffed!"

I take another bite of stew. Gross. The dwarfs must like Snow's company, because this is disgusting.

"What's the queen's real name?" Bob asks.

"Evelyn," Snow says.

"Evil Evelyn," I say. Makes it easier to remember.

"She's definitely evil," Snow says, then motions me to go on.

"So Evil Evelyn decided that instead of trusting someone else to kill Snow, she would just do it herself."

"Wait, Abby," my brother interrupts. "Where's the king in all this? Didn't you ever wonder about that? How could they write a whole story about a royal family and leave out the king?"

I look at Snow. "I think he's just kind of wimpy, right?"

Her eyes tear up again. "He's not wimpy. He's dead. He was killed in battle when I was five."

Me and my big mouth. Poor Snow! She lost her mom *and* her dad? "I'm so sorry."

"It's okay," she says sadly. She pushes her chair back and stands up. "Does anyone want more stew? I made a lot."

"No thanks," everyone says immediately.

Everyone except Jonah. "Me, please!"

Seriously?

Snow picks up Jonah's plate. "No one else? We're going to have lots of leftovers."

"So what happens next?" Bob asks.

"I forget exactly," I say, struggling to remember. "I think your stepmom disguises herself as an old woman and tries to kill you a few times? She uses laces?"

"It's true!" Alan says. "She tied them so tight Snow couldn't breathe. We came home and found Snow lying on the floor. We untied them just in time."

"And then she came back with that poisonous comb," Enid says, running her fingers through her pink hair.

"That was terrible," Alan says. "We came home and found Snow lying on the floor again."

"But we removed the comb, and saved her just in time," Alan booms.

Frances growls at Snow, stabbing her fork in the air. "You have to stop letting strangers into the house." Then she points her fork at me and Jonah. "Not counting you two. Maybe. I haven't made up my mind yet. Now finish the story."

"Right," I say. "So today was her third try. She was planning on giving Snow a poisonous apple to eat. In the story Snow actually eats the apple. And by the time that you all come home, it's too late!"

They all gasp again.

"Too late!" Enid shrieks.

"You mean . . ." Jon says, shielding his eyes. (His *sparkly* blue eyes. Jon really is cute. He could totally be a movie star. If, you know, they made movies in fairy tales.)

I nod, unable to say the words.

There's a moment of silence.

"Thank goodness you arrived when you did," Enid says. "You saved Snow's life."

"We should have a parade!" Bob says.

Maybe we should. We saved Snow White. We are awesome. We are heroes! Real heroes! Yay us!

"Not true," says Jonah. "The prince brings her back to life in the story. Right, Abby?"

Oh. Right. The prince.

"He does? How?" asks Tara.

"Well," I say, "after you guys find her on the floor again,

you put her in a" — I'm about to say *coffin*, but it sounds too scary — "box in the forest, and then the prince comes along and saves her."

"How can he save someone who's dead?" Frances asks.

"When he carries her off, the poisoned apple pieces fall out of her mouth and she comes back to life," I say. "Or something like that."

"I thought he kissed her," Jonah says. "And that's what brought her back to life."

"No," I say. "That's not the real story. That's the Disney version."

"Oh, right," Jonah says. "But it happened in Sleeping Beauty's story, right?"

"Right," I say.

"I like the kissing better," Enid says.

"But that's not what happened!" I say, getting annoyed. "I mean, happens. I mean, will happen."

"It's romantic either way," Tara says, swooning. I catch her glancing at Jon.

"So I don't die?" Snow asks.

I take a quick sip of water. "Actually, you do. But then you get better when the prince saves you. And then you get married and live happily ever after."

"Everyone lives happily ever after in fairy tales," Jonah says.

"Not everyone," I say. "Not the bad guys." Fair is fair.

"Are there fairies in the story, too?" Tara asks, wide-eyed.

"No," I say. "Not this one."

"Hmph," Frances says. "That doesn't make sense. Then why is it called a fairy tale?"

"Who cares?" Enid says, her eyes dancing. "So is it Prince Trevor? From the kingdom of Gamel? It has to be, right? He's the only single prince around."

Gamel and Zamel? Seriously? "I don't remember this prince's specific name. I think he's cute, though."

"As cute as Jon?" Tara asks, and then clamps her hand over her mouth.

"Not sure," I say, stifling a smile. "Snow, have you ever met the prince?"

"No," Snow says.

Frances snorts. "I once saw Prince Trevor throw a rock at a stranger."

"He did?" I ask. "That's not very nice."

She shrugs. "Well, he *was* two years old at the time. But still."

"A toast!" Alan calls.

They all lift their glasses.

"Snow is going to marry a prince!"

"Hip, hip, hooray! Hip, hip, hooray!"

Hmm. There is one small problem with all the hipping and hooraying.

Snow didn't eat the apple.

Which means she didn't get poisoned.

And if she didn't get poisoned, then she didn't die.

And if she didn't die, the probably cute prince didn't bring her back to life.

So she probably doesn't marry the probably cute prince.

Which means Jonah and I probably ruined her life.

# ✳ chapter ten ✳

## Oopsies

h ip, hip, hooray! Hip, hip, hooray! Hip, hip —"

"Stop!" I shout. "Snow isn't going to marry the prince!"

"But you just said she would," Alan says, confused.

"She was going to, but then we ruined everything. I'm so sorry. When we stopped Snow from eating the apple, we changed her story." By *we* I mean Jonah, but I'm not going to throw him under the bus in front of everyone. "If she doesn't get poisoned, the prince can't bring her back to life."

Jonah twists his bottom lip. "I didn't think of that."

"We're so sorry," I say. "Jonah, apologize to Snow."

"Sorry," he mumbles, beet red.

"It's okay," Snow says, lowering her head. "I don't need to marry a prince. I don't mind living with the dwarfs for the rest of my life."

"No," I say, feeling panicked. "No, no, no. That is *not* the way your story goes. You cannot stay here and clean up after them for the rest of your life!" We have to fix our mistake. We have to. Stories shouldn't change. They just shouldn't! Look what happens when they do: Snow loses out on her prince! And she has to stay and clean the dwarfs' house for the rest of her life! It's just not fair. And things need to be fair. Judges make things fair, and so will I. "And it's not fair that Evil Evelyn gets away with her evilness. In your story, she gets punished."

"What happens to her?" Snow asks.

"I don't remember exactly," I say, racking my brain.

"She has to put on burning-hot shoes and dance until she dies!" Jonah chimes in.

Sure, *that* he remembers.

Snow winces. "Ouch. That's awful."

Frances nods. "That sounds like something Prince Trevor would make her do. It's the rock all over again."

"He threw a rock when he was two! Jonah used to EAT rocks when he was two." I shake my head. "I have to fix Snow's story."

"Don't worry about me," Snow says. "I'll be fine. You two have to get home, anyway. Your parents are going to worry."

"No, you can't leave now," Bob says. "It's already dark out. It's way too dangerous. You'll stay here tonight."

"I guess you don't have a car to drive us home in?" Jonah asks.

"We have Yopopa," Bob says. "Our horse."

"He's a genius," Alan adds.

I can't help but giggle at the horse's name. And also: Can a horse be a genius? People, yes. Me, maybe. A horse named Yopopa? Doubtful.

"What's a car?" Tara asks.

"It's a horseless carriage," I say.

Frances narrows her eyes. "Are you sure you're not a witch?"

"Yes," I say. "But I don't even think a car — or Yopopa — could get us home." Who knows what will? Who knows what's even happening at home? I glance down at my watch. It says

12:15 A.M. How is that possible? It was just before midnight when we got sucked into the mirror. And we wandered around for at least a few hours. Maybe the watch stopped because the battery ran out? Or maybe the watch stopped because time has stopped at home. Well, why not? It makes as much sense as anything. When we finally get home, it will be the same time as when we left, and Mom and Dad won't have missed us at all. Perfect!

I look through the window and see that it *is* pretty dark outside. And scary. And anyway, I can't leave without figuring out how to fix Snow's story. I just can't. It wouldn't be fair.

"Are you sure you have room for us?" I ask. I don't want to impose.

"Of course," Alan says.

Hello, fairy-tale slumber party! "Then we'll stay."


"Jonah," I whisper angrily a few hours later. "You just kicked me in the face!"

Unfortunately, what Alan forgot to mention was that Jonah and I would have to share a bed.

My feet are hanging over the edge, and my brother's feet are way too close to my mouth. We're sleeping on opposite ends of a mini-dwarf-sized bed in Snow's room.

How am I supposed to sleep like this? And I need to sleep. I'm so very tired. I've been up for at least a zillion hours. Okay, I'm exaggerating. Actually, I don't know how long I've been up since my watch stopped. But I know I need to get some rest if I'm going to be able to come up with a plan to fix Snow's story. And then get us home.

"Sorry," he says. He turns. And tosses. And turns. And tosses. "I'm not tired. Can we go exploring? I want to see crocodiles. And dragons. And pirates. And —"

"Shush," I tell him, motioning to the bed next to ours. "Snow's sleeping. And you should be asleep, too. And no, we can't go exploring. We have to figure out how to fix Snow's story. And then we have to figure out how to get home."

"You don't need to fix my story," Snow declares. "I'm fine here."

"You're up," I say. "Did we wake you?"

"I'm not a great sleeper," Snow admits. "Ever since . . ." Her voice trails off.

"Since what?" Jonah asks.

"Since my father died," she says softly. Even in the dark, I can see the sadness on her face. "My mom died right after I was born, so I never really knew her. My dad remarried and then he died a few years later. And Evil Evelyn never liked having me around."

"What was it like living with Evil Evelyn?" I ask.

Snow sniffs. "She just ignored me. The castle had a lot of staff, so someone else would help me with my meals and clothes and things. And then one day she started glaring at me. I guess that's when the mirror told her I was pretty."

I sigh. I feel SO bad for Snow. We have to fix her story. It's not fair! Why should Snow have to clean and cook for the dwarfs when she should have her own palace? Why should Evil Evelyn get away with her evil behavior? And what about the prince? If we don't fix Snow's story, she'll never meet him and she'll never fall in love and live happily ever after.

"I'm sorry we interrupted Evil Evelyn yesterday," I tell her.

"Oh, don't worry," Snow says. "I'm sure my stepmother will try again. She's tried three times already."

"Why do you keep letting her in?" Jonah asks.

She looks at her hands sadly. "I don't know. I guess I keep hoping it's not really her. That she doesn't really hate me *that* much. My dad used to say that you have to believe the best in people."

"Of course you should believe the best in people," I say. "But not when they're trying to kill you. But you're right. Evil Evelyn will definitely try again. In fact, she's probably yapping it up with her mirror right now, asking who the fairest of them all is. When the mirror says it's you, she'll start plotting a new plan to kill you." An idea explodes in my mind like a firework. "Wait, that's great news! Yay!"

"Um, yeah," Snow says. "Yay."

"Not yay that she's going to kill you. Yay that we're going to fix your story. See, she'll probably put on another disguise and then come over. And this time we won't interrupt. We'll let her poison you."

"We will?" Jonah asks uncertainly.

"Yes! That's the point, right? Snow gets poisoned, you don't barge in asking for an apple, and the story goes on as planned."

"But how do you know she'll use poison again?" Jonah

asks. "The first time she didn't use it. She tried to lace her to death."

True.

Snow shivers. "And then there was the plan to eat my lungs and liver."

"Your stepmom has some serious issues," I agree. "But she did use poison the last two times. So hopefully she'll try it again."

"She *is* a fan of poison," Snow says.

"Exactly. So as long as it's poison again, that's what we'll do. Snow will eat the poison, she'll fall down, the dwarfs will put her in the box, the prince will find her and save her, she'll come back to life —"

"And they'll live happily ever after!" Jonah says.

Whew. I feel much better now. Everything will continue as normal. It's a perfect plan. I am such a good planner. I bet you have to be a good planner to be a judge. So you can plan people's punishments and stuff.

"When do you think she'll come?" Snow asks.

I flip my pillow to the cool side. "Good question. When did she come last time?"

"Today," Snow says.

"No, before today."

"Yesterday."

"And the time before that?"

"The day before yesterday."

"Perfect," I say with a yawn. "Then I bet she'll come tomorrow." Excellent. We'll take care of everything tomorrow.

First: We fix Snow's story.

Second: We figure out how to get home.

# ∗ chapter eleven ∗

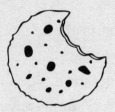

## Everyone Likes Cookies

**a**ll the dwarfs are at work when I hear a knock at the door. I'm not sure what they do, but they seem very dedicated.

"That's her!" I whisper, and put down my spoon. I'm not crazy about my breakfast, anyway. Snow's porridge is no Lucky Charms.

Snow turns even whiter than normal. "Maybe I shouldn't get it."

I place my hands on my hips. "You have to! That's the plan."

Jonah tugs on my arm. "When can we go exploring?"

"Not now, Jonah," I whisper.

"I know. But when?"

"Shush! When we're done."

"But I don't want to be poisoned," Snow whines. "I think I'd rather just live here. And stay un-poisoned."

"I bet you won't even feel it," I say, even though I have no idea if that's true. The story never said anything about the poison hurting, did it?

I peek behind the curtain, expecting to see the old woman from yesterday, but instead, there's a young girl standing there. She's wearing a white dress and has pigtails, and she's carrying a plate of gooey-looking cookies.

"False alarm," I say. "It's just a little girl."

"Abby —" Jonah says.

"I said shush, Jonah!"

Instead of shushing, he jumps up and down. "She changes into different disguises. It's probably Evil Evelyn dressed up."

"Oh, right." Duh. Of course. I should have noticed that she was still tall. It's the queen in disguise! She's so sneaky! She has poisoned cookies! "Snow, are you ready? Let's do this! Open the door and act normal. You don't want her to suspect anything."

"I'm sorry!" Snow yells through the curtains. "I'm not allowed to answer the door!"

What is she doing? "You have to answer the door! Otherwise she won't poison you!"

"You told me to act normal," Snow says back. "That's what I normally say."

"Fine, but don't let her get away."

"I have cookies!" the girl calls from outside. "Chocolate chip cookies! I'm giving them away for free! Would you like one? I'm just a little girl! A harmless little girl!"

"This is perfect," I whisper to Snow. "The cookies are just like the apple. You eat the cookie, you pass out, the story goes on as normal. Case closed." I take a step back so the little Evil Evelyn won't see me, but I pick up the corner of the curtain so I can watch. Jonah crouches behind the couch.

Snow takes a deep breath. "Here I go!" She opens the door and looks at the little girl. "Hello, little girl," she says in a meek voice.

Because the door opens inward, it's blocking my view a bit. I can still see out the window, though. There's an evil glint in the girl's eyes. I can also see her freckles. Evil Evelyn went all out on this disguise. I bet she rocks at Halloween.

The queen practically shoves the plate under Snow's nose. "Would you like one? Don't they smell delicious?"

My stomach grumbles. They *do* smell delicious. I kind of want a cookie. Especially since I didn't finish my porridge.

No poisoned cookie, no poisoned cookie!

"Well, um, all right," Snow says, her voice shaky. "I will eat one of your cookies."

"Here you go," the little girl says. "Take your pick."

I snort. I can't believe that Evil Evelyn thought Snow would fall for the same trick again. Obviously she's not that smart. Hmm. I almost fell for it, too.

"O-okay," Snow says. "Will do. I'm taking it. I'm taking it. Here I go." She reaches outside to pick up a cookie and slowly — *verrry slowwwly* — raises it to her mouth.

No turning back now! She is going to take a bite of the cookie. The story will continue like it's supposed to. Problem solved. Now all we have to do is figure out how to get home.

Snow opens her mouth and takes a bite.

That's when I see it.

The young girl is holding a hammer behind her back.

A hammer.

A hammer?

She's lifting the hammer and swinging it toward Snow's head.

*Noooooo!* This is not the plan! There is no hammer in my plan!

"Stop!" I scream at the tippy-top of my lungs. I jump toward Snow and push her out of the way. We both tumble to the floor.

Snow spits the cookie out.

At the same time, the young girl's hammer swings through the air and just misses its target. "Drat!" the young girl wails, spinning in a circle like a top.

"Why did you do that?" Snow asks me, pushing herself up on her elbows.

"She was going to hit you with a hammer!" She could have smashed Snow in half or made a dent in her head! Would a handsome prince fall in love with a smushed head? I mean, seriously. And who knows if a smushed Snow could be brought back to life?

"You again," the young girl spits, her lips morphing into a sneer. Her makeup starts to melt and I can see Evil Evelyn beneath the disguise. And yes, she's definitely wearing a key on a chain around her neck. What, does she have to wind herself up or something?

Evil Evelyn shakes a long black fingernail in my face. Hmm. There'll be no fooling me a second time. If that key doesn't give her away, those claws sure will. "Why are you ruining my plan?" she snarls.

Is she kidding me? "I'm ruining *your* plan? You're ruining *my* plan!"

Before she can smush *me* with the hammer, I kick the door shut with my bare foot.

Evil Evelyn tries to rattle it open. "I'm coming in! You can't stop me!" She pushes against the door and then kicks it. Then she stops. I peek out the window. Two seconds later, she starts muttering to herself and smashing the hammer against the door.

With the next bang, the hinges almost pop off.

"Maybe this will help," Jonah says, pushing the mini-couch against the door.

"Good idea," I say. "More!" The three of us heave over the mini–dining room table and the mini-chairs. They are much lighter (and smaller) than I wish they were.

I push, Snow pushes, and my brother pushes. We will not —
no, we will *not* — let Evil Evelyn in! On the other side, she's
yelling and grunting and hammering. We block the door with all
the furniture and appliances we can find. The garbage pail.
Chairs. A large pot. Fortunately, the windows are dwarf-sized.
No way is Evil Evelyn fitting through them.

"We have to scare her away," Jonah says.

"But how?" Snow asks.

"We have boiling water!" I scream. "If you don't go away in
three seconds, we're going to throw it at you!"

"We don't have boiling water," Snow whispers.

"She doesn't know that," I whisper back. I would never really
throw boiling water at someone. But Evil Evelyn probably thinks
all people are as evil as she is.

There's a pause.

"I'm going to throw it!" I yell, feeling a bit sick at the thought.
"You'll be covered in burns and blisters! You won't even be the
second-fairest person in the land. You'll be the first ugliest!"

"I'll be back," we hear.

Eventually the other side gets quiet.

"I think she's gone," I say finally.

Snow looks under the curtains. "I don't see her." She exhales with relief.

"Now what?" Jonah asks.

Good question.

"So can we take down the blockade?" Snow asks.

I crawl over to the couch and plant myself on a cushion. "Let's keep it up. Just in case."

"She only comes around once a day," Snow says. "We can try again tomorrow. Now help me tidy up before the dwarfs get back. Frances hates it when things are out of place."

I feel a little queasy. "This whole let-Snow-almost-die plan is not working. What if next time the queen comes back with a truck and mows down the cottage?"

"What's a truck?" Snow asks.

"A really big horseless carriage," Jonah says.

"But what if she comes back with a cannon? Or a dragon? What if she keeps coming back until she gets the job done?" I wonder aloud.

We need to save Snow's story — before there's no Snow left to save.

# ✳ chapter twelve ✳

## Puddle Jumper

After our poisoned-cookie plan fails, I lead us back into the forest and try to retrace our steps. Not that I'm ready to go home yet. I can't leave Zamel until I figure out how to change Snow's story back to the way it was. Snow's so nice. She deserves a happy ending. It's not fair if she doesn't get one because of us. And once the story is fixed, I want to skedaddle as fast as possible. I think time has stopped in Smithville, but what if it hasn't? I don't want Mom and Dad to worry.

But first we fix the story. We HAVE to. If we don't, Evil Evelyn could return and kill Snow for real.

I can't let that happen. Snow can't DIE because of us.

I feel cold and sick just thinking about it.

"This is it," Jonah says. "This is where we came out."

"How can you tell?" I ask. "All the trees look the same to me." Forget Yopopa. Is my brother a genius? A *nature* genius?

He points to a pile on the ground. "I see Mom and Dad's law books. And the computer chair is behind that tree."

Oh. Right.

"This is where you two arrived?" Snow asks. She picks up one of the law books and flips through it.

"Yup," I say. "Now all we have to do is figure out how to get back."

"To get here, I knocked on the mirror three times," Jonah says. "What if I do that again?"

"But there's no mirror here," Snow says.

"Good point," Jonah says.

"What about something else with a reflection?" I ask.

Jonah points in the distance. "Look, a puddle! Water! Water has a reflection, right?"

Yes! "Perfect!" The three of us run toward it.

"I'm going to try," Jonah says.

"Wait," I say. "But what if it works? We can't go home yet." What if the puddle starts to pull us all toward it and then we're back in our basement? "We still haven't fixed Snow's story."

What if Snow gets pulled back with us? How would I explain her to my parents?

Not that they'd mind. She *is* really nice. And her cooking might be gross, but she *does* clean. She could even stay in my room. We could be BFFs. Even better than BFFs — she could be the older sister I never had but always wanted. Yes! She'd lend me her clothes, French braid my hair, and teach me how to do a handstand.

Although she wouldn't be allowed to tell Jonah what to do. That's my job. She wouldn't be allowed to tell me what to do, either.

Maybe I don't really want an older sister.

"I won't knock more than twice," Jonah says. "The mirror in the basement hissed when I knocked once, and then turned purple when I knocked twice. If the puddle turns purple, then I'll stop."

"Perfect," I say. Except I doubt this will work. There's not much of a reflection. Just a lot of mud.

Jonah drops to his knees. He lifts his hand in knocking position. He knocks. Or at least, he tries to knock. But instead, he ends up putting his fist into the dirty water.

Snow and I giggle.

Jonah looks confused. Then he says, "Let me try again."

He does it again. *Splash.* We giggle again.

"It's not hissing *or* turning purple," he says, disappointment written all over his face.

I look down at the still-brown and still-silent puddle. "Nope."

"One more time," Jonah says, and lifts his fist.

"Don't," I say. "Just in case." What if it's too brown for us to see the purple? What if its hissing part is broken? It could still work on the third knock and drag us home!

Too late. His hand slices into the puddle. *Splash!* No purple. No hissing. Just a muddy hand.

Tee, hee. Thank goodness.

"Maybe we need to leave the way we came," I say as Jonah wipes his hand on a leaf.

"But the cottage doesn't have a basement," Jonah points out.

"Not a basement," I say. "An actual mirror."

"Enid has a mirror," Snow says. "You can try hers."

"Is it magic?" Jonah asks, his voice hopeful. "What we really need is a magic mirror."

Snow shakes her head. "Sorry. I only know one person who has a magic mirror. My stepmother."

My jaw drops. Of course! Evil Evelyn has a magic mirror! That's how Snow got into this mess in the first place. "I bet her mirror could take us home. Or at the very least, it would know how to get us home. Since it's magic and all."

Snow shakes her head. "She'd never let us use it. She's not big on sharing. And we'd have to sneak in."

"Where did Evil Evelyn get the mirror?" I ask. Maybe there are more around. Well, why not? I have one in my own basement.

"It came with the castle," she says. "It gets handed down from queen to queen." Her eyes get teary. "It used to be my mom's."

I can feel tears in my eyes, too. Poor Snow doesn't have a mom. Or a dad.

I feel a squeeze in my stomach. I miss my mom and dad. A lot. What if I was wrong about time stopping at home? What if right now they're missing me, too?

"But I'm sure my mom never used it for evil," Snow adds.

I blink away my tears. "I guess we'll have to sneak in."

Snow turns white with fear, which is no easy feat, considering she's already pretty pale. "I'm scared. If she catches us, she'll throw us in the dungeons. Or kill us. Probably kill us."

Jonah's eyes widen. "Do you think she'd eat our lungs and livers, too?"

Snow nods. "She might."

"Do you think she'd use ketchup? I bet they'd be pretty gross without ketchup."

I roll my eyes. "She's not going to eat any of us, okay? We're not going to let her see us. We're *sneaking* in, not *barging* in. Anyway, maybe the mirror at the cottage will work and we won't have to even go there."

On our way back to the cottage, Snow says, "I have an idea about how to fix my story. But it might be dumb."

"My teacher always says there are no dumb ideas," I say. "Only dumb people. Wait, no, I don't think that's how it goes."

Snow looks stricken. "Do you think I'm dumb?"

"Of course not!" True, she did fall for the queen's disguises multiple times. But that's because she's too nice. And anyway, I almost fell for it, too. But only once. "You're just too trusting," I say. "Sometimes you let people push you around."

She twirls her hair. "What do you mean?"

"Well, you're a princess living in a cottage with strangers instead of your own castle. There must be some way to get back what's rightfully yours."

She walks for a few moments without talking. "It's just that my stepmother is so much tougher than me. I'm weak."

"Snow, she's already tried to eat your lungs, suffocate you, poison you, and smush you with a hammer. But you managed to survive all those attempts. You're tougher than you think."

Snow's eyes widen. "I didn't think of it that way."

"Well, you should. You're one tough un-poisoned cookie. So what's your idea?"

She squares her shoulders and stands up taller. "Well, you said that the prince finds me dead, falls in love with me, and then brings me back to life, right?"

"Exactly."

"So why don't we just skip the dying part? I lie in the box, close my eyes, and act like I was just poisoned. He comes along, falls in love, carries me home, and I spring back to life. Except I was never dead!"

I stop walking and look at her. "So the story will basically stay the same, but you don't have to eat poison. Or have your head smushed."

She bites her thumb. "Dumb?"

I link my arm through hers. "Not at all. You know what? It might just work."


A few minutes later, we're back at the cottage and knocking on Enid's mirror.

Nothing happens.

We also knock on all the shiny pots, just to be sure.

Nope. No hissing or purple anywhere.

"Now what?" Jonah asks.

"First we'll fix Snow's story," I say. "Then we'll have to sneak into Evil Evelyn's castle and visit the magic mirror."

"So we get to spend another night? Yay!"

"Not yay. I'm not looking forward to another night of your feet in my face. And I don't want Mom and Dad to worry."

"But, Abby, you said that time stopped at home," Jonah says. "So that means they're asleep. They don't even know we're gone!"

"I know. . . ." I glance down at my watch. "Wait a sec. It says one oh five A.M. My watch is working again! But really slowly. We've been here one fairy-tale day, but my watch says only an hour has passed. Hmm. Maybe time hasn't stopped at home like I thought. Maybe it's actually one oh five A.M. at home. Maybe every day here equals an hour at home."

"So we can stay?"

"Well, Mom and Dad wake up at six forty-five and wake us up at seven. So as long as we only stay for just under six days, we'll get home before they realize we're gone."

He shrugs. "Easy, peasy."

"All right," I say. "We'll stay. But if you kick me in the face again, I'll pull an Evil Evelyn and I'll eat —"

"My liver?" he giggles.

I snap my teeth. "Your toes."

# ✳ chapter thirteen ✳

## The Hills Are Alive

he next morning, before we set off, I ask Snow if Jonah and I can borrow some clothes.

"I don't need anything," Jonah says, looking at Snow's dress with extreme panic.

"Um, yes, you do. We've been wearing the same pajamas for two days. We need to change." We also need to shower, but the bathtubs here scare me. You have to bring your own water. Using the outhouse was terrifying enough.

Ten minutes later, I'm wearing a blue skirt, pink top, and a pair of sandals that belong to Snow. Snow also lent me a red ribbon that I wear in my hair like a headband. Jonah's borrowed a pair of pants and a checkered shirt from Alan. Even though Alan's the biggest of the dwarfs, the pants come down only to Jonah's knees, and the shirt's so tight the buttons are popping.

"I'm packing everyone stew sandwiches for lunch," Snow calls out. "We had so much stew left over that I made sandwiches for everyone for the rest of the week. We have tons!"

Ladies and gentlemen of the jury: What is more disgusting? Stew sandwiches or smushed-banana sandwiches. It's a close call, huh?

Jonah offers to carry the sandwiches in a leather satchel that he borrowed from Bob. It has two straps, so he's wearing it like a backpack.

The dwarfs agreed with Snow's plan and built a box for her. They have a spot they like at the top of a nearby hill, so they guess that's where they would have put the box if Snow had actually been poisoned. Unfortunately, we don't know for sure, so we have to make the best of it.

I'm not happy about making the best of it.

I would rather know exactly where we should be.

Once we carry the box up to the top of the mountain, the dwarfs wish us luck and go to work.

The plan is for Snow, Jonah, and me to wait all day and then leave at night before it gets too dark. It's not like the prince is going to show up at night. I hope. Anyway, he wouldn't be able to see Snow, even in the moonlight.

Snow climbs into the box. I plump her hair and then leave the box open. He needs to see her, right?

Snow pulls out a book. It's called *Property Law 101*.

Hey! "Is that my parents' book?"

She blushes. "Yeah. I borrowed it from the forest. Is that okay?"

"Of course." If she marries the prince, she might be a queen one day. And queens should have a good education.

*Crack.*

"An animal!" Jonah cheers. "A dangerous animal!"

*Growl.*

My shoulders clench. It sounds like the animal from the other day! "What do we do?"

*Growwwl.*

"It's coming from behind that tree!" Jonah exclaims, and before I can stop him, he charges toward it.

"No, Jonah!" I yell.

*Growwwwwwwwwwwl.*

I make a mad dash toward my brother. I will save him! I will stop the evil beast from devouring my brother! I will do whatever it takes!

The growling beast pops out from behind a tree.

It's a wild piglet.

*"Growwwwwwwwwwwl!"* the piglet cries.

"Hi," Jonah says. "Want to play with us?"

The pig takes one look at us and scurries away.

"Boars are easily frightened," Snow calls out.

"Can I go chase him?" Jonah pleads.

"No," I snap.

"Please?"

"No." I sit down by a nearby tree and motion for Jonah to do the same.

He stomps his feet, but does as he's told.

We wait. And wait.

"When do you think the prince will get here?"

"No idea, Jonah."

"In five minutes? Next week?"

He's being SO annoying. "No idea, Jonah."

I draw a tic-tac-toe board in the dirt with a stick and motion to Jonah to go first. He wins. Then I win. Then he wins.

"Let's go exploring," Jonah says five minutes later.

"Not now, Jonah. We're waiting."

"I'm bored of waiting," he grumbles.

"I'm bored of you being annoying," I grumble back. "I'm going to check on Snow."

Her cheeks are bright red.

"Are you okay?" I ask. "You look hot."

She rests the book on her stomach. "I'm fine. Don't worry about me. Are you okay?"

"Snow, are you wearing sunscreen?"

Her face scrunches. "A screen for the sun?"

"I guess you don't have ozone problems here."

"Ozone?"

If only a modern-day dictionary had come back to fairy-tale land, too. Snow could study that.

"Let's move the box to the shade," I say. "We forgot water."

"I know," she says. "Sorry. I should have remembered. And I'm sorry for bothering you. I'm fine."

"Snow! It's not a bother. We don't mind. We want you to be comfortable. Come on, get out."

Snow climbs out and stretches. There's no way it's comfy in there. The three of us heave the box a few feet to the left so it's under a tree, and she climbs back in.

"So what was it like being a princess?" I ask her.

"Oh, you know," she says with a shrug.

"Not really. Did you go to lots of balls?"

"A few," she says.

"Did you have a crown?"

"Yeah."

"Lucky," I say.

She sighs. "You're the one who's lucky."

"Me? I never had a crown."

"You have a brother."

I snort. The girl who lives in a fairy tale is calling *me* lucky? Because of my brother? My oh-so-annoying brother?

I look over at Jonah, who's building a tower with sticks. He has a very determined look on his face and his lips are doing that twisty thing.

He must feel me staring at him, because he looks up and gives me a big smile. An adorable smile.

Aw. He's a cutie.

Sure, he can be annoying, but I'm glad he's here with me. He makes Zamel — and every place, really — a little bit more fun. "Yeah," I admit. "I guess I am lucky."

She nods. "I wish I had a brother. Or a sister."

"I wish I had a sister, too," I say. I look at her from the corner of my eye. "Hey, Snow?"

"Yes?"

"Do you know how to make a French braid?"

She shakes her head.

Hmm. "Do you know how to do a handstand?"

She nods.

"Will you show me?"

She sits up. "And leave the box?"

"I don't think you need to stay in there the whole time. We would hear a horse coming."

She practically jumps onto the ground. "Let's do it," she says.

Snow teaches my brother and me how to do handstands. Jonah learns right away. It takes me a little longer.

We're having so much fun that we barely notice when it starts to get dark.

"We should go home," Snow says, her cheeks flushed with happiness and handstands.

So we do.


It's the next day. My watch says it's almost three A.M. in the real world. We have four real-life hours left. We have four Zamel days to get home.

We hike back up to the clearing. This time I carry a big canteen of water. Snow packs more gross stew sandwiches in Jonah's borrowed bag.

As we reach the clearing, Snow points at the box. "Oh, look! A pillow! How nice." She skips ahead.

"I should have brought a pillow," I say. "Then I could have taken a nap. I barely got any sleep last night."

"Really?" he asks innocently. "I slept amazing."

"You certainly took up enough room." It wasn't just his fault

I didn't sleep. I can't sleep when I'm worried. And I *am* worried. About finding a way home. About saving Snow's story. About saving Snow's life.

Wait a sec. I turn to Jonah. "Did you bring a pillow?"

He shakes his head.

"I didn't bring a pillow," I say. "If you didn't bring a pillow, and I didn't bring a pillow, then who brought a pillow?"

"One of the dwarfs?"

Or . . . "Evil Evelyn!" we yell at the same time.

"Don't lie down!" I yell as we run toward Snow. "Poisoned pillow, poisoned pillow!"

Snow screams. Crumbs! It's too late!

Snow pops up, the tips of her hair burnt off like she stood too close to a fire. "Ow, ow, ow!"

I run toward her, lift the canteen, and dump it on her head.

Her hair fizzles. "Ow, ow, ow," she whimpers.

"Evil Evelyn is spying on us!" Jonah exclaims. "Creepy!"

"Are you okay?" I ask, shivering.

Snow nods.

"You're still the fairest of them all," I say.

"Sometimes I really wish I wasn't," she says with a sigh.

# ✲ chapter fourteen ✲

## He's Here, He's Here, He's Gone

**m**y stomach is a tangle of knots. We've been waiting for two days.

To help pass the time, we teach Snow how to play tag.

"Have you heard of freeze tag?" Jonah asks. "It's really fun. My new school friends taught it to me."

I glare at him. "Regular tag or nothing."

We play regular tag. It's not that much fun with only three people. But I'm sure freeze tag would be even less fun. Then we get bored. Snow returns to reading *Property Law 101*.

"Learning anything good?" I ask.

"I am," she says. "I'm learning about wills."

"What's a will?" Jonah asks.

"It's a legal document that tells people who gets a person's possessions when she dies," Snow says. She taps the cover. "According to this book, a wife automatically inherits all her husband's belongings after he dies. But not if it says otherwise in his will. So I'm wondering: Did my dad have a will?"

"Wouldn't you know if he did?" I ask.

"I guess," she says with a sigh. "It was just an idea."

We go back to playing with sticks. Then we get bored again.

"Abby, what if the prince doesn't come today?" Jonah asks.

"He's going to come soon," I say. He has to.

My brother fidgets with a stick. "But what if it takes him months to come? What if it takes him years? Mom and Dad will be really mad. I don't want to miss Hanukkah. And I definitely don't want to miss my birthday. I'm getting a new scooter!"

I glance at my watch again. It's after three at home. We don't have months to wait. Even if fairy-tale months are only a couple of days in real time, we can't let my parents think we're missing. They'll call the police! They'll hang missing-kid posters around town with our pictures on them. They'll be sick with worry. I roll a twig between my fingers. "I know we should wait for the story to unfold. I just wish we could hurry it along."

"So why don't we just bring Snow to him?" Jonah asks. "We'll go to his kingdom and introduce them."

I shake my head. "I think we should keep the story as close to the original as possible. That way we won't mess anything else up. I think it's better if he sees her in the box. The less changes from the real story, the better."

"What if we bring the box to the palace?" Jonah asks. "We'll put it outside his door. Then when he goes outside, he'll trip over it and the story will go back to normal."

I snort. "We can't carry the box all the way to Camel."

"Gamel," Snow says.

"Whatever." Oh! Oh! "I have an idea! We could send the prince an e-mail asking him to come here!"

Jonah laughs. "An e-mail?"

I blush. "A letter. I meant a letter. We send him a letter that he's wanted somewhere else, and we get him to come this way. Then he rides by and sees Snow in the box, just like in the story."

Snow bites her lower lip. "If he's going toward my old house, he would have to ride by here. We could tell him that he's wanted at the palace."

"Perfect!" I squeal. "Then he meets you along the way and the rest is destiny!"

In fairy-tale land, mail is sent by mailmen on horseback. We write and send a letter to the prince, telling him to come to the Zamel palace pronto, and then we wait.

And wait.

And wait.

Bor-ring.

Two days later, my watch says it's five o'clock back home. And I'm still sitting cross-legged on the forest ground, waiting.

Two more nights of Jonah's feet in my face.

Two more nights of eating Snow's gross porridge and stew.

Two more nights away from my mom and dad.

I like spending time with Snow, and I like hanging with the

dwarfs at night, but I miss my parents. I miss my bed. I might even miss Smithville. I definitely miss my couch. All this sitting in the forest is making my butt sore. I don't even want to discuss the ants trying to crawl up my legs.

I look over at my brother, who's scowling at a group of rocks. Even he's starting to get a little, well, antsy.

I know I have to try to fix Snow's story. It's the right thing to do. But we can't wait too much longer. We have to figure out how to go home.

*B-bam, b-bam, b-bam.* There's a thundering in the distance.

My heart speeds up. "That must be him!"

"Finally!" Jonah says.

Snow sits up. "*Him*, him?"

"*Him*, him! Places, everyone!" I yell. "Places! Go, go, go!"

Snow is supposed to run to the box. Jonah and I are supposed to climb a tree. Yes, one of the skills I've mastered while twiddling our thumbs in the forest is tree climbing. Jonah knows how since it's kind of like rock climbing, but easier. Snow wouldn't try it. She's afraid of heights. At least she's not claustrophobic. That would be bad, considering she's had to spend most of the past few days in a box.

Snow runs back to the box. I give Jonah a boost and he climbs to the top of the tree.

We hear the hooves of horses pounding in the distance.

I see a young man on a brown horse. He has blond hair, looks tall, and is really cute. He's wearing a crown and a red cape. It must be the prince. He looks like a prince. Not that I've ever seen a prince in real life, but he looks pretty prince-y to me. "It's him!" I cheer. "It's really him! Our plan worked!"

He's riding right toward the box. Now he's about a mile away! Now half a mile! He's a few yards away! He's slowing down! He's looking at the box! Any second now! Any second now, he'll see Snow and fall in love with her! The story will continue the way it's supposed to!

Wait. He's not stopping. Why isn't he stopping? He's speeding up. He's leaving. He's galloping away. Huh?

Dust flies everywhere as he gallops right past us.

I hold on to a branch, and as carefully as I can, I jump out of the tree. "Stop!" I yell at him. "You're supposed to stop!"

But he doesn't hear me. What, is he listening to an iPod or something? No, they definitely don't have iPods here. A Walkman, maybe?

I know it was him. It had to be. So what happened?

"That's it?" Jonah asks, sliding down to the ground. "He's gone?"

"It can't be!" I cry. "He saw the box. He looked right at it. Why didn't he stop?"

We hurry closer to the box. It's empty.

"Hello?" I call. "Snow?"

No answer.

No Snow.

"Snow!" I yell louder. My heart slams against my chest. Where is she? Did Evil Evelyn do something to her? Oh, no. Poor Snow!

*Squeak.*

Huh? What's that? Jonah pulls on my arm and points to a tree. A white sleeve peeps out from behind the trunk.

"Snow?"

*Squeak.*

"Snow, why are you hiding behind the tree?"

She doesn't answer. Instead, she lets out another squeak.

"Snow, are you okay?" I approach her and put my arm around her shoulder. "What happened?"

Her cheeks are pink. "I hid."

"I guessed that," I say. "But why?"

"I don't know!" she cries. "I got shy."

"You got shy? *You got shy?!*" What am I going to do with this girl? Now what? The prince — as well as the opportunity — passed us right by. And now that the prince didn't find Snow in the box, he's not going to fall in love with her. Her story is going to be totally different! What about destiny?

I glare at my brother. "This is all your fault."

"Me? What did I do?"

"It's your fault she didn't eat the apple!" I shout. "And why did you have to play in the basement in the middle of the night? Why couldn't you just go to sleep like a normal kid?"

He kicks a rock with his shoe.

"And you —" I turn to Snow. "I'm doing everything I can to help you, and you're messing everything up! Don't you want your happy ending?"

She pales. "Maybe not. Not if it's with some meanie."

"Throwing a rock when he was two doesn't make him a meanie!" I yell.

She crosses her arms in front of her chest. "It doesn't make him nice."

I stomp my foot on the ground. I am mad. So mad. Instead of going home to my family, I am sharing a bed with my brother and living in the middle of the forest so I can try to help Snow. And she doesn't even want to be helped. If she doesn't care about getting her happy ending, why should I? I shouldn't. I should just go home. It's almost morning! And what if time hasn't slowed down at home? What if my watch is just broken? Broken as in malfunctioning, not as in stopped. What if Mom and Dad have been looking for us for days? What if they're so worried they get *really* sick and have to go to the hospital? "Forget it," I say. "We're not helping you anymore. We give up."

Jonah's mouth drops open. "We can't give up!"

"Yes, we can," I snap. "It's time to go home." Sorry, Snow. I tried, I failed, and I'm sorry.

"You're right," Snow says, nodding. "We should be focusing on getting you home. Forget about me. I don't want to marry some rock-throwing meanie anyway. Even if he is a prince. I'm fine living with the dwarfs. We should go."

"Go where?" Jonah asks.

She takes a deep breath. "To my stepmother's."

# ✳ chapter fifteen ✳

## Snow's House

We are hiding behind a tree. Waiting.

"She's off!" I say, finally, as Evil Evelyn's carriage rides away. "How long do we have before she comes home?"

"She's usually gone for about an hour," Snow says. "So not long."

Evil Evelyn is on her way to see her masseuse. Snow said she goes twice a week to get a back massage. Apparently being evil is stressful.

We ride Yopopa the horse toward the castle gate. Luckily he's a giant horse and all three of us fit on his back. I'm at the rear, Jonah is in the middle, and Snow is holding the reins. Jonah begged for front place, but there's no time for Snow to teach him how to steer and stuff. I want to go home. Now. Enough is enough!

Except . . .

"Maybe we should wait," I say. "Maybe we should try something else to fix your story." Enough is enough, but I still feel bad for her. It's not her fault she's so shy that she blew her chance to ride off with the prince and live happily ever after.

And it's not her fault her story got messed up in the first place.

"Absolutely not," she says. "You need to be home with your parents. Besides, how do you know I won't get my happily-ever-after anyway? I can keep coming up with ideas on my own, you know."

"But —" I say.

"No buts," she says.

Wow. Is this really meek little Snow talking? She's getting tougher!

"Okay," I say. But I still feel bad.

"Okay," Snow says, and we trot toward the ginormous castle.

"I can't believe you grew up here," I say with a whistle. Or a kind-of whistle. Whistling is hard.

"What do you mean?" she asks as she steers Yopopa away from a bird.

"This place is huge!"

She shrugs. "Well, it *is* a castle."

And it is. A giant, beautiful castle. With guards and a draw-bridge and a moat.

The drawbridge is huge. Like, twenty-five feet across and ten feet wide. And it's hanging from the castle door with big chains. I wish we had a drawbridge at home. All we have are bushes and an old screen door that creaks. Although it would make having friends over a lot more difficult.

We are trying to break into a castle. What are the chances this works?

I was worried it might be too dangerous for Snow to come with us, but she said she wanted to help. Plus, she's the one who knows her way around the castle. And anyway, the queen's not even here. As for the rest of the people in the castle, we're not exactly sure what they think happened to Snow. Do they think she's dead? Do they think she's in hiding? Who knows what Evil Evelyn's told them.

We decided to disguise Snow just in case. Enid has a pink pointy hat that we used to cover her hair, and I coated Snow's very red lips with a dusting of flour. Plus, she's wearing my lime-green pj's instead of a dress. It's not as good as the queen's disguises, but it should do.

We are ready. Snow even packed us *another* picnic of stew sandwiches. Blah. For lunch and dinner. Jonah is carrying them in the borrowed satchel again. They're kind of stinky.

We pull up to the guard standing by the bridge. Luckily the bridge is still down, since the queen just left.

"That's Arnaldo," Snow whispers, pointing at the guard.

Arnaldo is very large. Very, very large. And he's using a sharp-looking weapon to scratch his extremely bushy black eyebrows.

"You," he barks at us. "Why are you here?"

My knees shake. "We're the new decorators?" I say, except it comes out as a question.

Okay, so I lied. Not nice, I know. Lying is bad. But we need to get into the castle, and this seems like the best way. Snow said decorators were always going in and out of the palace, so we decided that if we told them that's what we are, no one would look twice.

Arnaldo glares at us. Then he glares more at Snow. He is definitely looking twice. Five times at least. "Hmm," he mutters.

My stomach free-falls. He recognizes her.

"Hmm," he mutters again. We are so busted.

"Go ahead," the bushy-eyebrowed Arnaldo finally says. "But leave your horse here."

Phew! I guess my pajamas-and-pointy-hat disguise worked. We're in!

We tie Yopopa to a tree by the bridge. Then we cross the drawbridge and approach the palace.

There's a massive round gold knocker on the door.

"I'm nervous," Snow whispers. "I can't believe I'm back here. And I can't believe Arnaldo didn't recognize me."

A pretty, dark-haired maid in a gray uniform answers the door.

"It's Madeline," Snow whispers. "She's the maid. She knows me, too."

"You're in disguise," I remind her. "Arnaldo didn't recognize you and neither will she." I hope. I really, really hope.

"Can I help you?" Madeline asks.

"We're the decorators?" I say. Again, it sounds like a question.

"Oh," Madeline says with a frown. "We're not expecting you for another hour." She gives Snow a weird look. "Do I know you?"

"No," Snow says, hiding behind her floppy hat. "We've never met. Never, ever. I am not a princess. I'm a decorator."

I pinch her side. Way too obvious!

But Madeline seems to buy it, because she ushers us into the foyer.

The entire room is decorated in stripes. The marble floor is in black stripes. The ceiling has purple stripes. My slippers would fit right in. No wonder Evil Evelyn wants to redecorate. I've been here four seconds and I already have a headache.

"This is the room she wants to fix up?" I ask.

"No, she just did this room last month," Madeline says.

Seriously? "Then where? Her bedroom?" Please be her bedroom, please be her bedroom. That would make our lives so much easier.

"The kitchen," Madeline says.

Boo.

The kitchen is decorated all in red. Red sink, red table, red pots. I feel like I'm trapped in a giant bowl of cherry Jell-O.

"I'll leave you to it," Madeline says. "I have a lot of sewing to do. The queen's disguises don't make themselves, you know."

We wait for her to leave before we sneak out of the kitchen. We follow Snow up two winding staircases.

"This is it," she says at the end of a long, dark hallway. "Her room." She pushes open the door and we creep inside.

Hanging on the wall is the mirror.

# ✶ chapter sixteen ✶

## That's It?

the mirror is my size and framed in gold. If I didn't already know it could talk, I'd think it was an ordinary mirror. But then I notice a fairy carved into the bottom-right corner of the frame. Hmm. Maybe it's not so ordinary.

I hope it knows how to send us home.

Jonah runs up to it and knocks on the glass.

At first, there's no response, but then a loud voice from deep inside yells, "Are you trying to give me a concussion?"

The voice is definitely annoyed, but I can't tell if it's female or male. Two angry blue eyes glare in the reflection. There's no nose, no lips, and no chin. Just eyes.

Jonah freezes. "Sorry," he says in a tiny voice.

"You should be," the mirror says. "You have to follow the rules!"

This is my kind of mirror. I can deal with rules. I turn to Snow. "What rules?"

"It likes when you address it twice and then ask it a question. Like, 'Mirror, Mirror, how are you?'"

"I also like when you don't attack me," the mirror grumbles.

"My brother's really sorry," I say. "Mirror, Mirror, can you take us home?"

"Sure," it says. "Now?"

"Wow," I squeal, surprised.

"You're just going to take us home, Mirror, Mirror?" Jonah asks, sounding a little disappointed. "No quest or anything?"

"Nope. You want to go, you can go right now, but only right now."

"Why only right now?" I ask.

The mirror doesn't answer.

I roll my eyes. "Mirror, Mirror, why only right now?"

"Because the queen is coming home early."

Oh, no! "How early, Mirror, Mirror?"

"Soon," it says.

"How soon?" I ask.

The front door slams. "I'm home!"

"She can't find us here!" Snow shrieks. "She'll kill me and throw you in the dungeons!"

"No, she'd probably just kill you all," the mirror says. "The dungeons are already —"

It stops mid-sentence.

"Are already what?" I ask. "Mirror, Mirror?"

"Pretty full," it finishes.

I have a bad feeling about this.

"Mirror, Mirror," I say, "who's in the dungeon?"

"Xavier the huntsman," it says.

Snow gasps. "Oh, no! For sparing my life?"

"No, for spilling juice on the white carpet. Of course for sparing your life!"

"Someone woke up on the wrong side of the mirror this morning," I grumble.

"Excuse me?!" the mirror yells.

122

"Nothing, nothing. Mirror, Mirror, is anyone else down there?" I ask.

"Prince Trevor," it says.

WHAT?! Now all three of us gasp.

"That c-can't be," I stammer.

"But it is," the mirror says. "He came by yesterday claiming he'd been summoned by a letter. The queen thought he was attempting to overthrow her. She ordered her guards to lock him in the dungeon. Anyway," the mirror continues, "if you two kids want to get home, you'd better hurry up. You have about thirty seconds before she gets here."

ARGH! This is no good. I glance down at my watch. It's just before six in Smithville. We need to go home already. My parents are going to be up in less than an hour! We have to go home TODAY. But the prince is in the dungeon. Because of us. It was my idea to write him a letter. It's my fault. "We need to save the prince," I say solemnly.

Jonah's eyes light up. "A quest! Let's go!"

Snow puts her hand on my arm. "But, Abby, this could be your only chance to go home."

I can't go home knowing someone is in a dungeon because of

me. My heart thumps. "We have to save him. And the huntsman, too. We'll get another chance to go home."

"But —" Snow says.

"No buts," I say.

Jonah is jumping up and down. "We have to escape before Evil Evelyn finds us!"

I turn to the mirror. "Is there another way out?"

The mirror clucks its tongue. "Mirror, Mirror."

Seriously? There's no time for *Mirror, Mirror*! "Mirror, Mirror," I spit out. "Is there another way out?"

"There's the window."

"Let's go, let's go!" I whisper, hurrying to the window. I pull back the thick purple drapes and heave open the shutters. I look outside. We're two stories high.

"Now *that's* how you break your head," Jonah says.

I turn to Snow. "Right now I'm kind of wishing you were Rapunzel."

"Who?"

"Never mind. How do we do this?" I look around the room for ideas. All I see are the mirror, a wardrobe, a desk, and a four-poster bed. "Jonah, any chance you have a rope in your backpack?"

He shakes his head. "Just stew sandwiches. Hey. I'm hungry."

"Jonah, not now."

He looks around the room. "Let's use her sheet!"

"Good idea," I say, and start stripping Evil Evelyn's bed.

"But she'll notice it's gone," Snow says.

"She'll also notice if we're here!" I point out as I pull at the linens. "Which is worse?"

"Good point," Snow says, and she helps me strip the bed. "Now what?" she asks when we're done.

"She's coming, she's coming," the mirror says, taunting us.

"You guys go first," I say. "I'll hold the sheet. Just slide down as far as you can and then jump."

"What about you?" Snow asks.

"Don't worry, I have a plan. Now hurry!"

*Clomp, clomp, clomp.* Footsteps coming up the stairs.

We hear Evil Evelyn's voice as she trails through the hallway. "Oh, Mirror, Mirror," she sings. "I have a question for yooooou. . . ."

Snow looks like she might pass out, but I push her forward. She has to go first, because she's the heaviest, and Jonah can help me hold the sheet. Plus, I want her on the ground in case Jonah needs help. Jonah and I hold the sheet so tight that our knuckles turn white.

Snow hesitates.

"Go," I say. "You have to move!"

"B-b-but —"

"Go!"

With a sharp breath, she goes through the window. She slides down to the bottom of the sheet and then dangles in the air about five feet off the ground. "Now what?" she yells.

"Now you jump!" I say.

"I can't! I'm afraid!"

"You have to! Just do it!"

She closes her eyes, which I'm not sure helps, and jumps. She lands on her butt. A startled expression crosses her face, and then she smiles.

"You're next," I tell Jonah as I wipe the sweat from my forehead.

"But, Abby," he says, "who's gonna hold it for you?"

"Like I said, I have a plan. We'll do it hammock-style. You two will hold the corners and I'll jump into the sheet."

His face squishes. "I don't know if that's a good idea. What if you get hurt?"

Aw. He's worried about me! "I'll be fine. Go, go! We're running out of time."

Snow waves to him from the ground, and prickles of fear run down my spine. He's going to be okay, right? He has to be! I give him a quick hug. He climbs out the window and slides down the sheet. Then he jumps to the ground with a huge smile.

Now comes the tricky part.

Me.

Facing each other, Snow and Jonah are stretching the sheet as wide as it can go to give me room to land.

I look down. Oh, boy. Can I really do this?

I turn to the mirror. "Mirror, Mirror, please don't tell her we were here."

"If she asks, I have to."

Crumbs. We stripped the bed. She's going to ask.

I hear the doorknob turn. She's here! She's coming!

I try to aim myself as best I can and —

I jump.

# ✳ chapter seventeen ✳

## Soft Landing

I'm flying! I'm flying! I'm seriously, honestly flying!

Okay, maybe not *flying* flying, since I'm going down instead of horizontally. And whenever I imagine flying, it's usually soaring across the sky, not crashing to the ground. But still.

Yay!

*Thump.* I land in the sheet, and the next thing I know, I'm all tangled in it. It smells like mothballs. You'd think a fancy queen would make her stuff smell like flowers or at least fabric softener. As I remove the sheet from my head, I spot her in the window. "You three!" she cries. "Guards! Guards!"

I untangle myself and yell, "Run! Run, run, run!"

Before any of the guards realize what's happening, we make it back over the bridge. Tell me, what's the point of a draw-bridge if it's never raised? I'm holding Jonah's hand to make sure I don't lose him, and Snow is right behind us. She lost her hat somewhere along the way, but I guess the disguise-ship has sailed.

Yopopa. Where is Yopopa? Yopopa is gone. "I thought he was a genius," I complain.

"He is," Snow says. "He untied himself, didn't he?"

Great.

We run into the forest. I don't look back. I honestly have never done this much running in my life.

*Wzzzzz.* An arrow whizzes by my head and plants itself in a tree beside me. Ahh!

Another arrow! And another!

There are arrows flying at us from all directions.

We're bending. We're dodging. We're running.

"They're going to catch us!" Jonah says, holding my hand. "We need to hide!"

"Where?"

An arrow whizzes by. It grabs a piece of Jonah's sleeve, tears it off, and pins it to a tree trunk.

Jonah points to the top of the highest tree. "We need to get up there."

"But Snow can't climb," I say.

"Time to learn," he says. He grabs on to a branch and heaves himself up.

"Come on, Snow," I say to her. "You can do it."

I can see the fear in her eyes, but instead of saying no, she jumps for the branch. And makes it. Yay! I go next.

By the time the guards pass us, the three of us are safely hidden by a mass of branches and leaves.

We balance ourselves and catch our breath. The guards continue into the forest.

"Now what?" Snow asks.

"I'm going to have a sandwich," Jonah says as he unties the satchel-backpack. "I should have checked the palace for ketchup."

"I meant, what do we DO next?" Snow asks.

I take a deep breath. "Now we save Xavier and the prince."

# ✳ chapter eighteen ✳

## Castle, Take Two

We hide out in the trees and try to figure out a new plan. Our goal is to rescue both Xavier and the prince from the dungeons.

"But the guards will be looking for us," Snow points out. She's holding on to a large branch for dear life. "And both dungeons are locked."

"Of course they are," Jonah says. He's swinging from the treetop like he's on the monkey bars. "All dungeons are locked. Otherwise who would stay in a dungeon?"

"There's one key for the both of them," Snow says, her knuckles white.

I'm balancing on two branches. "So where's the key?"

She shrugs.

"In Evil Evelyn's room, maybe?" Jonah says. "If I had a key to the dungeon, I would keep it under my pillow."

I snicker. "It's not a baby tooth."

"I know where you'd keep it," he says to me. "In your jewelry box. That's where your diary key is."

"Jonah!" I shriek. "Why do you know that?"

"I was exploring." He bats his eyelashes all innocently. "Hey Snow, did you know you're on Abby's jewelry box? Cool, huh?"

I'm definitely going to have to move that key. A memory flickers in my head. A key. I saw a key. Where did I see a key? Oh! "Evil Evelyn was wearing a key! Around her neck!" I exclaim. In the excitement, I slip.

Snow screams, but I'm able to steady myself before I go crashing to the ground.

"Careful," Jonah says. "But how do we get it if it's around her neck?"

That's a very good question.

*  *  *

A few hours later, we head back to the castle. But this time it's the middle of the night. Luckily the moon and stars are super bright, so we can see our surroundings.

Our plan is to sneak back into Evil Evelyn's room while she's sleeping and slip off the key. The good news: The guards seem to be gone. The bad news: For the first time all day, the drawbridge is up.

"Um, how are we going to get to the castle without the bridge?" I ask.

"I guess we'll have to swim," Snow says.

"Cool!" Jonah says.

Uh-oh. Okay, I'll admit it. I'm no Little Mermaid.

"Wait till you see my front crawl," Jonah boasts. "It's awesome!"

At least we won't have to swim too far. The water is only about twenty feet across. I can definitely do this. Maybe.

"What if someone sees us?" Snow asks. She pinches her nose and wades in.

Jonah runs in after her. "How long can you hold your breath?"

I do not like where this conversation is going. "Let's just get this over with," I say. I take one step into the water and sink right in. Ugh, mud. And it's cold. "Let's go, fast, fast," I say. "And quietly."

Jonah is still wearing the satchel on his back. Those are going to be some very soggy sandwiches.

"Oh, no." Snow stops her breaststroke and freezes. "Oh, no. Oh, no. Oh no oh no oh no. I forgot about Crowly."

"Who's Crowly?" I ask. "A guard?" There must be some guards roaming the area.

"No. The crocodile that lives in the moat!"

I gasp, swallowing a mouthful of water. "This moat? Where we're swimming?" Is she kidding me?

Jonah points up ahead. "Is that him?"

Oh. My. Goodness. Up ahead is a crocodile. A ginormous crocodile. A ginormous, scaly crocodile that's currently munching on a large bird like it's a piece of celery.

"No," Snow says, still frozen. "That's way too small to be Crowly. She must have had a baby."

That's a baby? It's huge! I turn to Snow in disbelief. "How could you forget about two crocodiles?"

"I've had other things to worry about!" she huffs. "And when I left, there was only Crowly!"

On my left, an even bigger crocodile comes into focus. And then snaps her ginormous crocodile jaw.

"Maybe we should turn around," I say, my voice shaking.

Baby Crocodile blocks our path from behind and snaps her baby teeth. I would probably find the idea of a baby crocodile cute if she weren't trying to eat us.

Mama Crocodile lunges again.

Then Baby Crocodile lunges.

Then Mama. And this time, Mama practically flies through the air.

"A flying crocodile!" Jonah hollers. "Cool!"

Cool? Not cool! Their teeth look like steak knives!

Mama Crocodile lunges toward us. "Shore, shore!" I yell, grabbing on to Jonah and still-frozen Snow while trying to swim on my back. I kick my legs hard. It's not easy swimming without using your arms. And Jonah is really heavy. Why is he so heavy? It's that bag he's wearing! "What do you have in there, bricks?" I gurgle as water splashes into my mouth.

"The sandwiches!" Snow calls out. "Give them the sandwiches!"

Jonah reaches into the satchel-backpack and pulls out three of the now soggy stew sandwiches. He tosses two at Mama. He tosses a third at Baby. Will it work?

Baby looks startled. Mama nudges one of the sandwiches with her giant mouth. She does it again. Is she sniffing it?

Suddenly, Mama chomps into it. Baby tastes hers next.

"Even crocodiles need to eat," Jonah says, nodding.

"As long as they're not eating us," I say.

When my feet finally touch down, Snow and I collapse on the shore in relief.

Not Jonah. He's giddily waving good-bye to the crocs.

Dripping wet, I stand up, my legs still shaking. "We have to find an unlocked window on the main floor," I say. "I'll check these. You guys check those."

I try three. All the shutters are sealed shut.

"They're all locked," Snow says when we regroup.

Hmm. "Now what?"

Snow points upward. "Evil Evelyn's window is still open."

"Yeah," I say. "But how are we supposed to get there? Fly?"

Jonah looks back at the water. "I wonder if either of those crocs can fly. . . ."

"Jonah, NO. This is not one of your pretend basement games. This is not flying crocodile. Crocs can't fly. And even if they could you would not be allowed to ride them. Not on my watch, anyway." Speaking of watches . . . No. Mustn't look. It'll just upset me.

He shrugs and looks back at the castle. "Oh! Some of the stones stick out just like on the rock-climbing wall at the Y."

"So?" I ask.

Jonah claps his hands. "So, we rock climb!"

What? No! "No way," I say.

"Yes way," he cheers. "It's easy. Easier than tree climbing, even. I'm one of the best rock climbers in my class, you know."

"In class you have a harness."

"But I don't need a harness. I've never fallen."

"You haven't fallen *yet*."

"Abby," he says, his voice serious and his lips twisty. "I can do it. Trust me."

"I can't do it," Snow says, her face white. "No more heights for me."

"I can do it by myself," Jonah says. "I'll climb up. You guys spot me. I'll go in through the window. I'll take the key —"

"I am NOT letting you rock climb the outside of a castle," I say. "Case closed. Anyway, even if I did let you, what happens next?"

"Evil Evelyn's sleeping, right? So I carefully take off her necklace, then sneak back downstairs and open the shutters on the ground floor. You climb in and then we rescue Xavier and the prince. Then we go home." He wipes his hands together like he's cleaning them. "All done."

I do not like the idea of:

1. My little brother scaling two stories of a castle wall without wearing a harness.
2. My little brother in Evil Evelyn's room by himself.
3. My little brother coming up with ideas when my mind is a blank. Okay, fine. I'm proud of him. But still.

"Snow, you're on spot duty," I order. "I'm climbing, too."
How hard can it be?

# ✲ chapter nineteen ✲

## It's Hard. It's Really, Really Hard.

**m**y toes are sore. My fingers are sore. My whole body is sore. And we are only a foot off the ground.

Jonah gives me a thumbs-up. "You're doing great!"

"Both hands on the wall!" I order. I can't believe he does this for fun.

"Don't look down!" he shouts.

So of course I do. Ahh!

We climb, and climb, and climb some more. "Almost there," he says. At the top he pulls himself over the windowsill and disappears inside, behind the swishy purple curtains.

"Jonah," I whisper loudly. "I want you to stay in view at all times!"

He pops up a second later and raises his arms in a V for *victory.* "I did it!"

"Shhh!"

He leans over and helps me up and over the windowsill.

Right in front of us is Evil Evelyn. Luckily she's fast asleep.

*"Snoooooooooooortshhhhhhhh!"*

Evil Evelyn *snores.* Hahahahaha. Jonah and I giggle. We can't help it.

"What's so funny?" says a voice on the wall.

My heart stops. I spin to face the mirror. How could I have forgotten about the talking mirror?

"Shhh! Please don't wake her up," I whisper.

"Didn't hear you," the mirror says.

"Mirror, Mirror," I say, correcting myself. "Shhh. Please don't wake her up."

"That's better," it says. Then the mirror lowers its voice. "I won't. She's a really sound sleeper. And I don't want to get you in trouble. I like you two, and I like Snow."

"But, Mirror, Mirror," I say. "If you like us so much, why did you send Evil Evelyn to kill Snow in the first place?"

"I didn't have a choice. I have to tell the queen the truth. It's part of the —"

*"Snooooooooooortshhhhhhh!"*

Jonah presses his hands against the glass. "The what? Is it a curse? Wait — are you a real person stuck in a mirror?"

"Well, I'm not in a mirror because it's a fun place to hang out."

"That stinks," Jonah says.

"Tell me about it. All I do is reflect, all day long. It's a constant headache."

"What's your real name?" Jonah asks. "Mirror, Mirror."

"Ga-Gabrielle," the mirror says, choking up.

Oh! She's a girl. "Hi, Gabrielle," I say.

"Mirror, Mirror, can I call you Gabby?" Jonah asks. "It rhymes with Abby!"

"You may not," the girl in the mirror says.

I'll try not to take that personally.

I tiptoe over to the queen's bed. She's sleeping on her back.

Her covers are pulled up to her chin. I carefully lower them enough to see the necklace.

"*Snoooooooooortshhhhhhhh!*"

I jump. But then I lean in again. I see it! I see the key. But where's the clasp to the necklace? Oh, no! It must be at the back of her neck. How can I reach behind her head without waking her up? But wait! Someone with so many costumes would have scissors around for last-minute alterations, right? "Gabrielle, Gabrielle," I whisper. "Where can I find scissors?"

"In the drawer of the desk," she says.

I tiptoe to the other side of the room and open the drawer. It's a mess. There are papers, quills, bottles of ink, and — ta-da! — scissors! "Found 'em!"

I pick up one of the papers. It says: *the fairest of all* over and over and over again.

I think back to Snow's comments earlier. I ask, "Hey, Gabrielle, Gabrielle, do you happen to know if Snow's dad had a will?"

"Of course I know if he did," she says. "I know everything."

"So did he?" I ask impatiently. "Gabrielle, Gabrielle?"

"He did."

No way! "Can you tell me where it is?"

"Of course I can."

"Look, can you please stop playing games? Just tell me! Um, Gabrielle, Gabrielle."

"No need to get snippy, missy. It's hidden behind me. Just lift me up — carefully — and you'll see it."

Jonah and I lift the mirror up — carefully — and gently put it down on the floor. The wall is covered with loose stones.

"You move the stones," I tell Jonah. "I'll get the key."

I tiptoe back over to the queen's bed. I lean over her body . . .

*"Snoooooooooortshhhhhhhh!"*

I jump again. Her snores are terrifying. Must focus! Must cut the necklace!

*Snap!*

Done! I grab the key tightly in my fist. "Got it. Did you find the will?"

Jonah is staring at a round hole in the wall. "I found a bunch of papers," he says. "They look important."

"Okay, put them in your bag." I quickly help him put the stones back. "Let's go. Gabrielle, Gabrielle, thank you for all your help. We'll be back after we're done saving the prince and huntsman so we can go home." Now I can't help glancing at the watch. It's after six. We're running out of time!

"Good luck!" she calls after us as we hurry out of the room.

We run down the two flights of winding stairs to the main floor. We open the shutters. Snow crawls through the small window, and we follow her to a door at the end of the hallway.

I unlock the door and peer straight ahead.

Total darkness.

"We have to go down the stairs," Snow says.

"I can't see a foot in front of me, never mind stairs," I say. "Hey, Jonah, do you happen to have a flashlight in that bag of yours?"

He scrunches his nose. "No. But doesn't your watch have a light on it?"

"Oh! Right! Good thinking!" I press the LIGHT button on my watch and a super-scary, super-twisty creaky winding staircase pops up. "Yikes." This basement is SO much creepier than our basement.

"Let's go, let's go," Jonah calls out.

"Hold the banister," I tell him. "And your shoes had better be tied."

We wind down and down and down some more. I hold on to both the banister and the key for dear life.

When we finally reach the bottom, I take a deep breath and turn to Snow. "Now where?"

Something runs over my foot. A rat. I clamp my hand over my mouth to avoid screaming.

In the distance, we hear rattling and then: "Hello? Is someone there?"

"Prince Trevor?" I call out. "Is that you?"

Jonah jumps ahead. "We're coming, Mr. Trevor. We're coming to rescue you!"

We run toward a large oval door. We all crowd our heads at the small glassless window and see the prince. He *is* cute. Tall. Light hair. He looks very princely, even in this dungeon lighting. "Hey, Snow," I whisper, "fix your hair, fast!" I wish it hadn't gotten frizzled by the poisoned pillow. I unlock the door and it swings open.

"Hi," says the prince.

"Hi," Jonah and I say back.

Snow squeaks.

"I'm Abby," I say, and stick out my right hand to shake. But then I wonder if I should be curtsying or something, so I take my hand back. But his hand is already out, so I stick mine out again.

We shake.

"Nice to meet you," I say.

"You too," he says. "Thank you for rescuing me. I'm Prince Trevor."

"You're welcome. This is my brother, Jonah, and my very good friend Snow."

Snow squeaks again.

I think she *likes* him. Oh! Maybe now that he sees her, he'll fall in love with her and Snow can get her happy ending after all!

And still another squeak.

"Sorry, did you say something?" the prince asks her.

She shakes her head.

Hmm. He's not going to fall in love with her if she won't even talk. Although he fell in love with her in the original story, and she definitely wasn't talking then. Though her being dead probably had something to do with it. And looking pretty. Right now she's kind of a mess. She has seaweed on her forehead, and I wish she wasn't wearing my pj's. Hopefully after we finish rescuing him, they'll relax together and joke around, and they'll have a chance to talk and fall in love.

"Where's the second dungeon?" I ask Snow.

We follow her down a twisty, dark hall. She peers into another window. "It's him! At least, I think it's him. It's so dark."

I unlock the door and swing it open.

Inside is a guy around my dad's age. His hair is long. Really long. His beard is really long, too. He looks like Bob, but taller.

"Snow White?" he says to her. "You're still alive?"

"Lucky for you," I tell him. "Let's go."

We run back up the rickety stairs.

When we reach the main floor, I take Jonah's arm. "We saved them. Now we go home."

And then we hear:

*Goooong! Goooong!*

"What is that?" I ask, covering my ears with my hands.

Panic flashes across Snow's face. "The alarm gong! They know we're here!"

# * chapter twenty *

## Run!

Goooong! Goooong! Goooong!

"Someone must have heard us!" Snow shrieks. "We have to get out of here!"

I don't care how sound a sleeper Evil Evelyn is. There's no way she's sleeping through this racket.

"We have to get out of here. Now!" Prince Trevor declares.

Plan, plan, what's the plan? "To the moat!" I call. "We'll swim!"

Jonah pulls my arm. "That might not be a good idea. We're out of sandwiches."

Crumbs. New plan, new plan! Oh! I know! "Snow, can we lower the drawbridge?"

"Yes!" Snow says, and runs to the entranceway. "I need help!"

Prince Trevor hurries to her side. "What should I do?"

"Pull!" She points to the lever.

He pulls; she pulls. The twenty-five-foot bridge comes crashing down with a loud *KABLAM*.

If Evil Evelyn wasn't awake before, she is now.

"Go!" I yell, grabbing Jonah's hand. The five of us all make a run for it. Jonah and I are in the lead, Xavier is behind us, and Prince Trevor and Snow are in the back.

"Stop!" I hear.

Arnaldo and two of his fellow guards are blocking the drawbridge. They are all large. Very large. I think they even have tattoos. Snake tattoos. Or maybe they're wearing snakes. Not sure. Either way, they're scary. And their arrows are aimed at us.

We stop short. I guess there were guards roaming the grounds after all. Oops.

"Let's go back the other way," Xavier says.

New plan! We turn around. Except Evil Evelyn has taken

over the entranceway. Plus, she has a beefy guard on either side. With more snake tattoos. More arrows are pointed at us.

Now what? I look down to my right. Mama Croc has her jaw wide open and a hungry glint in her eyes. Baby Croc is on our left, looking equally hungry.

We are officially surrounded.

I am officially out of plans.

"Well, well, well," Evil Evelyn snarls. "Look who we have here. Guards! Put the prince and the huntsman in dungeon number one. Put the brother and sister in dungeon number two."

Oh, no! We can't go to the dungeon! How are we going to get home if we're in the dungeon?

We're not. If we're in the dungeon, we're not going home. Never ever.

"Dungeon number two is the better dungeon," Jonah whispers. "I think I saw a ball."

"That was a rat," I tell him. "And I don't want to be in either dungeon."

Evil Evelyn cackles. "As for Snow . . ."

"That's Snow? I thought Snow was in hiding!" one of the guards exclaims.

"I thought she was dead," Arnaldo murmurs.

"You're both right," Evil Evelyn says. "She was in hiding. And soon she will be dead."

And with that, something inside Snow appears to crack. "NO!" she yells at the top of her lungs. "NO, NO, NO! You are done trying to kill me. Do you hear me? DONE, DONE, DONE!!!" She points to the guards. "I command you to put down your weapons!"

The queen laughs. "You command them? You can't command them. I command them. You are nothing. You clean the house of dwarfs."

The dwarfs! Maybe they'll show up and save us! Isn't that how it always happens in the movies? The heroine thinks she's about to become cat food, and then her friends swing in from the branches and save her. The dwarfs have saved Snow in the past. They're going to do it again, right?

But how will they know to save us? Hmm. Yopopa's supposedly a genius. That's probably why he rode off earlier — to get the dwarfs! And now they're going to show up in the nick of time.

Any second now.

Now.

Jonah pokes me in the ribs. "Abby!"

"Not now, Jonah."

"But, Abby."

"I'm a little busy here, Jonah." Actually, not true. But I will be, any second now. As soon as the dwarfs show up.

"Abby!" he shouts. He takes off his satchel-backpack, opens it, and shoves some papers at me. "The will!"

The will? Oh! The will!

"We found the king's will!" I shout.

"You did?" Snow turns back to us, a look of surprise on her face.

I look at the first page, and then the second, and then the third. Please let there be something in here that helps Snow. Pretty please? Pretty please with a cherry on top? Pretty please with a hundred cherries on top?

"Are you done yet?" Evil Evelyn asks as she admires her black fingernails. "You're boring me."

I frantically flip through the pages. Nothing here, nothing here . . . Oh! Here! I found it! Page eleven, clause two! I found it! I clear my throat dramatically.

" 'In case of my demise, the kingdom of Zamel will become

the property of my one child, Snow White, the princess of Zamel. Queen Evelyn will remain her guardian until she is sixteen, and then Snow White will become queen.' "

Everyone gasps.

"I AM sixteen!" Snow exclaims.

"I don't care if you're thirty," Evil Evelyn snaps. "Zamel is mine."

"Apparently it isn't," Arnaldo murmurs. "You're an imposter. Snow's the queen! Get the imposter queen, boys!"

All the tattooed guards charge toward Evil Evelyn.

Yes!

"You haven't won yet!" Evil Evelyn shrieks back. "Snow can't be queen if she's dead."

She aims an arrow at Snow and pulls the bowstring.

"No!" I yell.

"No!" the guards yell. They jump on top of Evil Evelyn.

But it's too late. The arrow is already flying through the air.

"No!" Prince Trevor yells. In what seems like slow motion, he jumps in front of Snow.

Snow is saved! Yes!

But the arrow hits Prince Trevor square in the chest.

"Ah! Ah! Ah!" There is screaming everywhere. A lot of it is coming from me.

Prince Trevor is still standing, but his knees are shaking. After a few dramatic seconds, they buckle and he falls right over the bridge and into the water. *Splash!*

"Oh, no!" Snow cries as she jumps into the water after him. *Splash!*

"Snow!" I call out before I jump in after her. *Splash!*

"Me too!" hollers Jonah as he cannonballs into the moat.

"Jonah, NO," I command, but — *splash!* — it's too late. Why does he never listen to me? So annoying.

*Splash!* Xavier jumps in, too.

Now we're all in the moat.

Unfortunately, so are the crocs.

*Snap.*

*Snap, snap.*

Snow is struggling to hold up the bleeding Prince Trevor's shoulders while she treads water. Xavier is keeping afloat, too, while holding Prince Trevor's feet. I am holding Jonah. Mama and Baby Croc are coming toward us.

Their jaws are open.

They are growling.

They are hungry.

My mouth is dry. My heart is thumping hard against my chest.

This is it. This is really it. We will never go home again. We will never see our parents again.

I hug my shivering brother tight, close my eyes, and wait to become croc food.

# ✴ chapter twenty-one ✴

## Still Floating

**S**omething hits me in the face.

Croc teeth? No. It's smushy. Croc tongue?

I'm hit a second time.

"More stew sandwiches!" Jonah cheers.

My eyes pop open. Stew sandwiches are flying over the water. The crocs are happily chomping on them. Huh?

"I thought you were out of them," I say.

"I am!" Jonah cries.

"But how . . . ?"

Jonah points to the shore, where I see all seven dwarfs tossing sandwiches into the water.

They came! Yay! Yopopa preens beside them. He must have gone to get them after all. I guess he really *is* a genius.

While the crocs are busy stuffing their faces, we carry Prince Trevor out of the water and onto the shore.

Xavier removes the arrow. But it does no good.

Prince Trevor's eyes are closed. He's not breathing.

"Oh, no," Jonah says. I hug him against me. I don't want him to see.

"He's gone," I say. I can't believe it. He's really gone. And it's my fault. If we hadn't written him that letter, he wouldn't have come to the palace in the first place.

He's never going to be king.

He's never going to fall in love with Snow.

He's never going to do anything ever again.

Tears roll down my cheeks. Poor, poor Prince Trevor.

"No," a soft voice says beside me. "No, no, no."

I turn around and see Snow. She's kneeling beside the prince, tears streaming down her face. "No," she says again, her voice hardening. "No, no, no! You call this a happy ending? This is NOT a happy ending!"

"Snow," I say quietly, "there's nothing we can do."

"But in the story, I came back to life! So why can't my prince come back to life?"

"I . . . I . . ." I have no answer. Even if I did, I feel too choked up to speak.

But then she gets a determined look on her face. She kneels down beside the prince and presses her lips against his. And then it happens.

One eyelid flutters.

Then the other one flutters.

Then both his eyes fly open.

He's alive! He's alive?

"You," Prince Trevor says, looking at Snow. "You kissed me. I was dead, but your kiss woke me up."

Snow nods and smiles. "It wasn't a kiss, exactly. It was mouth-to-mouth resuscitation."

"You know mouth-to-mouth?" Jonah asks. "That is so cool!"

"Of course she does," Frances says. "With Evil Evelyn after her, we all had to learn some lifesaving measures."

Prince Trevor sits up and beams. "Whatever it was, you saved my life."

"You saved my life first!" Snow says, smiling brightly. "You jumped in front of the arrow!"

"You saved me from the dungeon first! You're amazing!"

"No, you're amazing!"

The two of them are staring dreamily into each other's eyes.

She really did save his life. And he saved hers. They saved each other.

We should have a parade!

Except this is definitely not the way the story goes. It's kind of the opposite of the way the story goes. Or at the very least, it's the story all tangled up.

Hmm. This version is different from the one in my book, but so what? Snow got a happy ending, didn't she?

Maybe sometimes different can be good?

Prince Trevor kneels on one knee. "Snow White," he says, "will you marry me?"

Yay!

"Seriously?" Snow asks, raising an eyebrow. "We just met five minutes ago."

The girl has a point. Also, she's only sixteen. That's crazy young to get married, at least in my world.

"And I don't know you that well," Snow continues. "I mean, did you really used to throw rocks at people?"

"What? No!" He blushes. "All right, maybe I did. But I was two. Can you ever forgive me?"

Snow tilts her head to the left. "Oh, all right. I did some silly things when I was young, too. I once poured glue all over my stepmother's hairbrush."

"She deserved it," I say.

Speaking of Evil Evelyn, in the distance I see Xavier carrying her, kicking and screaming, into the palace. "Let's see how *you* like the dungeon," Xavier sneers.

"Listen, Trevor," Snow says. "I'm not looking for a serious relationship right now. I need to focus on my duties here, now that I'm queen."

"I get it," the prince says, nodding. "Look, why don't we take it a little slower? How about dinner?"

That's perfect! Maybe it'll take them longer to get there, but Snow and Prince Trevor will get married one day. I just know it.

Snow's eyes light up. "I'll cook!"

"You don't have to cook anymore, Snow," I tell her. "You're the queen."

"I know," she says. "But I like cooking."

I hope Prince Trevor likes stew.

# ✲ chapter twenty-two ✲

## Back to Gabrielle, Gabrielle

*t*his place is awesome," Tara says, stepping into the foyer. "You are so lucky, Snow. You have a castle and a date with a prince." She glances wistfully at Jon.

Snow gives Tara a hug. "I'm glad you like it, since you'll be living here with me, too."

"We will?" Alan asks.

"Of course! I can't thank you enough for giving me a home when I needed one."

"We're going to have to get rid of the stripes," Frances grumbles. "They're giving me a headache."

Madeline the maid pops up behind them and clucks her tongue. "More redecorating?"

"Oh, yes," Enid says. "We're going to need some smaller furniture. And can we paint it pink?"

I get nervous as we climb back up the staircase. The mirror is going to be able to take us home, right? "This isn't going to be a *Wizard of Oz* situation, is it? There's not some guy hiding behind the mirror pretending to be all-powerful?"

Snow shakes her head. "No. It's real. Where's Oz? Near Smithville?"

"Not exactly," I say. I open the door to Evil Evelyn's room and walk straight to the mirror.

"Hi, Gabby, Gabby!" Jonah says.

"We're back. Gabrielle, Gabrielle, can we go home now?" I ask.

"You sure can," she says.

"I'm so happy for you," I tell Snow. "Everything worked out. Better than I could have hoped." I turn to the mirror. "Can Snow set you free now that she's queen?"

"I'm afraid not," Gabrielle says, and blinks away tears. "But thank you for asking. I appreciate it. Now it's time to say your good-byes."

I'm happy and sad at the same time. I hug Alan first. "Thanks for everything."

Then I hug Bob and Stan.

Then Enid. "Stay pink," I say.

Then Jon. "Stay handsome."

When I hug Tara, I can't help whispering, "Tell Jon how you feel." She blushes.

"You're not bad, kid," Frances says, hugging me next.

I shake the prince's hand. "Be good to our Snow," I say, swallowing hard to hold back tears.

"Good-bye, little man," Prince Trevor says to Jonah.

Finally, I hug Snow. "Will I ever see you again?" she asks.

My chest feels heavy. "I don't know. I hope so."

We hug tightly.

"Thank you for not letting Evil Evelyn poison me," she says to Jonah as she ruffles his hair.

He puffs out his chest. "No problem."

"All right already!" Gabrielle grumbles. "I have other things to do, you know."

"Ready?" I ask Jonah.

"Ready," he says.

I take his hand.

"The rest of you better get out of here or you might end up going, too."

"No thanks," Frances says. "Horseless carriages? How does that even work?"

"Good luck," Snow says.

I spot Tara take Jon's hand. Yay! We wave good-bye as they all leave the room.

"Hey, Gabrielle, Gabrielle, do you happen to know why the mirror in our basement brought us here in the first place?" I ask.

"You'll have to ask Maryrose," she says.

"Who's Maryrose?" Jonah asks. "Is Maryrose inside the mirror in our basement?"

"Maryrose will introduce herself when she's ready," Gabrielle says simply. "Now it's time to go."

I sigh. I want to know more. I need to understand what happened! But right now, I really, really, really just want to go home. "Are we going to take the furniture with us?" I ask. "Mom would love that four-poster bed."

"Snow would love it, too," Gabrielle says. "So hopefully not. But speaking of your parents, it's very important that you don't tell them anything about this."

"But why? We tell our parents everything." Mostly.

"It's too dangerous," she says solemnly.

"For who?" I ask. "Us? Them? You? Maryrose?"

"I've said too much," Gabrielle says.

The reflection in the mirror starts to spin around and around and around. I start to see images in the swirl: A desk. Boxes. It's our basement!

"Here we go," I say.

"What are you waiting for?" Gabrielle asks. "I'm an open door. Come on in!"

I take a deep breath and grab Jonah's hand. Then we step through the mirror.

*Zoom.*

We step right onto our basement floor.

I spin around to look at the mirror. It's calm. Normal. A regular mirror.

Like nothing happened. Like nothing's weird at all.

"Hello?" I ask. "Is anyone there?"

No one answers.

It's over. It's really over.

Well, kind of over. The basement is a mess. And all the law books are gone. So is the swivel chair. Oops.

"I wonder what happens if I knock on it again," Jonah says, reaching out his arm.

I stop his hand mid-motion. "Don't you dare!"

"We're home!" he cheers, running upstairs. "Let's go tell Mom and Dad!"

"Wait," I call behind him.

I follow my brother up the stairs. At the top of the staircase, I gently close the door behind me. The next level is awash in the morning light. I sneak into the kitchen to look at the clock on the microwave. It says 6:30 A.M. The same time my watch says. So I was right after all. Time passed slower here. Unless many days have passed?

I check my mom's iPhone. According to the date, it's the morning after we left! Perfect!

"Let's go see Mom and Dad!" Jonah exclaims.

I nod but press my finger against my lips. We creep up the last flight of stairs. I gently open their door.

"I want to get into bed with them," Jonah whispers.

"Me too," I whisper back. "But we're smelly and wearing other people's clothes." And sandals. Oops, I left my slippers at Snow's. Good-bye, slippers. I will miss you.

Jonah looks down at his too-tight outfit. "Oh, right."

"And I think getting into bed with Mom and Dad might freak them out." I close their door and head toward my room.

"Good night," Jonah says, following behind.

"Good morning," I say back, and give him a hug. "I'm going to miss your feet in my face."

He laughs, and I shush him again.

Once inside my room, I strip off my grungy clothes and toss them into the hamper. I kick off Snow's shoes. I pull on a clean pair of pajamas and get into bed. I have thirty minutes before my parents wake me up, and I'm going to use them.

# ✳ chapter twenty-three ✳

## Maybe Stories *Can* Change

W ake up, kids!" I hear. "Time to get ready for school!"

I open my eyes. I'm in my own bed.

Yes! I'm home! I'm home! I'm home! My watch and alarm clock say 7:00 A.M.

I can't help wondering: Was it all a dream?

I run to my laundry basket. Snow's skirt and top are crumpled in my hamper. Her sandals are by my dresser. It happened! It REALLY happened!

I look up and spot my jewelry box on top of my dresser. Aw, there's Snow. Wait a sec, she's wearing something new. She's wearing . . . my lime-green pajamas?! Oh my goodness! We really did change her story!

I run into Jonah's room. His clock might be green, but he's fast asleep. I yank down his covers. "It happened! It REALLY happened."

"Tired," he croaks. He opens one eye. "Of course it happened. Why wouldn't it have?"

I run downstairs. Mom and Dad are in the kitchen. They're drinking coffee and rustling through the newspaper. I throw my arms around both of them. "I love you guys!" I just hope they won't need their law books anytime soon. Or their computer chair.

My mom gives me a bowl of Lucky Charms. Yay! How I missed the marshmallow yumminess! Yay! No more gross porridge!

Jonah comes running into the kitchen, yelling, "Mom! Dad! Guess what? Abby and I swam with flying crocodiles!" He slides into his chair. "Cool, huh?"

I put down my spoonful of Lucky Charms and give him a look across the table. The mirror told us to keep it a secret. Not that I want to lie to my parents. But what if it puts them in danger? What if telling puts us *all* in danger? I'll have to give him a talking-to later.

"That sounds very exciting, Jonah," my dad says, giving me a wink. He obviously doesn't believe him.

"Wow, Jonah," Mom says. "You're looking kind of grimy." She looks at me, too. "So are you, honey. Didn't you take a bath last night?"

He nods his head. "I did, but —"

"We were looking for something in the basement," I say, jumping in. "It was very dusty."

"Did you find it?" Mom asks.

"Oh. Um. No," I say. "But we found other cool stuff instead."

"It's very cluttered down there," my dad says. "We should give away some of the stuff."

Cough, cough. "It's, um, not that cluttered." Not anymore.

"Well," Mom says. "You'd both better take showers before school. Abby, you first. Hurry, 'kay?"

I down the rest of my cereal and then squeeze her tight. "I'm so happy to be here," I say.

My parents smile at each other. "We're so glad to hear you say that," Dad says. "I know the move has been difficult for you — new things can be hard. Change can be hard."

"I'll be okay," I say. Change *is* hard. But it's not always bad. Take Snow, for instance. Her story is different now, but it's still good.

And take Smithville. It's still home, just a different home.

And freeze tag is still tag — just a different kind of tag.

Okay, fine. Freeze tag is still weird, but maybe it can be fun. I'll have to give it another try.

My dad squeezes my shoulder. "What do you want for lunch, honey? Banana and peanut butter sandwich?"

Anything that isn't stew. "Yes!" I say, nodding. "But slice the banana."

"Of course!"

I'm all for trying new things, but mushed banana and peanut butter glop are gross no matter which way you smush it.

I head back upstairs to take a quick shower and brush my very dirty teeth. I can't even remember the last time I used toothpaste. But on the way I hear a strange noise and I stop at the basement door.

*"Aaaaaaabby . . ."*

Was that my name? Should I go back downstairs and see what's happening? Is it Snow? Is she trying to tell us something? Is it Gabrielle? Or is it Maryrose? Who is Maryrose? Where is Maryrose? Is she in our mirror?

I'm about to open the door when I see my mom coming down the hallway. "What are you doing?" she says. "Go get ready. I don't want you to be late."

I let go of the door handle.

Tonight, I decide. Tonight I will find out why the mirror in our basement took us into a fairy tale.

*Hisssssssss.*

Definitely tonight.

# acknowledgements

Thank you thank you thank you to: Laura Dail; Tamar Rydzinski; AnnMarie Anderson; Abby McAden; Debra Dorfman; Becky Shapiro; Jennifer Black; Lizette Serrano; Becky Amsel; David Levithan; Elissa Ambrose; Tori, Carly, and Carol Adams; E. Lockhart; Lauren Myracle; Avery Carmichael; Courtney Sheinmel; Tricia Ready; Emily Bender; Aviva Mlynowski; Louisa Weiss; Larry Mlynowski; Targia Clarke; Anojja Shah; Lauren Kisilevsky; Susan Finkelberg-Sohmer; Judy Batalion; John and Vickie Swidler; Shari and Heather Endleman; Leslie Margolis; Meg Cabot; and BOB.

Extra love and kisses to Chloe, and my husband, Todd.

# Whatever After

## IF the SHOE FITS

## SARAH MLYNOWSKI

**■ SCHOLASTIC**

for my partners in crime,
lauren myracle and emily jenkins.

# ✴ chapter one ✴

## My Magic Mirror Might Be Broken

I have a magic mirror in my basement and I'm going to use it.

Jonah's hand hovers in front of the mirror. "Ready?"

"Oh, yes." I am definitely ready. I've been *trying* for three days. Four nights ago, Jonah and I accidentally got sucked through the mirror and landed in Snow White's fairy tale. Well, technically, we landed in the kingdom of Zamel. Rhymes with camel. That's where Snow White lives.

If I'd known we were going to Zamel, I never would have worn slippers and pajamas. I would have worn jeans, a cute sweater, and sneakers. But I didn't even know where we were until after we'd already messed up Snow's story.

But don't worry! Everything ended up fine. Different, but fine.

I did leave my slippers and pajamas at Snow's, though. The slippers were pretty beaten-up anyway, but the pajamas were my favorite pair. Snow borrowed them one night and loaned me a skirt and top. Getting my pajamas back isn't the only reason I want to visit Snow. I also want to know why Maryrose, the person who lives inside our magic mirror, sent me and Jonah there in the first place. There has to be a reason, right? And why did the magic mirror in Snow's bedroom tell us not to tell our parents about what happened?

Jonah and I decided to find out.

When we'd gone to Zamel, the mirror had sucked us inside at midnight, so the night after we got home, I set my alarm for 11:51 P.M. I put on jeans. A sweater. Sneakers. I woke up my little brother, Jonah. He put on jeans. A sweatshirt. Sneakers. We crept down the two flights to the basement and closed the door behind us.

Jonah knocked. Then he knocked again. Then he knocked once more. Three times, just like the first time.

But it didn't work.

We stood there, waiting, but nothing happened.

No swirling. No hissing. No opening up its big mirror mouth and swallowing us whole.

The next night we tried again. We got up close to midnight. Put on jeans. Sweatshirts. Sneakers. Crept down to the basement. Knocked and knocked again. Knocked a third time.

Nothing, nothing, nothing!

Tonight is Night Number Three. Everyone knows three's a charm. Especially when dealing with fairy tales.

So here I am. In the basement. Again.

Jonah's fist is up against the mirror. Again.

"Ready," I say. I brace myself. Here we go. It's going to work. I know it is.

Jonah knocks.

Once.

Twice.

Three times.

No swirling, no hissing, no nothing.

I stomp my sneakered foot. "I don't get it!"

Jonah sighs in disappointment, and his skinny arm falls to his side. "Do you think it's broken?"

I peer at the antique mirror. It looks the same as it did when we first went through it. It's twice the size of me. The glass part is clear and smooth. The frame is made of stone and decorated with carvings of small fairies with wings and wands. It's attached to the wall with heavy Frankenstein bolts. We just moved to Smithville — and into our new house — a few months ago, and the mirror came with the house. I used to think the mirror was creepy. I guess it's still kind of creepy.

But it's not *just* creepy. It's also fun. It's magic.

"It doesn't look broken," I say, seeing my brother and myself in the reflection. Jonah's brown hair is short and kind of a mess, standing up in different directions. Mine is shoulder-length and wavy, but still neat. "Let me try," I add.

I knock once. Twice. Three times.

The room is still.

"Hello? Maryrose? Are you there?" I know I said Maryrose lives inside the mirror, but truthfully, I'm not sure. All I know is that Maryrose has something to do with the mirror. I think. I really don't know much. I sigh. "Maybe we imagined the whole thing."

"No way," Jonah says. "We were there. I know we were. We met Snow! We ate her stew sandwiches! Yum. I wish Mom and Dad would make them one night for dinner."

I snort. First of all, Snow's stew sandwiches were gross. And second, the likelihood of Mom and Dad trying a new recipe these days is very unlikely. Like one in a bajillion. They haven't cooked in weeks. We've ordered pizza for the last two — no, make that three — nights in a row.

Don't get me wrong, I like pizza. What ten-year-old doesn't like pizza? What adult doesn't like pizza? Jonah LOVES pizza, even though he insists on dipping the crust in ketchup, which is totally gross. But three nights in a row is extreme. What happened to cooking? What happened to meat loaf? What happened to salad?

My parents used to cook all the time, before we moved to Smithville. They had time to cook then. Now they work all the time. They're lawyers and just started their own firm. I keep telling them I'm old enough to do the cooking, but they won't listen. Just because I nearly burned down our old house when I put my socks in the toaster ONE TIME. What can I say? I wanted toasty socks. They won't even let me near the washing machine, which makes no sense. Fine. I used too much detergent and turned the laundry room into a bubble bath, but also, only ONE TIME.

I yawn. "Let's go back to bed."

"But I want an adventure! Maybe the mirror can take us to other places, too. Like Africa! Or Mars! Or Buckingham Palace!"

"We've tried three times, Jonah. We can't do this every night. We're growing kids. We need our sleep."

He twists his bottom lip. "Just one more try."

I let him try one more time even though I KNOW it's not going to work. I am three years older than he is. I know these things. And I'm right. Of course I'm right. I'm always right. I march him up the stairs, back up to the top floor, and steer him toward his room.

He kicks off his sneakers and plants his face on his bed.

Back in my room, as I change back into my second-favorite pair of pajamas, I can't help but wonder if we really did imagine the whole thing.

But wait! My jewelry box is sitting on my dresser, and on the lid of my jewelry box are illustrations of fairy tale characters. Snow White is right between Cinderella and the Little Mermaid. Snow is definitely not wearing her puffy dress. She's wearing my lime-green pajamas, which means it really *did* happen.

So why isn't the mirror working?

# ✳ chapter two ✳

## No More Cereal, Please

blah, grumble, blah.

Yes, I'm cranky this morning. Why?

1. I'm tired from last night.
2. I'm having cereal for breakfast AGAIN when there is a full carton of eggs in the fridge.
3. I have nothing to wear because all my clothes are dirty.

It's not like I need a hot breakfast all the time, but the eggs are going bad TOMORROW. I know because I checked the carton.

Are my parents ever going to cook them? Why did they bother buying them?

And the laundry! They haven't done the laundry in more than a week! What is up with that?

"I am down to my monkey underwear," I say, shifting uncomfortably. My mother should know what this means. I have two pairs of monkey undies and I never, ever, EVER wear them unless I absolutely have to, since I am not a fan of wedgies. I should have just thrown them out. Of course, if I had thrown them out, then I'd have to go to school wearing dirty undies. Yuck. What I really need is for a) my parents to take me shopping, or b) for them to do laundry, but it's not like either will happen, since they barely have time to brush their teeth.

Seriously, I think my dad forgot to brush his teeth this morning. His breath smells like last night's pepperoni.

My mom ruffles my hair. "Sorry, honey. I'll try to get to the laundry tonight."

"If I run out of laundry, can I wear my Spider-Man bathing suit under my jeans?" Jonah asks.

"No, sweetie," Dad says. "You wouldn't be comfortable."

Like wedgies are comfortable?

*   *   *

It's the end of the day and I'm in bed and I'm not happy.

1.  We had pizza for dinner. Again. Forget smelling like
    a pepperoni. I might turn *into* a pepperoni.
2.  No one did the laundry tonight. I will have to wear
    my second pair of monkey underwear tomorrow,
    which means I will have a wedgie *again*. And after
    that — shudder, shudder — it's dirty undies for me.

Jonah, who is supposed to be asleep since his bedtime was an
hour ago, pops his head into my doorway and whispers, "See
you at midnight!"

I purse my lips. "Fine. I'll try again, but it's not like I expect
it to work."

"I bet it does!" he cheers.

"And what are you basing that on? The fact that it hasn't
worked for the past three days?" I ask in my best lawyer voice.
I'm going to be a lawyer when I grow up. Not because I want to
be a lawyer, but because I want to be a judge. You have to be a

lawyer before you can be a judge. That's the rule. For the record, when I'm a lawyer, I'm still going to do stuff like laundry and cook.

"It has to work at some point," Jonah reasons. "I'm setting my alarm."

I flump my head back on my pillow. "Fine. So will I."

I will humor my brother and return to the basement. But this is the last time. After tonight the mirror is dead to me. Enough is enough.


"Abby! Wake up! Let's go."

I open one eye, then the other. Doesn't my brother know that he's supposed to knock? That's the rule.

My alarm rings and I reach out to turn it off. Grumble. So. Not. In. The. Mood. But I swing my legs over the side of the bed anyway.

"Aren't you changing?" Jonah asks. He's wearing jeans. A red sweatshirt. Sneakers.

"Nope." I am staying in my pink pajamas with purple polka dots. Not anything I'd ever be caught in outside my house, but I'm not worried. It's not like the mirror's going to work.

Okay, here's the secret thing. Have you ever heard the expression "A watched pot never boils"? My nana says it all the time. It means if you're waiting for something to happen, it won't. But if you don't wait, it will. Like when you're waiting for your friend to call you back and you stare at the phone, hoping it will ring. It doesn't. But if you go off and do your homework, before you know it, your friend calls and — yay! — interrupts you.

So here's what I'm thinking: What if *this* is like *that*? When I get all dressed up expecting the mirror to let me in, it doesn't work. But if I wear the most RIDICULOUS pajamas I have, the only ones that happen to be clean, then the mirror will think I'm not expecting it and will finally let us in!

I shove the thought back down deep inside my brain. If the mirror knows I'm trying to trick it, then my trick isn't going to work.

La, la, la. No tricks here. Just wearing my ridiculous pajamas.

And sneakers. (No choice. The basement floor is cold, and my slippers are still at Snow's.)

I climb down the stairs with Jonah. I close the basement door. We stand in front of the mirror.

Jonah knocks once.

He knocks twice.

"Ready?" he asks.

"Whatever," I say, trying to sound bored.

He knocks a third time — thrice.

Ha, isn't that a funny word? It sounds like a kitchen utensil. To make the eggs really fluffy, I need to use the thrice. Except no one in my house eats eggs anymore.

"Abby —"

"It didn't work," I say. "Let's go back to bed. I'm tired."

"But, Abby —"

"Maybe we *did* just imagine the whole thing. Even the jewelry box. Or maybe Maryrose left town. Maybe she came with us to Snow's story and stayed there. Maybe —"

"Abby!"

"What?"

Jonah is pointing at the mirror. "Look!"

I look. It's spinning. It's hissing. It's turning purple. It's working?

Oh. My. Goodness. It's working!

"Wahoo!" Jonah cheers. "We're going back in!"

We're going back in! We're going back in! We're going back in and I'm wearing polka-dot pajamas.

# ✳ chapter three ✳

## This Is Not a Forest

Jonah jumps on his toes. "Let's just step inside before it eats us."

"Good idea," I say. "Maybe then it won't gobble up any more furniture." Last time, the mirror sucked up a swivel chair and most of my parents' old law books. I guess the plus side of our parents being too busy for even teeth brushing is they haven't come down here in the last few days. They'd have a million questions and I'd have no answers.

"I can't wait to see Snow!" Jonah exclaims. "And the dwarfs! And everyone!"

I grab my brother's hand. "Me too. Let's do it!"

We hold tight and walk in. At first it feels like we're stepping into a vacuum cleaner. I close my eyes. Then, *thump*.

I land on my butt and open my eyes. I expect to smell trees. Or ground. Last time, we arrived in the middle of a forest.

We are not in a forest.

Where are we? All I see is white. And NOT as in Snow White. "Jonah? You okay?"

"I'm tangled."

"In what?" I have no idea where I am. Why do I only see white? Am I in a marshmallow? I reach out to touch the whiteness. It's furry.

It's an animal. Crumbs! An animal ate me! "Help!" I scream. "I've been eaten!"

I try to push myself to safety. I end up petting it. Aw. So soft!

It doesn't move. I push the furry thing off me and stand up. The fur is on a coat hanger. "Oh! It's a coat!"

I glance around the small space. We're surrounded by coats. Wait a sec. "We're in a coatroom!"

There are about a hundred coats all around. Leather coats. Wool coats. Mink coats. Hats. Shoes. Ponchos.

"Are we at the dry cleaner's?" Jonah asks.

"It's a closet. A coat closet, I think," I say. The door to the closet is slightly ajar, and a stream of candlelight is shining in.

"I don't remember Snow having a closet like this," Jonah says.

"No. Hmm. What's that sound? Do you hear music?"

Jonah nods. There are trumpets and some drums. Dance music. Is it a party?

The closet door swings open. Holding a green cloth coat, a skinny young man with a goatee and wearing a purple uniform grabs a hanger off the pole.

I try to duck, but it's too late.

"What are you doing in here?" he screeches.

"We're not sure?" I say like it's a question.

"You kids better not be stealing coats!" he yells. "I'm up for a promotion and I can't get fired!"

"We're not, we swear," I hurry to say.

"We're here to see Snow," Jonah adds.

The guy blinks. "It's snowing? I should salt the stairs."

"Not snow, the weather," Jonah explains. "Snow, the person."

The guy shakes his head. "Snow is a name?"

"Yes!" I say. "She's the queen!" Who *is* this guy?

He hangs up the green cloth coat. "Clarissa is the queen of Floom."

"Floom?" I repeat.

"Yes, Floom."

"We're in Zamel," I say.

"No," the skinny guy says, tugging on his goatee. "Floom."

"Rhymes with room," Jonah says.

"And loom," the guy says. He eyes us suspiciously. "You're not from here, are you?"

"We're from Smithville," I say.

"Is that far?" he asks.

"About a mirror away," I mumble. "So there's definitely no Snow White here? I wonder where we are. Another story maybe. You said the queen is Clarissa?"

"And the king is Eugene, and the prince is Jordan."

"Is there a princess?" I ask.

"Not yet. Of course we're all hoping that will change. How old are you, nine?"

"Ten and a half, thank you very much." Humph. I try to push past him, but he blocks my way.

"What are you doing here?" he asks. He looks me over. "Are you the court jester?"

My cheeks burn. "No, I am not!" I really did not think this pajama-wearing plan through.

"Well, you're too young to be eligible for marriage."

"Um, no kidding."

A man and a woman, both wearing sheepskin coats, approach the coat man. "Don't go anywhere," the coat man says to us. "I have to help them."

Right. And where would we go? We're stuck in a closet.

He bows to the couple. The guy is wearing a tuxedo and she's in a long satin dress.

We *are* at a party. A fancy party.

"Oh my gosh, we're at a fancy party and I'm wearing pajamas!" I exclaim to Jonah. "How embarrassing. Maybe I should just stay in the closet."

"Do you think it's a wedding?" Jonah asks.

"Maybe."

"A sweet sixteen."

"Could be."

"A bat mitzvah?"

"I don't know, Jonah." I'm going to have a bat mitzvah when I'm twelve. There's no way it will be this fancy, though.

I peek at the woman as her escort hands her coat to the coat guy.

Speaking of fancy — her dress is covered in shiny beads and sequins, and has a huge poofy skirt.

She's wearing a ball gown. Which makes this a ball.

A ball. We're at a ball. My head nearly explodes. "Jonah! Look at her dress! Do you know what this means?"

"You're really, really underdressed?"

I wave my hand. "You're hardly wearing a tuxedo. But besides that. We're at a ball. Think. Who has a ball?"

"I have a soccer ball. I think it's somewhere in the back-yard, but I —"

"Not that kind of ball, Jonah. A *ball* ball. A party ball. We went through the mirror, but we're not in Snow White's story. We're at a ball and there's a prince. A prince looking for his prin-cess. We're in —"

His eyes light up. "Africa? Mars? Buckingham Palace?"

I smile. "No, Jonah. *Cinderella*."

# ✳ chapter four ✳

## Hello, Ball

do you know Cinderella?" I ask the coat guy.

He scratches his goatee. "Never heard of her."

"Maybe you're wrong. Maybe we're not in Cinderella's story," Jonah says.

"No, no, we are," I say, thinking fast. "The coat man works in the palace, which means he probably doesn't know Cinderella. Her family hides her away in the house!"

"If you say so." Jonah pauses. "Can we go explore?"

Jonah always wants to explore. Floom. Zamel. The basement.

"Wait a second," the coat guy says before Jonah can drag me away. "Are you supposed to be here? Were you invited?"

"Not exactly —" Jonah begins.

I shoot him a look. If the coat guy kicks us out, we're in big trouble. The mirror that will take us home is probably here in the palace. Also, I want to see Cinderella. What girl doesn't love Cinderella? That awesome dress! The glass slippers!

I've always wanted a pair of glass slippers. Also ruby slippers. Hmm, I wonder why we call the glass slippers *slippers*? They're not slippers. They're high heels.

The coat man is staring at me. Oh, right. I need to come up with a reason why we're here. "We're um . . . looking for our parents!" I say. "They brought us here and told us to hang out while they talked to their friends."

Okay, fine. So I stretched the truth a bit.

A lot, actually. But desperate times call for desperate measures. We just got here. We can't get in trouble already!

The coat guy frowns. "Well, I suppose the king will enjoy your outfit."

Humph. I guess he's being sarcastic.

He narrows his eyes. "You're sure your parents are here?"

Jonah and I both nod.

The coat guy shrugs. "All right. Go ahead. Have fun."

We step out of the closet. We're standing in some sort of

entranceway. The ceilings in this place are really high. Soaring. It reminds me of my school gym. Except it's much, much nicer. And less smelly.

"Look," Jonah says. "There's a painting on the ceiling!"

I look up. It's a painting of people. Royal people. Hundreds of royal people. I can tell they're royal because they're all wearing crowns. I guess this royal family has been around for a long time. I feel eyes on me and look back down. The man and the woman who just checked their coats are staring at me.

Or, more likely, staring at my pajamas.

How rude. This can't be their first time they ever saw pajamas. They don't have to *stare*.

"Let's go inside the ballroom," Jonah says excitedly.

I notice an elderly woman eyeing me, too.

"But people are looking at me," I whisper.

"So?" Jonah asks.

"They think I'm weird!"

"You are! Who cares? Let's go to the party!"

"But I'm too obvious in my pajamas! And you, too! You're wearing a red sweatshirt and jeans. Do you see anyone else wearing a sweatshirt and jeans? We're at a ball!"

"No one is noticing me with you in that outfit, trust me."

"Thanks," I retort. "We have to be careful. What if someone says something to the prince? What if Cinderella sees me? What if I mess up the whole story?"

Jonah ignores me. "Do you think they have snacks? I bet they have dogs-in-a-blanket. It seems like the kind of party that has dogs-in-blankets."

"Do you mean those mini–hot dogs? They're called pigs-in-a-blanket."

"No, they're not." He adamantly shakes his head. "Why would they be called pigs-in-a-blanket when they're *hot dogs*? They're not *hot pigs*."

"I didn't make this up, Jonah. I'm just correcting you."

"Who cares what they're called? I just want to eat them. Let's go!" Instead of waiting for me to respond or grant him permission, he takes off.

Why doesn't he realize that I am the older sibling and therefore responsible for making all the decisions?

I run after him into the ballroom.

Wow. There are, like, a thousand people here. No wonder Cinderella was upset that she wasn't invited.

"Look," I say, pointing. Up on a stage are two people sitting on two purple thrones. "They must be the king and queen."

The queen is smiling a perfect smile. Her teeth are the color of white chalk, and she has long wavy blond hair. She looks like a real-life Barbie. Or maybe a beauty pageant contestant.

The king is sitting next to her, looking bored. He keeps yawning.

Between him and his wife is a humongous flag.

The Floom flag, probably. The design? Pink with purple polka dots.

I look down at my pajamas. I look back at the flag.

I look down again. I look back up.

I look around and see that a crowd of people are waving and smiling at me. "Great outfit!" one woman cheers.

Oh my goodness! No wonder no one has kicked me out. I am wearing the Floom flag! I'm their mascot.

I'm going to blend right in!

Wait. Maybe that's why the mirror finally let us through. Yes! We never would have been accepted here if I wasn't wearing this Floom flag pair of pajamas.

Our magic mirror sure is smart.

Out of the corner of my eye, I spot the prince.

I can tell he's the prince because:

1. He's handsome.
2. He's youngish (like an older teenager).
3. He's wearing some sort of royal purple robe. (Or maybe it's just a bathrobe over *his* pj's, but I highly doubt it.)
4. He's wearing a crown.
5. He's surrounded by a ton of girls. There are many giggles and a lot of hair flipping. It's like watching one of those dating reality shows that my mom used to watch when she had time for TV. The girls look so silly. I'm *so* embarrassed for them.

"Princes wear crowns, too?" Jonah asks. "Can I wear a crown?"

I snort. "Are you a prince?"

"Mom says I'm *her* prince."

"Then ask Mom to get you a crown. Maybe she'll make you one out of tinfoil."

"Never mind," he says. "It looks kind of heavy. Hey, is that Cinderella?" he asks, pointing to the girl standing next to the prince.

"Her? No way." The girl he's pointing to is wearing a beige dress with a gold choker around her neck. She's definitely not Cinderella.

"How do you know?" Jonah asks.

"Because . . . because . . ." Her hair isn't straight and it's not curly. It's more zig-zaggy. A little frizzy.

And it's not blond. Or brunette. It's in the middle.

And her eyes aren't blue or green or sparkly. They're small. And her lips are kind of thin. "She's average-looking," I answer. She's not ugly or anything — she's just ordinary. Plain. And Cinderella is supposed to be the MOST beautiful girl in all the land.

"Are you sure?" Jonah asks. "The prince is talking to her. He seems to like her. Isn't that how the story goes?"

I look more closely and have to agree. The prince *is* talking to her. He's even laughing at something she's saying. But it doesn't mean he wants to marry her, does it? I mean, I laughed when Zach Rothenberg stuffed an edamame up his nose in the school cafeteria, but it doesn't mean I want to marry *him*.

There's a sudden trumpet sound at the door. Everyone in the room turns to look.

Then one of the doormen announces, "The gorgeous stranger princess has arrived!"

The gorgeous stranger princess?

Cinderella!

## There She Is, Miss America. Oops. Miss Floom.

I study the prince to see how he reacts. First, he turns to look at his dad, the king, who motions to the door. I'm guessing that's his royal order to Go Get the Stranger Princess. The prince nods and makes his way outside.

And the girl he was talking to? Her face falls. Aw. I can't help but feel bad for her. But come on! How can a regular girl compete with Cinderella?

Cinderella! I'm going to see Cinderella!

The entire crowd drifts out the door to see.

Oh. My. Goodness.

First we see a gold coach. "That used to be a pumpkin!" I whisper to Jonah.

Then I motion to the six gray neighing horses. "Those were mice!"

Standing by the coach are six footmen and a plump coachman.

"What were those?" Jonah asks.

"The coachman was a rat, I think. But I forget what the footmen were. Spiders? No, lizards, maybe?"

Here she comes! First her foot. Her glass-slippered foot. The crowd oohs and aahs.

She steps out of the coach just like a movie star at a Hollywood premiere.

Everyone gasps.

I gasp. She really is gorgeous.

Her dress is gorgeous, too.

She looks just like she does on my jewelry box, in her ball gown. She's so sophisticated. So stunning. So sparkly!

"She's breathtaking," a young man with thick black glasses says.

"But who is she?" a woman with bright pink lipstick asks. "Is she really a princess?"

"She's not from around here, that's for sure," an older woman leaning against a cane says, then clucks her tongue. "Trust me. I would know. I know everyone."

"Her dress is real silver!" pink-lipstick woman says.

"No, it's platinum," the older woman declares. "That's better than silver. It's even better than gold. Trust me."

The dress glitters. Cinderella glitters. Her blond hair is pulled up and back in some sort of super-awesome knot, and her face is made up. Red lipstick. Blush. Silver eye shadow.

Or maybe it's platinum.

You can see her blue eyes even from here. They're practically glowing.

The prince appears beside her. "Hello," he says gallantly. "Nice to see you again."

"Hi," she responds, batting her mascaraed eyelashes. "It's nice to see you again, too."

Huh? Again?

"I don't get it," Jonah says. "He knows her already?"

That is weird. How does he already know her? I tap the cane woman on the shoulder. "Excuse me," I ask. "How does the prince know Cinder — I mean, the beautiful stranger princess?"

She rolls her eyes. "They met at the first ball."

Oh! Right! There were a whole bunch of versions of *Cinderella*, and some of them had more than one ball. My nana is a literature professor and she used to read all the original fairy tales to me when we lived near her in Naperville.

I just don't remember how many balls there were. Hmm. Probably three. Of course — everything in fairy tales happens in threes.

"So there are three balls?" I ask.

She clucks her tongue. "*Noooo.* Two. Yesterday's and today's. That's it."

I guess not *everything* happens in threes. I turn back to Cinderella. She looks so beautiful. He looks so handsome. They are a perfect fairy tale couple. "Isn't it romantic?" I swoon. "Isn't it wonderful?"

"The other girl doesn't think it's so wonderful," Jonah comments, pointing with his chin toward the girl who was talking to the prince before he dumped her for Cinderella.

The average-looking girl.

She does look kind of devastated. I don't blame her — she was making the prince laugh before Cinderella showed up. If she would have asked me, I would have told her to back off — she was asking for heartbreak.

Really, everyone should consult me before making decisions. It's for their own good.

"Abby, what now?" Jonah asks.

"One sec," I say. I can't help but follow Cinderella and the prince as they walk back into the ballroom. They're magnetic. All the guests point and gasp. Even the music stops.

Everyone's mesmerized. Everyone except my brother, but he's a seven-year-old boy. He can't be expected to appreciate epic romance.

The prince wraps his arm around Cinderella's waist and takes her hand.

Sigh.

The music restarts. My heart soars. They begin to dance.

Rumors and whispers swirl.

"I heard she's the heiress to a diamond dynasty!"

"I heard she's the youngest princess in Roctavia!"

"I heard she's turned down thirteen marriage proposals, but thinks our prince is the one!"

I cover my mouth so I don't laugh.

"Abby," Jonah whispers. "They're wrong, right? Isn't she just an ordinary girl whose fairy godmother made her look pretty to come to the ball?"

"She was always pretty," I say. "But her mom died and then —"

"How come the mother always dies in fairy tales? Snow White's mom died, too."

"I don't know, Jonah. I don't write these things, I just read them. Where was I?"

"Dead mother."

"Right. Her mom died and her dad remarried an evil stepmother."

"Again with the evil stepmother!"

"Tell me about it."

"But the evil stepmother had daughters?"

"Yes. Two. And they're not as beautiful as Cinderella."

"And why is she at the ball again?"

Luckily I paid attention to Nana's stories 100 percent of the time. Jonah, about 30 percent.

"The stepmom was invited. She was planning to go with her stepdaughters, hoping that the prince would fall in love with one of them and make her a princess. Cinderella wanted to go, too, but her stepmom said no way. She made her sleep in the attic and do all the housework. Cinderella cried, and then presto, up popped her fairy godmother who said she was going to help her. She turned a bunch of animals into the coach and footmen, and her rags into a beautiful dress. She gave Cinderella glass slippers. She's an awesome stylist, this fairy godmother. Wish I had one. Anyway, she told Cinderella to leave the ball by midnight."

"Why?"

"Because that's when all the magic ends."

"But if she's a fairy godmother, why can't she make it last longer?"

I shrug. "I don't know. But what happens next — what happens now — is that Cinderella's having so much fun that she nearly forgets it's midnight. She runs and drops her shoe —"

"I thought there were two balls?" Jonah asks.

"Oh. Right. I don't remember every single detail, but I think at the first ball Cinderella danced with the prince but then remembered to leave before midnight. But the final ball is when she loses track of time and then drops her shoe. Her dress turns back into rags, and the coachmen and the footmen and the coach turn back to mice and rats and lizards and a pumpkin. Meanwhile, the prince picks up the shoe and promises that whoever the shoe fits will be his wife. Over the next few days, his assistant goes around to all the households in the kingdom and makes the ladies try on the slipper. It fits Cinderella perfectly. She shows him the second shoe as proof and all is well. She gets married to the prince and is rescued from her mean stepmother. And they live happily ever after." Sigh. I love this story.

"What happens to the stepsisters?"

"In the classic version, I think it was written by some French guy, Perrault or Poutine or something, Cinderella forgives them. That's the one Nana liked the best. In the others I think it's kinda grosser."

His eyes light up. "Tell me!"

My brother loves the gross parts.

"Well, in the Grimm brothers' one, the stepsisters try to cut off their heels and toes to fit into the slipper. And then they die."

"No way! Awesome!"

I roll my eyes.

"Snack?" a waiter interrupts us, waving a plate in front of us.

"Dogs-in-a-blanket!" Jonah cheers.

I roll my eyes again. But I take two.

Jonah takes three and stuffs them all in his mouth. "So what do we do now? Explore?"

"Can you swallow before talking, please? Where are your manners? We're at a ball."

"Why should I listen to you? You're wearing pink pajamas with purple polka dots."

Humph. "I think we should find the magic mirror that will take us home first so we're not rushing around later."

"Then we can explore?"

"Yeah. But let's start with the mirror. It's probably somewhere in the castle. Looking for it is exploring, right? Now's our best chance anyway since the royal family and the staff are distracted by the ball. But we have to be careful not to get in Cinderella's way. We can't risk messing up the story!"

He wiggles his eyebrows. "You don't want to say hi? Even quickly?"

"Of course I do, but we can't. We learned our lesson with Snow White. We will NOT mess the story up this time around!" No way, no how, no thank you.

## ✳ chapter six ✳

## Mirror, Mirror, Let Me In

We find twelve mirrors in the castle:

The mirror in the queen's room. The king's room. The prince's room. The guest rooms. The maids' rooms. There are even two in the ballroom.

None of them work.

And knocking on them isn't always easy, either.

There was a maid in the queen's room. We told her that Her Majesty requested her presence downstairs so that we could continue "exploring."

If we don't stop exploring soon, we are definitely going to get caught.

"Now what? We've tried all of them!" Jonah huffs after we've visited every room — thrice.

"Maybe the magic mirror isn't at the palace," I say. "Maybe it's at Cinderella's house. Snow White lived in the palace before she had to run away. So maybe the portal is where the main character originally lives, before she gets to live happily ever after."

"But we don't even know where Cinderella lives!"

"We can follow her home," I say. "*She* knows where she lives."

"Do you think she's still here?" Jonah asks.

"Wait, what time is it?" I glance down at my watch. Oh, no! I'm not wearing my watch! I took it off last night before bed. Not that my watch would tell me what time it is here. But it would tell me what time it is at home so we could get home before my parents wake up. And now I have no idea what time it is in Smithville!

ARGH.

Jonah follows me sneakily down the hallway back into the ballroom, and I spot a huge round clock hanging on the far wall.

It's 11:55.

I scan the room for Cinderella and spot her dancing with the prince.

Now the clock says 11:56. Hmm. Does Cinderella not realize what time it is?

"It's getting late," Jonah says. "We should tell her to go. Doesn't she turn into a pumpkin at twelve?"

"Her coach turns into a pumpkin, not her." I grab hold of his sleeve. "But no, don't do anything! We don't want to mess anything up."

We wait. We watch. 11:58. 11:59.

My heart thumps. What if our just being here messed things up? What if we don't have to do anything but be here and the story changes anyway? What if she changes back into her rags right here and everyone gasps and freaks out and the prince doesn't want to marry her after all?

Twelve!

*Ding Dong! Ding Dong! Ding Dong!*

Cinderella looks up at the clock. Her face pales when she sees the time. She looks at the prince, says good-bye, and then — sprints!

Like really fast!

She makes a mad dash right out of there.

She doesn't look back, she just goes, goes, GOES!

Zoom! Rhymes with Floom!

"We have to follow her," I order Jonah, and sprint right behind her. "If we lose her, we won't know where she lives!"

"At least we didn't mess up the story," Jonah calls out.

We follow her outside. She's running down the steps of the palace, and the prince is chasing after her. She's in the front, Jonah and I are to her left, and the prince is behind us. We're a triangle on the move.

On the bottom step, her glass slipper falls off, just like it's supposed to. Yes! We didn't mess anything up!

She glances back for a second, but sees the prince behind her and doesn't stop moving.

She just goes, goes, GOES!

"Wait! Wait! WAIT!" the prince yells.

I look behind and see that he's stopped. He bends down and picks up the slipper.

Jonah and I, however, keep on running.

Cinderella jumps into her coach and shouts, "Go, go, GO!"

The footmen and horses go, go, GO!

"Oh, no!" Jonah exclaims. "How are we going to keep up on foot?"

"Run," I order. "Fast, fast, FAST!"

We chase the coach down the block. I'm huffing and puffing, and I really need to do more exercise because I am not in very good shape and —

I see a spark up ahead. Like someone is lighting a match.

The coach begins to glimmer. The horses are shaking. Something is happening.

*Kabam!*

The coach is shrinking! The horses are shrinking! The footmen are shrinking!

*Poof!*

Cinderella is sitting on her butt in the middle of the street next to a squashed pumpkin.

The horses are mice. The footmen are lizards. The coachman is a rat.

The whole transformation only took about two seconds. I wish I had my dad's video camera so I could put it on YouTube.

Jonah is standing beside me with his jaw wide open. "Did anyone else see that? Someone else must have seen that!"

I look around the empty moonlit street. We're the only witnesses.

"Oh well," Cinderella says to herself. She looks nothing like the Cinderella of two minutes ago. No wonder her own family didn't recognize her. Her hair hangs around her shoulders, and she's no longer wearing any platinum eye shadow or red lipstick or any makeup at all. Her dress is plain brown. Her jewelry is gone, too. She stands up and brushes her dress off. She takes off her right glass slipper and starts walking barefoot.

"What do we do now?" Jonah asks.

Isn't it obvious? "We follow her home."

# ✳ chapter seven ✳

## Just Pretend You Don't See Us

We follow her for the next thirty minutes, all the way to her house. It's a good thing there's a full moon because this town doesn't have any streetlights.

We keep a safe distance. We only whisper. We duck into the shadows whenever Cinderella turns around. We're really good at this sneaky thing. I bet we could be spies when we grow up. We'd be the cool brother-and-sister team that gets to go to exotic places like New York or Japan to steal nuclear power secrets. They'll make a movie about us! It'll be called —

"WHY ARE YOU PEOPLE FOLLOWING ME?"

Oops.

Cinderella is glaring at us from her porch, her hands on her hips.

"We're not following you," I squeak.

"Um, yes you are. You followed me all the way from the palace."

"No, we —" I stop in mid-sentence. We *are* following her. I'm not sure what to say.

"We need to use your house," Jonah says.

"There's a public bathroom three blocks over," Cinderella says.

"No, so we can go home," I say.

"What? Who are you?"

"I'm Abby, and this is my brother, Jonah."

"Don't you have your own house?" she asks.

"We do, but we need to use yours to get back to it."

"I don't understand," she says. "Anyway, I can't let you in. My stepmother is really strict, and if I don't listen to her, I get into trouble."

"Your stepmother is still at the ball," I say. "We'll be in and out before she gets home."

"Yeah," Jonah pipes up, "but even if you did get into trouble, it won't be for long 'cause you're going to marry the prince!"

Her eyes widen. "Excuse me?"

Uh-oh. "Jonah, no!"

Jonah turns to me, cheeks reddening. "What? Was I not supposed to tell her?"

Cinderella steps down from the porch. "Why would you say I was going to marry the prince?"

"I don't see what the big deal is," Jonah says to me. "Why shouldn't she know her future?" He grins at Cinderella. "You were at the ball, right? You danced with the prince and he thinks you're the prettiest girl around. You're going to get married."

"But — but I don't understand!" she sputters. "How would he find me? He'll never recognize me! Even my own stepmother and stepsisters didn't recognize me!"

I sigh. Since the cat is out of the bag, I guess there's no reason to keep it all a secret. "You dropped your shoe, right? He picked it up. Tomorrow he's going to make an announcement that he's going to marry the person who fits the shoe. He sends his assistant to make every girl in the kingdom try it on. It only fits you."

A slow smile spreads across Cinderella's face. "Seriously?"

"Seriously," I say. "You're going to be a princess — and then you'll get married and be his queen. Well, at first you'll just be a princess, but eventually you'll get to be queen once his dad . . .

you know." No need to be morbid. "Anyway, my point is that even if your stepmother is ticked off at you for a few days, it won't matter in the long run."

"Squee!" Cinderella squeals. "That is absolutely the best news ever. I can't believe the prince picked up my slipper!"

"It was lucky," I say. It probably would have been luckier if the prince had caught up with her, but who am I to judge?

One day I'll be a judge. But not yet.

"It's also lucky that it only fits you," Jonah says.

"They're perfectly molded to my feet." She lifts the remaining shoe so that it's eye level. "See?"

And there it is. Right in front of me. The infamous glass slipper. "Can I hold it?" I ask breathlessly.

"Sure," she says, and passes it to me.

Whoa. It's heavier than I thought. And it's really made of glass. Completely see-through. It feels like I'm holding one of my parents' for-company-only wineglasses. But it's a shoe. A really high-heeled shoe. I'm not sure how she even walked in them. And they're tiny, too. For an adult. Or an almost-adult, anyway — I'm guessing she's about sixteen. The weird thing about the shoe? There are toe marks where the toes go. This shoe was perfectly molded to fit Cinderella's foot. I guess that makes sense for the story — if they were just a size five, then other girls with size-five feet could fit in them, too.

I hand it back. I really don't want to drop it by accident.

"Why didn't the glass slipper disappear like the rest of the stuff?" Jonah asks.

"My fairy godmother changed the dress and coach and horses from something else," Cinderella explains. "But she gave me the shoes as a gift. The slippers are made just for me, you know."

"High heels," I say.

"What?"

I wave my hand. Never mind.

"Anyway, how do you know what's going to happen to me?" Cinderella asks. "Are you some type of fairy?"

"No," Jonah says. "But we're in a fairy tale."

She scrunches her nose. "Does that mean a fairy told you what happens to me?"

"Well . . . kind of," I say. A fairy *tale* told us what happened. Close enough. "Can we come in? We don't have much time. We need to get moving before your family gets home."

"All right," Cinderella says, and unlocks the door.

We step into a fancy foyer. Not as fancy as the palace, but still fancy. The tiles on the floor are checkerboard, black and white. There's a big couch, a love seat, chairs, a fireplace, and a wood grandfather clock up against the wall.

There's a lit chandelier above us, and a big rectangular mirror right by the entranceway.

"Let's try it," I say. "Cinderella, stand back. We definitely can't take you home with us. That would mess up your life for sure."

Jonah knocks. Once. Twice. Thrice! Nothing.

Boo. "How many other mirrors do you have in the house?"

"My stepmother has one in her room, and my stepsisters have two. That's it. But why do you need to use a mirror to get home? Where do you live? I don't understand."

"Neither do we," I say. "But that's the way the magic works. Why do we need a mirror to get home? Why did you have to leave the ball by midnight?"

"Magic is weird," she says. "Let's go."

On the second floor, there are two rooms and another staircase.

"Where's your room?" I ask Cinderella.

She points up. "The attic. Let's start in my stepmother's room." She throws the door open and motions to the large mirror by her bed.

I knock. Once. Twice. Thrice!

225

Nothing.

"Argh!" I say.

There's a noise outside. It's a carriage.

"Look who it is," Cinderella says with a smirk. "My step-mother and stepsisters returning from the ball. Wait until I tell them what you told me."

My mouth goes dry. "No, no, no. You can't say anything to them!"

"Why not? You said it's going to happen! Were you not telling me the truth?"

"I was telling you the truth, but who knows what will happen if you say something? What if they try to stop it? What if they mess something up? You have to keep it a secret! Promise me you'll keep it a secret!"

"Okay, okay," she grumbles. "If you think I have to."

"*We* have to hurry," Jonah says. "We don't want them to see us, right?"

"Let's go. To the stepsisters' room! One of those mirrors had better work."

"Abby, what if they don't? How will we get home?"

"I don't know!"

Last chance. Here we go.

# ✳ chapter eight ✳

## Double Trouble

I can see in the moonlight that the room is all pink. Two pink beds, two pink carpets, two pink desks, two pink wardrobes, and two pink pillows — one embroidered with the name *Kayla*, the other with the name *Beatrice*.

But best of all: two full-sized pink-framed mirrors.

I have a good feeling about these mirrors, I really do.

Jonah runs straight to Kayla's mirror. "Maybe they both work. We each get our own portal, how cool is that?"

"Do you really think I'd let you walk into a mirror by yourself?" I say. "What if you actually end up on Mars or something? Not happening. Let's just choose one and go for it."

Cinderella is looking out the window. "Hurry! They're getting out of the coach! They won't like this one bit! Last month they caught me napping in here and they locked me in their closet for two hours!"

I shiver. They sound awful. I take Jonah's hand and knock. "One . . . two . . ."

And now for the final knock . . .

"Three!"

Nothing.

"Cinderella, are you awake?" cries a voice from downstairs. "Where are you? Make us some tea!"

Oh, no! They're home!

And we're still here.

I hear the *clomp-clomp-clomp*ing of their walking around downstairs.

"I have to go," Cinderella whispers urgently, and turns to leave the room. "You guys have to get out of here!"

"We will," I say with more optimism than I feel. "There's still another mirror."

"Bye, Cinderella!" Jonah says.

"It was nice to meet you," I add.

I grab Jonah's hand. "This mirror is going to work. It has to. Ready? One . . . two . . ."

And now for another final knock . . .

"Three!"

Still nothing.

This is NOT good. Not good at all.

I hear more clomping. *Clomp-clomp-clomp* coming up the stairs.

The sisters are going to walk into their room any moment. We need to *do* something.

We need to hide.

I signal to Jonah for him to slide under the bed. It looks like I'm waving at him.

"Huh?" he says.

"Shh! And don't say huh. Say excuse me."

"Excuse me, what are you doing with your hand?"

*Clomp-clomp-clomp.*

"I'm trying to motion you to — Oh, forget it! Just slide under the bed!"

He nods and does it. Finally. I slide under Kayla's bed. The bed skirt reaches the floor, so unless they look for us, they won't catch us. Ouch! I just scraped the top of my arm.

What if they see us? What will we say? What will happen to us? Will they call the fairy tale police? Will we go to fairy tale jail?

The room is suddenly lit up.

"Cinderella, were you in our room?" someone asks in a high nasal voice. "Our door is open."

"Yes," Cinderella calls back. "I was, um, cleaning up." I hear footsteps coming closer — not the *clomp-clomp-clomp* kind, but the dainty kind. Cinderella's footsteps.

"Is that what you did all night?" the same person says.

"No. I was pretty busy," Cinderella says. I hear a smile in her voice.

At least she's not telling them the truth.

I hear the window opening and feel a flush of cool air. "So, tell me all about the ball," Cinderella says, and I detect a little bit of an edge to her voice. "Did either of you get to talk with Prince Jordan this time?"

Hmm. That wasn't very nice. She knows neither of them got to talk to the prince. She danced with him the whole time. Is Cinderella rubbing it in?

"Kayla got to talk to him," the same person — must be Beatrice — says.

"Really?" Cinderella says. "I didn't . . . I mean, that's nice. So what happened?"

"The beautiful stranger showed up again and interrupted them," Beatrice says.

"Really?" Cinderella says again.

"I heard she was a princess," Kayla says.

"She wasn't a princess," Beatrice says. "We'd have heard about her if she was a princess. I bet she was an heiress. Those clothes were expensive."

"The prince danced with her the rest of the night," Kayla says. "Again. I was really hoping she wouldn't show tonight."

"*Reeealllly?* The prince danced with the beautiful stranger? And that's why he stopped talking to you? How sad for you!"

I put two and two together and realize that the ordinary-looking girl we saw talking to the prince was Kayla. Also, is it just me, or is Cinderella being mean?

"Yes," Kayla says, "it was pretty sad." She sits down on her bed, and the mattress sags so that it's an inch from my face.

Uh-oh.

If she bounces, she's going to break my nose. DO NOT BOUNCE, KAYLA. DO NOT BOUNCE.

I hope she's not a bed jumper. I think back to all the times Jonah and I have jumped on our beds. What if there were kids from other dimensions hiding under our bed skirts and I had no idea?

My nose tingles.

Do not sneeze. Abby, whatever you do, DO NOT SNEEZE.

"Prince Jordan was *obsessed* with the beautiful stranger," Beatrice says. "He's in love with her, surely. How could he not be? She's gorgeous."

Ah-ah-ah —

*Don't-don't-don't* . . . I squeak a sneeze.

"Did you hear something?" Beatrice asks. "We better not have another mouse problem. Anyway, guess what happened at the end of the night?"

"I have no idea," Cinderella says. "Did Prince Jordan ask Kayla to dance?"

I can practically see Cinderella batting her eyelashes all fake-innocently.

"No," Kayla squeaks.

"Did he ask you to dance, Beatrice?"

"No," Beatrice huffs.

"I give up," Cinderella says.

"When the clock struck midnight, the beautiful stranger made a run for it. And no one could find her."

"No way," Cinderella drawls.

Way.

"The prince ran after her and found her glass slipper! It fell off while she was running, surely."

"Yes, it did," Cinderella says. Then she clears her throat. "It did?"

"Yes," Beatrice says, "And the prince is determined to find her. He'll be able to, surely."

Surely, surely, surely. She's such a know-it-all.

"I think I'll let you guys go to sleep," Cinderella says. "Or maybe you're not that tired. It doesn't sound like you did much dancing."

Yup, that was definitely mean.

She closes the door behind her. Uh-oh. She thinks we made it through the mirror. She thinks we're gone. And now we're stuck in the stepsisters' room! Argh!

I hear some shuffling on the bed above me. And then I hear . . . crying?

Why is one of the evil stepsisters crying? They're supposed to be evil, not sad.

The crying is coming from directly on top of me. It must be Kayla. The one who was talking with the prince.

"What on earth is wrong with you?" Beatrice asks.

"I just thought . . . I thought the prince might have liked me. I thought we had a connection."

"Oh, please. What did you expect? You can't compete with a girl like that. Get real. You're just not pretty enough."

My stomach hurts, and it's not from the pigs/dogs-in-a-blanket. I can't help but feel bad for Kayla. I know she's supposed to be evil and all, but she seems to really like Prince Jordan. And no one wants to like someone who doesn't like them back.

"Just go to sleep," Beatrice says, and the lights go back out.

Okay, at least they're going to sleep. Once they're out cold, Jonah and I can sneak out. They must be exhausted. It's well after midnight, their time at least. I have no idea what time it is at home, which is a little bit scary. I'm hoping time works the same way it did in *Snow White* — about one fairy tale day for every hour at home. Which means it's only about twelve thirty at home.

We just have to get home before Mom and Dad wake up, around seven.

Nothing I can do now. Nothing but wait.

And wait some more. When I finally hear not one but three sets of snoring, I decide it's safe to make a move.

I pull myself out from under the bed with my elbows and crawl over to Jonah. "Come on," I whisper. When he doesn't answer I give him a poke.

"What?" He jumps and hits his head on the mattress. "Ouch."

I shush him. When the sisters don't react, I motion to Jonah to follow me out the door.

I make the motion very, very clear.

He lifts his eyebrows, not getting it.

"Just follow me," I whisper, and roll my eyes. I carefully open the door. *Creeeak.*

We step into the hallway. Phewf!

The stepmom's door is closed. Guess she's asleep. How mean — she didn't even say good night to her daughters. I might be running out of underwear, but no matter how busy my parents are, they always come into our rooms to say good night.

"What do we do now?" Jonah whispers.

"I guess we go to sleep," I say. "Maybe Cinderella can help us find the right mirror tomorrow."

"But where will we sleep?"

I point to the winding stairs. "The attic. Cinderella's room."

When we reach the door, Jonah asks, "Should we knock?"

"Um, yeah." Now if he'd only knock on *my* door at home.

"But what if she gets scared?"

"She's probably already asleep," I say. "Hopefully, she has a couch up there we can curl up on. So I won't knock."

I turn the handle and quietly open the door. Cinderella is standing in the middle of the room, admiring the glass slipper.

"Hi," I say. "Glad you're still up."

Startled, she jumps. As she jumps, the glass slipper slips from her hands and drops directly onto her left foot.

"OWW!" she screams. "Ow, ow, ow!"

"Are you okay?" I ask, hurrying over to her.

"Do I look okay?" she snarls, holding onto her foot and hobbling over to a chair. "That really killed. You guys scared me. I thought you were gone!"

"The mirror didn't work," I say.

"Ow, ow, ow. That landed right on my foot."

"I'm so sorry," I tell her. "Do you want some ice?"

"It'll be okay. Just give me a sec. Ouch." She closes her eyes. "Only another day or so and then I'm outta here, right?"

"Right," I say. "Again, sorry."

"Can you bring me the slipper? Did it break?"

I look for the slipper on the ground and gulp when I see it. The heel has cracked off. In one hand, I'm holding a four-inch heel, in the other a flat glass boat. "It doesn't look so good," I admit.

Her eyes fly open. "Oh, boo," Cinderella says. "That isn't going to mess anything up, is it? The shoe being broken?"

"It shouldn't," I say, but I'm not so sure. "No — you have to try on the shoe the guy brings — at least, that's the way I remember it."

"The way you remember what the fairy told you?"

"Um, yeah. Right." I look around the room for a safe place to put the slightly broken shoe and rest it on top of the only shelf next to a tin bucket.

"Oh well." She closes her eyes again. "I'm really tired. And my foot really hurts. Like *really* hurts."

"It will feel better in the morning," Jonah says with a yawn. "That's what my mom always says."

"Then let's go to sleep," Cinderella says. "I have to be up in a few hours to make breakfast."

"Where's your bed?"

"I don't have one — I just sleep on the straw on the floor."

"That stinks," Jonah says. "You really need a mattress."

"I'll get one when I'm a princess," she says with a sigh.

"You'll get as many as you want when you're a princess," I tell her. "You can have a whole stack of them. Like *The Princess and the Pea*!"

"The who and the what?" she asks.

I shake my head. "Never mind."

"I hate peas," she adds.

"Forget I even mentioned them."

"Tomorrow," Cinderella says wistfully, "I'll be a princess."

"And we'll find our way home," Jonah adds.

"Everything will work out tomorrow," I say.

We each gather up some straw and mold it into beds. It's a little scratchy. Actually, a lot scratchy.

Well, at least I'm already in my pajamas.

# ✳ chapter nine ✳

## This Isn't Looking Good

I wake up to the sound of screaming.

"My foot! Ouch, my foot! What happened to my foot?"

I bolt upright to see Cinderella clutching her left foot and howling.

"What's wrong?" I ask.

"My foot is wrong! Look at it!" She thrusts it in my face.

I have never seen a foot quite like this.

It is black.

It is blue.

Her toes are the size of marshmallows and the entire thing is bloated.

Is it a foot or a balloon?

"Is that from dropping the glass slipper on it?" Jonah asks.

"No, it's from playing the piano with my toes," she replies sarcastically. "Of course it's from dropping the glass slipper on it! It's completely swollen. And it hurts!"

I shake my head. "I knew we should have put ice on it."

She tries to stand up, but then grimaces and falls back down onto the straw. "How am I supposed to do my chores? I can barely stand."

"Cinderella! Cinderella! Where are you? Are you still sleeping?" yells a voice from downstairs.

"Oh, no," Cinderella wails. "That's Betty! My stepmother! I must have overslept! I have to make breakfast!"

Excuse me for a second. Betty? Her stepmother's name is Betty? That doesn't sound right. Betty sounds like a nana. Or someone who bakes cakes. It doesn't sound like an evil stepmother.

Cinderella tries to stand up again, but she winces as she puts weight on her foot. "I need to get dressed. And you two need to get out of here. I'm not allowed to have guests."

"Where are we supposed to go?" I ask. "We have to find the mirror that takes us home."

"You tried all the mirrors here," Cinderella says. "Go try other ones."

"But we don't know where else to go!" I say. "If the mirrors here don't work and the mirrors at the palace don't work, which mirrors will?"

Cinderella shakes her head. "I am not a mirror expert!" She hobbles over to the closet, opens the door, and stands behind it for privacy. When she closes it again, she's wearing a long-sleeved gray dress. "Now where did I put my shoes?"

"Your glass slipper?" Jonah asks.

"No, my work shoes. There they are." She spots a pair of loafer-like shoes at the door and limps toward them. She slides the right one on, no problem, and then tries to put on the left shoe. "Oh, crow, my foot is too swollen. I can't get the shoe on. I'm going to have to go barefoot."

Uh-oh.

I steal a look at the broken glass slipper that's lying by the wall. It's the right shoe.

Which means the prince has the left shoe.

If the loafer doesn't fit her left foot, then the glass slipper won't, either.

Crumbs.

If the glass slipper doesn't fit Cinderella, she isn't going to be able to prove she's the girl the prince danced with at the ball. They won't get married. She'll be stuck here forever.

I look at Jonah. He looks at me. He knows. He knows I know.

We did it again. We landed in a fairy tale and we messed things up.

Now what?

"Uh-oh," Jonah says. "Her foot is a basketball."

"Everyone shush!" I say. "I need to think. We need to fix this."

Cinderella waves her hand in the air. "Fix what? I feel like there's something you're not telling me here. Can you fill me in?"

I really don't want to.

"Your foot isn't going to fit the glass slipper," Jonah blurts out.

"It won't fit *today*," I say. "We'll take her to a doctor. Or it could still heal in time. We don't know when the prince is coming. Maybe he's not coming for another week. Her foot won't stay like this forever. It'll heal. It's probably not broken. It's probably just a sprain."

"Abby," Jonah calls out pointing to the wall. "It's okay! Look!" He's pointing at the slightly broken slipper on the shelf.

"We can show the prince's assistant that one. Cinderella will try it on her good foot and it will fit and our problem is solved."

Oh! Yay! "Jonah, you're right! Shoe problem solved!"

"Cinderella!" the voice from downstairs yells. It's getting closer. "You missed breakfast! We had to butter our own bread and brew our own tea! Where are you?"

"I'm coming!" Cinderella calls. "It's my stepmother!" she hisses to us. "She can't come in here! She'll see you!"

"Cinderella, I'm coming in," the voice says.

"Hide!" Cinderella whispers to us, her eyes wide with fear.

I look around the room. Hide where? There is nowhere to hide! There is just straw! No beds! No curtains! No nothing.

Oh, wait. There's the closet. We can hide in there. We'll be super quiet. She won't even notice us! We'll be invisible! Like mice! Instead of bothering to motion to Jonah, I jump up, grab his arm, and hustle toward the closet.

We can make it! We can make it!

The door to Cinderella's room swings opens just as Jonah and I are scrambling into the closet. I'm about to close the closet door behind us when — *Bam!* Jonah bumps his head into my back, I lose my balance, I fall against the wall, I extend out my arms try to stop myself from crashing to the floor, I knock over the tin bucket that's sitting on the shelf — and *clang! Smash!*

The tin bucket knocks over the only-slightly broken glass slipper. The only-slightly broken glass slipper crashes to the floor and smashes into a million pieces. It's now a VERY broken glass slipper.

Crumbs.

Shoe problem unsolved.

# * chapter ten *

## It Is Not a Pleasure to Meet You

Cinderella, what are you doing —" Betty stops in mid-sentence. "Excuse me! Young man! Young lady in the Floom flag! Who are you people?"

She's taller than I expected. Taller than Kayla. And scarier. She's wearing a long brown skirt and a tucked-in green blouse. She has thick straight gray hair that falls past her shoulders, straight bangs across her forehead, a narrow nose, thin lips, and beady brown eyes.

Betty definitely does not look like a Betty. A Betty would smile at me and offer me milk and cookies. Or maybe some brownies. A Betty would never glare at me like I was some sort of cockroach dashing across her floor.

Think fast, Abby, think fast. Why are we here? I know! When in doubt, be polite! "Hi," I say. "It's so nice to finally meet you."

"It is?" Jonah and Cinderella both ask.

"Jinx," Jonah calls.

Betty takes a step closer to me. "Who are you?"

"I'm Abby," I say, "and this is my brother, Jonah."

"We're from Smithville," Jonah adds.

Betty frowns. "And you are here, why?"

"Be-because . . ." Hmm. Long-lost cousins? I glance back at the bucket that unsolved my shoe problem and get an idea. "We're Cinderella's replacements!"

Betty clicks her tongue. "Do tell, why are we replacing Cinderella? Is she going somewhere?"

"As a matter of fact I am," Cinderella says haughtily. "I am going to —"

Oh, no! She can't mention the prince! "She's going to need help —" I interject while pinching Cinderella's arm.

"Ow!"

"— since she busted her foot. We're not really replacements," I add. "We're more like helpers."

Betty's beady brown eyes nearly bug out of her head at the sight of the overstuffed toes. "How did that happen?"

"Well," Cinderella begins. "Last night I dropped a glass sl —"

Nooooooo! "Sled," I interject, pinching her again. "She dropped a glass *sled* on her foot." Oops. That just came out.

"What is a glass sled?" Betty asks.

"You know," I say, stalling. "A sled. For sledding?"

"Down a hill!" Jonah adds. "I love sleds! We have one at home! It's wood, though. But I bet glass ones are slippier."

"Yes," I say. "Exactly. Much slippier." I really can't believe the words that are coming out of my mouth.

"But there's no snow outside. Where was she using a sled?" Betty asks. "And where did she get it?"

Right. Good points. "She found it in the neighbor's trash," I say. "Now we know why they were throwing it away. Dangerous things, these glass sleds. Especially when used down staircases."

Betty stares at me.

"Obviously she would have used it outside if there'd been snow," I add. "But there isn't." That kind of makes sense, doesn't it?

Do I sound as ridiculous as I think I do? Cinderella is bright red. Jonah is twisting his bottom lip. So yeah, I probably do.

247

Betty scans the attic. "Then where is said sled now?"

She's got me there. No. No, no, no. I will not let her win this! Where is the glass sled now? I know! "After it busted Cinderella's foot, I had to throw it out. Like the neighbors did. Wise people, those neighbors."

Jonah wags his finger like he's talking to a dog. "Bad sled. Bad, bad sled."

"But how did you two end up here?" Betty asks.

How did we end up here? Good question. I'm guessing that the magic mirror explanation isn't something I should share.

"She delivered the newspaper," Cinderella offers.

Way to go, Cindy! "Yes!" I cheer. "I was delivering the newspaper. Exactly. And I heard Cinderella scream when she landed at the bottom of the staircase."

"That makes no sense. Why is her foot swollen? You don't get swollen feet from falling down the stairs. You get a broken back or a concussion or —"

"Um, because when she picked up the sled to throw it out, she dropped it on her foot." There. Whew. "And then she screamed a second time, and I came running in. Your door was unlocked, by the way. Not a safe practice." Oh, I'm good! "She told me she had chores to do, so I offered to help her until she gets better."

Betty looks at me suspiciously. "Where are the rest of the newspapers?"

"We gave them out," I say quickly. "And then we came back."

Betty throws up her hands. "But why are you helping her? What's she giving you in return?"

"We're helping her because we're nice," Jonah says. "We don't mind. That's what nice people do. They help each other."

Betty's beady brown eyes narrow. She's not buying it. She doesn't understand what nice is! I need to speak her language. "Also," I add, "she's teaching us to speak English."

Betty raises an overly penciled-in and slightly uneven eyebrow. "It sounds to me like you already know how to speak English."

"She's teaching us to speak gooder," Jonah pipes up.

"Cinderella is a . . . a . . . a . . . *dortun jombi*," I say. "That's means 'good teacher' in Smithvillian. That's the language we speak in Smithville. Also —"

"Okay, I don't care," Betty says, looking bored. "If you want to help Cinderella while her foot is out of commission, knock yourself out. We're going to be busy, anyway. Since you delivered the paper, I assume you've all read the news?"

"Absolutely," I say, nodding. "Can you just remind us what it says?"

"Only that the prince has announced that he will marry whoever fits the glass slipper he found at the ball. His assistant will begin to visit all the households in the kingdom later today. So you three had better get started cleaning the house. Start in here. There's glass all over the floor."

Oh, no! Today already?

I look at Cinderella's foot.

Uh-oh.

"We have a *relamo*," Jonah says, after Betty leaves.

"A what?" I ask.

"*Relamo* is Smithvillian for problem," he says.

Hardy har har.

# ✳ chapter eleven ✳

## We Need Magic, Pronto!

**W**hat are we going to do?" I ask.

"This really *is* a *relamo*," Cinderella says, frowning. "If the prince's assistant comes today, my foot is definitely not going to fit in the glass slipper."

"Right," I say.

"What should the Smithvillian word for 'trouble' be?" Jonah asks. "*Dessinsty*?"

"Jonah," I say. "Try to focus."

"Maybe he won't come today," Cinderella says wistfully. "Maybe he'll come tomorrow."

I check out the state of Cinderella's foot. "I don't think it's fitting tomorrow, either."

"So what do I do?" she asks. "I need it to fit!"

"You could always cut off one of your toes," Jonah says. "Like in the Grimm story."

Cinderella gasps. "That is, indeed, a grim story."

"Jonah, that's disgusting!" I say.

"I was just kidding," he says. "That would hurt. Although it would be really cool."

There has to be a solution. "Oh! I know!" I say. It's so easy! "You have a fairy godmother, right?"

Cinderella nods.

"So ask her to fix it! That's what she's there for. To fix things."

"I guess I could do that," Cinderella says.

"How do you get her to come?" Jonah asks. "Do you just call her?"

"Call her? Yes! Exactly. I call her name and she comes." Cinderella tilts her head toward the chimney, "Farrah! Farrah! Yoo-hoo, you there?"

"She's like Santa!" Jonah says.

A second later, a big puff of yellow is sparkling in the center of the room. Then the sparkle slowly trickles to the ground, and I see her — the legendary fairy godmother.

She is not what I expected. I thought she'd be plump.

But she's not. Instead, she's super skinny. And she has big wide eyes that are green and smiling. Her hair is wild and curly and perched on her head in a loose bun. Instead of wearing a twirly dress, she's wearing black leggings and a yellow sweater. She's like a human bumblebee. Or not human, exactly. Are fairies human? At least I think she's a fairy. I don't see any wings. She's holding a yellow-and-black swirly wand that looks like a candy cane. If candy canes were yellow and black.

"You're the fairy godmother?" Jonah blurts out.

"I am. And you must be Abby and Jonah."

"How did you know?" I ask.

She laughs. "Word gets around. So, Cinderella, what can I do for you?"

"You need to fix her foot," I say. "It's busted. It's never going to fit the glass slipper the way it is now. And if it doesn't fit the glass slipper, then she won't be able to marry the prince."

Farrah looks at Cinderella. "Is that what you want? To marry the prince?"

"Of course that's what I want!" Cinderella says. "Why do you think I wanted to go to the balls? For the pigs-in-a-blanket? I need the prince to rescue me and get me out of this place."

Farrah blinks. And then blinks again. "Excuse me?"

"I need him to rescue me," she repeats. "Marrying him will save me from this miserable life."

"And if you don't mind," I pipe in, "can you please direct us to the nearest magic mirror? We need to get home. Thank you for your time."

This is perfect. All of our problems will be solved with one burst of yellow sparkle! Farrah will fix Cinderella's foot and then send us home with a poof.

Farrah crosses her arms. "No."

"Exqueeze me?" Did I hear her right?

"No," she repeats.

Cinderella blinks. And then blinks again. "I don't understand. Why not?"

"First of all, I don't like being told what to do," Farrah says, glaring at all of us. "And second, Cinderella, I don't like this attitude of yours. Not one bit. You need to learn to rescue yourself! You need to learn to stand on your own two feet!"

"But my foot feels broken!" Cinderella whines. "I can't stand at all!"

"Well, you'd better learn. You can't rely on a prince to save you. You have to be self-reliant!"

"What's self-reliant?" Jonah asks.

"It means relying on yourself," I explain.

"I'm self-reliant," he says.

I snort. "Please. You don't even make your own bed."

"Does that mean you're not going to fix my foot today?" Cinderella asks meekly.

"I am not going to fix your foot today," the fairy godmother says. I can't believe how mean Farrah is being. None of the fairy tale versions mentioned this!

"We really need you to fix Cinderella's foot *today*," I say. "If the slipper doesn't fit, we won't be able to prove that Cinderella's the right girl! Isn't that why you sent her to the ball in the first place? So she could snag the prince?"

"Noooo," Farrah says. "I sent her so she could have a night out on the town!"

"You never thought that the prince might fall in love with her?" I ask.

"I'm fine with the prince falling in love with her — I just don't want her to be so needy about it." Farrah shakes her head at Cinderella. "You're not my only charge, you know. I'm the prince's fairy godmother, too. I've known him since he was a baby — no way do I want him getting stuck with a whiny damsel in distress. He needs a partner in his life. After all, a queen must be strong. If you can prove to me you won't be hanging on to his shirttails, I'll help you snag him. Got it? Show me you can stand on your own two feet and I'll fix your foot. I'm willing to help you — but only if you help yourself first."

"But it will be too late!" I say. "The prince's assistant is on his way now!"

"The assistant is at the other end of the kingdom. He won't make it here until Tuesday afternoon. I'll give you until Tuesday at noon to call for me and prove your self-reliance. It's Sunday morning. You have two and a half days. Make them count."

But — but — but . . . "Wait! Farrah? What about us? Can you help us find a magic mirror so we can go home?" I ask.

It's too late. She's gone in a puff of sparkle.

# ∗ chapter twelve ∗

## Now What?

there's no time for brainstorming ideas. We have to get right to work. Cinderella hobbles around the kitchen cleaning up the breakfast dishes while Jonah and I sweep the living room.

More precisely, I hold the dustpan while Jonah attempts to sweep.

He is the worst sweeper ever. He's just running around with the broom, swishing it in every direction. I think he might be making the dust worse than it was before.

"Focus, Jonah, focus!"

He sweeps a piece of dirt into my mouth.

"Jonah!" I say with a spit.

"Sorry," he says, but he's laughing so I don't really believe him.

His face turns serious and he twists his bottom lip. "Abby, how are we going to get home?"

"I, um, have a plan," I say. Although to be honest, I don't have a plan yet. I'm making it up right now. But I think it's important for Jonah to trust that I always have a plan. It's my job as the big sister.

"Yeah?" he says. "What is it?"

"Oh. Right. Well . . ."

"You don't have a plan, do you?"

"I do, I do! We help Cinderella prove to Farrah that she can be self-reliant before noon on Tuesday."

"What is it about twelve o'clock in fairy tales?" Jonah asks. "Whether it's noon or midnight, something always happens at twelve."

"That is true. I don't know why. So back to my plan. How about this — when Farrah comes back she'll be so amazed by the new and improved Cinderella that she'll happily tell us where the magic mirror is."

"But what if she doesn't know where it is?"

"She must know," I declare. "At the very least, she could zap us home herself. She does have a magic wand."

He nods. "Okay. Decent plan."

I hear footsteps in the hallway. It's Beatrice, the meaner sister. She looks a lot like her mother. Exact same thin nose and lips, exact same straight hair and bangs. Except hers is brown instead of gray. And she's the tallest of the three.

"Why are you two here?" she asks.

"We're here to help Cinderella."

"Good. Go help her with the wash. I'm low on underwear."

That makes two of us.

"Uh, okay."

"Kayla!" Beatrice yells up the stairs. "Do you need Cinderella to do your wash?"

"Yeah," Kayla calls back.

"The hampers are in our closet," Beatrice tells us. "We're going to visit friends now. Surely you'll see to it that the laundry is done by today so it'll be all ready for tomorrow. The prince's assistant is coming, you know."

"Fine." Must be a really slow washing machine.

I go upstairs. The stepsisters' door is closed so I knock. After what happened with Cinderella, I will never not knock again.

"Come in," I hear.

Kayla is lying facedown on her bed.

"Hi, Kayla," I say. "I'm just getting your laundry."

She turns her face toward me. "How do you know my name? Have we met?"

Well, I saw you fawning over the prince at the ball and then spied on you from under your bed. But no, technically, we haven't met. "You're Beatrice's sister, right?"

"Yes."

"We're helping Cinderella out while her foot heals," I say. "We're going to do your laundry and then make you dinner."

She nods. "Okay," she says, and then turns her head the other way.

"It's nice to meet you, too," I say sarcastically.

She doesn't bother to answer.

I bump Kayla's hamper down the stairs. "Cinderella?" I ask, popping my head into the kitchen.

But she's already done cleaning the kitchen and has managed to sweep and dustpan the entire marble entranceway by herself.

On one foot.

She's a cleaning machine.

"Wow," I say.

"Yes?" she asks.

"Where's the washer and dryer?" I ask.

"The what?"

"The washer and dr —" I stop in mid-sentence. "Do you guys not have a washer and dryer?"

"*I'm* the washer and dryer," she answers. "I wash the clothes by hand, then hang them up to dry."

Yikes. Even if my parents never bother using it, I have never felt more thankful for our washer and dryer in my entire life.


Cinderella and I are on all fours washing her stepsisters' clothes in the tub in the basement. At least they have running water in Floom, otherwise we'd be standing on a riverbank.

I'm soaping, Cinderella is rinsing, and Jonah is hanging. We have a whole production line going on. Next we're ironing wrinkled dresses. Cinderella is going to show me how to use the ironing board and everything.

"I don't understand what Farrah wants from me," Cinderella says. "How can I rescue myself?"

"Let's think about it," I say. "You said you were stuck here, right?"

"I *am* stuck here. I have nowhere else to go."

"But you're not chained to the house," I say. "You can leave if you want to."

"Where's your dad?" Jonah asks. "Is he dead?"

"He's not dead," Cinderella says. "He's just gone."

"Gone where?"

"Just gone. He left us. He left me. My mom's death was just too much for him."

"But he got married again," I say.

"I think he just wanted to find a place for me to live, since I was only twelve. And once he did — he took off. We used to get postcards, but we haven't heard from him in three years."

"That's terrible!" Jonah says. "I can't believe a dad would do that."

"He's a sailor," Cinderella says. "And he sailed away. I doubt I'll ever see him again. And he left me here. Stranded. I have no money and nowhere to go. That's why I need the prince to rescue me."

"Why don't you get a job?" I say, rinsing a pair of striped socks. "Then you'll have your own money and you can get your own house."

"But she's going to move into the palace when she gets married," Jonah says. "She doesn't need her own house."

"She won't get to marry the prince if Farrah doesn't fix her foot," I argue. "And Farrah won't help unless Cinderella helps herself. If Cinderella gets a job and moves out, it should prove to Farrah that she can be self-reliant. But if Farrah gets all weird and says it's not enough, at least this way Cinderella won't be stuck here anymore. It's a no-lose plan!"

Cinderella cocks her head to the side. "But what kind of job could I get? I'm not good at anything."

"That's not true," I say. "You're the world's fastest cleaner. You tidied that whole living room in forty-five seconds flat."

"You could be a cleaning lady!" Jonah says.

"We need to think bigger," I say, my eyes widening. "You could start a cleaning service! You could train a whole bunch of cleaners to clean superfast like you do and then send them out to people's houses! You taught us to clean; you can teach other people, too! You'll start a company. You'll make a fortune. You can call it . . . Mess Be Gone. No wait, Cinderella's Cleaners!" I pump my arm in the air, feeling proud of myself. I am a big fan of alliteration. Although I don't remember if alliteration has to be the same first letter or the same first sound. Whatever. It's still cute. From now on maybe I should go by Awesome Abby.

Cinderella shudders. "No way. I hate cleaning. I do it so fast so I can be done with it. I don't want to clean other people's houses for money. I don't want to clean this house, and if I had my own place, I wouldn't want to clean that, either. If I had my own money, I'd hire Cinderella's Cleaners."

"They probably wouldn't use your name if you weren't part of the company," Jonah points out.

Cinderella nods. "True."

I'm pretty sure she's missing an excellent business opportunity, but whatever. I think harder. "What about something with animals?" I say. "Aren't you really good with mice?"

"Farrah is good with mice, not me. Actually, I'm not all that great with any animal. Plus, I'm allergic to dogs. They give me a terrible cough and make me sneeze. Cats, too."

"Can you be a lawyer?" Jonah asks. "That's what our parents are."

"That takes a lot of schooling," I say, a little bit huffy. "Not everyone can be a lawyer, you know."

"I don't want to be a lawyer," Cinderella says. "Too much

arguing involved." She squeezes water out of one of Beatrice's shirts. "This is missing a button. I'll have to sew on a new one."

Hmm. "You can sew?"

She nods. "Of course. Can't you?"

"I've never tried," I say. "But I probably could. But this is about you. What about becoming a seamstress?"

"Think bigger," Jonah says, echoing my previous statement. "You could make clothes. You could be a fashion designer."

"That's perfect!" I say. Way to go, Jonah! "You'll make clothes and sell them. A perfect plan!"

"But what should I make?"

"You have to make something unique," I say. "Something that someone else isn't already making. What do you know how to make?"

Cinderella shrugs. "I've never made anything entirely from scratch, but I'm really good at stitching. I've hemmed skirts. Sheets. Shirts. Dresses."

"Can you make underwear?" I ask. Mine are giving me a wedgie.

"Um, I guess."

"Never mind. Let's focus on things people in Floom want."

"Floom people wear underwear," she says, sounding insulted.

"No, I mean special clothes," I say. I think about the people of Floom. What do they all like? Oh! "They loved your dress! Everyone loved the dress you wore to the ball. They couldn't stop gushing about it!"

She nods. "They did love my dress. I *loved* my dress. I wish I still had my dress."

Ding ding! "That's what you'll do! You'll make a Cinderella dress! You'll make a bunch of Cinderella dresses and then you'll sell them!"

"And make one for yourself," Jonah adds. "Maybe the prince's assistant will recognize you if you're wearing it when he comes by with the glass slipper."

Cinderella's eyes light up. "That, my little friend, is a perfect plan."

And once she's done with that, maybe she can make me a pair of jeans, a sweatshirt, and some new undies.

# ✴ chapter thirteen ✴

## Project Cinderella

We take a break from the wash to search the house for material.

"The living room curtains!" I say. "They're platinum!"

"They're more of a silver," Cinderella says.

"Is there really a difference?" Honestly, I can't tell. "The curtains are perfect." It'll be just like in *The Sound of Music* when Maria makes the kids' clothes!

"I can't dismantle the curtains," Cinderella says. "Betty would notice."

"Is there anything else silver-ish that she has and won't miss?" I ask.

"I think she might have some extra tablecloths," Cinderella says. "Let's look in the closet."

We trudge over to the closet and find a stack.

"This one isn't bad," I say. "It's not exactly silver. It's more gray. But we can accessorize."

"But we still need to finish the wash," Cinderella says.

"We'll finish the wash," I say. "You make the clothes."

"I'll be in the attic," she says. "Wish me luck."

I peek into the room ten minutes later. "How's it going?"

"Great," she says from under the gray tablecloth.

"Did you sketch it out?"

"Um, no. Should I?"

"I think that's what designers do."

"I'm not really good at drawing," she says. "So I just started cutting."

"Okay," I say. She probably knows more about this dress stuff than I do. "What should we do next?"

"Can you make the beds?"

That I can definitely do. Unlike my brother, I make my own bed every morning.

Since Betty and the stepsisters have gone to "visit friends" (I know — they have friends? I'm shocked, too) I take my time making their beds and snooping through their stuff.

Kayla has *Jordan + Kayla* written in hearts all over her notebooks. I'd feel bad for her if she wasn't so mean.

I go back downstairs and find Jonah reading the newspaper at the kitchen table. And by the newspaper, I mean the comics. "Let's go," I say.

"Guess what I found," he says.

"Big Nate?"

"No, but there is a comic strip called Big Tate. Do you think they're related?"

"Maybe. Come on. We have to make the beds."

"Wait, I found something else you're going to like." He flips the pages back. "Look!"

*Apartment in private home for rent*

*33 Slipper Street*

*Cozy, 600 square feet*

*Private bathroom, big kitchen, and big windows!*

*Ground floor! Great light! Wonderful location — near shops and palace.*

*No pets.*

*$100/month*

"Isn't this perfect for Cinderella?" he says. "It's on Slipper Street. I think that's a sign. And no pets! She's allergic to pets."

"Rent is so cheap in Floom!" I say. "That's amazing!"

We clomp up the stairs to tell her the news.

"Sounds heavenly," she says.

I look around the room. All I see is a heap of tablecloth. "How's it going?" I ask, a little concerned. But she looks pretty intent, so I guess that's a good sign.

"Great. I'm a natural. I'll probably need another hour or so, though."

"Let us know if we can help! Good luck!"

An hour later: "Cinderella? How are you doing in there?"

"Wonderful! I need another hour! Do you think you could start dinner? Maybe make a chicken Caesar salad? We have leftover chicken from last night."

"Um, I don't know how to make Caesar salad," I say.

"Can't we just order a pizza?" Jonah asks.

"The cookbook is on the counter! It tells you how to make the dressing," Cinderella calls out.

"Oh. Okay."

How hard can it be?

We follow the recipe. We mince. We chop. We whisk. We finish the dressing. Then we make the salad.

"This was easier than I thought!" I say, munching on some loose lettuce.

And who knew? Cooking is fun! Cookbooks make it so much easier, though. Cinderella has the *Official Floom Cookbook*. There is a section on stew. There is a section on pizza. There is a section on something called *Kingslingions*, a Floom specialty, which calls for rice, shark fin, olives, and pineapple (which I never, ever want to try). There is also a section on desserts. Chocolate chip cookies! Lemon meringue pie! White chocolate cake! Yum.

When all the prep is done, we go back upstairs.

I knock and call from the hallway, "Cinderella? You still there? How's it going?"

"All done!" she says. "I'm just trying it on. Come in!"

"I can't wait to see it!" I squeal.

"Here I come!" She steps out from the closet and cheers, "Ta-da!"

Oh.

Oh, no.

It is not good.

It is not good at all.

The edges are jagged. The sleeves are uneven. There are random slashes in places that shouldn't have slashes. It looks about seven sizes too big.

She looks like the bride of Frankenstein.

She pirouettes. "Is it gorgeous? This was easier than I thought."

Jonah tugs at my arm. "That's what you said about making the Caesar salad."

Very true. Except the Caesar salad actually looks like Caesar salad. This dress does not look like the dress she wore to the ball. It doesn't look like a dress at all. It looks like a tablecloth that got attacked by a class of preschoolers with scissors.

Cinderella does another twirl. "I'll make you a pair of undies with the leftover material."

Thanks, but no thanks. "Cinderella, I don't know how to tell you this but —"

Her face falls. "What?"

I sigh. "You really need a mirror in here."

# * chapter fourteen *

## And the Next Plan Is . . . ?

"Oh my," Cinderella says. We're in the stepsisters' room, examining the dress in one of the mirrors. She looks at herself from all angles. "Oh my, oh my. I am really not a good designer."

"No," I say. "You're really not."

"You can keep practicing," Jonah says. "You don't get good at something overnight."

"That's true," I say. "But it's already Sunday evening. It's almost dinnertime. We only have a day and a half left to raise a hundred dollars!"

Cinderella sighs.

"What?" I ask.

"It just seems like an awful lot of work for something that's not going to be needed in the end. I mean, if this convinces Farrah to help me, I'm going to marry the prince and live in the palace. I won't need the apartment after all."

"You could keep the apartment for your office," Jonah says.

She makes a sad face. "My office for what?"

"Your job," I remind her. "I want to get married one day, but I still want to be a judge. Even if you do marry the prince, you might discover you like being self-reliant. Even a princess should feel self-reliant. In the meantime, you still need a job. Are you sure you don't want to be a cleaning person? Or maybe just a clothes washer?"

"I hate washing clothes," Cinderella says. "My hands are all chapped. And it's boring. I want to *make* something."

"You're making something cleaner," I say.

Cinderella shrugs. "Is the chicken Caesar salad done?"

"Yup. All set.

"Oh, good. Did you make anything for dessert?"

"No, were we supposed to?"

"I can do it. But we'd better hurry. They'll be home soon, and they eat at seven."

My stomach grumbles. "When do *we* eat?"

"After they eat."

"Oh, man," Jonah wails. "I'm hungry."

We help Cinderella back down the stairs and into the kitchen. We hear the front door open, and then Betty butts her head in. "I hope dinner is almost ready," she says.

*"Gezuty!"* Jonah says.

"Hmm?"

"That's Smithvillian for 'almost,'" he explains.

She rolls her eyes and steps out.

"So what should we make?" I ask, flipping through the cookbook. "Cake? Lemon meringue pie? Cookies?"

"What about brownies?" Jonah asks.

"Yum, I love brownies," I say. "Let's make them."

Cinderella's face scrunches up. "What are brownies?"

Both my brother's and my jaws fall open. "What are brownies?" I yell. "Are you joking?"

She shakes her head. "I've never heard of them."

"You've never tried a chocolate brownie?" Jonah repeats, dumbfounded.

"I've never tried any kind of brownie," she says with a shrug.

"You really need to get out more," I say. "I'm sure they're in the book." I flip through the pages. Cinnamon cupcakes, pineapple tarts, chocolate chip cookies, apple muffins . . . but no brownies. NO BROWNIES?

"I can't find a single brownie recipe. This should be illegal."

"What is a brownie, exactly?" she asks.

"It's a small square of deliciousness," I say.

"So let's make some," Cinderella says. "Do you know how?"

"It's easy," Jonah says. "You take the brownie mix off the shelf and give it to your mom and dad and they mix it with some stuff." His face falls. Either he just realized that Cinderella doesn't have any brownie mix or he remembered that our parents don't have much time for brownie making right now.

"Oh," he says. "I guess that won't work. You probably have to make it from scratch."

"So what's the recipe?" Cinderella asks.

I look at Jonah. He looks at me. "I don't know," I say. "Our parents never made them from scratch."

"Okay, why don't you tell me what it tastes like?" Cinderella asks. "Maybe I can figure it out."

"They're chocolaty. They're like a cross between a cookie and a cake," I say.

Cinderella ties an apron around her waist and pulls out a mixing bowl. "I do a lot of baking, so we'll have some trial and error. Do you mind being my tasters?"

"That is something I wouldn't mind at all," Jonah says. "Bring on the brownies!"

Hmm. I'm getting an idea here. "You do a lot of baking?"

"Yup," she says, turning on the oven. "Lots."

"Do you like baking? Is it something you could do even more of?"

"Sure," she says. "I find it relaxing."

Here's the big one: "Are you any good at it?"

"I'm not bad," she says with a shrug.

"Are you a better baker than you are a sewer?" I ask.

She laughs. "Much better. Are you guys thinking what I'm thinking?"

My mind is racing. "I'm thinking that this could be your job! You can bake brownies and sell them! All of Floom would come and buy them because you're the only person who makes them."

"Where would I sell them?" Cinderella asks.

"Your apartment!" I say. "It'll be an apartment *and* bakery. It's on the ground floor — it's perfect."

"You want me to start my own shop?"

"Yes! Wouldn't that be cool? You could call it Cinderella's Brownies! Wait. No. That doesn't have alliteration. Hmm. It's really too bad you're not making cookies. Cinderella's Cookies has alliteration." Maybe not alliteration. But close enough.

"Floom already has cookies," Cinderella says.

I drum my fingers against the counter. "Right. And you have cakes and cupcakes, too, huh?"

She nods. "We do."

"Oh, well. Brownies it is. I'll keep thinking about the name."

"But I need to sell these brownies before I have the money to get the apartment," Cinderella says. "I guess we could sell them at the market. We could set up a booth."

"Perfect!" I say. "We'll go tomorrow!"

"Hurray!" Jonah cheers.

"Our problems aren't solved yet," Cinderella says, her forehead wrinkling. "I still don't know how to make the brownies."

Oh. Right. "You will. I have complete faith in your baking skills."

I hope I don't have to eat those words.

# ✳ chapter fifteen ✳

## If At First You Don't Succeed, Keep Eating

While Cinderella bakes in the kitchen, Jonah puts the chicken Caesar salad on plates and I serve it in the dining room.

"You didn't give me enough chicken," Beatrice complains.

*Excuuuuuuuse me.*

"Do you want me to get you more?" I ask.

"Surely I do. Why else would I have complained?"

Um, because you complain about everything? So far she's told me that there's:

1. A speck of dirt on her fork.

2. A draft in the room.

3. No pepper on the table.


"Anything else?" I ask. I look at Kayla, but she's too busy staring at her plate. What's up with her?

"You need to refill our water, too," Betty snaps. "I'm thirsty."

"No problem," I say with fake cheer. As long as they're not coming in the kitchen, I'm happy.

I keep a fake smile on my face until I'm back in the kitchen and then groan. "Betty and Beatrice are so annoying. More water! More chicken! Clean forks! Blah, blah, blah!"

"Don't forget about Kayla," Cinderella says, pulling her first batch of brownies from the oven. "Hasn't she complained about the food needing more salt yet? She always complains about the food needing more salt."

"She hasn't actually." Kayla's barely said two words. She's barely eating, either. She's just moping into her food.

"Maybe she's getting sick or something," Cinderella says. She cuts out two chunks of brownie and hands one to Jonah and one to me. "Here, try this."

"Blah," Jonah says, spitting it out in the garbage.

"Jonah, that's so rude," I say.

"But it tasted gross!"

"Can you try to be constructive, please?" I ask.

He looks thoughtful. "It needs to be less bad."

I take a small bite. I second the blah, but keep it to myself.

"Very constructive, Jonah, thank you. I actually think it needs more sugar. And maybe more chocolate chunks."

"Will do," Cinderella says, dancing around the kitchen. I think she's having fun. Now all we need is for her to make a decent brownie and we'll be all set.


The next batch is disgusting, too. And way too gooey. I didn't know it was possible to have brownies that were too gooey, but it is.

"Should I feed it to the evil ones for dessert?" I ask.

"Yes," Jonah says. "Maybe it will make them barf."

I shudder. "But then we'd have to clean up the barf."

"I actually don't know what to give them for dessert," Cinderella says. "We have nothing ready."

"Do you have any fruit?" I ask.

"Fruit isn't dessert," Jonah says, looking horrified.

"It is, too," I say. "I saw some clementines. They can have those."

"Make sure to peel them," Cinderella says.

"Seriously?" I groan. "Jonah, help me."

"I'm kinda busy," he says. By busy he means, he's dipping his finger in the brownie bowl and licking it. "After you make chocolate brownies, can you make caramel brownies? And chocolate chip brownies? And blondies?"

"And some with nuts," I add.

"Yuck," Jonah says. "No one really likes nuts in their brownies. They just eat them because they have to."

"Why would you have to eat brownies with nuts?" I ask.

"Parents think they're healthier. Like carrot cake. People think it's healthy just because it has carrots in the name. Blah. Please do not put nuts in your brownies."

"Got it," Cinderella says. "No nuts."

"And no carrots," Jonah adds.


The clementines do not go over well.

"Fruit is not dessert!" Beatrice cries.

"I expect you to make something more dessert-y tomorrow," Betty says. "There are three of you in there. You have no excuse."

Grumble, grumble, grumble.

Kayla just stares at her clementines.

Back in the kitchen I discover that batch three of the brownies is burnt.

I'm beginning to get nervous.

"What about ketchup brownies?" Jonah suggests.

"That's disgusting," I say. "And stop eating the brownie mix!"



"I think these need vanilla," Cinderella says, sampling batch four. I've just cleared the plates off the dining room table.

I have no idea what vanilla does to brownies, so I am happy to take her word for it.

"Cinderella?" Kayla says, poking her head into the kitchen. "I'd like another glass of water."

Seriously? Can she not pour the water herself?

"Of course," Cinderella says.

Kayla eyes the many plates of brownies. "What are you doing in here?"

"Preparing dessert for tomorrow," Cinderella answers, which is not a lie.

"Oh," she says. She looks like she's about to say something more, but she doesn't. When Cinderella hands her a glass of water, though, she whispers a tiny "Thank you." Then she hurries out of the kitchen.

Cinderella looks stunned. "What was *that*?" she says. "Kayla never says thank you. None of them do."

"That's so rude," I say.

"That's the least of it," Cinderella says. "Last week Kayla dripped tomato sauce on the chair and then blamed me. Betty made me scrub it with my toothbrush. She and Kayla just laughed. Then Beatrice spilled more on purpose. The two of them are the worst. Sure, Beatrice's usually the instigator but Kayla's no angel."

I put my arm around her thin shoulders. "You'll be out of here soon. I know it."

"You will," Jonah says, helping himself to another spoonful of batter. "This stuff isn't bad. It's not as awesome as dogs-in-a-blanket but —" His eyes light up. "Can you make dogs-in-a-blanket brownies? That would be awesome."

"Please don't," I say.

"We could dip them in ketchup!"

Sometimes I'm not sure how we're even related.

Cinderella finishes batch five at around eleven.

I chew carefully. It is chocolaty. It is the perfect amount of gooey. It is melt-in-my-mouth delicious. Hurray!

"Cinderella," I say slowly. "This is the best chocolate brownie I have ever had in my entire life."

The next morning, we wait for Betty and her daughters to leave to visit more friends before we start baking. (I know — more friends?)

We use up all the chocolate and all the flour and all the eggs and make ten trays of brownies — one dozen brownies per tray. We wait for them to cool down, pack them up, and get ready to go to the market.

If we sell them for a dollar each, we'll even have extra money. Cinderella is going to need extra cash for supplies and stuff.

Except . . .

"Um, guys?" I ask. We're all ready and standing in front of Cinderella's house. We have the brownies, some signs, and even the ironing board. That was my great idea. We need some sort of table for the booth, right? "Where is the market? And how are we supposed to get there?"

"Cinderella," Jonah says. "Don't you have a car or something you can drive?"

She shakes her head. "My coach turned into a squashed pumpkin, remember?"

"How do you normally get there?" I ask.

"I normally walk. It's not that far. Maybe twenty minutes. No problem."

"Um, yes, problem. We're carrying ten trays of brownies." I look down at her still swollen foot. "Even if Jonah and I carry your share, I don't think we're walking anywhere."

"Maybe she can stay behind and bake more brownies?" Jonah asks. "And we can do the selling?"

"I don't know if that's gonna cut it with Farrah," I say. "How is she walking on her own two feet if we're leaving her behind?"

We stand there, not sure what to do.

One coach goes by us. And then another one.

"Can we call a taxi?" Jonah asks.

"A what?" Cinderella asks.

Hmm. If this brownie thing doesn't work out, she can start a taxi service.

"We can always take the parriage," Cinderella says.

"I hate porridge," Jonah says. "Stick to brownies, please."

"The what?" I ask.

"The parriage! Don't you have parriages in Smithville?"

"I don't know what that is," I say.

She looks at me with disbelief. "This Smithville place sure sounds backward."

Humph. At least we have brownies.

"Oh, look," she says, pointing down the street. "Here comes a parriage now!"

Up ahead is a green carriage being pulled by two horses. On the front of the carriage it says 5: CROSSTOWN.

"Oh!" Jonah exclaims. "It's a bus!"

"It's a parriage," Cinderella says. "You know. Public carriage."

"Cool," I say. "But how much does it cost? We don't have any money."

"Fifty cents a person," she says. "Each way."

"Maybe we can pay in brownies." I wave at the driver as the parriage approaches, but he doesn't stop.

"Don't be silly," Cinderella says. "You have to be picked up at the parriage stop."

"Where is it?" I ask, annoyed. We're never going to make it!

"At the end of the street," Cinderella says.

I see a sign in the shape of a diamond at the corner. "Jonah, you run, and I'll help Cinderella. Go, go, go!"

Jonah runs up ahead, carrying his share of the brownies. I don't know if he's going to make it.

Cinderella and I follow behind as fast as we can.

"Ouch," she says with every step. "Ouch, ouch, ouch."

"We're almost there!" I encourage. Poor Cinderella.

He runs . . . he runs . . . and he makes it!

Jonah steps onto the carriage. He steps back out a second later. "He'll take us," he shouts. "For a half dozen brownies!"

"Six brownies? That's highway robbery! That's six dollars' worth!"

"It's worse than that. I had to give him a whole brownie to taste first. He liked it — a lot — but that's his final offer. He says take it or leave it."

"It's not like we have a choice," Cinderella says.

Grumble. Sounds like brownie blackmail to me. "All right. Six more brownies it is," I say. I wish we had saved some of our gross ones from last night.

We reach the bus, hand over the brownies, and squish into a seat.

"These are really good," the driver says. Crumbs are caught in his beard. "What are they called again? Crownies?"

"Brownies," Jonah says.

Hmm, I kind of like *crownies*. And since no one here knows what brownies are we can call them *crownies* if we want. Why not? We invented them! And then we could call the store Cinderella's Crownies!

"Cinderella's Crownies," I announce. "We'll be at the market. Tell your friends."

Cinderella puts her foot up on the seat. Her toes are still the size of marshmallows.

Hmmm. Marshmallow crownies?

I look back at her toes. Yuck. Never mind.

# ✳ chapter sixteen ✳

## Step Right Up

the market has all kinds of cool stuff. Food, clothes, furniture, old people in puffy outfits. We set up on the ironing board. Jonah hangs a sign that says, CINDERELLA'S BROWNIES! $1 EACH!

I take out the marker and turn the *B* into a *C*. Much better.

The brownie-crownies look amazing. They smell amazing.

Only problem? We've sold:

Zero.

"Why is no one buying any?" Jonah whines, finishing off a brownie-crownie.

"Maybe they're too expensive," Cinderella says.

"Yes, but this way we don't have to sell as many," I say.

"Yes, but right now we're not selling any," she says. "If they cost less, more people will buy them."

When did she get so business-savvy? "Fine. We'll try selling them for fifty cents apiece."

I change the sign to two for a dollar. It doesn't help.

Do you know what's also not helping? Jonah eating all the brownie-crownies.

"What time does the market close?" I ask.

"We have a few more hours," Cinderella says. "We have to get home and make dinner."

"At least we have dessert," Jonah says.

One older woman comes up and sniffs at the table. "What are you selling?" she barks.

"Brownies!" Jonah says.

"Crownies!" I correct him. "Would you like to buy two? Only one dollar."

"What's a crownie?"

"It's a yummy dessert!"

"No, thanks," she says, and walks away.

"You don't know what you're missing!" Jonah calls out after her and helps himself to another brownie-crownie.

Wait a sec. "That's the problem!"

"What is?" Jonah asks.

"They don't know what a crownie is!" I say.

"No one knows what a crownie is," Jonah says. "It's not a real word."

I ignore him. "They don't know how good crownies are. We need to give them samples. That's what you did to convince the parriage driver, right? It'll work here, too!"

"You want us to give away crownies for free?" Cinderella asks eyes wide.

I nod. "Except not whole ones. We'll cut them even smaller. Once people taste them, they'll buy them! It'll be like Whole Foods or Costco! I love when they give you samples. Jonah, you'll go into the crowd and pass them out. Make sure to tell them that we're selling them right here, okay?"

He salutes me. "Aye, aye, captain."

I break some crownies into pieces, put them on a plate, and hand them to my brother. "And, Jonah —"

"Yeah?"

"No munching!"

\* \* \*

293

We've given away a total of twenty crownies in samples. And we've sold ten crownies at fifty cents each. Meaning, we've made five dollars. Except we're out ten dollars in merchandise.

"It's better than nothing," Cinderella says.

"True," I say. "Rome wasn't built in a day."

"What's Rome?" she asks.

"You really need to get out more," I say.

"I'm out of samples," Jonah says, coming back to our booth.

"We definitely have more of those," I say. "Wanna switch?"

"Sure," he says.

I cut up the crownies into even smaller pieces and start walking down the rows. There's a butcher selling meat. A couple selling silver necklaces that have a dangling green eye on them. A little bit creepy. Oh! A woman with red hair is selling seriously cute dresses for ten dollars! I wish I had money so I could get one. Right now I'm wearing one of Cinderella's drab gray dresses. It's kind of itchy. And about two sizes too big.

"Crownies!" I chant. "Come have a free crownie! A brand-new dessert like you've never had before! It's a mix between a cookie and a cake! The chocolate will melt in your mouth! Goes great with a glass of milk!"

A few people take samples and I remind them to come by our booth.

"I'll try one," says a little freckled boy.

I hand him one and watch as his eyes widen with joy. "Delicious!" he says.

"Excuse me, would you like a tasty treat?" I offer a pregnant woman. "We're selling them for fifty cents at our booth!"

"Absolutely," she says. "Hey, these are amazing!"

I give her an extra one since she's tasting for two.

"Excuse me, would you like to taste Cinderella's Crownies?" I say to the back of a young woman's head. "They're delicious! They're homemade! Come meet the baker!"

She turns around.

Her hair isn't blond or brunette. It's in the middle. And frizzy. Her eyes aren't blue or green or sparkly or really big. They're average. And her lips are kind of thin.

My jaw drops.

Her jaw drops.

It's Kayla.

# ✴ chapter seventeen ✴

## Nowhere to Hide

AGHHHH!

The first thing I think is: *RUN, ABBY, RUN!*

So I run.

I run past the redheaded dressmaker and the butcher.

Maybe she'll think she imagined me? I run and duck and stop and hide behind a group of teenagers and then run some more. I don't want to return to Cinderella's Crownies in case Kayla is following me. I can't lead her to the evidence!

I crouch to the ground behind a cookie booth to catch my breath. She's probably not following me. She probably didn't even see me. And I ran really far. I definitely lost her. I'm a really good spy.

I stand up carefully. Mmm. Those cookies smell good. I wonder if I could trade a brownie sample for a chocolate chip cookie?

I look across the counter. Kayla is staring right at me.

"Hi, Abby," she says.

It's over. Kayla is going to tell her mother. They'll drag us home and lock Cinderella and Jonah and me in the attic, and Cinderella's Crownies will be over before it ever really began.

"What are you doing here?" Kayla demands. "What are Cinderella's Crownies?"

"They're . . . they're . . ." I try to come up with some sort of lie, but instead I shove the plate under her nose. "Try one."

She shrugs. Takes a bite. Chews. "Wow," she says. "These are great! Crownies, they're called?"

"Excuse me," says the cookie lady. "Would you mind going to the other side of the counter? We're selling cookies here, not cookie imitations. Please remove yourself from the premises."

These are crownies, not cookie imitations, thank you very much. I walk around the counter to Kayla.

"Yup," I say to Kayla. "Crownies."

"And Cinderella made them?"

I nod.

"I'm impressed! And she's selling them at the market?"

I hesitate but nod again.

"What for? Oh, I know. I bet she's trying to make money so she can move out."

My mouth drops open. "How did you know?"

She shakes her head. "It's not easy living with my mom. And my sister's no picnic, either. I should know."

I can't help but be surprised. "What do you mean? Don't you like living with them?"

"I don't have a choice. I can't leave my mother and sister. But Cinderella can. She should. They treat her like a slave!"

"Um, she does your laundry, too. And makes your meals. And your bed. You kind of treat her like a slave, too."

Her cheeks turn red. "I guess you're right. I shouldn't. I don't mean to." She sighs. "But you're right. I do. Correction. I *did*."

"I don't understand. How have you only realized this now? It's been going on for years!"

She sighs again. "This is going to sound strange, but something unfair happened to me recently and it made me think about all the other unfair stuff that happens all the time."

I wonder what she's talking about. I guess she means what happened with the prince. "Unfair stuff happens all the time," I say, "but what's happening to Cinderella is super unfair."

"I know." She bites her lower lip. "How can I help?"

"You really want to help?" I want to believe her. I really do. But what if she's setting us up?

"I really, really do," she says, eyes wide.

"What about your mom and sister? Are they here?"

"No, it's just me. They dropped me off. Told me I was moping too much. Told me to buy something to make me feel better. I picked up a new pair of shoes." She motions to her satchel. "I'm taking the parriage back home later."

I give her a long, hard stare. She seems earnest. I want to believe her, really I do. But I don't want to be gullible. "Okay," I say, finally. "You can help."

I'll give her a chance, but I'm still going to keep an extra-special eye on her.

Maybe I need one of those creepy green eye necklaces after all.

"Step right up, step right up!" Kayla hollers. "Cinderella's crownies for sale!"

I can't believe it — Kayla is selling Cinderella's crownies. And she's selling a lot of them. She's a natural. She even bought a few for herself — for a dollar each! It was her idea to jack up the price back to a dollar.

Jonah and Cinderella almost had heart attacks when I brought Kayla over, but I vouched for her and so far so good.

It seems she really has changed. I do feel bad that she's still pining for the prince. But Cinderella and the prince are meant-to-be. You can't get in the way of meant-to-be.

I'm sad she's sad, but I'm also happy she's becoming a nicer person. Sometimes tough experiences change you for the better, I guess.

"Cinderella, your crownies are really amazing," she says.

Cinderella flushes with pleasure. "Thank you. It means a lot to hear you say that."

"I'm sorry I don't say nice things more often. I've been the worst stepsister ever."

"Well . . ." Cinderella hesitates.

"Yes," I fill in for her. "You have been."

"I've had it so easy and you've had it so tough," Kayla says. "I'm sorry."

I wonder if she'd still feel sorry if we told her the *whole* plan. All she knows is that we're trying to raise a hundred dollars so Cinderella can move out. She has no idea that Cinderella wants to move out to prove to Farrah that she can rescue herself. No clue whatsoever that Cinderella wants to marry the prince, who just happens to be the guy Kayla is pining for.

"You haven't had it *that* easy," Cinderella says. "Your dad died when you were really little, and you have to share a room with Beatrice, who's incredibly bossy. And your mom . . . well, your mom is really . . ."

"Mean?" I say.

Kayla snorts. "That's the understatement of the year. She yells at puppies. What kind of a person yells at puppies? But at least I have my own money. My dad set up a big trust fund for me and my sister. I don't have to rely on anyone for anything."

"Still," Cinderella says, "it must be tough being in your shoes."

I look down at Kayla's shoes. They're black and shiny. They're definitely nice. They're also really big. Her feet are about twice the size of Cinderella's. Even the swollen one.

No, the glass slipper is definitely not fitting on *her* foot.

"I need another crownie," she says. "Here's a dollar."

I hand her an extra-chocolaty one. "Don't worry," I say. "This one's our treat."

# ✻ chapter eighteen ✻

## Keep On Bakin'

$e$ ven though we sold most of our crownies, we only made thirty dollars. Then we had to use ten dollars of that money to buy more crownie ingredients, which only left us with twenty dollars' profit.

Which means we have to go back to the market tomorrow morning and make eighty dollars. Which seems kind of impossible.

And we only have until noon at the latest.

Then I subtract the time it takes to get to and from the market, and I get really worried. "Do you think Farrah would meet us at the market at noon?" I ask.

Cinderella shakes her head. "She really seems to like chimneys and fireplaces."

Long story short? That night, instead of sleeping, we bake.

Chocolate chip crownies, blondies — or *clondies* as we call them — and walnut crownies, even though Jonah keeps shaking his head in disapproval.

It's a good thing I'm busy mixing ingredients all night, because there's no way I can sleep. I'm way too nervous. What if our plan doesn't work? Will Farrah think we failed our mission? Will she not help Cinderella? Will she not help Jonah and me get home?

We really have to get home. Technically it's only been a few days in fairy tale land, so probably only a few hours have passed at home.

The key word here is *probably*.

What if I'm wrong? What if time is going faster at home? What if *days* have passed? Or what if Farrah doesn't help us find the magic mirror that will lead us back to Smithville? Then what?

Then we're stuck in Floom . . . forever.

It's seven o'clock Tuesday morning. I'm navigating through the many booths at the market. Jonah and Cinderella have been here since six. I stayed behind to wait for the last two batches of crownies to cool and to leave the stepfamily their breakfast.

But who knows what'll happen when Betty wakes up and realizes we're not there. We asked Kayla to tell her that we had some errands to run. I hope Kayla doesn't change her mind and tell on us.

As we approach our booth, I feel an explosion of butterflies in my stomach. What if it's slower than yesterday? What if no one buys anything? What if we can't pull it off?

Wow, it's really busy here today. Look at that booth near the entrance! They have a line. It snakes around the block.

I wonder what they're selling?

As I step closer to the booth, I realize something amazing.

The people are standing in line for Cinderella's Crownies.



By nine o'clock, we've sold forty crownies.

By ten, sixty-five.

By eleven-thirty, we're sold out.

We've made a hundred and twenty dollars.

"You did it!" Jonah cheers, giving Cinderella a high five.

We actually had six crownies left, but we let ourselves have a snack. Of course, the six crownies left had walnuts. But that didn't stop Cinderella *and* Jonah from eating their share. I'm saving one of mine for later.

"*We* did it," Cinderella says. "You guys are the best. I couldn't have done it without you."

That's true, though technically she shouldn't have had to do it at all. It's because of us she hurt her foot. No need to remind her of that, though. "You're going to be a princess!" I tell her instead.

Cinderella puts the money in an envelope, which I carry in one of the extra satchels.

We give each other a group victory hug and then run, run, run to catch the parriage.


The grandfather clock in the living room says 11:45 when we open Cinderella's front door. We only have fifteen minutes left to call Farrah!

"Where have you been?" Betty snaps when we step inside. "The prince's assistant is on his way and I had to prepare the tea myself!"

Oh, no. I don't want to anger Betty. What if she somehow messes up the plan?

"We were at the market," Cinderella says.

"Doing what?" Betty barks.

"Getting dinner." It's the truth. Cinderella bought a pot roast from the butcher for later. Betty has an account there, so she charged it.

Though if everything goes her way by the time dinner rolls around, she won't be the one cooking it. She'll be engaged to the prince.

Betty looks at her with suspicion.

"We just need to freshen up," Cinderella says, "and then we'll make lunch."

"What *I* need is for you to finish preparing the tea and cakes for the prince's people. I've just heard that they're only a few houses away. They should be here within the hour. So you need to hurry. Beatrice and Kayla are making themselves presentable as we speak."

"We'll be right down," Cinderella says cheerfully.

It's 11:50.

Jonah and I run up the stairs while Cinderella hobbles up behind us. We pass Beatrice and Kayla's room on the way. Their door is open, and I peek inside.

"Cinderella!" Beatrice yells. "I need your help!"

"Can't now," Cinderella says, giving Kayla a thumbs-up.

Then up to the attic we go. We close the door behind us.

Cinderella knocks on the chimney. "Farrah? Are you there?"

My heart races. I hope this works. It HAS to work.

There's a burst of yellow sparkle. Here we go.

# * chapter nineteen *

## Now or Never

S o," Farrah says, twirling her wand between her fingers like it's a cheerleading baton. "How'd you do?"

"She did great!" I say, but then wonder if I should let Cinderella do the talking. A person who stands on her own two feet should definitely use her own tongue, right? "I'll let her tell you about it."

Farrah nods. "Good idea."

Cinderella takes a step forward. "We decided I would get a job so I could afford an apartment of my own. And Jonah — um, I mean *we* — found a great place that's a hundred dollars a month. You said that if I could prove to you that I can rescue myself, you would fix my foot. And if you fix my foot, then I'll fit the glass slipper like Abby said I was supposed to. So I started a crownie company called Cinderella's Crownies to raise a hundred dollars for the apartment."

"What's a crownie?" Farrah asks.

Jonah rolls his eyes. "It's really called a brownie. My sister's just weird."

"Crownies are little square cakes," Cinderella explains. "I baked a bunch and then we sold them at the market. I really enjoyed making them and selling them, and we made a hundred and twenty dollars, which is enough to —"

"Rent an apartment!" I shriek. I'm sorry. I'm just not good at containing myself. "Which proves she can stand on her own two feet! She's self-reliant! She is, she is!"

"Exactly," Cinderella says.

Farrah nods. "I'm impressed. You can afford to rent your own apartment? That does prove to me that you're not just a damsel in distress. Maybe you're a worthy partner for the prince after all."

"Yay!" I cheer. "And, Farrah, not that I'm not focusing on Cinderella and her issues right now, but we really need to talk about finding a magic mirror."

She smiles. "Let's take care of Cinderella first, okay?"

She lifts her wand. She makes three circles in the air and then sends a zap toward the table. The glass slipper that had been smashed reappears in a puff of sparkle. Oh, yay! She fixed it!

"And now for your foot," she says.

Yes, yes, yes! Everything is going to be back on track now. Hurray!

The door bursts open. "Not so fast. Stop whatever you're doing!"

Betty! What is she doing here? Beatrice is behind her. Beatrice and . . .

Kayla.

"See, Kayla?" Beatrice says, pointing to the glass slipper on the table. "I told you she was the mystery girl from the ball. She stole your prince!"

"How did you know?" Cinderella asks.

"It wasn't that hard to figure out," Beatrice says. "Also I'm a very good eavesdropper. You guys aren't exactly quiet."

Kayla's eyes tear up. "I don't understand. I thought you were trying to raise a hundred dollars so you could move out."

"Technically, she was raising a hundred dollars to prove to me that she's worthy of the prince," Farrah says.

"You lied to me," Kayla says, her mouth turning down. "You stole my prince!"

"I'm sorry, Kayla," Cinderella says. "But he was never *your* prince. If he was your prince, he wouldn't have spent both nights dancing with me."

"But he liked me! I know he liked me. . . ." Kayla's voice trails off. She juts her quivering chin at Cinderella. "I can't believe I helped you! Prince robber!"

Betty smiles a seriously evil smile. "Don't get all worked up, Kayla. Cinderella isn't marrying the prince. She couldn't raise the hundred dollars."

"Yes, she could. It's right here." I pull out the envelope with the money. "See? There's enough in here for the apartment plus twenty dollars extra."

"Let's see about this, shall we?" Betty walks over to me. "Tell me something, who paid for the ingredients that Cinderella used to bake the crownies?"

"We bought the ingredients for the second batch at the market," Jonah says.

Betty raises an eyebrow. "What about the first batch?"

"We found the ingredients in the house," I say, my voice shaking.

"So that means you used *my* ingredients for *your* crownies. Without asking my permission. Which, in my book, is stealing. I don't know what kind of laws you have in Smithville, but here in Floom stealing is a crime." She laughs. "Forget the attic. You should see what a jail cell feels like."

"Take twenty dollars." Cinderella says quickly. "Then we'll be even."

"Will we now?" Betty says. "Twenty dollars hardly seems enough for all the ingredients you stole. And what about the paper you used to make the signs? And the ironing board you used as a table? I'd say you owe me, including penalties and interest . . ." She pretends to be hard at thought. "Hmm. How much did you say you made? A hundred and twenty dollars? I'd say you owe me a hundred and thirty." Her mouth twists into an evil smile. "Aw. You don't have that much. Too bad. I guess this means you and your little Smithvillian friends are going to jail."

"Mom, no!" Beatrice yells.

Can it be? Did I have it all wrong? Is Beatrice the nice one and Kayla the bad one?

"If they all go to jail," Beatrice whines, "who's going to do the cooking and the laundry?"

Betty smiles. "Think, Beatrice. Whichever one of you marries the prince will move me and your sister into the palace with you, yes?"

Beatrice nods. "Surely,"

"Then we'll each have our own maid to tend to us — who needs Cinderella?"

My heart pounds. I turn to Farrah. "Can't you stop her? She's being ridiculous!"

Farrah shakes her head. "She's the lady of the house. Cinderella should have asked her permission before taking her things. There's nothing I can do."

"Your choice," Betty says with a grin. "A hundred and thirty dollars — or jail."

I look at Kayla, my eyes pleading. "I know you're mad, but can't you convince them to go easy on us? Remember how crummy you felt for treating Cinderella badly for so long? Haven't you changed at all?"

Kayla's lips quiver but then she takes a deep breath. "Mom," she says finally. "You're being unfair. Cinderella didn't know she was stealing. She lives here, you know. She just assumed it was her stuff, too."

"Well, it wasn't, and now she has to pay," Betty spits out.

I send Kayla another pleading glance. "I know you think Cinderella marrying the prince is unfair," I say. "But the way you treated her since she was twelve is even MORE unfair. You owe it to her to help! You know you do!"

Kayla face falls. "I know, I know. Mom, I'll give you the hundred and thirty dollars, okay? Just don't send Cinderella to jail. She's suffered enough."

"Excuse me," Farrah pipes up, "but that breaks the rules."

Cinderella and I exchange a look. "What rules?" she asks.

Farrah frowns. "The rules about being self-sufficient. If Kayla just gives her mother the money, she'd be rescuing Cinderella. Haven't you been listening? Cinderella has to prove she's self-reliant. That's the whole point."

"See?" Betty says. "Even the skinny fairy woman agrees. I think it's time I called the police."

Wait. "You have a phone?" Can I call home?

"Phone! Crownies! Are you guys just making up words to confuse me?" Beatrice asks.

I guess that's a no.

Wait. Did she say crownie? Oh, oh, oh!

"Farrah," I say slowly, "if Cinderella earns the money to pay back Betty, that would prove she's self-reliant?"

"How can I earn the money?" Cinderella says. "I have no ingredients to make more crownies and no money to buy them, and even if I did, we're almost out of time! The prince's assistant is going to be here any minute!"

I reach into my bag and pull out the one remaining crownie. "You still have one crownie left to sell. Kayla, please, please, please would you be interested in buying this crownie for a hundred and thirty dollars?" I turn to Kayla and hold my breath. Who's she going to side with?

"She would not," Betty snaps.

Kayla's cheeks redden. "Actually, Mom, I would."

"Really?" Jonah asks. "You know it has walnuts, right?"

"I can't believe you'd betray your own mother," Betty snarls at Kayla.

"I'm sorry, Mom. I don't want to betray you. I want to make up the last few years to Cinderella."

Farrah looks at her watch. "Five . . . four . . . three . . . two . . . one! You made it! I'm very impressed."

"Think again, fairy freak," Betty says. "Do you see money in my hand? You do not. Cinderella goes to jail."

"Um, actually?" I say. "Speaking as her lawyer, the

negotiations were completed before the deadline, so I would say she's in the clear. Right, Farrah?"

In response, Farrah raises her wand, points it at Cinderella's foot, and zaps it. There's a puff of sparkle, and before our very eyes, Cinderella's foot shrinks back to its normal pre-marshmallow size.

"I'm healed!" Cinderella says, wriggling her toes. "Thank you, Farrah!"

"As for you two," Farrah says to me and Jonah, "it's time to tell you how to get home."

"Really?" I ask.

"Really," she says, twirling the wand between her fingers. "The portal is actually —"

She's interrupted by a loud knock at the front door.

Jonah rushes to the window. "There's a carriage outside! It must be the prince's assistant!"

"Get her!" I hear.

The next thing I know, Beatrice jumps onto Farrah's back, the wand flies out of Farrah's hand, and Beatrice and Farrah tumble to the ground. The wand goes rolling across the floor.

Betty scoops it up. "Now where were we?"

# ✻ chapter twenty ✻

## Squeak

Give that back immediately," Farrah commands.

Betty's evil-scary smile returns. "I don't think so. Let's see. Now that I have the power, what shall I do with it?"

"I'm guessing you're going to abuse it," Cinderella says wryly.

Betty swishes toward Cinderella and hurls a zap her way.

There's a burst of yellow sparkle and then Cinderella starts to shrink. She gets smaller and smaller and then even smaller. And turns gray. And grows a tail.

"Cool," Betty says. "I must have pressed the mouse-making button."

Oh. My. Goodness. She turned Cinderella into a mouse. A mouse wearing itty-bitty clothes.

"Stop that," Farrah demands, her hands on her hips.

Betty just laughs and turns to Jonah.

"Don't you dare," I yell as I jump in front of him. Zap! Sparkle!

All I can see is yellow, and then zoom! The room is suddenly increasing in size. I feel sick. It's like I'm on a Tilt-A-Whirl. And then — *plunk*. I'm on my tush, with my legs in the air in front of me.

Except they are not my legs. They are little twig legs. They are gray. And I have a tail.

I'm a mouse.

ARGHHHH!

I look at Jonah.

He's a mouse, too. A baby mouse in a red sweatshirt and jeans. A baby mouse who is currently trying to catch his tail.

"Achoo!" sneezes the Cinderella mouse.

I try to say *bless you*, but instead what comes out is, "Squeak!"

"Hand that wand back to me this instant," Farrah warns, taking a step toward her.

Betty turns the wand on Farrah next. "I don't think so." Zap! Sparkle!

Farrah yelps as she starts to shrink and turn green and scaly.

"A lizard button!" Betty says gleefully. "This thing is fantastic!"

What are we going to do? Farrah's a lizard in a yellow top and black leggings! And we're mice! What if we're stuck like this forever? Even if the Farrah lizard somehow shows us how to get home, we can't go back to Smithville as mice! My parents will never know it's us! They'll catch us with traps and hurt us and not even know it!

There's another knock on the front door. "Is anyone home?" we hear.

"Mom, turn them back into people right now," Kayla demands.

"Sorry, sweetie, I couldn't hear you. Did you say squeak?" And with that she turns her wand on Kayla and zaps her.

This is insane. Betty just turned her own daughter into a mouse. A very *large*, brown mouse with very sharp teeth. Wait a sec. Is she a —

"You're a rat! How fitting," Betty snarls. She smiles and then yells downstairs, "Coming!" She turns to Beatrice. "But first things first. Let's resize those feet." She points the wand at her daughter's left foot and zaps it.

It *resizes* all right. It expands. And expands some more. It expands into the size of a basketball. And then turns orange. It's a pumpkin!

"Mom!" Beatrice shrieks.

"Sorry, sorry. Hold on." Betty pulls out a pair of glasses from her pocket and studies the wand. "Aha! There it is. Reduction button." She zaps her daughter's left foot again and it shrinks back to its original size and color. Then she zaps it once more and it shrinks even smaller. She zaps the right foot next. "That should do it. Grab the slipper, will you, dear?"

"With pleasure," Beatrice says, and then cackles.

"Coming!" Betty calls again, and the mother and daughter hurry downstairs, slamming the attic door behind them.

"Squeeeeeak!" I yell. Which really means, *We have to follow them!*

"Squeak!" say Cinderella and Kayla at the same time.

"Squinx," says my brother gleefully, which I'm assuming is mouse for jinx.

We all scurry to the door. Um. Small problem. We are way too short to reach the handle. Now what?

"Squeak," Jonah says again, and proceeds to try to squeeze himself under the door. Oh, no. What if he gets stuck? But he doesn't. He goes right under. Mice are very squirmy.

I squeeze through to the other side, too. Cinderella goes next. Then Kayla. Then Farrah. I guess rats and lizards are squirmy, too.

We made it! They all follow me as I scamper down the stairs and into the living room.

Betty is standing by the couch, her arms behind her back holding the glass slipper that Farrah fixed. Beatrice is sticking her foot out as the prince's assistant crouches in front of her with the other glass slipper.

And the prince. I did not expect him to be here, too, but the prince is sitting on the love seat looking regal and princely in his very purple robe.

"Squeak!!!!" cries the Kayla rat.

"Thank you so much for the tea," the prince says. "That was very thoughtful of you."

"I'm sure everyone is showering you with treats," says Betty.

The assistant nods. "The last house we were at had these amazing little cake things. They're called crownies, I'm told.

Cinderella's Crownies. They bought them at the market. Have you ever had one?"

"They're quite delicious," the prince says.

Betty grunts. "I've heard they make a lot of crumbs."

Cinderella squeaks.

Wait a sec. The assistant looks familiar. He's skinny and he has a goatee. It's the guy from the coat check! I guess he got promoted. Way to go!

"Time to do the shoe thing," the goatee guy says. He lifts the glass slipper to Beatrice's left foot.

*Please don't fit, please don't fit, please don't fit.*

It fits.

Crumbs is definitely right.

# ✳ chapter twenty-one ✳

## Hickory Dickory

Prince Jordan," goatee guy says, "say hello to your bride."

No, no, no! We have to do something to stop this!

Beatrice slides the right slipper onto her foot and does a little victory dance with her shoulders.

Prince Jordan smiles as he approaches her. "Hello, um — who are you again?"

Beatrice curtsies and then straightens up. "Beatrice."

"You're much taller than I remember," he says, sounding perplexed.

"It's your imagination," Betty says. She's stuck the wand

behind her ear like a pencil. Is that any way to treat a wand? No, it is not.

Kayla-rat scurries up the couch, jumps on her sister's shoulder and tries to bite her.

"Mom, we really need to get an exterminator in here," Beatrice says tossing her sister to the ground.

And *we* need to steal back the wand. I scurry across the room and assess the situation. A couch, a love seat, a fireplace, a chandelier, and a grandfather clock. I need to get at Betty from above if I want to snatch the wand. If I can somehow make it to the chandelier, maybe I can jump on her head? But how will I get to the chandelier? I'm pretty sure mice can't fly.

Still, if fairy tales have taught me anything, they *can* run up a clock. Like in "Hickory Dickory Dock"!

Okay, so technically that's a nursery rhyme, but it's still worth a shot.

I can do this. I scurry over to the ledge at the bottom of the clock and dig right in. This is easier than I thought. I use my itty-bitty nails to claw and climb to the top in just a matter of seconds. Ha! And they say *time* flies.

Except here I am, perched on top of the clock. Now what?

The chandelier is too far away for me to make the jump. What I really need is for Betty to take a few steps backward. Come on, Betty, move it!

Jonah looks up and sees me. "Squeak?" he asks, which I interpret to mean, *What are you doing up there?*

I'd squeak right back at him, but I don't want to draw attention to myself. Instead, I try to use my little mouse-hands, pantomime style, to tell him what to do.

So far I haven't been successful with any of my hand gesturing, but this time we have liftoff. He seems to understand, because the next thing I know, he's bashing himself against Betty's shoe like a bumper car.

She takes a step back. Go, Jonah, go!

Bash!

Step back.

Almost there . . .

Bash!

Except she's getting annoyed. She swings her foot back and — no! — kicks Jonah with the pointy toe of her shoe and sends him flying across the room. He somersaults through the air and lands in the fireplace.

Hey, that's my brother you're kicking around!

"Squeooonah!" I yell, and before I realize what I'm doing, I'm flying, supermouse style, straight for the top of Betty's head.

Plunk.

"What —" Betty says.

Before she figures out what's happening, I grab the wand with my pudgy little mouse-fingers and yank it from behind her ear.

Now the wand and I are on a collision course with the ground.

# *chapter twenty-two*

## Kazam

Ohmyohmyohmy!

The floor is coming at me fast and I'm holding on tight to the wand.

We land with a thud and a burst of sparkle.

Yay!

"Yes, we definitely need an exterminator," Betty growls, reaching down for the wand, a terrifying expression on her face.

No, no, no! She is not getting back this wand. I transfer it to my mouth and run, run, run toward lizard-Farrah, who's currently helping mouse-Jonah out of the fireplace. He's covered in ashes, but otherwise fine.

"I'll catch it," goatee guy says, chasing after me.

There's a straight line from me to Farrah. All I have to do is run. Or, maybe scurry is the right word.

"Just step on the thing," Betty says, which chills my spine and sends me running even faster.

But then — whoosh!

My tail! Goatee guy has my tail! He's picking me up by my tail!

My feet are lifting in the air, and I realize I only have one shot. I harness all my energy and give the edge of the wand the strongest shove I can muster, sending it skidding across the room.

"Is that mouse wearing a dress?" goatee guy asks.

Betty is too busy running toward the wand to answer.

I strain my neck to see the wand barrel toward Farrah and the fireplace. And . . . it makes it! She jumps on it!

There's a huge burst of yellow sparkle and Farrah stretches into her normal self.

Goatee guy gasps and drops me, and once again I plummet to the ground. Ouch. I'm getting tired of all this plummeting.

"Farrah, is that you?" Prince Jordan asks.

"Hey, Jordy," Farrah says. "Good to see you again. You're looking well." She holds the wand up in the air and spins around and around and around. A splatter of yellow sparkle flies around the room.

Everything changes at once. I feel like I'm on that Tilt-A-Whirl again and I'm stretching, stretching, stretching until I look down at my legs and realize I'm no longer mouse-Abby.

I'm person-Abby once again.

Yay!

Jonah and Cinderella have morphed back as well.

Yay and yay again!

And then there's the sound of cracking glass.

"OWWW!" Beatrice screams.

Her feet have doubled in size, and the glass slippers have cracked right open because of the pressure.

"This is not the girl I danced with," says the prince. "I fear you're trying to trick me. Our shoe doesn't even fit, and neither does the other one! Come on, Gary, we're leaving."

"No, wait!" Betty exclaims, a wild look in her eye. "I have another daughter you can marry. She's running around here somewhere. . . ."

"Mother, I'm right here," Kayla says, stretching back into her human form.

"Can someone please tell me what's going on?" Prince Jordan demands.

"I'd be happy to," I say. "You're right. Beatrice is not the girl you danced with. Her mother stole Farrah's wand, turned us all into animals, and zapped her daughter's feet so they'd fit in the glass slippers."

"So then who do the shoes belong to?" His gaze falls on Kayla. "Is it you? I *know* you. We talked at the ball, right? You made me laugh."

She hesitates, but then shakes her head. "Yes, I did," she says. "But no." She kicks up her heel. "These tootsies are size nine. No way they're squeezing into those teeny-sized shoes."

Prince Jordan's face falls. "But then who —"

"They're Cinderella's!" Jonah yells, pointing at her.

He turns to her. "You?"

Cinderella nods nervously.

"Let me just repair the shoes with a zap and you'll see for yourself," Farrah says. She waves her wand toward the slippers, enveloping them in a burst of yellow. "There you go. Try them on, dear. You've earned it."

"But — but — but —" Beatrice stutters.

"No buts," I say. "Now please get out of Cinderella's happy ending."

Beatrice lets out a loud *humph*, and then tries to follow her mother, who is slowly backing toward the door.

"Why don't you two hang around for a while?" Farrah says, and sends a sparkle-zap their way.

They instantly shrink into two little birds. Two caged little birds. Two caged little birds in drab gray dresses.

The prince turns to Cinderella. "Hi, again," he says.

"Hi, yourself," she says softly.

"Ready for the shoe test?"

Cinderella sighs and takes a seat on the couch. She kicks off her loafers. "Let's do this."

He picks up the first shoe and it slips perfectly onto her foot. He picks up the second and it does the same.

"Hurray!" we all cheer. Jonah and I high-five.

Farrah grins.

Even Kayla says, "Congratulations. I'm happy for the two of you." But she has a sad look on her face.

The prince takes Cinderella's hand and pulls her to her feet. He crouches on one knee. "Cinderella, will you do me the honor of being my wife?"

Finally! It all worked out! The story can go on as planned! We saved the day!

Cinderella looks at Prince Jordan and then at Kayla and then back at the prince and then back at Kayla and then down at her glass slippers. "Prince Jordan, I'm so sorry, but —" She takes a deep breath. "No."

# * chapter twenty-three *

## Huh?

everyone gasps.

Jonah tugs at my arm. "Abby, why did she say no? Isn't she supposed to say yes?"

"I don't know!" I say. I really don't. What happened here?

Cinderella sits back down and pulls off the slippers. "I'm so sorry," she says. "Two days ago, there was nothing I wanted more than to marry you. I wanted you to rescue me. But since the ball, I got to stand on my own two feet and make my own money, and now everything is different. I love making crownies. I want my own place. And I don't really love you . . . not the way Kayla does. You deserve someone who loves you for the right reasons. Everyone does."

We all look at the prince for his reaction. I kind of expect anger. Or bafflement. But what I see instead surprises me.

He looks relieved.

"To be honest," he says, "it was my father who was so taken with you. Not that you're not beautiful. You are. But I really enjoyed the time I spent with . . ." He turns to Kayla. "Excuse me, what's your name again?"

Kayla squeaks. Nope, she's not a rat again, she's just excited. "Kayla," she finally sputters.

He smiles at her. "I was secretly hoping the slipper would fit you, not Cinderella." He looks at Cinderella. "No offense, okay?"

"None taken," she says.

"This is wonderful," Farrah says. "I'm so happy for you three!"

It is a super-happy ending. Different from the original ending, but I like it anyway.

Prince Jordan hesitates. "But . . . I've already made a royal proclamation that whoever fits the slipper will be the new princess. I can't undo that."

No, no, no! They will have this happy ending! "Maybe you can't undo it," I say, "but I can." I pick up both slippers and throw them hard against the brick fireplace, smashing them to smithereens. "Oops."

"Yay!" Jonah cheers. "No more slippers! I guess Kayla can't try them on."

"You do know that I can fix them," Farrah points out.

We all stare at her, holding our collective breath.

She smiles. "Of course, if I do, there's no guarantee they'll be the same size as before."

"In that case," the prince says, "I'm officially declaring the slipper test invalid, since it's so inaccurate." He bends back down on one knee. "Kayla, will you do me the honor of being my bride?"

"Yes," she says as a tear trickles down her cheek.

Hurray!

"Isn't it romantic?" goatee guy says. I notice that he's gazing at Cinderella.

"It is," she answers him with a shy smile.

"I really enjoyed your crownies," he says. "I'm Gary, by the way."

"Thank you. I'm Cinderella"

"I'll have to come by your bakery and get some for myself."

"That would be lovely," she says, and then . . . bats her eyelashes?

Cinderella and Gary the Goatee Guy? Who would have thought?

Farrah puts her arm on my shoulder. "I guess it's time for you and your brother to go home now."

"Yes, please." I say. "Can you tell us where the magic mirror is?"

"Abby!" Jonah says. "Abby, I think —"

"Not now, Jonah," I say. "I'm trying to get us home."

"But, Abby —"

"Jonah, please hold on. Farrah? The mirror?"

Farrah shakes her head. "There is no magic mirror."

"Don't say that." My panic is rising. "Sure, I like it here in Floom, but we need to get home! I'm not even one hundred percent sure what time it is at home."

"Abby," Jonah says a little more forcefully. "I know how we get home."

I turn to him. "You do?"

"Yes."

"How?"

"The fireplace!"

I look at the fireplace and then back at him. "Are you crazy?"

"No! It's true! When I fell into it, I'm pretty sure I heard it hiss."

"No way!" I say.

I turn to Farrah for confirmation that my brother is crazy, but see that she's nodding. "Way?" I ask her.

"Way," she says.

"But how?"

"Fairies can enchant different household objects and appliances. It doesn't always have to be a mirror."

I stare at her, trying to comprehend what she's saying. "Are you telling us that Maryrose is a fairy?"

"Of course she's a fairy! How else could she enchant your basement mirror? Didn't she tell you she's a fairy?"

We shake our heads.

"Oh. Oops. She's very mysterious that Maryrose. So do you guys want to go home or what?"

We both nod.

"Let's do it!" Farrah says. "I have places to be, you know."

"We may want to sweep up the fireplace first," I say. "It's covered in glass."

"I'll do it!" Cinderella calls out.

"Don't worry," Jonah says, going to get the broom. "I've got it."

We're never getting out of here.

When we're ready, we give big good-bye hugs to Cinderella and Kayla and shake hands with Gary the Goatee Guy and Prince Jordan.

"What are you going to do about Betty and Beatrice?" I ask Farrah.

She frowns. "I suppose I'd better turn them back before they peck each other to death. But it's your call, Kayla."

"All right," Kayla says. "Turn them back. But in about an hour or so. You can do it remotely, right? By then Cinderella and I will be long gone. They are definitely not moving to the palace with me." She turns to Cinderella. "You don't mind if I crash at your new digs until the wedding, do you?"

"Of course not," Cinderella says.

"I'll do the cleaning," Kayla says.

"I'll do the cooking," Cinderella says. "Ever since my mouse experience, I'm kind of craving mac and cheese. Or a four-cheese pizza. And cheese and crackers. Pretty much anything with cheese."

"So what do we do?" Jonah asks Farrah. "Should I knock?"

"No need," Farrah says. "We know you're there. Both of you crouch inside and tell me when you're ready."

We wave good-bye and squat in the fireplace. I notice there's a fairy — with wings — carved into the stone. Didn't the magic mirror at Snow's have that, too?

"We're ready!" Jonah says.

There's a burst of yellow sparkle and the next thing I know, we're zoom, zoom, zooming up the chimney.

# ✻ chapter twenty-four ✻

## Home Sweet Home

We pop right up the chimney and pop out of our basement mirror.

"Ow," I say. "That hurt. You okay?"

Jonah is already hopping on his feet. "I'm great. That was so much fun! Can we go back?"

"Now?"

"I'm wide awake," he says. "It's only two in the afternoon in Floom."

"On our last trip, one day in fairy tale land turned out to be about one hour at home. So that means it's about two thirty in the morning here. We should probably go to sleep."

But first I turn back to the silent mirror. "Maryrose? Are you there? Can we talk? We'd love to know why you keep sending us into different fairy tales."

No answer.

"Maybe tomorrow," Jonah says.

I roll my eyes. "Why do we keep coming back if she won't even tell us what's going on?"

"Because it's fun," Jonah says. "And she'll tell us eventually. She'll have to."

We hike up the stairs and I peek at the microwave clock. Wait a sec. "It's not two in the morning. It's *six* in the morning."

His eyes bulge. "That was close. Mom and Dad wake up in one hour!"

I don't get it. Last time, every day in fairy tale land was an hour back home. This time we were gone for two and three-quarter days, which is about . . . sixty-six fairy tale hours. It doesn't add up!

"I guess time depends on the story," Jonah says.

"I guess."

"Next time, bring your watch," he says.

"What next time? Did I agree on a next time?"

He nods knowingly. "There will be a next time."

We climb back up the stairs to the top floor and open the door to my parents' room to carefully peek in. *Creak*.

"Shush!" I whisper, but they don't budge.

"Don't worry," Jonah says. "They won't wake up. They're really tired."

"They've been working really hard," I say. I suddenly feel guilty about all the grief I've given them. They just started a new law firm — that's why we moved to Smithville. And starting a new business — is *hard*. I know, because I just helped start one. There are so many details to think about! And running a home is tough, too.

"I guess it's kind of tough to be in their shoes," I say.

"Bed?" Jonah asks.

"Bed," I say, and I close the door. "A real bed, too. Straw on the floor, I will not miss you."

"Good night, Ab," Jonah says.

I give him a tight hug.

Then I step into my room and over to my jewelry box. I want to see Cinderella.

She's there, smiling. But now instead of her poofy platinum dress, she's wearing a poofy baker's hat. And an apron that says CINDERELLA'S CROWNIES.

Aw! Yay, Cinderella!

Snow is standing beside her, still in my lime-green pajamas.

Oh, no! I forgot my polka-dot pajamas in Floom! Oh well. They were ridiculous pajamas anyway. And I guess they belong in Floom, since they're the flag and everything.

I strip off my dress, which is covered in gray soot. I'm about to toss it into the hamper when I realize something.

My hamper is full.

And I'm wide awake.

I have an idea. I pull my overstuffed laundry bag out of the hamper and drag it out the door.

I knock on Jonah's door.

"Yeah?"

"Laundry run," I say, opening it. I take out his bag and drag it all downstairs to the laundry room off the kitchen.

If I can do it by hand in Floom, I can figure out the machine in Smithville.

But how much detergent to use?

I read the directions. Easy, peasy. It's like following a recipe.

Not that I'm agreeing to another adventure or anything, but it's always good to have clean non-wedgie undies ready.

Just in case.

# acknowledgements

Thank you, thank you, thank you:

Laura Dail, my super agent who never gave up on (Farrah/Keri) Abby; and Tamar Rydzinski, the queen of foreign rights.

My excellent editors, Aimee Friedman and AnnMarie Anderson, and the rest of the Scholastic team: Abby McAden, Becky Shapiro, Janet Robbins, Allison Singer, Bess Braswell, Emily Sharpe, Lizette Serrano, Emily Heddleson, Candace Greene, Becky Amsel, and David Levithan.

Joel Gotler and Brian Lipson for all their hard work in Hollywood.

First readers and editors Elissa Ambrose, Courtney Sheinmel, and Emily Jenkins. (Rock stars, all three of you.)

Also, Louisa Weiss, Leslie Margolis, and Aviva Mlynowski, for their awesome notes.

Special callout to Tori, Carly, and Carol Adams for their support and enthusiasm. Yay, Torly Kid!

Targia Clarke for taking such good care of my family.

Also thanks to: Larry Mlynowski, Jess Braun, Adele Griffin, Jess Rothenberg, Julia DeVillers, Lauren Myracle, Joanna Philbin,

Emily Bender, Alison Pace, John & Vickie Swidler, Robert Ambrose, Jen Dalven, Gary Swidler, Darren Swidler, Ryan and Jack Swidler, Shari and Heather Endleman, the Steins, the Mittlemans, Bonnie Altro, Farrin Jacobs, Robin Wasserman, Tara Altebrando, Meg Cabot, Ally Carter, Maryrose Wood, Jennifer Barnes, Alan Gratz, Sara Zarr, Maggie Marr, Susane Colasanti, Elizabeth Eulberg, and Jen Calonita.

Thanks and love to my husband (also my tech support, life manager, and Prince Charming), Todd. Extra love and kisses to my sweet little Chloe, who always wants just one more story.

# Whatever After

## SINK or SWIM

# SARAH MLYNOWSKI

**SCHOLASTIC**

for anabelle,
my littlest princess

# * chapter one *

## My Parents Are in the Way

Should I pack a bathing suit?

Yes. I definitely should.

I stuff my bathing suit — it's pale blue with cute white ruffles — into my bright-red suitcase. I'm going to visit my nana in Chicago! I can't wait. My nana is the best. Chicago is the best. And, yeah, I know it's cold to be swimming in Chicago, but my nana lives in an apartment building with an indoor pool and a hot tub.

I'm not really into pools, since I'm not the world's best swimmer.

But hot tubs? I love hot tubs. What's not to love about a big, bubbling bath that melts all your worries away?

Mom and I are flying to Chicago this Friday, only three days from today. It's a long weekend, so I won't miss any school, which is important because I am not a fan of missing school. I am an excellent note-taker and I like hearing everything the teachers say. Also, I don't want to give my new friends the opportunity to forget about me.

So far I have packed:

• the bathing suit
• two bottoms (one pair of jeans, one pair of stretchy black leggings)
• three undies
• three tops (one purple hooded sweatshirt, one white sweater, one light-green shirt with a collar)
• two pairs of pajamas (my orange pair and my navy pair — not my favorites, but they're practically all I have left; I am dangerously low on pajamas.)

The reason I am low on pajamas: When the magic mirror in our basement took my seven-year-old brother, Jonah, and me to

Zamel (where we met Snow White), I accidentally left behind my lime-green pj's. When the magic mirror in our basement then took us to Floom (where we met Cinderella), I accidentally left behind my polka-dot pink-and-purple ones.

Yes, we have a magic mirror in our basement. It came with the house.

I open my jewelry box. My nana bought me a pretty mother-of-pearl necklace for my tenth birthday and I think I should pack it. I don't really understand what the difference between pearl and mother-of-pearl is, to be honest. My nana said mother-of-pearl was more age-appropriate for me. Personally, I think they should call it *kid-of-pearl* if they want it to be more age-appropriate. Anyway, I don't normally wear the necklace to school because I'm afraid it will catch on something and all the mother-of-pearls will go flying across the classroom. But it'll be safe in my suitcase.

My nana bought me my jewelry box, too. The outside features images of all the fairy tale characters. Like Rapunzel with her long hair, the Little Mermaid with her tail, Cinderella in her poofy baker's hat, and Snow White in my lime-green pajamas. Cinderella and Snow White weren't always dressed like that, obviously. Only after Jonah and I changed the endings of their stories. Which was a total accident. We didn't *mean* to change the fairy tales. But everything ended up okay, so no need to worry.

I gently place the mother-of-pearl necklace on top of my navy pj's. I really need to go shopping. But what am I going to tell my parents about my missing pajamas? Maybe that the dryer ate them? It's not like I can tell them *the truth*; Gabrielle, the fairy who lives inside the magic mirror in Snow White's world, told us not to. Maryrose, the fairy who lives inside *our* mirror, has never said a word to us — so who knows what she thinks.

Last Thursday, Jonah and I woke up just before midnight with the full intention of either talking to Maryrose or getting her to take us to another fairy tale.

We got dressed. We snuck down the stairs. We opened the basement door.

And we saw that the lights were on.

My parents were in the basement.

My parents were not supposed to be in the basement at midnight.

Sure, *technically* the basement is their home office. So of course they are *allowed* to work in it. But how were we supposed to get sucked into the magic mirror when our parents were awake and standing right there? We couldn't. It was a problem.

Why were my parents working at the ridiculous hour of midnight? No, they do not work for a twenty-four-hour call center. They do not work for a bakery, either, and they are not getting up to make the doughnuts. Or brownies. (Or crownies. That's an inside joke between us and Cinderella.)

No, my parents started their own law firm when we moved to Smithville a few months ago. And now they're working like crazy people. Jonah and I haven't been able to get to the mirror all week. My parents had a lot more free time when we lived in Chicago.

Now I sit down at my desk and take out my math textbook and notebook. Time for homework. This desk was with me in my old bedroom back in Chicago, but it looks different — bigger — in my new room. I'm still kind of getting used to my new house. I'm not going to lie — it helps that I have a magic mirror.

It also helps that I've made new friends here: Robin and Frankie. Frankie is a girl, although I know it doesn't sound like it. When I have a little girl, I am not going to name her a boy's name. It's too confusing. On the first day of school, Ms. Hellman, the gym teacher, divided up our class into boys and girls and put Frankie with the boys. Frankie's face turned the color of a tomato.

We laugh about it now, though. The three of us: Frankie, Robin, and me, Abby. We're a trio. The terrific trio. Or maybe the tremendous trio. Or . . . I can't think of another word that means awesome that starts with T. There would be a lot more options if we were four or five. Fantastic four. Fabulous four. Famous four. Fun four. But two new friends are good. Two friends are great.

You get what you get and you don't get upset, right? That's what my mother always says. That and: There's nothing to fear but fear itself. And also: You've made your bed, now you have to sleep in it.

For the record, I make my bed every morning. Unlike my brother.

Anyway, I'm going to use all those expressions when I'm a judge. Oh, yeah, I'm going to be a judge when I grow up. Well, first I'm going to be a lawyer, and then I'm going to be a judge, because that's the rule.

I pretend my pencil is a gavel and bang it against my math textbook. "That's my ruling and it's final!" I say out loud. Not bad.

My door swings open and Jonah barges into my room. "What are you doing?"

"Homework," I say.

"Then why are you talking to yourself?"

"Because I feel like it," I snap, embarrassed that he caught me.

He sits on my bed and swings his legs. "Why is your stuff already in your suitcase?"

I turn around to face him. "Why would it not be? Why are you asking me a million questions?"

"I'm bored," he says. "Want to see if we can rock-climb up the side of the house?"

"No, Jonah, I do not. I have to finish my homework, and then I want to finish packing. I'm leaving in three days, you know."

My dad's friend from college and his son are coming to visit this weekend, so my mom and I thought it was the perfect time for some girl bonding. But even if my brother was coming to Chicago, he is the kind of person who would pack the morning of a big trip, not three days before. Actually I take that back. My brother would not pack *at all* because my parents would not trust him to pack. Last time we went away for a weekend, he packed one pair of underwear, two socks, and Kadima paddles. No T-shirts. No jeans. No shoes.

"I don't think you have to pack," Jonah says. "I heard Mom telling Dad that she's exhausted and that her brain is getting fuzzy and that she should probably postpone the trip to Chicago until after the case."

I jump out of my chair. "What? Postpone the trip? *Noooo!*"

He shrugs his thin little shoulders. "Sorry, that's what I heard."

"Are they in the basement?"

Jonah nods.

I run right out of the room and down the two flights of stairs.

Jonah is on my tail. We reach the basement in approximately two seconds flat.

"Mom!" I shout.

I can't help but glance at the mirror. It's still attached to the wall with heavy Frankenstein bolts. Same stone frame engraved with small fairies with wings and wands. Nothing has changed.

Good.

"Yes, honey?" my mom asks, swiveling her chair to face me.

I turn away from the mirror fast before my parents see me staring and realize it's a magic mirror that slurps us up into fairy tales.

No, they probably wouldn't guess all that just by seeing me look at it. Especially since they're so preoccupied with work that they haven't noticed that I'm short two pairs of pajamas, or that their law books are gone from the basement bookcases, or that we're missing one swivel chair. Actually, the swivel chair they noticed, but they just assumed they'd left it in Chicago. The truth is all these things got sucked into the mirror when we visited Snow White.

Anyway. "Mom. Please don't tell me we're canceling the trip to Chicago. Please, please, please don't."

"Oh, honey," my mom says, her forehead wrinkling. "I'm sorry. I was going to talk to you about it tonight, but . . ."

"No buts!" I cry. "It's too late to change your mind. Nana is expecting us! We already have plane tickets! And I already packed!" I stomp my foot on the floor for effect. I know it's babyish, but I can't help myself.

"I spoke to Nana this morning — she understands. She said we should come the next long weekend. And I called the airline and we can switch our tickets, too. Maybe then Dad and Jonah can come with us. We'll stay in a hotel and everything!"

Tears fill my eyes. "I don't want to wait until next time! Next time is months away. And I don't want to stay in a hotel. I want to stay with Nana."

She shakes her head. "I'm sorry, honey. But I'm just too busy. Please try to understand."

I don't want to understand. I cross my arms. I pout. I stomp my foot one more time, just because I feel like it.

I don't want to act like a baby, but . . . but . . . but . . . *Sigh*. I know my mom is *really* busy. And it's my job as the older sibling to act mature. I am ten, after all.

"I *am* sorry," my mom says. "But you know what they say. You get what you get, and you don't —"

"Get upset," I grumble.

Although right now, it's a saying I wish I could *forget*.

# ∗ chapter two ∗

## Grumpy Pants

*t*hat night, I toss and turn and turn and toss. I can't sleep.

My still-packed suitcase is sitting on my floor. Seeing it there just makes everything worse, but I don't have the heart to unpack it.

It's 11:45 P.M. and my dad and mom are asleep. They turned in about an hour ago.

Hmm.

I feel a tingle in my belly.

I may not be able to visit my nana, but I can definitely visit fairy land.

I sit up and push my covers off. Yes! I'm going to visit fairy land right now. Why not? I'm wide awake. My parents are not in the basement. Tonight is the night. I know it. I should go!

I look down at the pair of pajamas I'm wearing. Maybe I should change into regular clothes. Although last time, the mirror finally let us in *because* of the pajamas I was wearing. They were the same design as the Floom flag: pink with purple polka dots. But how do I know what clothes will help us get into the mirror if I don't know what story we're going to?

I guess I'll stay in my pajamas. That way if the mirror doesn't let us in, I can at least go straight back to bed.

I spot my open suitcase. Oh! I'll bring my suitcase with me! Why?

1. We are usually in the stories at least a few days. I may as well have a change of clothes with me.
2. It's already packed.
3. Maybe something inside will help us get into the mirror.

So the suitcase is coming, too. I strap on my watch (last time I forgot it and had no idea how much time had passed), then zip my bag and roll it into Jonah's room.

He's fast asleep.

"Hey!" I say, gently shaking him. "Mom and Dad are sleeping. Let's go see the mirror."

He opens his left eye then sits up. "Sure! But why are you bringing your suitcase?"

"To have extra clothes. You can put some of your stuff in it, too."

He climbs out of bed and disappears into his closet. "Like Kadima paddles?" he asks.

My brother is obsessed with playing Kadima. I do not know why. When I'm on the beach, I like to read and relax, not chase a bouncy blue ball with wooden paddles.

"I was thinking more along the lines of clean underwear, jeans, and a T-shirt. You know what, I'll pack for you. You put on your sneakers."

(My sneakers are already on and double-knotted.)

I pack two pairs of his Batman underwear, one pair of jeans, one blue shirt, our toothbrushes, and cinnamon toothpaste. Then I tiptoe down the stairs to the main floor. I lift my suitcase up so that it doesn't bump and wake my parents. It is SO heavy. I motion for Jonah to grab the other end, but he's too focused on his tiptoeing to notice.

I stop at the landing and take a deep breath — there's no sound from our parents' bedroom. We've come so far — we can't get caught now. I open the basement door, turn on the lights, and then we creep down the rest of the way.

In front of us is the antique mirror, twice the size of me. The glass is clear and smooth. My brother and I are in the reflection, of course. We're both wearing pajamas and sneakers. What's worse — we're wearing matching black-and-white pajamas. I hadn't noticed in Jonah's dark bedroom. We look like twins. Like Oompa Loompas. Like Dr. Seuss's Thing One and Thing Two.

"We look like zebras!" Jonah says. His short brown hair is a mess. It's standing up in different directions. I pat down my own curly brown hair. I like to look neat. Also, not identical to Jonah.

I try to look deeper into the mirror to see if I can see Maryrose. She lives inside. At least, we think she lives inside. We don't really know that much about her. Only that she's a fairy and that when we knock three times, she takes us inside different fairy tales. Sometimes. I hope we're wearing — or have with us — the right thing.

"I'll do the knocking," Jonah says. "Ready?"

This better work. It will be pretty annoying if I have to drag this suitcase all the way back upstairs tonight.

"One —"

"Wait! Jonah?"

His hand freezes in midair. "Yeah?"

"Let's try not to mess up the story again, 'kay? We just want to visit and see what's happening. We don't want to change anything."

"Uh-huh," he says. "One —"

"Don't 'uh-huh' me," I state. "I do not want you touching ANYTHING or talking to ANYONE. Not without my permission. Got it?"

"Yes, Mom."

I wag my finger. "No messing the story up. That's a rule."

He twists his bottom lip. "What story do you think it'll be?"

"Hmm. I don't know."

"I like *Jack and the Beanstalk*." His eyes widen. "How cool would it be to meet a giant?"

I nod. As long as he doesn't step on us.

"Or Aladdin! Then we could fly on a magic carpet."

Flying on a magic carpet sounds a little scary. What if I fall off? On the other hand, then I wouldn't need airplanes. "I could take the magic carpet to visit Nana!"

Jonah grunts. "So I can't talk to anyone or touch anything, but you can steal the magic carpet and take it to Chicago?"

"I was kidding," I say. Kind of.

He shifts from foot to foot. "Can we go now?"

"Yes. Just remember: No touching."

"Unless it's stealing a magic carpet."

"Right." Then I shake my head. "No. No touching. No stealing. No anything."

He laughs. "Okay, okay. Can I do my three knocks now?"

"Go."

He does. Almost immediately, there's a hissing sound. The mirror starts swirling and casts a purple light over the room. A second later, it's pulling us toward it like it's a vacuum cleaner.

"It's working!" Jonah exclaims.

"Then let's go!" I grip Jonah's arm with one hand, my suitcase with the other, and step inside.

# ✳ chapter three ✳

## Splash

*t*he second I go through the mirror, I inhale a mouthful of water.

What is happening? Am I in my bathtub? Why can't I breathe?

Everything is blurry, and my eyes sting, so I close them. The water is salty. Bathtub water isn't salty. Also, I'm horizontal, on my stomach, and my elbows are rubbing against the ground.

A sandy ground.

Need air! Can't breathe! Lungs exploding!

I open my eyes, look for the light, and push my face toward it.

And then . . . *cough, cough, cough!* Ahhhhhhhh.

Air. I'm breathing air. Gulps and gulps of air. Who knew air could taste so good? Who needs ice cream when air is so incredibly delicious?

Once I've finished gorging on the air — it's an all-I-can-eat air buffet! — I realize I'm looking at a sandy beach. But I'm not on the beach. I'm in the water, looking at the beach. It's bright out here, too — around noon. What is going on? I twist around and see that a huge wave is about to smash into me. "No!" I yell, and try, unsuccessfully, to get out of its way.

*CRASH.*

No, no, no, I will not drown! *Cough, cough, cough!*

My heart is thumping, and I push myself to my feet before I can get attacked again. What in the world is happening?

I turn back to face the beach. It's empty. No tourists, no sand castles, no bright-colored beach towels. Just pure-white sand sparkling in the midday sun. Beyond the beach are trees and beyond the trees are mountains. When I turn the other way, there's blue ocean as far as the eye can see. Even as far as my *stinging* eyes can see. Wait a sec. One thing my eyes can't see is my brother.

"Jonah! Jonah, where are you?" Where is he? My heart sinks to the ocean floor.

Just as I'm about to panic for real, he bursts out of the water and gives me a thumbs-up. "How cool is this?" he cries, sopping wet and grinning.

He's here! He's okay! Hurray! "Jonah, get over here now!"

"I'm fine!" he yells back.

Unlike me, my brother loves to swim.

According to my parents, when I was a kid, not only did I refuse to swim in the ocean, but I would cry hysterically when anyone else tried to. My parents. My brother. Strangers. Obviously I'm over that *now*.

Kind of.

*CRASH.*

Another wave sends me toppling back under the water.

AHHHHHHHH!

*Cough, cough, cough!*

Okay, fine, I'll admit it: I AM AFRAID OF WATER.

Not hot tubs or baths, but oceans, lakes, and rivers. Also moats, when I happen to come across them. Basically, I am afraid of bodies of water that have animals in them.

I am also afraid of pools.

They seem shallow but then BOOM the bottom's gone, and you're gulping chlorine.

Right now, I need to get out of the ocean, pronto, before it sucks me under for good. As I stand, my pajamas feel like they weigh two-hundred pounds. My sneakers are no longer sneakers. They are now bricks attached to my feet.

"I wonder where we are," Jonah says, swimming up behind me. "Do you think we're in *Jack and the Beanstalk*?"

Oh! Right! We're in a fairy tale! There must be a fairy tale reason for the water, then. My shoulders relax. "Do you *see* Jack or a beanstalk?" I ask. There's no ocean in *Jack and the Beanstalk*.

He scrunches up his nose. Hmm, his nose is looking a little red. He might need sunscreen. Crumbs, I don't think I packed any.

Speaking of stuff I packed — where's my suitcase?

I spin around and around until I spot it a few feet away, floating in the other direction. "Our stuff! We have to get it!"

"I'll get it," my brother says, diving after it. Except the waves are quick and I can see my red suitcase drifting away faster than Jonah can swim.

"Forget it, Jonah!" I don't want him swimming so far out. It's too dangerous.

"But I don't want to lose my Kadima paddles!" he calls.

"You didn't pack them!" I yell back.

"I did when you weren't looking!"

Now I know why my suitcase was so heavy.

Eventually, when the suitcase is nothing more than a red dot in the distance, Jonah gives up and swims back.

Great. Just great. I have nothing to wear but soggy pajamas and hundred-pound shoes. With a large sigh and a lot of effort, I heave myself onto the dry sand.

*SQUISH.* When I pull off one of my sneakers, a piece of seaweed and a gallon of sandy water spill out.

Jonah is right behind me. "Abby! I see someone! Is that Jack?" He points to the ocean. In the distance, there's a blob moving toward us.

I squint toward the water. I see a head! A guy's head! But it can't be Jack. Jack climbs; he doesn't swim. Also, Jack is about my age, and this guy looks like a teenager. Wait! Behind the guy's head another head keeps bobbing in and out of the water. A girl's head. At least I think it's a girl's head. I can see long blond hair. They're getting closer . . . and closer . . . and . . . Yup, it's a girl. And then behind her is something green and orange. A towel? A floatie?

It's shiny and triangle-shaped and reminds me of a paper fan I had as a kid.

Oh! It's a tail! The girl has a tail!

Which can only mean one thing.

"She's a mermaid!" I exclaim. "We're in *The Little Mermaid*!"

"But who's the mermaid holding?" my brother asks. "Maybe it's Jack?"

"I am one hundred percent sure it is *not* Jack," I snap.

The guy has dark-brown hair and his eyes are closed. His head is rolling from side to side. That's not a good sign.

I can't tell if this mermaid is *the* Little Mermaid or just *a* mermaid. I need to remember the original story. My nana read it to me a million times. I just have to focus, and it'll all come back to me. Too bad there's no *time* to focus.

From about twenty feet away, the mermaid's head bobs above the surf. She looks right at us, gasps, and disappears under the water. A second later, she pushes the guy toward us and swims in the other direction.

"We scared her," Jonah says.

"Wait!" I call to the mermaid. "Don't leave!"

"I thought we weren't supposed to talk to the people in the story!" Jonah exclaims.

Right. Crumbs.

No time to worry about that now.

The guy is sinking under the surface and it's up to us to save him.

# ∗ chapter four ∗

## The Real Story

We jump back into the water and each grab one of the guy's arms. He's wearing a yellow shirt and dark-brown pants that are soaked and torn. He's handsome. Really handsome. Floppy brown hair, chiseled cheekbones. Full lips that are tinged blue.

Uh-oh, that's not a good sign.

"Don't drop him!" I order.

Jonah's eyes are wide with worry. "Is he okay?"

A wave crashes into my back and I ignore the question. "Let's just get him to the shore!"

We pull and we heave, and a few minutes later we lay him

down on the sand. I cup my ear against his mouth. He's breathing! "He's okay! Just unconscious, maybe?"

Jonah exhales in relief. "Who do you think he is?"

As I collapse on the hot sand beside him, the original story floats back to me. Prince . . . shipwreck . . . the Little Mermaid saved the prince . . . "Oh! That *was* the Little Mermaid! And this is the prince she saved from the shipwreck!"

"But why was the prince in the water?"

"Don't you remember?" I ask. Nana read him the same stories she read to me. Although I paid attention 110 percent of the time and he paid attention about 10 percent of the time.

He shrugs. "Just start at the beginning."

"Fine," I say. I lie down on the sand and close my eyes, suddenly exhausted. "There was a mermaid. And she was, um, little."

"What was her name?" Jonah asks.

Hmm. Good question. "I don't think she has a name in the actual story."

"Who wrote the story? Was it the Grimm brothers again?"

"No, it was a Danish guy. Hans Christian Andersen."

"He liked Danish? The cheese kind?"

I open my eyes just long enough to roll them at my brother and then close them again. "No, he was from Denmark. The country."

"But the Little Mermaid lived in the ocean, right?"

"Obviously."

"Why are you being mean?" he whines.

"Because you're asking dumb questions!"

"I'm sorry. I'll stop talking. Just go on with the story."

"The Little Mermaid really wanted to swim to the surface but she wasn't allowed until her fifteenth birthday. She had a bunch of older sisters and they'd already done it. When the Little Mermaid was finally allowed to peek out above the water, she saw a prince fall off a boat. Instead of letting him drown, she brought him to shore and saved him."

"That's what we just saw!" he exclaims.

"Exactly."

Beside us, the prince coughs up some seawater. Both of us spring up, but the prince's eyes stay closed.

"So what happens next?" Jonah asks.

"Well, after she saved him, she fell in love with him."

"And then they got married?"

"No," I say. "It's kind of a long story, actually, but what happened is that she hid. She didn't want the prince to see her since she was a mermaid. So when he woke up, he didn't know she had saved him. She went back underwater and asked around and discovered that the only way to get a human on land to fall in love with her was to have two legs. And the only way for her to get two legs was to make a deal with the sea witch. So she went to the sea witch and —"

The prince lets out a loud snore.

"And," I continue, "the sea witch offered to give her legs, but the witch wanted payment. So the Little Mermaid gave her —" I stop. This part is gross.

"Her allowance?"

I squirm. "No."

"Her sneakers?"

"What sneakers? She had a tail."

"Oh. Right. Then what?"

"Her tongue."

"Are you kidding me?" he gasps. "The Little Mermaid gave away her tongue?"

I nod, trying not to picture it.

Jonah's eyes light up. "That's disgusting! Awesome!"

My brother tends to like the gross parts of these stories. He has a stronger stomach than I do. He loves roller coasters. Especially the ones that go upside down. Not me, thank you very much. I prefer staying upright.

"Well," I say, "technically, it was the Little Mermaid's voice that the sea witch wanted. The Little Mermaid had an amazing singing voice. But she gave that up for legs. Forever."

Jonah shakes his head. "I can't imagine never speaking again."

"Me neither," I say. I doubt you can be a judge if you can't speak. How would you sentence people? "Also, the sea witch added an extra curse to the spell — if the prince married anyone else, the morning after the wedding, the Little Mermaid would . . . would . . ."

"Would what?" Jonah asks. "Have to give the sea witch her fingers? Her nose?"

"*Snoooort!*" groans the prince, but his eyes stay closed.

"Worse than that," I say gravely. "If the prince married anyone else, the morning after the wedding, the Little Mermaid would die."

Jonah pales. "But we don't have to worry, right? Because there must have been a happy ending. The prince fell in love with the Little Mermaid, they got married, and they lived happily ever after?"

"Well . . ." I hesitate.

Just then we see a splash in the distance. It's the mermaid again. The *Little* Mermaid. Her blond hair, her green bikini top, and her green-and-orange tail peek out of the water and then disappear.

"I see her," Jonah whispers. "Should we hide? Maybe if we run away she'll forget she saw us and the story can continue the way it's supposed to?"

"Yeah," I say, remembering what I'd said back in the basement. That we should stay out of the way so that whatever fairy tale we landed in wouldn't get messed up.

Except maybe I want to mess this one up.

I look at the Little Mermaid and then back at the prince. "Here's the thing. The ending of the real story of the Little Mermaid isn't good. It isn't like the happy ending in *Cinderella* or *Snow White*. In the end of the Little Mermaid's real story, the Little Mermaid *doesn't* get the prince. She doesn't get her happy ending at all. In the end of the real story the prince marries someone else, another princess, and the Little Mermaid . . ." I take a deep breath. "The Little Mermaid dies."

"You're wrong," Jonah tells me. "I saw the movie. The Little Mermaid doesn't die!"

"The movie isn't the real story," I say. "Haven't you ever heard of a Hollywood ending? When the movie writers give the story a happy ending even though that's not what happens?"

"But she can't die," Jonah cries, and bangs his fist against the sand. "That's the worst ending I ever heard!"

I nod. "It definitely is a bummer."

Okay. I think I *do* want to mess up the ending. "I have a new plan. I think we should change the rest of the story."

He twists his lower lip. "I thought that was against the rules."

I throw my hands up in the air. "Maryrose has never even spoken to us! Whose rules?"

He cocks his head to the side. "Your rules."

Oh. Right. "Yes, well, technically changing the ending is against my rules. But maybe that rule is a mistake. I don't want the Little Mermaid to die. I want to give her a new ending — a happy ending."

# ✳ chapter five ✳

## That's What Happened

there's another groan beside me. This time the prince's eyes flutter.

"I think he's waking up," my brother says.

The prince's eyes open all the way. He looks at Jonah and then at me. "Where am I?" he asks, his voice gruff.

"You're on a beach," Jonah says.

"How did I get here? I was on a ship." The prince sits up slowly and rubs his forehead. "I don't remember what happened. Wait. I do remember. There was a storm. I fell overboard. How did I survive?" He notices our soaking wet clothes. "Did you two save me?"

I crouch beside him. "It wasn't us. It was the Little Mermaid!"

His eyes crinkle. "The what?"

"The Little Mermaid!" I point to the water. "She was right there a few minutes ago."

He twists to look but the water is smooth. "What's a mermaid?"

"You know," Jonah says. "Half fish, half person?"

The prince shakes his floppy hair, and I wonder if he lost his crown in the ocean.

"There's no such thing as a half person, half fish," he says. "That's ridiculous."

"It isn't," I say. At home, I'd have to agree with him. If one of my new friends told me that she'd seen a mermaid at the beach I would have to ask her if she'd hit her head recently. But we aren't in Smithville. "Where I live, you'd be right," I say.

"You don't know that," Jonah tells me. "We might have mermaids at home."

"We do not," I say.

Jonah shrugs. "You don't know for sure. He thinks there are no mermaids here, and he's wrong."

Fair point, I guess. I motion around me. "Where are we, anyway?" I ask. From the beach, I spot a path that leads toward a big stone building in the distance. Just as I'm trying to figure out what it is, a bell rings from it. A school?

The prince stretches his arms up above his head. "The kingdom of Mustard."

Jonah and I both laugh. "Seriously?" I ask.

The prince squints into the sun. "Why would I joke about the name of my kingdom?"

"Your kingdom is named after something you put on a sandwich?" Jonah asks.

"Maybe they don't have mustard here," I tell Jonah. "Like how in Floom they didn't have brownies."

The prince shakes his head. "We eat mustard. It's our favorite condiment. We eat brownies, too. We even dip them in mustard."

"That's disgusting," I say.

Even Jonah agrees. "Yuck," he says. "I wish we were in the kingdom of Ketchup."

My brother is obsessed with ketchup. He puts it on everything. Fries. Mac and cheese. Plain bread.

Seriously, plain bread. Now, that's disgusting.

"Brownies in ketchup," Jonah says. "That I'd try."

Now, that's *really* disgusting.

The prince wobbles to his feet. "Who are you?" He eyes our outfits. "You didn't escape from a prison, did you?"

I look down at our matching pj's. Our matching black-and-white-striped pj's. We do look like inmates.

"No," I say quickly. "We're just in our pajamas."

"So if you two didn't save me, how did I survive? Maybe a fisherman brought me in? Or I washed up on a piece of drift-wood? Or are you two just being modest?"

"No," I say. "I can barely swim. It was the Little Mermaid — we just dragged you in."

"Aha! So you DID save me! Then I, Prince Mortimer, am in your debt. Would you please accompany me back to the palace so you can be celebrated?"

"But Prince Morty . . . can I call you Prince Morty?" Jonah asks hopefully.

"Only my parents call me Morty."

Jonah pouts, then continues, "But Prince Mortimer, it really wasn't us who saved you."

*Hold on.* I elbow Jonah in the side.

"Ouch!"

"I just need a minute to talk to my brother," I say, and yank him a few feet away. "We may as well go to his palace," I whisper.

"We might not be able to find the Little Mermaid tonight, and we're going to need somewhere to sleep."

Jonah shrugs. "I'm game if you are. But we're definitely going to mess this story up."

I look out at the water. "Let's hope so."

# ✷ chapter six ✷

## Celebration Time

We're walking up the path toward the building when we run smack into three teenage girls. They all start shrieking the second they see us.

At first I think they're making fun of our matching prison pajamas, but then I realize they're shrieking at the sight of the prince.

"Oh! My! Goodness!" swoons one.

"It's him! It's him! It's him!" cries another, looking like she might faint.

Jonah and I aren't the only ones dressed in matching outfits — the girls are all wearing white collared shirts, yellow skirts, white kneesocks, and yellow patent-leather shoes. A uniform? I guess the building is a school after all.

"Prince Mortimer!" the third girl cries out. "Everyone is looking for you! I'm, like, so happy that you're okay!" The girl has a mouth full of bubble gum and super-curly brown hair. Each curl looks like a Slinky.

I wish my curls did that. I also wouldn't mind a piece of gum. Especially since my toothbrush drowned with the rest of my suitcase.

"I'm fine," the prince says. "But I need to get back to the palace."

"Let me get help!" the girl with curly hair says, and then runs back up the path. The rest of the girls just continue to stare.

A few minutes later, she's back with a bunch of important looking grown-ups, and soon we're on our way to Prince Mortimer's palace.

The hour-long carriage ride swerves us around the beautiful coast. All along the beach are small villas with big outdoor decks and docks and boats. The waves crash against the white sand. The water sparkles like emeralds. The sky is bright blue. Leafy green trees sway in the distance. It kind of looks like the pictures my parents took of their tenth anniversary trip to St. Thomas, which is an island in the Caribbean. Even though Nana came to stay with me and Jonah, we were NOT pleased about being left behind. Jonah was bummed to miss out on the Waterinn Resort's many activities — snorkeling! swimming! kayaking! — while I was bummed that we missed out on the hot tub. Also, I love tall frosty drinks that come with tiny umbrellas, and I'm pretty sure that's what all the drinks are like in the Caribbean.

When we arrive at the palace, there is a crowd of people waiting for us out front. At the center are the queen and king. They're both wearing gold crowns, but they're not dressed like a typical queen and king. Instead of robes, the king is wearing yellow shorts and a yellow-and-white flowered shirt. The queen is wearing a yellow tank dress with a gold belt, gold flip-flops, and big gold sunglasses.

These people really like yellow. Oh — it's probably their official color, since it's the kingdom of Mustard!

Both the king and queen have sun-bleached hair and leathery-looking skin from too many hours spent on the beach. Which is the kind of skin I don't want to have when I'm older. Which is why I always wear sunscreen.

Except for now. Because I didn't realize I'd be going to a beach.

After grabbing the prince in a bear hug, the king turns to us. "Dudes! We are so grateful that you saved our son," he says.

Dudes? I'm not a dude. "It wasn't just us," I say. "A mermaid brought him to shore."

The king laughs. "Sure, dude. Whatever you say. We're just grateful that he's okay. After he disappeared off the ship we assumed the worst."

"You'll be our guest for a few days, won't you, darlings?" the queen asks, not letting go of her son's hand.

"Sure!" Jonah exclaims, gesturing toward the tennis courts to the left of the palace and the volleyball court to the right. "It's awesome here."

He's not wrong.

The palace is amazing. All windows and marble. Yellowish marble. These people take the name of their kingdom seriously.

"Darlings, would you like something to drink?" the queen asks. "Maybe a banana smoothie?"

We nod. That definitely sounds tall and frosty. A minute later a tall, icy yellow drink — with a teeny, tiny yellow umbrella — is plunked into my hand. Hurray!

I slurp it down in twenty seconds. Yum.

Jonah nudges me. "Not bad, eh, darling?"

I laugh. "Pretty good, dude, pretty good."

A maid named Vivian leads us inside the palace. She's about my mom's age, and her brown hair is tied back in a tight bun. She's wearing a perfectly pressed yellow uniform.

Inside the palace, there are yellow flowers everywhere. The rooms are decked out with gold chandeliers and ginormous paintings. Paintings of the ocean, of the king and queen, of the prince, and of other people in crowns.

Vivian leads us upstairs. She opens the door to my room. And by *room*, I mean *suite*. Huge, gorgeous suite.

It's the size of the entire top floor of my house in Smithville. In the middle is a king-sized yellow canopy bed. The room even has a balcony that overlooks the water. From the window I can also see a pool. And a mini-golf course. And a baseball diamond. And a hot tub.

Yes. A hot tub.

Forget the Waterinn — this might be the best hotel ever. Except it's not a hotel. It's Prince Mortimer's house. Our house for the next few days.

Jonah's room is right next door. There's a door between our rooms that connects us if we want to be connected.

"You can unpack here," Vivian says, motioning to a chest of drawers.

"Thanks," I say. "But we lost our luggage. I don't have anything to unpack."

Speaking of stuff in my suitcase, now that I think about it, I bet the reason Maryrose let us in the mirror right away was *because* I had packed a bathing suit. It's a must-have piece of clothing for this fairy tale. She must not be very happy that I let my suitcase vanish in the ocean.

"Nothing to unpack?" Vivian echoes. "I'll ring for the royal tailor at once! You absolutely need something for the prince's welcome-home party tonight!"

I can't help but think about that fairy tale, *The Emperor's New Clothes*. Wasn't there a fake tailor who pretended to sew all these new outfits for the emperor, but the emperor was really walking around naked? Hopefully this tailor will make me *actual* clothes.

A few minutes later, the royal tailor knocks on my door to take my measurements. Then he takes Jonah's and hurries away to get to work.

"In the meantime, get in the hot tub and relax," Vivian orders. "I'll bring you an extra swimsuit."

Okay. If she insists.

I slip on the suit — it's yellow with gold, red, and green polka dots — and make my way outside in a plush yellow robe and matching slippers.

The hot tub overlooks the ocean. I dip my big toe in first. *Ahhh*. Hot and delicious.

As I sink under the steaming water, I think, *I could get used to this*.

After Jonah — in new yellow swim trunks — joins me for a bit, we both return to our rooms to get ready.

My closet is now filled with outfits. Real ones — nothing invisible here. There's a beautiful long, flowy yellow dress with a beaded top and a silky skirt. There's also a simpler cotton yellow sundress. Two yellow nighties. A few pairs of yellow undies. I'm going to look very sunny. Good thing they also gave me a new pair of red sunglasses.

I put on the fancy dress and step out onto my balcony, calling to Jonah to meet me outside.

Jonah steps onto his balcony, which is connected to mine with a short divider between them. He's wearing new yellow pants, a striped yellow-and-white collared shirt, and a massive smile. "I love it here," he says. "This is the best vacation ever!"

"It's not a vacation," I remind him. But honestly — it does kind of feel like a vacation. The view from here is incredible — blue, blue water that goes on forever. Even though it's warm and sunny, the ocean breeze is gentle and amazing. But still. "We have a job to do. We *really* have to find the Little Mermaid before it's too late." I look out into the water, hoping for a glimpse of her. Is she swimming up the coast looking for the prince right now? Where is she?

Jonah pumps his fist in the air. "We have to stop her from dying!"

"So, here's the plan," I say, rubbing my hands together. "We're going to nip this problem in the bud. We're going to stop the Little Mermaid from making the deal with the sea witch in the first place. If she stays a mermaid, then she won't die, even if the prince marries someone else."

Jonah cocks his head to the side. "That's not what I think we should do. I think we should let her make the deal with the sea witch and then help her get the prince to fall in love with her so she can live happily ever after."

What? He can't be serious. "Jonah," I say, "that is the worst plan ever."

He motions around him. "But it's so nice here! I bet the Little Mermaid would really like it."

I wag my finger in his face. "That is a bad plan for many reasons. First of all, it's very risky. If the Little Mermaid visits the sea witch, then she *has* to get the prince to marry her, or bye-bye mermaid."

"Everything has risks," Jonah says. "We keep going through the mirror even though we never know where we're going to end up or if we can get home. Living on land with the prince is the Little Mermaid's dream. We can't tell her not to dream. Everyone has to dream big, right?"

"Of course we have to dream," I say, annoyed. "But if you know your dream is impossible, then you give it up. You find a new dream and you make it work. You get used to it."

He frowns. "That's so sad."

My brother's just not getting it. "Jonah, we didn't want to move to Smithville, did we?"

He shakes his head. "*You* didn't want to move to Smithville."

"Fine, *I* didn't want to move to Smithville. But we did, and now we're okay. We have friends. We have a magic mirror. It's not so bad. You have to learn to make the best of what you have. You get what you get and you don't get —"

He smirks. "Wet!"

"Upset," I say. "Hmm. Maybe that's the whole point of the original *Little Mermaid* story. That she should have been happy with being a mermaid. The Little Mermaid gave up her whole life — her family, her home, her tail, and even her voice — for a guy who didn't appreciate her."

Jonah nods. "That's true. She even gave up her tongue."

"Exactly. If she'd learned to be happy with what she had, she would have been much better off." I squeeze the railing. "We have to stop the Little Mermaid from making the biggest mistake of her life."

He nods. "You're right."

Of course I'm right. I'm always right. Well, not always, but usually. "Now the only issue is — how do we find her?"

"Maybe she'll be at the party?" he asks.

"I doubt she'll be hopping around on her tail," I say. "But maybe someone at the party will know how to find her. Before she makes the deal with the sea witch."

If she hasn't made the deal already.

# * chapter seven *

## Party Hearty

As we hurry down the marble stairs, I glance at my watch, which says it's twelve fifteen at night. Huh? It doesn't feel like it's twelve fifteen. Oh, right, that's the time it is back home.

I look for a clock and see that it's six P.M. here. I guess every hour at home is a day here. We have to be back home by seven A.M., the time Mom and Dad wake us up. So we have six-and-three-quarter hours. Which means six-and-three-quarter days here. That's tons of time to find the Little Mermaid a new happy ending and find our portal home.

As long as my watch is right. We did take a bit of a swim — I hope this watch is waterproof.

We hear the music from the ballroom and discover that the event is already in full swing. Since we're both starving, we make a beeline for the buffet. Vivian introduces us to Carolyn, the chef, who's setting up the plates of lobster sandwiches, mac and cheese, corn, and, of course, mustard. Lots and lots of mini bowls of mustard.

Carolyn is wearing a poofy yellow chef's hat and a yellow apron. She's about my nana's age.

"Have you guys even tried ketchup?" Jonah asks Carolyn. "I think you'd like it."

She makes a sour face. "Ketchup? Too tomato-y."

Jonah sighs.

As we munch on the delicious food, we chat with the guests. Everyone wants to meet us, the children who saved the prince.

"It wasn't just us!" I tell anyone who will listen. "A mermaid was the one to actually save him — we only helped with the last step."

"A mermaid! What's that, darlings?" asks the queen.

"A half fish, half human," I explain.

"That's impossible," the queen laughs. "You two darlings have fantastic imaginations!"

"Have you ever heard of mermaids?" we ask Vivian as she folds yellow napkins. "Half fish, half human?"

"No such thing," she snaps.

How are we going to get someone to tell us how to find the Little Mermaid if no one has ever heard of mermaids?

"Psst! Hey!"

Jonah and I turn around to see Carolyn the chef beckoning from a long hallway.

"Does she mean us?" I ask.

"I guess so," Jonah says. "Let's go!"

Before I can respond, Jonah has already taken off after her. And of course, I follow. I can't let him chase kind-of strangers by himself.

"I heard your questions and I have something to show you," Carolyn whispers.

"About mermaids?" I ask.

"Shhhh!" She opens a door that leads to a winding staircase. "Follow me."

We take the stairs down a floor until we're in the basement, and then we follow her into a small room.

"You should see this." In the center of the room is a small bed covered with a yellow comforter. To the left is a dresser. She opens the bottom drawer and takes out a drawing that's about the size of my hand.

"Look," she says. "Careful."

I take the drawing and realize that it's of a woman — a woman with a fish tail.

"It's a mermaid!" Jonah exclaims.

"It definitely is," she says, squaring her shoulders.

"I thought no one here had ever heard of mermaids," I say.

"They haven't," she says. "But I have. My mother gave this drawing to me. She used to tell me stories about the mermaids all the time."

"Had she seen them?" I ask.

"No," she says. "But my great-great-grandmother Edith did. She was lost at sea and a mermaid saved her. She told my great-grandmother about her mermaid friend, who told my grandmother, who told my mother, who told me. I know everything about them."

"Tell us!" Jonah exclaims.

"They live under the water. In a beautiful kingdom. With streets and houses and restaurants and clothes and everything. The girls are called mermaids and the boys are mermen. And they all have silver tails. And —"

"That's not true," I interrupt. "We saw one. She didn't have a silver tail."

"She must have," Carolyn huffs. "That's what my mother told me. And what my grandmother told her. And what —"

"Did your mom say anything about how to get the mermaids to come on land?" I ask.

"They can't," Carolyn says. "Whenever my great-great-grandmother Edith wanted to see her friend, she had to swim into the sea. The mermaid even gave her a potion that let her breathe underwater for twelve hours."

"Ohhhh," Jonah's eyes light up. "Let's take that! Do you know how to make it?"

I shiver. I am not going underwater with or without a potion, thank you very much. There are sharks underwater. Sharks and other animals that want to eat me.

Carolyn nods. "I do know how to make it, but I can't because one of the ingredients is mermaid spit."

Gross.

"Find me a mermaid," she adds, "and I'll make you the potion."

*　　*　　*

Vivian spots us as we return to the party.

"Where have you been?" she asks.

"Just looking around," I say.

She scowls. "I hope you're not making a mess for me. Russell! Russell, come here!"

A boy about Jonah's age appears at her side. His skin is suntanned and freckled. Like everyone else in Mustard, he looks like he spends a lot of quality time on the beach.

"This is my son," Vivian explains. "He can keep you two company. Russell, why don't you show Abby and Jonah where you play tetherball?"

"Let's go sailing instead," the boy says. "I think the royal boathouse is still open."

Yes! That's a great idea. If we're on a boat, we'll be able to find the Little Mermaid. We may not have an underwater potion, but that doesn't mean we can't search the sea.

"No boats!" Vivian snaps. "It's almost dark out, and the sea is too rough."

Oh well.

"I love tetherball," Jonah says.

Russell nods. "Let's go!"

"I'm going to stay here," I say. The last time I played tether-ball I almost broke my nose.

Tomorrow, we'll take out a boat. Nothing that will tip over. A rowboat maybe. Then we'll find the Little Mermaid. How hard can it be?

# * chapter eight *

## Row, Row, Row Your Rowboat

*f*irst thing the next morning, Jonah and I head for the royal boathouse.

We find the yellow hut right on the beach. A suntanned guy in mirrored sunglasses is manning the booth. All around him are different kinds of boats. Windsurfers, sailboats, canoes, banana boats.

"We'd like to borrow a rowboat," I say.

"Of course," the royal boatman says, handing us a ledger. "Just sign one out."

The royal boathouse seems a lot like a library.

"And two life jackets," I add. "And do you happen to have some sort of radio? In case the boat drifts off and we need to get in touch?"

The boatman shakes his head.

"Do you have goggles?" my brother asks.

"Yup, those we got." He reaches under the counter and hands us two pairs.

"What do we need these for?" I ask my brother.

Jonah scrunches his eyebrows as though the answer is obvious. "To look underwater for the Little Mermaid."

"Underwater?" I ask, slightly incredulous. "Are you crazy? We're not going *in* the water."

He snorts. "How else are we going to find her?"

"With our eyes!" I exclaim. "From the boat!"

"That's just silly," he says, taking both pairs of goggles and dangling them from his arm. "We'll swim around."

My mouth gets super dry. "We'll see," I say, but what I really mean is NO WAY.

Jonah turns back to the boatman. "Do you have snorkels? Or scuba equipment?"

"Are those types of boats?" he asks back.

"I guess not," Jonah says.

"You don't know how to scuba," I remind my brother.

My brother shrugs. "Not yet, but I wanna learn."

So not happening.

As we make our way to the shore, I see that half the palace is already out on the water. Including the prince, king, and queen. All three of them are windsurfing.

"Let's take Windsurfers out instead," Jonah begs, his eyes following them with longing. "It looks fun!"

The three royals are being pulled by the wind in all directions. Suddenly, the king flies headfirst into the ocean.

It does not look like fun. It looks terrifying.

"Not a chance," I snap.

"Enjoy," the boatman says as we step into the rowboat and sit side by side. He pushes us out into the water, and off we go.

Five minutes later, sweat is dripping down the sides of my face.

The sun is beating on our heads.

"Push! Pull! Push! Pull!" I order.

It turns out that oars are really heavy. Who knew?

The massive yellow life jackets we're both wearing over our

bathing suits do not help the heat. Between the next push and pull, I catch Jonah trying to take his life jacket off.

"Don't you dare!" I warn.

"But I know how to swim."

"I don't care. You're my baby brother, and it's my job to make sure you don't drown."

We push-pull for another ten minutes before I call out, "Enough." The water is somewhat calm and we're away from the other boats. Might as well stop here. Also, I'm too tired to go on. My arms feel like rubber. I guzzle water from my canteen and motion for Jonah to do the same. I made sure we both filled up before we left. No getting dehydrated on my watch. Still, I feel like there's something I forgot. But what?

Anyway, it's time to find the Little Mermaid. "Oh, Little Mermaid!" I call. "Are you there, Little Mermaid?"

I do not see the Little Mermaid. I just see a lot of blue water.

"We're not going to see her from up here," Jonah says, putting on one of the pairs of goggles. "Let's jump in."

My heart races. "No, Jonah, that is not the plan."

"That's my plan," he says.

"But . . . but . . . but. . . . the water has sharks!"

He stands up and looks like he's ready to cannonball in. "It also has mermaids. And it's not like I'm going to drown. I'm wearing a life jacket."

He swings his arms back and forth.

"Jonah, you're going to flip the boat!"

"I won't," he says. And then he hollers, "Geronimo!" and launches himself over the edge.

Water splashes into my face. "You're so annoying!" I yell.

He ignores me and waves. "Come on in! It's so warm!"

What choice do I have now? I can't let him be in the water by himself. What if he needs me? I hug my life jacket to my chest. At least I can't drown with this on.

I can't, right?

Okay. I can do this. My legs shake as I adjust the goggles on my nose. I carefully — very carefully — dip my big toe in. Anything could be hiding underwater. Not just mermaids. But sharks and stingrays and jelly fish and barracudas and croco-diles, and did I mention sharks?

"Just jump!" Jonah yells. "Don't be such a scaredy-cat!"

My face burns. "I am not a scaredy-cat!"

"You are, too," he says. "You're scared of everything. Sharks. Jumping in the water. Flying by yourself."

"What are you talking about? I'm not afraid of flying by myself."

"So why don't you go see Nana on your own this weekend?"

Is he crazy? "I can't go by myself!"

"Yes you can! My friend Isaac flies by himself once a month. His dad lives in Miami."

I pause. "They let a seven-year-old fly by himself?"

"Yup. He's a UM. Unaccompanied Minor. If he can do it, you can do it."

Flying by myself does sound a *little* scary. What if I got lost at the airport? What if there was turbulence on the plane? "Mom would never let me," I say, my heart hammering.

"It doesn't hurt to ask," he says. "Scaredy-cat."

"I'm not a scaredy-cat!" I snap. And then, before I can change my mind, I jump into the ocean.

I did it! I jumped in! Hurray! Who's a scaredy-cat now, huh? The water is cold. But considering how hot it is outside, it feels good. Really good.

I scream. Something swam by my leg. I take a deep breath. Just a minnow.

I make sure my goggles are on tight, take a deep breath, and peer into the murkiness.

A school of shiny red fish swims by us at top speed. They are very pretty. They are not mermaids.

"Oh, Little Mermaid!" Jonah calls. "Where are you?"

She does not answer.

We watch as all kinds of fish swim by us. Neon-orange ones. Bright-blue ones. A pink one that looks like a balloon with porcupine needles. Lots of fish, but no mermaids.

"We should head back," I say eventually. "This isn't working. We'll have to think of another way." I help Jonah climb into the boat and then heave myself up behind him.

We both drip water everywhere.

"Where are the towels?" Jonah asks, rubbing his wet arms.

Crumbs. I knew I forgot something.

Dejected, we row our way back to the palace.

"I'm hungry," Jonah whines.

"We're almost there," I say. "You can ask Carolyn to make you a grilled cheese."

"I'm not having a grilled cheese without ketchup. That's just sad."

That morning Carolyn made us delicious omelets. And served them with a side of mustard. Jonah had almost started to cry.

"You're crazy," I say.

"Crazy about ketchup," Jonah says.

"Can we focus on rowing, please?" I ask. "The shore is right there! Then I have to figure out a Plan B."

"Maybe she'll come to us," Jonah says.

"Push, Jonah, push! Why would she do that?"

"She loves the prince, right? She probably wants to see him."

"You know," I say, "I think you're right. I remember something in the story about her swimming by the shore and trying to get a glimpse of him. Pull, Jonah, pull!"

"I'm pulling," he snaps. "More than you're pulling."

"I guess we'll have to watch the water as much as we can," I add as the bottom of our boat smashes into the sand.

As we're towing the boat to shore, the queen waves us over to join her for lunch.

"We should change first," I say.

"Don't be silly," she says.

So we join the king, queen, and prince at the oval table outside for lunch. There's a yellow silk tablecloth, and the dishes and silverware are all made of gold. I put my yellow silk napkin on my lap like you're supposed to. I elbow Jonah to do the same.

It seems silly to be so formal when we're all in our bathing suits, but whatever. The king and prince aren't even wearing shirts — they're just in bright-yellow trunks. The queen's swimsuit is pale yellow with a little skirt.

Carolyn serves bowls of squash soup, followed by lemon chicken and yellow rice.

"How was rowboating?" the prince asks while chewing a mouthful of rice. For a prince, he doesn't have the best manners. I'd mention it, but you know. He's a prince. He could probably have me beheaded.

"Hard," I admit. "We were looking for the Little Mermaid, but we didn't find her."

"Ha, ha, ha," they all laugh. "A mermaid! You two are so funny!"

Sigh.

Carolyn gives me a knowing look as she serves me a bowl of banana sorbet.

After lunch, Jonah and I head to our balconies to try to catch a glimpse of the Little Mermaid from there.

Jonah starts to fidget.

"What's wrong?" I ask.

"We don't *both* have to sit here, do we?"

"Why, do you have other plans?"

He smiles sheepishly. "I was going to play with Russell. Wanna come?"

"I have to look for the Little Mermaid!"

"Oh," he says. "Okay."

"If you really want to go, you can," I say, but I don't really expect him to leave me alone.

Jonah jumps up. "Great! I'll see you later!"

I can't help but feel annoyed. He still thinks this is a vacation! We have work to do.

As I stare at the ocean, I wonder if I'm wasting my time. The water is so busy with all the boats and swimmers. We know the Little Mermaid doesn't want to be seen — so then why would she swim close to the surface during the day? She probably does it at night.

I get to my feet. Maybe instead of watching the water, I should spend the day searching the palace grounds for portals to get back home. Make that: *Jonah and I* should spend the day searching the palace grounds.

I find my brother playing Ping-Pong with Russell outside. "Jonah, I need your help. We have to find the portal home." I whisper the last part so Russell doesn't hear. I don't know anything about the kid — I'm not going to trust him with our situation yet.

"Let me just finish this game." Jonah leans over the table and tries to return a shot.

"Jonah! Now!"

"Okay, okay," he grumbles. "Sorry, Russell. Wanna come help us knock on all the furniture to find our way home?"

I purse my lips. I guess we're not keeping our situation a secret.

Russell wrinkles his nose. "Not really. My mom doesn't like when I touch the furniture."

I lead Jonah back inside.

"How great is it that Russell gets to live in the palace?" he asks. "Imagine getting to be here every day."

"Don't get too comfy," I say. "We need to go home eventually. And remember: The portal can be anything. *Any object.*"

We step into the main hallway and Jonah looks around. "So it could be a — door?" he asks.

I nod. "Or a mirror. Or a fireplace. Or a table. How are we supposed to know?"

Jonah motions to all the frames on the wall. "Maybe it's a painting."

"Maybe," I say. "Let's try knocking on them to see if any of them make any sounds or start spinning. But don't let them take you yet, 'kay? Stand back."

I start with the full-body portrait of Prince Mortimer. He's wearing his crown and a yellow wet suit. It's really life-like. His eyes seem to follow me around the room. I knock on the painting three times. It's creepy, but I don't think it's enchanted.

It takes about an hour, but we knock on at least a hundred portraits and paintings.

"Guess it's not the paintings," I say.

"Are we done?" Jonah asks eagerly. "Can I go windsurfing?"

"No, Jonah! We have to check the doors and mirrors."

We hurry around the palace knocking on all of them. We are almost done when —

"Come in!" Vivian yells when we knock on one of the spare bedroom doors.

Oops. "Hi," I say. Inside, I head to the mirror over the dresser and knock three times.

"What in the world are you doing?" Vivian asks, putting down her duster.

I give a small smile. "Um, knocking? See, the way we got here was through a mirror, so a mirror might be our portal home."

"Well, stop it!" she barks. "You're making the frames uneven. Go play outside!"

"I agree," says Jonah.

"Sorry, Vivian," I say. I pull Jonah back downstairs. We're never going to be able to knock on every object in the house. The palace has a lot of stuff. And Vivian is going to kill us.

"What we need," Jonah says, sitting down on a marble step, "is a fairy."

"This story doesn't have a fairy!" I cry. "The only magical person in this story is the sea witch, and we can't go see her since she lives underwater. And I don't happen to have any mermaid spit on me."

"We should try a bat signal."

"Huh?"

"You know how in *Batman* they put up a signal in the sky when they need Batman? That's what we need. A bat signal. But in our case, a mermaid signal."

I'm confused. "For the sea witch?"

"No, for the Little Mermaid. Something to get her to come faster."

"But what would draw the Little Mermaid to us?"

"There's only one thing," Jonah says.

We look at each other and both say it: "Prince Mortimer."

# ✳ chapter nine ✳

## The Prince of Portraits

We try to convince Prince Mortimer to hang out on the beach that night, but he says he's too tired from his day of windsurfing. So we use the next best thing we can find.

Prince Mortimer's wet-suit portrait.

We wait until the middle of the night.

Then we sneak downstairs and very, very, very carefully lift Prince Mortimer's portrait up and off the wall.

"Careful!" I whisper as it leans toward Jonah and almost turns my brother into a pancake.

It's a good thing Vivian lives in the basement with Carolyn and the other staff, or she would definitely hear us right now.

"Got it?" I ask. "Lift on three and then we'll carry it out. One! Two! Three!"

We lift. But it's so heavy that we end up dragging it across the foyer and out the back terrace to the sand, as close to the water as we can get.

"Do you really think this is going to work?" Jonah asks when we're finally outside.

"Hopefully the Little Mermaid will see this and want to swim right up to it," I say. "She *is* madly in love with him."

"Unless she hates him now that the story's already different," he says.

"Then all of our problems would be solved," I say. "But I doubt it."

"I just hope she can see it," Jonah says. "I could figure out how to build a fire."

I snort. "You could not."

"I could so," he huffs. "You just need the sun and a piece of glass. How hard could it be?"

"Hard, considering it's the middle of the night."

"Oh, right."

Luckily it's a full moon, so we don't need to rely on my brother's nonexistent fire-starting skills. Everything on the beach is lit up. Including the portrait. Including the water lapping at the base of the portrait. Wetting the paint.

"Quick! Jonah! The prince is losing his feet!"

We hurry to move the portrait back a few feet. I doubt we'd be the royal family's welcome guests if we ruined one of their prized paintings.

"So, what now?" Jonah asks.

"We wait. She'll see the portrait and swim up to us and we'll talk to her. I'll sit behind the painting and hold it up while you keep watch."

At least an hour passes. Jonah's eyes are drooping.

Another hour.

Jonah's eyes are closed.

"Jonah, wake up!" I yell. "I can't do both jobs at once!"

"Not sleeping!" he announces, and opens his eyes wide.

"Let's switch," I say. "That way you can pretend not to sleep while you balance the portrait, and I'll look for her."

We switch. Jonah dozes. I scoop sand from one hand to the other, keeping watch.

When I feel my own eyes start to droop, I decide it's time to call it quits. This is getting us nowhere. I'll give it ten more minutes, and then we're going to —

*Splash.*

Did I just hear that? Or is it my imagination? I spring to my feet and run closer to the shore.

I see her! I see her! Long green-and-orange tail. Really gorgeous blond hair. It goes down to her waist and is almost the color of butter.

She's treading water by a rock, gazing at the wet-suit portrait of Prince Mortimer.

I want to yell, "Hello!" but I'm afraid of startling her and sending her back under the water. She's not too far out — maybe twenty feet. The water is calm.

If only I could swim out twenty feet. If only I had on a life jacket.

Maybe I can swim out a little. Not too deep. Just to where I can still stand.

Luckily I'm wearing my bathing suit under my sundress. I slip off the dress and wade into the water. Slowly. Carefully. Without making a sound. Without making a splash. Wow, the water is cold at night. I wish *I* had a wet suit.

I almost reach her when the water hits my waist. That's as far as I'm going to go.

"Abby?" Jonah's voice echoes along the beach. "Where are you?"

Uh-oh.

Jonah stands up on the shore, still holding the painting. "Abby!" he yells, blinking the sleep from his eyes. "Where did you go?"

I want to yell, "SHHHH," but I don't want to scare the Little Mermaid.

"Abby! Abby!"

The Little Mermaid sinks her shoulders and tail under the surface.

"Wait!" I cry. "Little Mermaid! Please don't go! We want to help you!"

She disappears under the water.

I lunge toward her. "No! Don't go! We know you love the prince! That's why we brought his painting! To get your attention!" Suddenly my feet no longer touch the ground. Oh, no.

"Abby!" Jonah hollers. "I see her! She's in the water."

"No kidding, Jonah! Can you lend me a hand here, please?"

"You're the girl from the other day, right?" a voice asks timidly. The Little Mermaid! She's talking to me!

"I am," I say, frantically doggy-paddling to stay afloat. "Don't be afraid. We want to help you."

Her face peeks out from behind the rock. "Is that your brother?"

"He definitely is," I say, finally finding the sand with my tiptoes. "You only have sisters, right?"

She nods.

"Lucky." I laugh. "And you're the youngest, huh?"

She nods again and runs her fingers through her wet hair. "How did you know that?" she asks. "Humans never know anything about me."

"Yeah, well, I've read your story. That's what I want to talk to you about. I know that you're a mermaid and that you love the prince and that you want to trade your tail for two legs."

She gasps. "I haven't told anyone that."

"I read it. In a book."

"You know how to read?"

My eyes widen. "You don't?"

*Splash.* I turn to see Jonah swimming toward us.

The Little Mermaid shakes her head. "No one underwater does. Books and ink don't last underwater. They disintegrate."

That makes sense. "Well, we read. And that's how we know who you are. And what happens to you. And it isn't good."

She pulls on a lock of her hair. "What happens?"

"You go to the sea witch and make a deal with her. She turns your tail into two legs but makes you give her your voice as payment."

She touches her throat. "My voice?"

I nod.

"Your tongue!" Jonah adds, now beside us.

"That's disgusting," the Little Mermaid says.

I agree. "That's why we don't want you to do it."

"Is your name really Little Mermaid?" Jonah asks.

She shakes her head. "It's Lana."

"I'm Jonah," my brother says. "And my sister is Abby."

"Nice to meet you, Abby and Jonah. I've never spoken to humans before."

"We've never spoken to a mermaid before," Jonah says. "Most people here haven't even heard of mermaids. They're weird. They don't use ketchup, either. Is there ketchup where you live?"

It's very late, I'm very cold, and I do not feel like chatting about ketchup. "Lana, let's get back to business. Are we all clear? You can't trade your voice and tail for legs to make Prince Mortimer fall in love with you. It doesn't work. He marries someone else and you end up . . ." My voice trails off. A wave hits me and I struggle to steady myself.

Lana squints. "I end up what?"

"Dead," Jonah says matter-of-factly.

She shivers. "I don't want to be dead."

"Exactly," I agree. "That's why you have to learn to be happy with your life in the water. You get what you get and you don't get upset."

In the moonlight, I see Lana's eyes tear up. "But I don't want to stay where I am! I love Prince Mortimer! And I want to live on land! Where there are sunsets and flying fish!"

"What are flying fish?" Jonah asks.

"You know," she says. "Fish that fly through the air. My sisters told me all about them!"

"You mean birds?" I wonder.

"Flying fish!" she insists. "And shoops!"

"What are shoops?"

"The things you put on your feet. You know — shoops."

"You mean shoes," Jonah says.

She shakes her head. "Shoops!"

"Forget about shoops," I say. "Didn't you hear what I said? You're going to lose everything! Your tongue! Your life! You can't make a deal with the sea witch! You can't give up everything that makes you who you are. It's just not right."

Lana crosses her arms and pouts. Her tail slaps against the water. I guess that's her way of stomping her feet. "But I love him."

She's being ridiculous. "You've never even spoken to him!"

"You don't need to speak to someone to know you love him," she insists. "You don't know what it's like. You're just a kid."

I snort. "You're practically a kid, too."

"I'm fifteen," she huffs.

"That's not even old enough to vote!"

"Vote on what?" she asks.

"The president," I say.

"We don't have presidents here. My father is the king. He runs the ocean. And I'm a princess. And I want to marry the prince."

Jonah floats on his back. "Maybe she could still marry the prince, without making a deal with the sea witch. Maybe they can have a long-distance relationship. Or maybe she can live in the pool. Or he can go live with her in the ocean. He can use the underwater spit potion!"

Lana cocks her head to the side. "There's an underwater spit potion?"

"That's what Carolyn said," I say. "But she hasn't been right about everything. She's the chef at the palace. Apparently her great-great-grandmother met a mermaid."

"I've never heard of a potion," Lana says, "but if it really worked, then the prince could stay with me!"

"Carolyn said it lasted only for twelve hours," Jonah says. "So he'd have to come back on land eventually."

"Maybe we could alternate," Lana says hopefully. "He could spend some time underwater with me, I'll spend some time in his pool . . ."

"It's doable," I say.

"But . . ." Lana hesitates. "Do you think he'll love me even if I'm a mermaid?"

"A guy should love you for who you are," I say. "If you have to change yourself, he's not right for you."

We all nod. Sounds right, doesn't it?

"I like the potion-plus-pool plan," I say. "That way you can still be together without trading anything with the sea witch. I think the prince has to meet you. Once he sees that you're real, and once you tell him that you're the one who saved him from the shipwreck, I'm sure he'll fall in love with you."

"Yeah?" Lana asks.

"Absolutely," I say, and hope that it's true.

# \* chapter ten \*

## The Ocean Can't Hide Everything

*t*he next morning, Jonah, Prince Mortimer, and I head out to the beach, as planned.

"Is she really going to be here?" Prince Mortimer asks.

"Yup. She can't wait to see you again," I say.

Jonah and I told him that the person who swam him to shore is here to see him. We left out the mermaid part, since he didn't believe us the first time we told him. He'll find out the truth soon enough.

My plan is totally going to work. He's going to meet Lana and fall hopelessly in love. So what if she's a mermaid? That won't stop true love! In a few weeks, he'll propose, they'll get married, and — *ta-da!* — happy ending. I glance at my watch. It's only two o'clock back home. We'll get Lana and Prince Mortimer together, and we'll still have five days to find our way back!

We are really getting good at this fairy tale stuff.

As we walk down to the shore, I spot Lana already waiting in the ocean. Her upper body is above the water and her tail is underneath. From this angle, you can't even tell she's a mermaid.

Prince Mortimer's eyes light up. "That's her?"

"Yup," I say.

"She's beautiful." He practically skips all the way down to the water. "Hello!"

She smiles back. "Hello!"

"Are you really the one who saved me from the shipwreck?" he asks.

She nods. "I did. I brought you to Crescent Beach, and then Abby and Jonah pulled you ashore."

"I am forever in your debt," he says, tipping his head. "Come out of the water so we can talk."

"It's so hot out," she says, blushing. "Why don't you come in the water?"

Nice one, Lana!

"I don't have my bathing suit on yet," he says. "Tell me more about how you saved me. You happened to be in the water that night?"

"Yes," she says simply.

"I guess you were on another boat?"

She smiles. "Something like that."

"You have beautiful hair."

"Thank you," she says, batting her eyelashes.

"So you brought me all the way to safety?"

She nods.

His eyes are all shiny and moony. "That's amazing. You saved me, and you're so beautiful."

"Thanks again," she says.

He clears his throat. "Will you marry me?"

Wow, that was fast! I thought it would take a few weeks, but it only took a few minutes. Maybe it really is true love!

Lana's smile lights up her face. "I will!"

"Fantastic," he says, his eyes twinkling. "You will be my princess."

"I should tell you something," she says. "I am already a princess."

Surprise crosses his face. "You are? Princess of where?"

"Of the sea," she says, and with that she dives into the water and shows him her tail.

His face turns white.

Uh-oh.

She reemerges, still smiling.

"You have a t-t-tail!" he spits out.

"I do," she agrees. "I'm a mermaid."

He shakes his head repeatedly. "There is no such thing as mermaids."

Jonah laughs. "Prince Mortimer, she has a tail. You can't argue with that."

The prince waves his hands in front of his face and takes a few steps back. "I can't marry a half person, half fish."

What? No! "Why not?" I ask. "She can sleep in your pool! Or the hot tub! The hot tub is really relaxing!"

He keeps walking back toward his palace. "I just can't! I need a wife who can walk and dance. Someone who can live with me on land. I'm sorry, but this will never work. I take back my proposal!"

"You can't take back a proposal!" I yell.

"Yeah!" Jonah hollers. "Finder's keepers!"

"There's a potion," I tell him. "A potion you can take. You'll be able to live part-time with her under the water."

"There are sharks under the water!" he exclaims. "And I'm not giving up my palace to live in some underwater cave!"

Hmph. What a romantic.

And with that, he turns and storms back to the palace.

"But, but, but . . ." Lana's voice trails off. "I don't live in a cave. My father's palace is just as nice as this palace."

I hurry toward her. "Lana, I'm so sorry."

She winces. "I told you this wouldn't work. I need legs to marry him. And the only way to get them is the sea witch."

"Lana, I don't get it. Why are you so crazy about him? He just insulted your palace! And he's not willing to give anything up for you! Why are you going to give everything up for him?"

She purses her lips. "Because I love him!"

I roll my eyes. I can't help it. She's hopeless. "There has to be another way." I rub my fingers against my temples. "I need to think about it."

"Well, I need legs. I have to go, anyway. My dad is having a party tonight, and I said I'd be there."

"Good." At least a party will keep her from visiting the sea witch. "By tomorrow I'll have another plan. Trust me, I'm very good at planning."

Jonah nods. "She is very good at planning."

"Just whatever you do, don't go to the sea witch. Deal?" I ask.

"Whatever," she says. And then, without even a good-bye, she disappears under the water, leaving me to come up with another plan. Fast.

# ✳ chapter eleven ✳

## That Hurts

Once again, I toss and turn and turn and toss. I can't sleep. Lana is going to come by in the morning, and I have no idea how to get her a happy ending. My only option is to convince her that her current life is super awesome *without* the prince.

And it *so* is. She's a princess! She has great hair! If she lived where we do, she could be in a shampoo commercial. She has five sisters — I wish I had *one* sister, never mind five. Legs just aren't *that* great. I look down at mine. Sure, they can run and dance and stuff. But I've seen her swim, and she moves a lot faster than I do.

There's a loud noise outside the window. It sounds like, "Oooooh!" but it's more of a moaning.

I bet it's quieter underwater. Land has all kinds of creepy sounds.

"Ooooh," I hear again.

Wait. That sounds like a person.

I run out to the balcony and look down at the beach.

"Oooooooooh!" I hear a third time. I look around in the moonlight and eventually see that the sound *is* coming from a person. From Lana. She's lying on the sand.

As I try to figure out what's going on, she starts to flop from side to side. Her tail starts to quiver. And then as I watch, her tail splits right down the middle into two.

OH. MY. GOODNESS.

I have seen a lot of crazy things in fairy tale worlds. But I have never seen anything like this.

I step over the divider and pound on Jonah's balcony door. "Wake up!" I yell. "We have to help her!"

When I turn back to Lana, the green in her legs is slowly fading to the same light color of her skin. Her hair is the same. Her upper body is the same. But now she has legs. LEGS!

And green bikini bottoms.

"What's up?" Jonah asks, opening his balcony door.

"That's what's up!" I say, pointing to Lana. "She made the deal with the sea witch! Why would she do that when I told her not to?" I stomp my right foot. I am mad. So very mad.

"Oooohhhh!" Lana moans.

"We need to help her," I say. "Get a towel."

We hurry down to the beach and find her still twisting in pain on the sand.

"Does it hurt?" Jonah asks her.

"Obviously, it hurts!" I exclaim. "She wouldn't be making those sad sounds if it didn't hurt!"

Lana just nods.

I put my hands on my hips. "Did you go to the sea witch?"

She nods again.

"Why would you do that?" I wonder. "I told you *not* to!"

She opens her mouth to say something but then immediately closes it.

I gasp in horror. Since she has legs and went to the sea witch . . . the sea witch has her . . . has her . . . has her tongue. "Did you give her your . . . ?" I can't even say the word. It's too gross.

Lana nods. But then she points to her legs.

My stomach churns. She really did it. Gave away her tongue for legs. Why would she do that? Why would anyone do that?

I take a deep breath. I take the towel from a very wide-eyed Jonah and wrap it around her wet shoulders. "Can you stand?" I ask.

She shrugs, which I take to mean *I don't know*. Communicating with someone with no tongue is *not* going to be easy. She holds my hands, and I gently lift her up.

She's shaky on her feet, but it seems to work. At the same time, she grimaces, so I guess it hurts. After a few seconds, she is able to walk on her own.

We take her back to the palace.

I want to yell at her. To tell her that she made a huge mistake.

But by the pained look on her face, I think she already knows it.

"Come sleep in my suite," I tell her. "We'll deal with this in the morning."

She looks like she wants to say something, but then just nods. Without a word, she follows me to my room.

# ✳ chapter twelve ✳

## Nice to Meet You Again

Lana is up before I am. She's sitting on the floor of my room, examining her toes.

"How are you feeling?" I ask.

She gives me a big smile and a thumbs-up.

She motions to her body. I have no idea what she's trying to say.

She motions again.

"You're cold?"

She shakes her head.

"Hot?"

She tugs on the yellow nightie I lent her last night. Maybe she's saying thank you.

"You're welcome," I tell her.

She shakes her head again and then makes a waving motion with her hands.

"You want to go swimming?"

Her cheeks turn red and she stomps her foot. She pulls at the nightie again and grunts.

"Oh, you want to get dressed!"

She gives me a big nod. Then she makes a show of patting down her hair.

"You want to wash your hair and then get dressed and then see Prince Mortimer?"

She claps. I guess I got it.

The door bursts open. "Who are you?" Vivian looks at Lana and demands.

Lana's eyes widen in fear. She opens her mouth to answer but then seems to remember she can't say anything.

"She's a mermaid!" I say. "Remember I told you I was looking for a half fish, half human?"

Vivian clucks her tongue. "She doesn't look like she's half fish. She has legs."

Good point. "Well, she used to be half fish," I say.

"I don't approve of lying, Miss Abby," Vivian says. "Does your friend with legs have any clothes, or did she lose her luggage, too?"

I shake my head. "No luggage."

"I'll call the tailor," Vivian barks.

Twenty minutes later, Lana has been measured and has showered and is wearing a brand-new sleeveless yellow sundress. She still smells a little salty, but I guess that's what happens when you live most of your life in the ocean.

"Now get outside, both of you, so I can clean," Vivian orders.

Through the balcony window, we spot Prince Mortimer already out on the beach, standing by the royal boathouse. Jonah is up, too — he and Russell are building sandcastles.

Prince Mortimer looks up, and Lana waves at him.

Prince Mortimer waves back and gives Lana a slightly quizzical look.

Lana curtsies. Then she pulls my hand and hurries me outside.

Prince Mortimer watches us as we approach.

"Hi," I say. "Do you remember Lana? She gave up her tail to be with you, so I hope you're happy." I don't mean to sound as grumpy as I do, but I guess I can't help it. I feel grumpy.

"You have legs!" the prince exclaims.

She blushes and nods.

"She gave up her voice for those legs," I say.

Lana gives me a sour look.

What? She did! Lana should be thanking me. In the original story, the Little Mermaid had no translator, and the prince never knew that she was the one who saved him and he ended up marrying someone else. The only reason he knows what's going on here is because of me.

And maybe Jonah. My brother who is currently making snow angels in the sand.

Mostly me.

"Who cares about your voice?" the prince exclaims. "You look gorgeous."

I have no choice but to roll my eyes.

He takes Lana's hand and twirls her around. Then he drops to one knee. "I will honor my earlier proposal. Will you marry me?"

She nods happily.

Lana and the prince embrace. Everyone on the beach — the king, queen, Jonah, Russell, and the guy manning the royal boathouse — claps and cheers.

And me? Honestly, I'm not sure how I feel. On the one hand, I'm happy that Lana got what she wanted. She wanted to marry the prince, and now she will. She's getting her happy ending.

But on the other hand, she:

1. Lost her tail!
2. Lost her voice!
3. Lost her underwater kingdom! Will she ever even see her family again?
4. Is marrying a guy who only likes her for her legs!

Even though she seems happy, I can't help feeling sad.

The prince takes Lana's hand. "We'll get married immediately. Three days from now. We'll do it in the ballroom, of course."

Of course? I had so expected him to stay on the beach.

Lana follows him into the palace. For someone who just got legs, she looks very glamorous as she walks.

"See?" Jonah says, running up to me, covered in sand. "It all worked out."

"Not all of it," I say. I can't shake the sad feeling.

"So now what?"

"I guess we go home."

"Already?" He looks longingly at the water. "Don't you think we should stay a few more days? Just until the wedding? That way we can make sure Lana gets married and has her happy ending. What time is it at home?"

I glance at my watch. "Three A.M."

"Great!" he cheers. "Then we have four hours until Mom and Dad wake us up. Which is four days. I'm going kayaking."

I grab his arm before he runs away. "We need to look for the portal!"

"We will, we will," he says. "How about we split up?

"All right," I say. "That sounds reasonable."

He scrunches his nose. "You go check the furniture," he says.

"We already checked the mirrors. I guess I can check the tables and chairs. What are you checking?" I'm glad he's finally willing to do some work.

As he runs toward the beach, he calls over his shoulder, "I'm going to check all the kayaks!"

I walked right into that one.

# ✳ chapter thirteen ✳

## Lost in Translation

*t*he next day, we're in the dining room having tea and discussing wedding details.

Chef Carolyn can't stop staring at Lana. "She's really a mermaid?" she asks, eyes wide.

"She was, but she gave it up," I explain.

"I wish she could talk! I have so many questions!"

The prince clears his throat. "Back to the menu," he says. "Chef Carolyn, I'd like you to prepare sole, tilapia, and yellowfin tuna. Fish, in honor of my little mermaid!"

Lana's eyes widen to the size of her teacup.

"What's wrong, my pet?" Prince Mortimer asks, patting her knee. "You don't like tuna?"

She shakes her head frantically.

"What about sole?"

More head shaking.

"Then what would you like to serve?" he asks.

She shakes her head no, and then makes a weird squiggly motion with her hands.

"She doesn't want fish. She must want lobster. Perfect!" He kisses her on the forehead, gets up, and leaves the room.

Lana's eyes fill with tears.

"Did you not want lobster?" I ask.

She shakes her head.

"Wait, I'm confused," Jonah says. "You did want lobster or you didn't?"

She shakes her head again.

"Which one?"

Lana drops her head down on the table and sighs.

What can I say? It's tough to talk without a voice.

Since they got engaged, the prince and Lana don't seem to understand each other at all. Lana does a lot of nodding and shaking her head, but it's tough to answer questions like: What do you want to serve for dinner? You can't answer that with a nod or a head shake.

Vivian hurries into the living room clutching a paper card. "Look," she calls out. "The calligrapher just finished the wedding invitations. Don't they look nice?" She places one in Lana's hands. "I'll send one to your family."

Lana shakes her head. I notice that her eyes fill with tears but that she blinks them away.

"You're not inviting your dad?" I ask, shocked.

She shakes her head again.

Communicating would be so much easier if mermaids knew how to read and write.

"What about your sisters?" I ask. "Aren't they going to be your bridesmaids?"

She points to me.

"Me?" I ask. "You want me to be your bridesmaid?"

She nods.

Wow! I've never been a bridesmaid before. But I've always, always, ALWAYS wanted to! The dress! The bouquet! I don't know what else bridesmaids do, but I'm sure it's fun.

"I accept!" I cheer. "I'm going to be an amazing bridesmaid. The best bridesmaid ever. But wait — if I'm the only bridesmaid, does that make me the maid of honor?"

Lana nods.

This is the most exciting thing that has ever happened to me. Besides falling into fairy tales through my magical mirror, obviously.

I am going to be *the* Little Mermaid's maid of honor! Who else can say that? No one! Only me! "But are you sure you don't want to ask your sisters?"

She shakes her head and looks down at the invitation.

"Read it out loud!" Jonah says.

I shoot him a look across the table.

He blushes. "Oh, right. I keep forgetting you can't talk."

"She can't read, either," I say. A lightbulb goes off in my head. "I have an idea! An idea that's going to fix everything. Okay, not everything, but definitely your communication problems."

Lana looks up at me eagerly.

I wait for Jonah to make a drum roll or something, but when none comes I turn to Lana and announce, "I'm going to teach you to write! If you can write, then you'll be able to communicate with Prince Mortimer. And with everyone. Then you won't be so frustrated. When anyone asks you a question you can just write the answer down!"

"Great idea, Abby," Jonah says. "I think I'll go play tennis while you do that. Russell is having his tutoring lessons now, but maybe I can get him to sneak away."

I sigh.

Lana points to the invitation.

I don't understand what she wants. "You want me to read it to you?"

She shakes her head no. She nods. She shakes her head no again. She points to herself and then her eyes and then the invitation.

"I think she wants you to teach her to *read*, too," Jonah says.

"Of course! Reading and writing go hand in hand." I square my shoulders. "Just call me Professor Abby." All I need now is a pair of eyeglasses and a blazer. Oh, and pencils. And paper. "Jonah, before you disappear for the day, please find me some paper and pencils."

Jonah hurries off. When he comes back with paper and different-colored pencils, I spread them all out on the table.

Pencils, check! Paper, check!

Now what? I've never actually taught anyone to read before. Where do I start?

"Okay, bye!" Jonah calls.

"Wait! Jonah. You just learned to read, right?"

"Right," he says. "This year."

"Can you, um, tell me how to start?"

He fidgets with the door. "How about with A?"

I nod. "So we'll go through all the letters, and I'll teach Lana the sounds. Thanks. You can go now."

Jonah bolts out the door.

I write a capital A. No need to confuse her with small letters yet. "A makes an 'ahhhh' sound. Ahhh!" I overemphasize. "Also, sometimes 'ay.' A is for . . . 'Abby'! That's me. A is also for 'at' and 'animal.' Why don't I write it down and then you copy it?"

I write a big A, and then she copies it ten times.

I smile. "A is for 'awesome.' Now let's do B. Do you know what B is for?"

She shakes her head.

"B is for 'brother,'" I say. "And 'ballroom.' And best of all, 'bridesmaid.'"

# ✳ chapter fourteen ✳

## Read It and Weep

Lana is a fast learner. By the end of the day, she knows the whole alphabet. By the day before the wedding, she can pretty much read and write.

It helps that we recruit Russell's tutor. I'll admit it: I'm no reading and writing expert. But it was all my idea, so I'm taking credit for it anyway, thank you very much.

Lana decides not to tell Prince Mortimer what she's up to. She wants it to be a surprise. Since he's always outside surfing, canoeing, or windsurfing, it hasn't been much of a problem.

When Lana takes breaks, we are very busy with wedding prep. We go to dress fittings with the palace tailor. Lana's dress is the perfect bride's dress — white, strapless, and fitted on top, with a big, poofy skirt. My maid-of-honor dress has capped sleeves, a sweetheart neckline, and a short skirt. It's pretty gorgeous — and yellow, of course.

Also, as maid of honor, it is my job to help Lana prepare for her big march down the aisle. I make her practice walking. Heel-toe, heel-toe, heel-toe. I read a book about a model once, and that's how she was told to walk down the catwalk. I'm guessing it's the same for a wedding.

I even practice my own walking — as maid of honor I have to make sure not to trip.

Being maid of honor is pretty important, you know. And time-consuming.

My job is to keep Lana happy and worry-free all day. Also to get an updo, manicure, and pedicure on the morning of the wedding. Yup, the bride and the maid of honor both get their hair and nails done! I've never had an updo, manicure, or pedicure, so I'm psyched.

Now, the day before the wedding, while Lana studies with Russell's tutor, I try and find the portal home. I knock on everything I see. Bedposts. Bowls. Stairs. Nothing works.

Jonah is supposed to be helping, but he's too busy vacationing.

"Can you please help me?" I ask him, finding him doing handstands in the pool.

"Abby, I'm sure it will be something at the wedding. The portal usually pops up at the *end* of our adventure."

"Jonah, of course it pops up at the end of our adventure! Once we find it, we leave!"

"Not true," he says, floating on his back. "We wait until the happy ending is all straightened out, and then we leave. The happy ending here isn't all straightened out yet."

"It practically is," I tell him.

"Then I'm sure we'll figure it out tomorrow," he says. "Why don't you come swimming?"

"Just because you're taking a break doesn't mean I can," I huff. Although it is very hot. And the pool does look very refreshing. But also deep. Anyway, I have other things to do.

I leave my brother to feel guilty in the pool while I go check on Lana.

She's scribbling on a piece of paper. She's writing! My plan totally worked!

"What are you writing?" I ask.

She takes a clean piece of paper and writes, "RITING PRESINT FOR PRINS."

Okay, so she's not the best speller yet, but come on. Two days ago she didn't even know that her name started with the letter L. Give her a break.

"Cool," I say.

She nods. Her cheeks are flushed with happiness.

"What is it?"

She points her pencil at her notebook.

It says:

"ONCE UPON A TIME THER WAS A MERMAD PRINCES. ON HER 15 BIRTHDA SHE SAW A PRINS FAL IN THE WATER —"

"Oh!" I squeal. "It's the story of how you met!"

She nods.

"He's going to be so impressed," I say. "Wait, Lana, I want to ask you a question. How come you don't want to invite your family to the wedding?"

She sighs. She pulls out a fresh piece of paper and writes, "THEY CANT COM ON LAND. AND THEY MUST

BE VERE MAD AT ME. AND NOT FEEL LIKE CELEBRATING."

"Are you sure? We could send them the invite — you never know what they might say."

"NO," she writes. "THEY CANT REED."

Oh, right.

That's so sad! She seems to think so, too, because I catch her frowning and gazing toward the window that overlooks the water.

On the bright side: I'm still the maid of honor!

# ✳ chapter fifteen ✳

## Your Bed Has Been Made

*t*hat night we all eat together in the dining room.

It's a pretty delicious dinner. Chef Carolyn makes a barbeque. There are cheeseburgers and corn and grilled salami. Of course, there's mustard. For dessert we have banana pie and lemon cake. These people really know how to eat, even if most of the food is yellow.

During dessert, Lana stands up and hands a box to Prince Mortimer. There's a yellow ribbon tying it closed.

"What's this?" he asks.

She smiles.

"It's her wedding gift to you," I explain, not wanting to give away the surprise but bursting with excitement. How amazing is she that she learned to write in two days? She's amazing! And it was all my idea! I am the best maid of honor ever!

Prince Mortimer unwraps the ribbon, opens the box, and takes out pretty papers laced together with ribbon. The first page reads: *Our Story, by Princess Lana.*

"How nice," the prince says before placing it beside his plate. He goes right back to his lemon cake.

Lana looks shocked.

I *feel* shocked. "Aren't you going to read it?"

"I'm in the middle of dessert," he explains, taking another forkful. "Yum."

Lana's face falls.

No. No, no, no. "But don't you see what a big deal this is? Lana wrote that! Herself! She learned to read and write so you guys can communicate!"

Prince Mortimer takes a big gulp of pineapple juice before continuing. "What does Lana need to read and write for? She's a princess. She just needs to smile, dance, and be beautiful."

I drop my fork and it clatters against my plate.

Jonah's jaw drops open.

Lana gasps. She looks at Prince Mortimer and then back at me. She shakes her head. Then she pushes her chair back and runs out of the room.

Everyone else at the table shrugs.

"Guess she doesn't like lemon cake," the prince says, and continues eating. "You know what we should have at the wedding? Lemon meringue pie."

I can't listen to one more minute of this. I excuse myself from the table and hurry after Lana. I do kind of hope they have lemon meringue pie at the wedding, though. I love lemon meringue pie.

When I walk into her room, just down the hall from mine, she is pacing.

"Sorry about that," I say.

Lana throws her arms up in the air. She picks up a paper and pen and writes, "I THINK I MAD A BIG MISTAK!!!"

I think she made a big mistake, too. Which I told her from the beginning. Not that I'm going to say "I told you so" now. Even though I really want to.

But I won't.

Her eyes tear up, and she continues writing:

"I GAVE UP EVERETHING TO BE HERE. MY FAMI-
LIE. MY HOME. MY VOICE. MY SISTERS!! MY DAD! OH
MY POOR DAD."

"What's wrong with your dad?" I ask. "Isn't he the king?"

She nods. "HE IS LONELY SINCE MY MOM DIED 10
YEARS AGO."

Her poor dad. First he lost his wife, and now he pretty much
lost his daughter. I sit down on her perfectly made bed. I'm
impressed. She makes a good bed.

"WHAT SHUD I DO?"

As I glance down at the bed, I remember one of my mom's
favorite expressions. "You made your bed, and now you have to
sleep in it," I say.

She shakes her head and then writes, "VIVIAN MADE
MY BED!"

Oh. Right. She probably made Jonah's, too. I, on the other
hand, made my own bed, thank you very much. Anyway, that's
not the point. "It's an expression," I say. "What I mean is, I'm not
sure what you *can* do except get married." And this isn't because
of the maid of honor thing. I swear. "You can't go back to your
family. You don't have a tail. Can you swim in the ocean the way
you are now?"

She shakes her head no.

"And, anyway, if you cancel the wedding, he'll marry some-one else. And then . . ." my voice trails off.

And then.

Although maybe the deal with the sea witch changed. It's possible, isn't it? Since the story has changed? "Did the sea witch tell you that if the prince marries someone else you'll . . . you'll . . . stop living the next morning?" I can't bear to say the word *die*.

She nods.

Crumbs.

We can't let that happen. No matter what.

# ✻ chapter sixteen ✻

## On the Other Hand

It's W-day. Wedding day.

And M-day: Maid-of-honor day.

Also, G-day: Go-home day. Assuming we can find the portal. My watch says it's just before six, so technically we have until tomorrow, but I don't want to be late.

I spend the morning in the royal salon getting ready. When they wash my hair with yummy lemon-scented shampoo and conditioner, I lean back and admire the gold chandelier above my head. Then they set my hair in curlers, and while it dries, they place my feet in a little claw-foot tub for a warm pre-pedicure foot bath.

Ahhhh.

Even more melty than a hot tub, if you can believe it.

They file and paint my toes gold. Then they do the same to my fingernails.

It's all very glamorous. I feel like Dorothy in *The Wizard of Oz* when she's getting all prettied up before she meets the wizard.

Lana and the queen are both in the royal salon, too.

Lana doesn't say much. Obviously, she can't talk. She doesn't write much, either, though. She just stares into the distance, looking miserable.

On the other hand, the queen doesn't *stop* talking.

"Everyone is coming," she says. "Even the royal family of Watermelon will be here. They're bringing their lovely daughter Alison. Lana, darling, she's about your age and goes to school here in Mustard. I hope you two will become friends."

Lana just shrugs.

A pretty princess named Alison? I can't help but wonder if that's the girl Prince Mortimer marries in the original story. Whatever. She's not marrying him in *this* story.

And: Watermelon? Really?

Once my nails are dry, my hair is arranged in a very cool and elaborate updo, with gold barrettes to keep it in place. They even sprinkle in gold sparkles to make it shine. Then they get to work on my makeup.

Makeup!

I've used some of my mom's blush before, just for fun, but I've never gotten my *makeup* done. They use pink blush! And gold eye shadow! And mascara! And pink lip gloss! By the time they're done, I look years older. At least thirteen.

Lana is still getting her makeup done, so I tell her I'll meet her in her suite in half an hour to help her get dressed.

One hour until the wedding!

The people around the palace are buzzing and hopping and getting everything ready. I peek into the ballroom to see what it looks like, and there are at least a hundred gold chairs set up with an aisle down the middle.

I practice my wedding walk all the way back to my room. Heel-toe, heel-toe. Slow and steady. I try to keep my shoulders down like my nana always tells me to.

I miss my nana. She would be so proud to know that I'm *the* Little Mermaid's maid of honor.

I change into my yellow maid-of-honor dress in my room, and then hurry over to Lana's door to see how she's doing. I knock once. Twice. Three times. I can hear her inside, but she's not answering.

Oh, right. She can't talk.

Finally she throws open the door.

She's in her full veil and wedding gown. Her hair hangs loose and curly around her shoulders. She looks gorgeous. Sure, she always looks gorgeous, but now she looks *extra* gorgeous. Like a princess. Like a *real* princess. No — like a fairy tale princess.

"You look beautiful," I breathe.

She shrugs.

Then I notice her face.

Her eyes are wide, her skin is pale, and she's biting her lower lip so hard, I think it might be bleeding. She also has her right hand wound through her hair and appears to be pulling on it. Hard. She looks terrified.

"Lana, you don't look so good. I mean, you look gorgeous, but you also kind of look like you're about to barf."

Just what every bride wants to hear on her wedding day. Maybe I'm not the world's best maid of honor, after all.

Lana closes her eyes and then opens them again, looking even sicker.

I'm not sure what to do. Or what to say. As maid of honor, it's my job to make her feel better. To get her to the altar. But how can I convince her to go through with a wedding when she's so clearly unhappy? On the other hand, if she doesn't marry Prince Mortimer, what will happen to her? Nothing good. Something bad, in fact.

Someone pounds on the door. "Guys, it's me! Jonah! Can I come in?"

"Yup," I say, nervously watching Lana.

"Everyone's waiting," he says, waltzing in. "Are you two ready?"

Jonah looks adorable. He's in a black tux with a mustard-colored bow tie. I wish I had a camera to take a picture and show my parents. Although then they would wonder why we were at a fancy event without them. It might be hard to explain.

Lana takes a deep breath. Then she nods. She marches out of the room, and we trail behind her. She'll be happy, right? This will all work out.

It has to work out. Has to, *has* to, HAS to.

And the pit of fear in my stomach has to go away.

We follow Lana down the stairs and toward the ballroom. For some reason, this feels more like a funeral march than a wedding. Maybe that's just how weddings always are? It's not like I've ever been in one before. What do I know?

Vivian is waiting for us at the bottom. "You look beautiful, Princess Lana! You, too, Abby. Take your bouquets." She hands us both bunches of yellow roses and white baby's breath, tied together with gold ribbon.

Ohhhh, pretty.

Jonah waves to us and slips inside so he can sit down with the rest of the crowd.

I peek through the open doors and see that the room is packed with at least a hundred people. Prince Mortimer is also in a black tuxedo and a mustard-colored bow tie, and he's already at the altar. Yellow flowers are everywhere — roses, tulips, daisies, and other kinds that I don't know the names of. The room looks really beautiful. I can't believe they put this all together in three days. It must be a world record.

Violin music begins to play.

"Abby," Vivian says. "You're first. Then Lana."

My turn! I look back at Lana. "You're okay?"

She nods and motions for me to go.

I don't want to leave her by herself, but I guess that's my job. I take a step. Heel-toe, heel-toe, heel-toe. I'm doing it! I'm doing it! This is fun! I am *so* acing this. Heel-toe, heel-toe, heel-toe! I did it! I made it the whole way without tripping!

When I get the altar, the prince is smiling at me.

I smile back. Maybe he's not so bad. He loves her, right? He'll make her happy?

He is smiling at me, right? I look behind me and realize he's actually smiling at his reflection in the stained-glass window.

Hrm. Well, at least he's smiling. Smiling's still good, right? He could be frowning at his reflection. That would be worse.

I look up and spot Lana, waiting at the doors.

Everyone stands up and turns to her.

She really does look stunning. She only looks a little bit like she's going to barf, and I'm probably the only one who notices.

The violinist begins to play the "Here Comes the Bride" march.

Lana doesn't move. She just stares. And stares.

Uh-oh. I motion for her to come.

She stares some more. She pulls her hair. She takes one step forward.

She takes one step back.

And then another step back. Then she spins on her heels and runs the other way.

# ✳ chapter seventeen ✳

## Better Now Than Later

**a** rumble goes through the room.

The prince looks at me in surprise. "Did she just leave?"

"Um . . ." It definitely seems like she did. "Maybe she had to pee or something?"

"She couldn't have waited until after the wedding?"

"A girl's gotta go when she's gotta go," I say, not really believing that:

1. I'm talking to a prince about pee or
2. Lana actually had to pee.

"Why don't I go see what the issue is?" I say nervously. And then, without waiting for a response, I hurry back down the aisle — no time for heel-toe now — and run out of the ballroom.

Should I really check the bathrooms? I realize there's no need to, because as soon as I step out of the ballroom, I see that the front door is wide open.

Lana left the palace. She's officially a runaway bride.

I run right after her and spot her already at the shore, holding up her dress, up to her knees in the water.

"What are you doing?" I ask. "You're supposed to be getting married!"

She shakes her head.

"You're not getting married?"

She shakes her head again.

"But what about the prince?"

More shaking.

"But you know what this means! If he marries someone else, you'll die!"

Her eyes fill with tears and she nods.

I pace up and down the sand. This is not good. Not good at all. If the prince does marry someone else, she's in serious trouble. We're all in serious trouble, because that's not a happy ending at all. That's a terrible ending. That's the same ending as the original ending! I take a deep breath and try to calm down. It's not like he's going to marry someone else *today*. We have some time to figure this out. Maybe the prince will learn to be less of a jerk and she'll change her mind. Maybe we can find another prince that she would want to marry, and *that* would work instead.

I hear Jonah's voice from the palace door. "Abby! What's happening?"

I guess I have to tell them the wedding's off. Had I known that canceling a wedding would be part of my maid-of-honor duties, I might not have been so excited about the job. "You stay here," I say finally. "Don't go in the water. I don't want you drowning. I'm going to talk to Prince Mortimer."

She closes her eyes in relief and I slowly make my way back to the palace.

Everyone looks up at me as I enter the ballroom.

"She better be coming now," Prince Mortimer barks. His face is bright red. He looks furious.

"Um, I don't think she is," I say timidly from about halfway down the aisle.

466

"Darling, how long will she be?" the queen asks, checking her gold wristwatch.

"A pretty long time," I say. "I think she wants to . . ." I have to just say it. "I think she wants to cancel the wedding."

Several hundred gasps echo through the room. I wince.

"You're kidding!"

"Cancel the wedding?"

"Not marry the prince?"

"Is she *crazy*?"

Prince Mortimer's face falls. "I can't believe she would do that to me," he cries, looking genuinely pained.

As insensitive as he's been, I can't help but feel bad for him. No one wants to be left at the altar.

The queen jumps up. "How dare she run off like that!"

The king stands up beside her and turns to the crowd. "Dudes, we know you all came to see a royal wedding today, and we *will* have a royal wedding today. Morty, there must be someone else here that you could marry."

My heart stops. What? Is he kidding? He must be kidding.

The queen nods. "Yes! Princess Alison is here today. Morty, would you marry her?"

"Let me see her," Prince Mortimer says.

The queen motions to Princess Alison. "Sweetie, will you stand up, please?"

Princess Alison stands up and curtsies. She has tight spiral curls and looks familiar. I know! She's the girl from the school, the one who got help after we found Prince Mortimer on Crescent Beach! She's the princess of Watermelon? Not surprisingly, she's wearing a satiny red dress, with a green sash and green shoes.

The prince nods. "I'll marry her. I like her hair. She's pretty."

The king claps. "Fantastic. Alison, would you like to marry our son?"

"Yeah, okay," she says, twisting a curl around her finger and snapping her chewing gum. "He *is* cute."

"And your parents? The king and queen of the kingdom of Watermelon? Do you agree to this union?"

"We do!" the king says, a big, smug smile on his face, a red-and-green checkered bow tie around his neck.

This isn't happening. THIS ISN'T HAPPENING.

"This isn't happening!" I yell.

Jonah tugs on my arm and whispers, "I'm pretty sure it *is* happening."

"Great," Prince Mortimer says. "Let's start the music over.

Do you want to do the whole walk-down-the-aisle thing, or just come up?"

"I'll just come up," Princess Alison says. She maneuvers her way through the crowd, fluffs her dress, and begins walking down the remainder of the aisle. "Excuse me," she says to Jonah and me as she squeezes past us.

"What a perfect match," a woman sitting near us says. "She's a princess, he's a prince. He's handsome, and she's beautiful. They go together like French fries and mustard!"

"What is wrong with you people?" I shriek. "Mustard does not go on French fries! Ketchup goes on French fries! Ketchup! Or mayonnaise, in some countries. Or maybe a mixture of the two, if you're into that. But not mustard! Never mustard!"

Everyone stares at me.

Am I losing it?

"I totally agree," Jonah says. "C'mon, Abby, let's go. We need to help Lana."

Yes, we definitely need to help her. Because Prince Mortimer is marrying someone else, which means that Lana is going to DIE in the morning.

Unless we can save her.

# * chapter eighteen *

## Night Swimming

We find Lana sitting on the sand, staring sadly into the sunset.

"You need to go talk to the sea witch," I tell her. Lana needs to convince the witch to reverse the spell.

She points to her mouth and then her chest.

"You can't breathe underwater," I say.

She nods.

"Any way we can get the sea witch to come ashore?" I ask.

Lana shakes her head and shimmies her hand so it looks like a tail.

"She doesn't have legs," I confirm. "But she's a witch; she can do whatever she wants."

"She probably doesn't want to come on land," Jonah says. He can be annoyingly logical.

Argh! We have to fix this! We're running out of time!

"Maybe Princess Alison won't *really* marry Prince Mortimer," Jonah says. "Maybe she'll pull a Lana, and bolt at the last minute."

Just then we hear loud clapping inside the palace and choruses of "Congratulations!"

"There goes that idea," I mumble.

"Oh! Oh!" Jonah shrieks. "What about that potion Carolyn talked about? Remember? The one that her great-great-grandmother used to go underwater? The spit potion?"

I shake my head. "Do you think that even works?"

"Well, she should try it. What other choice do we have?"

He has a point.

We find Carolyn in the kitchen, slicing lemons.

"Remember that potion you said your great-great-grandmother used to go underwater?" I ask.

"How could I forget?" she says with a laugh.

"Do you know how to make it?"

"Do I remember the ingredients? Of course I do. Mermaid's spit, a tablespoon of sea salt, three fish eggs, a tablespoon of water, a teaspoon of club soda, and a pinch of algae. I've always wanted to make it, but finding the mermaid's spit has been difficult."

"We have the spit," I say. "We need some potion so Lana can go underwater."

"Of course," she says, putting down her knife. "Anything for my favorite mermaid."

She gathers all the stuff from the kitchen, mixes it up in a glass, and then runs with us outside and hands the glass to Lana. Lana spits inside, then takes a sip. Then she turns and hurries into the ocean, diving underwater. Two seconds later she pops up, gasping and shaking her head.

"I guess it doesn't work," I say.

"Maybe now that Lana has legs, her spit isn't mermaid-y anymore," Carolyn says.

Lana leans over and carves into the sand: "I DON'T HAVE A TAIL BUT I WILL ALWAYS BE A MERMAID."

"In that case," Jonah says, "maybe a mermaid can't use her own spit. Or maybe the spell only works on humans."

"Lana's a human," I say.

Carolyn shakes her head. "She's a mermaid. She just said so herself."

Jonah tugs on my hand. "You know what that means, right? It might work on us."

Huh? "Us?"

"Us," he repeats. "We're human."

"*I* am, yes. I'm not always so sure about you."

"Seriously, Abby. *We'll* try the potion."

"I doubt it will work," I say, my heart hammering.

"I bet it will," he says. "We'll get to breathe underwater! It'll be fun!"

"Sharks. Waves. Salt in our mouths. That doesn't sound like fun. And it's going to be dark soon. How will we see anything?" I can't do it. I just can't.

"Don't you have a light on your watch?" he asks.

"Yeah." As if one probably-waterproof-watch light is enough for me to go up against the entire ocean.

"Let's just try. It's our only chance."

"Are there any other options?" I ask, my voice squeaky. "There must be. Maybe Carolyn wants to try it?"

Carolyn shakes her head. "Me? Are you crazy? I eat shark. I don't let them eat me!"

"You eat shark?" Jonah asks, eyes wide.

She nods. "I'll make it for you. It's delicious."

"No thanks," we say in unison.

Jonah looks at me. "I think it's up to us, then. Let's do it!"

Goose bumps cover my whole body. He wants me to go underwater. No life jacket. No air.

I can't. I can't. I can't.

I *have* to.

Slowly I nod.

Lana hands Jonah the cup.

"Cheers!" Jonah cries, and takes a big sip. "It tastes like sushi!"

I roll my eyes. "Have you ever even had sushi?"

"No, but I bet this is what it tastes like. It could use some ketchup." When Jonah's done, he hands me the cup and scurries toward the water, diving right in.

"Wait, Jonah!" I yell, but it's too late. He's under.

He pops up. "It works! It really works!"

"Great. Just, um, great!" My hands shake. Before I sip, I ask, "But how will we ever find the sea witch?"

"Lana can make us a map," Jonah calls.

Carolyn takes a pen and paper out of her apron and hands it to Lana. "Here you go."

Lana starts to sketch. When she's done, she writes "2 HOURS" on top.

"It'll take us two hours to get there?" I ask.

Lana nods.

That's a long time for us to be swimming. Two hours to the sea witch's place, two hours back, plus how long to convince the witch to help us? At least we have twelve hours to work with.

"Bottoms up," Carolyn says.

I nod, and then I swallow a gulp of the potion. I almost gag. But I keep swallowing because I have to.

P.S. My brother's not wrong — a little ketchup *would* go a long way.

I hand Lana the glass and then carefully wade into the water. The *dark* water. This can't be a good idea. I barely swim well during the day; how am I going to swim well at night?

"Just dunk!" Jonah orders me.

I bristle at being bossed around by my baby brother, but I know he's right. Getting into the water is like taking off a Band-Aid. It always hurts less to just rip it off. I'm in up to my waist. I should go under now.

Okay, *now.*

"Time is ticking," Jonah calls. "I'm going under again!"

"Jonah, hold on!" I yell, but then he disappears under the surf. At first I see bubbles rise to the surface but then they stop.

I don't like bubbles that stop. My heart feels like it might pound out of my chest.

Now I have no choice. I grip the map in my hand, hold my nose with the other, seal my eyes shut, and go under.

Cold, cold, cold! I carefully open my left eye. At first it's blurry, but then it clears up. This is a hopeful sign. It doesn't sting or anything. I open the right eye.

Around me I see blue. Lots and lots of navy blue. I'm glad the sun isn't completely gone yet.

"Hi!" Jonah says, swimming over to me. "How cool is this? We can talk!"

I am afraid to open my mouth in case I swallow a gallon of water and drown. But I do it. I open my lips in a little circle and take a tiny breath in. I do not choke.

"It works!" I say, amazed. I have no idea *how* it works, but it is working. I am breathing and talking underwater. No scuba equipment necessary.

I thought I would sink to the bottom, but I'm not. I'm just floating. It's like I'm in one of those gravity-less spaceships and I can go up or down or anywhere I want.

We swim farther into the deep.

There are brightly colored fish swimming in all directions. A family of turtles meanders by us. And coral is everywhere. It looks like pipe cleaners gently blowing in the wind. Yellow, red, orange, blue, green. The water doesn't even feel cold anymore, just like a really nice bath.

Jonah is having the time of his life. He's laughing, somersaulting. He's even yodeling. Does he really have to let every sea creature know we're here?

"Can you try to be quiet?" I ask him, as a neon fish that's shaped like a trumpet smashes its nose against my knee. It does not seem to like me.

"Why? This is awesome."

"Jonah! This is serious business! You've been acting like a two-year-old since we got here!"

"You've been acting like a forty-year-old!" he snaps back. "This is supposed to be fun."

"No, it isn't!" I yell back as the trumpet fish goes after my big toe. "We're helping Lana."

"Why can't helping Lana be fun?"

"Because . . . because . . . You're impossible," I say, and turn my back on him. "Let's go to the sea witch and get this over with." We have to stay on schedule. We have to see the sea witch. But first we have to *find* the sea witch.

I pull the map up to my eyes. Unfortunately, the map has disintegrated in the water.

"Crumbs!" I yell.

Jonah turns back to me. "What's wrong?"

"Unlike us, the map was not waterproof."

He bites his lower lip. "I think I remember the way. Follow me."

"You think, or you *know*?"

He shrugs. "I think."

"Time is ticking, Jonah!"

"Well," he says, swimming forward, "then we'd better get kicking."

I nervously follow Jonah through seaweed, around coral, and over a cave. I feel bad for snapping at him, but honestly, he doesn't take anything seriously.

By now the water has started to get dark. Really dark. I press the light on my watch to illuminate our path and pray that the batteries don't die.

We swim for what feels like at least another hour.

I could really use a snack. That sushi potion was just not enough. I wish I'd had time to pack a picnic lunch from the wedding buffet. I'm going to miss that lemon meringue pie.

At the end of the cave, Jonah turns left and points.

"That's it," he says.

I shine my light up ahead. I have no doubt that he's right. If someone asked me to design a sea witch's house, this is what I'd create.

The walls are gray stone and covered in black sea-sludge. The path to the doorway is surrounded by barracudas and floating fish skeletons. There's a low moaning sound all around us. Jonah slows down and takes my hand.

"Maybe we should find a doorbell or something. The sea witch might not be the type of person who likes to be surprised." I see a big knocker in the shape of a human skull. With a trembling hand, I bang the knocker against the door.

Slowly the door creeps open.

"Come in," we hear. The voice is definitely female, but low and raspy.

We swim through the entranceway, terrified.

There she sits in the middle of the room. Well, not sits. Lies sideways on a black couch. She is not what I expected at all. She's beautiful. She's a mermaid just like Lana, but her tail is dark purple instead of green and orange. She's younger than I expected, too — she looks about my mom's age. She has black, waist-length hair.

Beside the couch is a large gray pot. No, it's not a pot. It's a cauldron. It's made of stone, and bubbles are steaming out of it. It looks like a hot tub — but a really, really scary one. I do not want to go anywhere near that cauldron if I can help it. I take a step back.

"Who are you?" the sea witch drawls. Her voice is smoky. It makes me want to move closer, but I resist.

"I'm-I'm-I'm Abby," I stutter. "And this is my brother, Jonah."

"Hello," she says. "I'm Nelly."

I nod. "We're here on behalf of Lana. I'm her —" I pause. "I'm her lawyer."

The sea witch cackles. "Her lawyer? Lana has a lawyer?"

I nod. "And I'm here to negotiate a deal."

"How are you even down here? Did you take the underwater potion?"

We nod.

Nelly laughs again. "Well, you'd better start negotiating before your time runs out."

"Right." I nervously clear my throat. It's been about two hours, which means we have ten hours left. We can convince her to help us in ten hours, can't we? "We would like you to reverse the spell you put on Lana," I say, my voice trembling.

She raises a perfectly arched eyebrow. "Which one?"

I half smile. "All of them?"

"Let's see," Nelly says. "There's the spell that changed her tail into legs. There's the spell that took away her voice. Then there's the spell that says that if the prince marries anyone else, she'll die before the next sunrise, which is at six oh five A.M."

"All of them would be good," I say. "But the dying one is definitely our priority."

"Reversing spells isn't cheap. What will you give me?"

I clear my throat. "What do you want?" Oops. This may have been a tiny oversight on my part. I came to negotiate with the sea witch but I didn't bring anything to trade. Never mind being a failed maid of honor — I'm a failed lawyer, too.

Nelly eyes Jonah. "The boy?"

Jonah scoots into my side.

"Um, no." Even though we're kind of in a fight, she still can't have my brother. "Is there anything else you want?"

She looks me over. "What is that on your wrist?"

I look down. "You want my watch? I can give you my watch." Not that I really want to give away my watch, but of course I'll do it to save Lana's *life*. I'm not sure how we'll find our way back to the shore without any light, though. I guess I'll worry about that problem later.

The sea witch nods. "Here's my offer. You give me the watch."

"Okay," I say. Maybe this won't be so hard after all.

"And in return for the watch, I'll give you a knife. You'll use the knife to stab the prince in the heart. Then I'll undo all the spells. Lana can go back to her life as a mermaid."

Is she kidding me?

"Um, that's not going to work, either," I say. "I am not going to kill someone." Sure, the prince is a bit of a jerk, but that doesn't mean I want him dead. And that definitely doesn't mean that I would ever consider killing him. I want to *be* a lawyer, not *need* a lawyer. "Can't I just give you the watch, and you'll reverse the spells?"

She snorts. "Reverse all the spells for one measly watch? No. One of you stabs the prince, or nothing. You know what? I don't even want a watch. The girl and I had a deal. She's the one who wasn't satisfied with her life even though she had *everything*. She had family who loved her! She was a princess! She was beautiful! But no, no, no, she wanted to give it all up to be *human*. She's a jerk! Just like her father!"

"But she wasn't happy!" I say. "She risked everything for a different life. She's not a jerk. She's . . . she's . . . brave! And you're a coward. You just hide in your cave and steal from people. You want everyone to be as miserable as you are."

Nelly blinks. And then blinks again. "Unless you have something better than a watch to trade, then we're done here."

Now what are we supposed to do? Wait. "Why is Lana's dad a jerk?" I wonder.

She ignores my question and instead says, "I guess we're done. Samuel! My dear Samuel! Show these children the door!"

My dear Samuel? "Don't tell me she has a boyfriend," I say.

But no. Just then a shark — an actual shark — swims up to us with a menacing look on its face.

I'm not that surprised her only companion is a shark — no person could love someone that mean.

"We're getting out of here," I say, and pull Jonah straight out of the house.

By the time we reach the black water, my heart is beating about three thousand miles a minute.

"That didn't go well," Jonah says.

"No, it didn't," I say, leaning against something soft and squishy that I hope won't eat me. I try to catch my breath. "Now what?"

"I can think of one person who might help us," Jonah says.

"Who?"

"The Sea King."

I nod. "It's time to find Lana's dad."

# * chapter nineteen *

## Sticks and Stones

I remember that, in the movie, the king offers to trade places with the Little Mermaid," Jonah explains as we start swimming again. "Maybe he'll want to do that now."

My heart clenches. "So the king dies instead of Lana? We don't want that, either!"

"Hopefully he'll have a better idea than that," Jonah says. "But we have to find him and ask. Don't you think our parents would want to know if we were facing a life-or-death situation?"

"We face life-and-death situations every time we go into the mirror!" I say.

"True," Jonah says. "But still."

"Okay," I say. Maybe the king can force the witch to recant her spell. Or maybe he'll have something to trade. Clearly he knows the sea witch — she called him a jerk.

So we're going to talk to him. But first we have to find him. Which we can't seem to do. We swim and swim, but we keep passing the same cave.

We're lost. We're very, very lost.

And there's something really freaky about being lost underwater in the dark. Beige coral reef sways in the wind and looks like fingers trying to grab us. Silvery fish appear to have teeth.

I light up my watch. It says six thirty, which means it must be around midnight here. How much longer can we swim in circles?

"We know you," a voice says.

"Did you say something?" Jonah asks.

"No," I say. "I thought it was you." A chill creeps down my spine. "Hello?" I say timidly. "Is someone there?"

"Yes," another voice says.

"We are," says a third voice.

We're surrounded.

"Who are you?" I ask, and aim my watch light at the voices. The light reveals a mermaid. No — five mermaids. All with green-and-orange swishing tails. The tops they're wearing look familiar, but I can't figure out from where.

"We're Lana's sisters," the one in the middle says. She has short, butter-colored hair and she's wearing a white sweater. "We've been spying on her, but we can't get too close to the shore. Is Lana okay?"

"Not exactly," I say, before explaining the whole story.

"We have to go talk to my dad!" one sister wearing a purple hoodie cries. "He has to help."

"We were trying to find him," I say. "Isn't it the middle of the night? What were you guys doing?"

"We were at a party," another one says, giving the necklace she's wearing an anxious twirl. Her brown hair is tied back in a tight braid and she's wearing a light-green shirt with a collar. "It's past curfew, though — we're definitely going to get in trouble."

"It's worth it for Lana," the mermaid in the hoodie says. "Follow me!"

We follow her through a winding path, past schools of striped and speckled fish, sparkly red coral, and even a twenty-foot-long shipwreck that's jammed into a bunch of rocks.

Two of the sisters swim by me, both wearing what look a lot like pajama tops.

Familiar pajama tops.

I glance at all the sisters. Purple hoodie. Green shirt. White sweater. Wait a sec.

"Those are my clothes!" I exclaim. "You found my suitcase!"

They spin around. "That was yours?" the one in the hoodie asks.

"Yes!" I say. "I thought I lost it."

"You did lose it," the one with the braid mutters. "Finder's keepers." She looks like the youngest of the bunch.

"Sasha," the one with the short hair and white sweater scolds. "We'll give them back their stuff." She looks like the oldest.

"Can we keep the wood paddles and the ball?" the one in my hoodie asks. "We made up a whole game with them where we hit the ball back and forth."

"That's how you're supposed to play," Jonah says. "It's called Kadima."

"We love Kadima," she says.

"Me too!" Jonah says. "We should play if we have time."

"There's no time for Kadima!" the oldest sister and I both yell. We look at each other and smile.

Soon we get to what appears to be a town. It's pretty empty because it's the middle of the night, but there's one restaurant still open.

"Where are we?" I ask.

"That's Salties," one of the sisters tells me. "It's the nicest restaurant on the Main Canal."

A few mermaids and mermen are sitting outside, enjoying the night. Instead of being pitch-black, like I expected, there are little sparkling lights lining the canal.

"Where do the lights come from?" I ask the oldest sister.

"Bioluminescence," she says. "Underwater life that glows in the dark."

Everyone looks at us curiously as we swim past — we are the only ones without tails — but we don't stop to sightsee.

Finally we spot what has to be the castle.

It's just as nice, if not nicer, than Prince Mortimer's palace. It's made of stone and cliffs and covered in protective coral.

"Let's go straight to Dad's room," the oldest says. "Follow me!"

No need for stairs in this palace. We swim right up into the king's windowless room. Not much security here.

"Dad! Dad!" the oldest one cries, swimming over to his bed.

"What's wrong, girls?" the king asks, opening his eyes.

He has dark hair that's gray at the temples. He also has one of those chins with a cleft in it.

He spots us. "Why did you bring humans?"

"They're friends of Lana's. And Lana needs our help."

Quickly I spill out the whole story. ". . . So you see," I say once I've finished, "we didn't know who else to go to. Do you have anything the sea witch would want? Or could you command her to reverse the spell? Maybe threaten to put her in ocean prison?"

The king looks shocked, yet I notice a determined glint in his eye. "Poor Lana! We must save her at once. Girls! Collect all the family jewels. The necklaces! The rings! All of Mom's old stuff!"

"Not the jewelry!" one of the sisters cries. "It's all we have left of Mom!"

"Your mom would want us to use it." The king throws off his covers. "Everyone, follow me."

# * chapter twenty *

## We're Back

It's not the most inviting décor," I say as I push a floating fish skeleton out of the way and knock on the door. I glance at my watch. We have to move fast. We've been underwater for almost nine-and-a-half hours. We still need two hours to get back to the beach.

"Go away!" Nelly yells from inside. "Didn't I tell you to stop bothering me?"

The door swings open and the sea witch has a scowl on her face. But suddenly her expression changes. Softens. She blinks. And then blinks again. She's looking above my head and I turn to see that she's staring at the king.

And he's staring at her.

"What do *you* want?" she asks.

The king blushes.

"Nelly," I say, "the king is here to offer you jewelry. If you'll save his daughter."

"Right!" the king says, snapping out of his trance. "May we come in?"

Nelly tears her eyes away from the king and checks out our whole group. "All of you?"

"Yes," I say. I put my hands on my hips and clench them into fists, hoping I look defiant.

"I guess." Nelly sweeps her arm to the side in an exaggerated gesture of welcome, and all eight of us float-march in.

"I haven't seen you in years," the king says.

"No, you haven't," Nelly says, tight-lipped.

"How do you know each other?" I ask.

"We went to elementary school together," the king says.

"We certainly did," Nelly says, crossing her arms and slapping her tail against the ground. "How could I forget? You used to call me a horrible name."

The king's eyes widen in surprise. "What are you talking about? I called you Jelly Nelly!"

She scowls. "Exactly. Jelly Nelly. Because I reminded you of a jellyfish."

"So why is that horrible?" the king asks, his forehead wrinkling.

"Because jellyfish are annoying and poisonous," Nelly spits out.

I'd have to agree. Jellyfish are kind of the mosquitoes of the sea.

The king shakes his head. "Jellyfish are smart. And beautiful. And fascinating."

"They are not," Nelly says, but her voice wavers.

"They are so," he says. "I called you Jelly Nelly because I had a crush on you."

Nelly blushes. "You did?"

"You did?" we all echo.

Now it's the king's turn to blush.

Nelly makes a strange sound. Was it a giggle? She clears her throat. "Oh. I just assumed . . ." Her voice trails off. "I had no idea." She wraps a strand of her dark hair around her finger. She giggles again. Is Nelly flirting? Does the sea witch *like* the king?

"Well, now you know," he says. He's all flushed. "It's nice to see you again." Oh. My. Goodness. Does he still *like* the witch?

But then he shakes his head. "No. It's *not* nice. You have to help my daughter."

Nelly crosses her arms. "I don't have to do anything."

He straightens up, flirting forgotten. "We have jewels to offer you. In exchange for you changing the spell you put on Lana. Girls, show her what you have. Nelly, take whatever you want. But please, spare my daughter."

The oldest steps up and opens her hand to reveal a sparkling ring. "I have a diamond engagement ring."

The second oldest opens her hand next. "I have emerald earrings."

The third shows us a chunky bracelet. "It's fourteen-carat gold."

The fourth has two hoop earrings dangling on her thumb. "They're platinum."

Sasha, the youngest, steps up and points to her neck. "I'm wearing a mother-of-pearl necklace. I guess you can have it."

Hold on a minute. "That's my necklace!" I exclaim.

Sasha shrugs. "Don't you want to help Lana?"

I sigh. "You can have it," I tell Nelly.

Nelly eyes the goods. "Hmm," she says. "They're pretty, but I already have my own jewelry." She wiggles her fingers in front of us, and we see that they are glittering with jewels. "Do you have anything else?"

"Um . . ." We look at each other. We are empty-handed. We are out of stuff.

"You can have my Kadima paddles," Jonah offers.

"What's Kadima?" Nelly asks, intrigued.

"It's a game," Jonah says. "You and another person hit a ball back and forth. It's very fun."

Nelly's face clouds over. "I don't want a game," she snarls. "Who am I going to play it with? Samuel doesn't have hands. If you have nothing else to offer, I think we're done here."

A lightbulb goes off in my head. She doesn't want Kadima *paddles*. She wants someone to play Kadima *with*.

Before I thought no one could love her because she was mean. But maybe she's so mean because no one loves her.

I know how to save Lana.

"Would you consider reversing the spells on Lana in exchange for a date?" I blurt out.

Nelly blinks. "Excuse me?"

"A date," I repeat. My mouth feels dry. This has to work. It just has to.

Nelly blushes and looks down at the sandy floor. "A date with whom?"

I glance at the king. His cheeks are just as red as Nelly's. He's just as lonely as Nelly.

He swims forward. "With me," he says.

Their eyes meet across the room.

"Really?" she asks softly.

He nods. He takes another step toward her. "Would you like to go out sometime, Jelly Nelly? Or I can just call you Nelly."

"Just Nelly is good," she says. And then giggles.

Yes! This is going to work! Way to go, me! Speaking of going — we have to get a move on.

"So do we have a deal?" I ask. "A date in exchange for reversing the spells? You can go to Salties!"

"What if she hurts our dad?" the youngest mermaid cries. "She's a witch, and he's all we have left!"

Good point.

"Can you give us some sort of collateral?" the oldest mermaid asks, running her fingers through her short hair.

Nelly nods toward the shark. "You can keep Samuel as a pet until the date is done. He needs a babysitter, anyway. He eats the couch when he's lonely."

Better the couch than me.

"So," I ask again. "Do we have a deal?"

We all hold our breath.

Nelly and the king nod. "Deal," they say simultaneously, and then they both laugh and turn red again.

"Let's shake on it," the king says, putting out his hand.

"Abby," Jonah says, tugging at my sleeve.

"One sec, Jonah," I say, wanting to see how this ends.

Nelly takes his outstretched hand.

We wait for them to shake, but instead, they both just stand there, holding each other's hands. And holding.

Still holding.

All righty, then.

"Abby," Jonah says again. "I don't feel so good. My chest feels heavy."

I glance at my watch. The potion is going to run out in two hours! We have to go.

"Abby," Jonah says again, and crumples into a heap on the sandy ground.

I lunge after him. But before I can reach him, the room starts to spin. I feel intense pressure on my chest. Like someone's sitting on me. Or like I'm underwater and I can't breathe.

Oh, no.

The potion ran out early.

"Jonah!" I try to yell — but nothing comes out. The people around me look murkier and murkier until I don't see anything at all.

# ✻ chapter twenty-one ✻

## Ashore

"Abby, Abby. You have to get up."

The next thing I see is light. A very bright light.

I open my eyes. Where am I? What happened?

I sit up, cough, and notice Lana kneeling beside me.

"Finally," she says, her eyes squinting in concern. "How do you feel?"

The last thing I remember, we were underwater. And now it's just me and Lana on the beach. I'm so confused. "How did I get here?"

"My family brought you up, and then I pulled you onto the beach."

I'm still a bit dizzy and disoriented.

Wait a sec. I'm on the beach. Jonah's not. Oh, no. Oh no, oh no, oh no. "Where's my brother?"

She hesitates. "He's, um . . ."

My heart stops. He drowned. He drowned, and it's all my fault. Plus I was so mean to him today. I was awful. He was just being his totally awesome fun self, and I yelled at him. I try to breathe, but I can't.

". . . There he is," she says.

What? He's alive? I jump to my feet and spot him hopping his way down the beach.

"Jonah!" I shriek. "You're alive!" I throw my arms around his neck.

"Of course I'm alive," he says. "I was just getting myself a snack. I'm starving." He's munching on French fries and mustard. "Glad you're finally awake."

I let go of his neck even though I don't want to. "How long was I out for?"

"A few hours."

"What happened?"

"Either we didn't take enough potion each, or the recipe wasn't exactly right."

I hug him hard. "I'm so sorry I was mean to you."

"I'm sorry I made you do all the work," he says. "Want a fry? The mustard isn't as awful as you'd think."

"Sure," I say.

"Me too," Lana says.

"What time is it?" I wonder.

"Almost ten A.M."

I look at Lana in surprise. "It's ten o'clock, and you're still alive!"

She nods. "I am."

"And you can talk!"

She nods again. "Nelly reversed the spell. And gave me back my voice."

"That's amazing!" I cheer. "We did it! We fixed the story! Everything is back the way it was!"

"Not everything," Jonah says.

"What do you mean?" I ask, munching on another fry. Jonah's right. The mustard isn't that bad.

He motions to Lana. "She still has legs."

He's right. She *does* still have legs. "What happened? Nelly wouldn't let you have your tail back? She's making you stay on land forever? I thought we had done so well! Did your dad cancel the date or something?"

501

Lana shakes her head. "No, that's not it. She offered to give me my tail back, but I told her I didn't want it."

Huh? "Why not?"

"I love my family, but I don't want to leave the surface. Prince or not, it's my home. I love to walk and dance. And I really love sunsets. And shoops — I mean, shoes. And books. And paintings. And have you tried a cheeseburger with mustard and that yellow-y American cheese? They're amazing."

I nod.

She goes on. " And even though I have my voice back, I have another voice now that I'm not ready to give up."

I don't understand what she's talking about. "You have a second voice?"

"Yes! Thanks to you, I can write! And that's given me a whole new voice. I want to stay on land and write stories about the world under the ocean. I want to write books about mermaids and share them with humans so they don't think merfolk are make-believe!"

"I would love to read those," I say. "Is your dad okay with you staying?"

She nods. "He said he was going to miss me, but he also gave me these." She opens her hand, and I see the diamond ring, the emerald earrings, and the bracelet. "They belonged to my mother. He told me I can sell them and buy a house with a big dock so he and my sisters can always visit."

"That's amazing," I say, throwing my arms around Lana in a hug. "Everything worked out."

"Almost," Jonah says. "We still have to get home."

Oh, no! If it's almost ten here, we only have two hours to get back, and we still have no idea how. "What are we going to do?" I ask.

"It's all taken care of," Jonah says smugly. "By me."

"But, Jonah, we're sitting on the beach. Not in our basement."

"Not for long," Jonah says, and then he points to the water.

In the distance, I see the five mermaid sisters, plus Nelly, plus the king.

"She's finally awake!" the oldest mermaid says.

"Hi, guys!" Lana yells. She splashes out into the water and hugs them all. Aw. We got them back together.

"Carolyn made us more underwater potion," Jonah says. "She made double, just to be safe."

"How does that help?" I ask. "We don't live underwater."

"Nelly's cauldron is underwater. It's going to take us home."

"But Nelly isn't a fairy," I say. "Is she?"

He shrugs. "She said she could do it."

"She did? Did you have to trade her something?"

He shook his head. "She said it's payment for reintroducing her to the king."

"Oh!" If being a judge doesn't work out, maybe I can be a matchmaker. "When do we go?"

"Now!"

I look back up at the palace. "Should we say good-bye?"

"I said good-bye for both of us. Carolyn said she'll miss us. And she promised to teach Lana how to cook."

"Don't worry," Lana says. "I promise not to make shark."

"And Vivian packed up all our stuff and put them in your suitcase."

"Whose suitcase?"

"Your suitcase! The mermaids gave it back."

"Oh! Great! What about the stuff inside the suitcase?"

"They gave that back, too. Lana put your necklace around your neck when you were sleeping. I tried to do it myself, but that clasp is really confusing."

I reach up and feel my necklace. "Thanks, Jonah. Thanks, Lana."

"No problem," Lana says.

"I gave Lana's sisters my Kadima paddles," Jonah says. "They seemed to really like them."

"That was sweet of you, Jonah." I turn to Lana.

Lana takes the cup of potion, spits in it, and then hands it to me. "I'm going to miss you two. Thank you for everything."

I chug the still-disgusting potion, and then give Lana a tight hug. "Your stories are going to be amazing."

"Thanks. I can't wait to write them."

Jonah gives her a hug, too.

"I'll see you tomorrow, everyone!" she calls to her family. "Have fun on your date, Dad! But don't make any trades, okay? And I'll miss you, Abby and Jonah!"

We wave. Here we go. With one hand, I hold on to my brother, and with the other, I hold on to my suitcase. Just like when I came, but now with extra yellow clothes. I dunk right away.

Sometimes you just gotta go for it.

This time when we go underwater, the ocean is alive with activity. Mermaids and mermen everywhere. Everyone's busy, swimming this way or that. It's like we were dropped in the busiest aquarium in the world.

I wish we had more time to explore. Maybe we'll come back one day?

When we arrive at Nelly's house, everything looks different. Maybe because it's bright outside. Or maybe because she did some spring cleaning of the skeletons and stuff.

"Thank you," Nelly whispers to me.

I try not to stiffen as she gives me a hug.

"Because we reintroduced you to the king?" I ask.

"Yes. And because you were right. Instead of changing my own life, I wanted everyone to be as miserable as I was. I *was* a coward."

We hug all the sisters, and then we are ready to go. "What do we do?" I ask, eyeing the bubbling cauldron with a little bit of fear.

"Just swim right into it," Nelly says.

"We won't burn?"

"You shouldn't."

"But I don't understand," I say. "I thought only fairies could get us home."

"I *am* a fairy," she says.

Huh? "We thought you were a witch," Jonah says.

"A witch is a fairy who does bad things," she says. "See, it depends what you use your magic for."

Aha. That makes sense. I look toward the cauldron. "We can't both fit in," I say. Not together.

"I'll go first," Jonah says.

"I'm not letting you go alone!" I say.

"Then hold on to my foot."

"Okay," I say. I grab hold of his very wet sneaker with one hand and the suitcase with the other. "Ready?" I ask.

"Ready!" he says. "Hold on tight!"

He swims, swims, swims right toward the cauldron. It squeezes but doesn't hurt. I close my eyes and trust Jonah to get us home.

# ✳ chapter twenty-two ✳

## Dry, Again

𝓽he next thing I know, I'm in a very large puddle on my basement floor, still holding Jonah's foot. We've slid across half the floor like we're at a water park.

"Well done," I hear.

"You too," Jonah and I both say at the same time.

"That wasn't me," I say. My spine tingles. "That wasn't you?"

He shakes his head.

"But, Jonah, if it wasn't me, and it wasn't you . . ." I look back at the mirror. It's still swirling. "Maryrose? Was that you?"

She doesn't answer. But that had to have been her! It must

have been! She talked to us! She finally talked to us! And she said "well done"!

What does "well done" mean? "Was changing the tale what we were supposed to do?" I ask the mirror. "Do you have a plan for us?"

She still doesn't answer.

"Abby, what time is it?" Jonah asks.

I look at my watch. "It's four minutes to seven."

"We gotta go!"

He's right. Our parents will be waking us up any minute. I turn back to the mirror. "I have a lot of questions for you," I say. "And next time, I would really appreciate it if you could answer them." I leave the wet suitcase downstairs because it's filled with water and ridiculously heavy. I cross my fingers and hope I have a chance to deal with it before my parents find it.

We dash up the stairs. When we're on the main floor, I hear the ringing of my parents' alarm clock. "Run! Run!" I whisper to Jonah. "Go put on your pj's, hide your wet clothes in the back of your closet, and get into bed! Love you! I'm glad you didn't drown!"

"Love you, too!" Jonah says as he sprints toward his bedroom. "I'm glad you didn't drown, either!"

Our doors close just as I hear my parents' door opening. Oh no, oh no, oh no! I rip off my clothes, look for a clean pair of pajamas, remember I don't have any, jump under my covers, and pull them up to my neck as my doorknob starts to wiggle.

About half a second later, my door creeps open. "Morning, honey," my mom says. "Time to get up."

I fake a yawn. "Thanks, Mom!"

I hear a bang from Jonah's room. Mom looks quizzically in his direction. Oh, no! He's not ready yet. I need to distract her! What do I do?

"Wait! Mom?"

She leans against the doorway. "Yes, honey?"

"I want to talk to you about something."

"Yes?" she asks expectantly.

At first I have no idea what I want to say, but then, suddenly, I do.

I spot my jewelry box on my dresser and think about Lana. I had wanted her to accept her life as is, but she wanted to fight for her dreams. Sure, sometimes you have to get what you get and not get upset. But maybe other times, you have to follow your heart and go after what you really want. Take a risk. Be brave.

I guess part of growing up is learning when to do which.

"Mom," I start. "I know you're really busy. I understand. But I think I'm old enough to go to Chicago by myself. There's a program where they let kids fly by themselves — they call them UMs. Undercover Minors? No, Unidentified Minors. No —"

"Unaccompanied Minors!" Jonah screams out from his room.

"Thanks!" I yell back. "Jonah told me that his friend Isaac takes airplanes by himself to visit his dad, and he's only seven. Can I do that to visit Nana?"

"Oh, honey! By yourself? Are you sure you're up for that?"

I nod. If I can navigate the deepest part of the ocean, I can definitely get around the airport. I don't say that part to my mom.

"You wouldn't find it scary?"

"I might," I say. "But being a little scared is worth it to see Nana."

Mom sighs. "I'll tell you what — I don't know much about this UM program, but it sounds like a possibility. I'll look into it, okay?"

"Thanks, Mom. I can do it, I swear."

"I have no doubt that you can," she says softly. She inhales deeply. "You smell delicious. Like the beach."

I laugh. I can't help it.

She looks at me quizzically. "Do you have a suntan?"

511

"Er, no," I say. "It's just the light."

She nods and tousles my hair. "Maybe when all this work is done, we should go to Florida for a week off."

"Sounds good to me," I say. She may wonder where we got our new swimsuits.

"Hey, honey, why aren't you wearing any pajamas?"

"Oh . . . um . . ." I think back to the story of *The Emperor's New Clothes*. If I tell my mom I'm actually wearing pj's will she pretend to believe me? Probably not. "They're too tight," I say, suddenly inspired. "I need new ones. I'm a growing girl, you know."

"Oh, I know," she says, and smiles. "I'll have to take you shopping. Now go get dressed and then come down for breakfast, 'kay? Time for school."

I nod. Even though I'm tired, I'm excited to see Frankie and Robin. I wish I could tell them what I've been up to, but I don't think we're supposed to tell anyone.

Hmm. Are we not supposed to tell anyone, or just not our parents?

Could I bring Frankie and Robin with us next time? Would the mirror let them in?

Once my mom leaves, I jump out of bed and pick up my jewelry box.

Lana is no longer a mermaid. Instead, she has legs. She's lying on her stomach, propped up by her elbows, wearing a yellow sundress and strappy sandals. She's writing in a notebook.

She's a real writer! Yay!

I wonder if she found a worthy prince. Or maybe a worthy surfer. I wonder if I'll ever see her again. I wonder where the mirror will take me next.

I study the other characters on my jewelry box. I've always wanted to meet Sleeping Beauty. And Rapunzel. And that flying carpet really does look like fun. I'll just have to hold on extra tight.

I'm ready, Maryrose. For answers. For excitement. For our next adventure. Wherever it may be.

# acknowledgments

Thank you to my awesome agents, publishers, first readers, and friends: Laura Dail, Tamar Rydzinski, Brian Lipson, Aimee Friedman, Abby McAden, David Levithan, Becky Shapiro, Becky Amsel, Bess Braswell, Allison Singer, Janet Robbins, Elizabeth Parisi, Lizette Serrano, Emily Heddleson, Candace Greene, AnnMarie Anderson, Courtney Sheinmel, Emily Bender, Anne Heltzel, Lauren Myracle, E. Lockhart, Tori, Carly and Carol Adams, Avery and Whitney Carmichael, Targia Clarke, Jess Braun, Lauren Kisilevsky, Bonnie Altro, Susan Finkelberg-Sohmer, Corinne and Michael Bilerman, Debbie Korb, Joanna Steinberg, Casey Klurfeld, Jess Rothenberg, Adele Griffin, Leslie Margolis, Robin Wasserman, Maryrose Wood, Tara Altebrando, Sara Zarr, Ally Carter, Jennifer Barnes, Alan Gratz, Penny Fransblow, Maggie Marr, and Farrin Jacobs.

Love and thanks to my family: Aviva, Mom, Robert, Dad, Louisa, Gary, Lori, Sloane, Isaac, Vickie, John, Gary, Darren, Ryan, Jack, Jen, Teri, Briana, Michael, David, Patsy, Murray, Maggie, and Jenny. Extra love and extra thanks and lots and lots of kisses to Chloe, Anabelle, and Todd.

**READ ON FOR A SNEAK PEEK AT ABBY AND JONAH'S NEXT ADVENTURE!**

# Whatever After #4

# DREAM ON

ow Abby and Jonah are in Sleeping Beauty's story, along with Abby's friend Robin. Before they know it, Sleeping Beauty is wide awake and Robin is fast asleep. How will Abby and Jonah make things right?

"Robin, is everything okay?" I ask. "What are you doing? Did you forget something down here?"

She doesn't answer. She just continues walking in a circle.

"Is she sleepwalking?" I wonder out loud.

Jonah rubs his eyes with the back of his hand. "Don't sleepwalkers keep their arms out? Like zombies? Maybe she's a zombie."

"Robin is not a zombie," I say. Though she does look a bit like a zombie. "Robin, you're creeping us out! Talk to me!"

Instead of answering, Robin bumps right into the mirror.

The magic mirror.

I hear a low hissing sound. *Sssssssssss.*

Oh no oh no oh no. The mirror is waking up.

Robin takes a step back.

She bumps into the mirror again.

My whole body tenses as a warm purple light radiates from the mirror. If Robin hits the mirror one more time, it is going to suck her up and take her into a fairy tale. I CANNOT let that happen. I have to stop it!

"Maryrose, are you there?" I cry. "Are you listening? Please don't take my new best friend! STOP, ROBIN, STOP!"

I reach out to grab on to her again, but she steps forward and out of my grasp. It's too late.

Robin bumps into the mirror a third time.

First her reflection starts to swirl like it's been caught in a washing machine.

No, no, no!

Then the mirror turns into a vacuum, pulling Robin toward it. Finally, I manage to get a grip on her wrist.

"No! Don't go!" I shout. I feel like I can't breathe.

Jonah is holding on to the banister. I grab on to him with one hand, and on to Robin's wrist with the other. But it's like I'm playing tug-of-war and losing. Robin's right foot disappears inside the mirror first. Then her whole leg. Then half her face disappears inside.

It's too hard to hold on! I let go of her wrist, and the rest of Robin gets slurped by the mirror.

Getting my best friend swallowed into a fairy tale was so NOT part of my sleepover plan.

**Each time Abby and Jonah get sucked into their magic mirror, they wind up in a different fairy tale — and find new adventures!**

**Read all about the**
**Whatever After**
**series!**

### Whatever After #1: FAIREST of ALL

In their first adventure, Abby and Jonah wind up in the story of Snow White. But when they stop Snow from eating the poisoned apple, they realize they've messed up the whole story! Can they fix it — and still find Snow her happy ending?

### Whatever After #2: IF the SHOE FITS

This time, Abby and Jonah find themselves in Cinderella's story. When Cinderella breaks her foot, the glass slipper won't fit! With a little bit of magic, quick thinking, and luck, can Abby and her brother save the day?

### Whatever After #3: SINK or SWIM

Abby and Jonah are pulled into the tale of the Little Mermaid — a story with an ending that is *not* happy. So Abby and Jonah mess it up on purpose! Can they convince the mermaid to keep her tail before it's too late?

## Whatever After #4: DREAM ON

Now Abby and Jonah are in Sleeping Beauty's story, along with Abby's friend Robin. Before they know it, Sleeping Beauty is wide awake and Robin is fast asleep. How will Abby and Jonah make things right?

## Whatever After #5: BAD HAIR DAY

When Abby and Jonah fall into Rapunzel's story, they mess everything up by giving Rapunzel a haircut! Can they untangle this fairy tale disaster in time?

## Whatever After #6: COLD AS ICE

When their dog Prince runs through the mirror, Abby and Jonah have no choice but to follow him into the story of the Snow Queen! It's a winter wonderland . . . but the Snow Queen is rather mean, and she FREEZES Prince! Can Abby and Jonah save their dog . . . and themselves?

### Whatever After #7: BEAUTY QUEEN

This time, Abby and Jonah fall into the story of *Beauty and the Beast*. When Jonah is the one taken prisoner instead of Beauty, Abby has to find a way to fix this fairy tale . . . before things get pretty ugly!

### Whatever After #8: ONCE *upon* a FROG

When Abby and Jonah fall into the story of *The Frog Prince*, they realize the princess is so rude they don't even *want* her help! But will they be able to figure out how turn the frog back into a prince all by themselves?

### Whatever After #9: GENIE *in* a BOTTLE

Abby and Jonah get to meet Aladdin — but then they accidentally stop him from getting the magic lamp! Will a genie of their own be enough to make all of Aladdin's wishes come true?

# Don't miss this MAGICAL new series!

NORY, ELLIOTT, ANDRES, and BAX are students in
Dunwiddle Magic School's UPSIDE-DOWN MAGIC class.
In their classroom, lessons are unconventional, students are
unpredictable, and magic has a tendency to turn wonky at
the worst possible moments . . .

From *New York Times* bestselling authors
SARAH MLYNOWSKI, LAUREN MYRACLE (*Life of Ty*),
and EMILY JENKINS (*Toys Go Out*) comes a new, offbeat series
about a group of misfits who set out to prove that life on the
other side of ordinary has its charms.